D1564402

THE ROYLES

Also by Virginia Coffman
in Thorndike Large Print

Dark Winds
The Candidate's Wife
Orchid Tree

This Large Print Book carries the
Seal of Approval of N.A.V.H.

The Royles

Virginia Coffman

Thorndike Press • Thorndike, Maine

Library of Congress Cataloging in Publication Data:

Coffman, Virginia.
    The Royles / Virginia Coffman.
        p. cm.
    ISBN 1-56054-331-0 (alk. paper : lg. print)
1. Large type books. I. Title.
[PS3553.O415R68   1992]   92-28074
813'.54—dc20   CIP

Thorndike Press Basic Series Large Print edition
published in 1992 by arrangement with Severn House
Publishers Ltd.

The tree indicium is a trademark of Thorndike Press.

This book is printed on acid-free, high opacity paper. ∞

Many thanks to Edwin Buckhalter for the idea, Jay Garon for the mood, and my sister, Donnie Coffman Micciche, my best critic and best friend

PART ONE

CHAPTER ONE

They were still pushing and shoving, the women especially. They stood on the tiptoes of their cracked and worn shoes to get a better look at the forest of flowers and the mysterious packages arriving at the servants' entrance of Tiger Royle's Fifth Avenue mansion.

Watching from the third-floor window of her bedroom young Alix felt ashamed that she was the cause of all those eagerly watched preparations.

"Why do they care?" she asked Mattie Fogarty, her maid, who was almost dancing with excitement. "Why don't they hate Pa and me for having the house and the food and flowers and all? Pa says some of them are starving."

"Mr Royle's a right kind gentleman," Mattie reminded her. "Nobody as good to the poor as him. What I been hearin', you don't find them Astors and Vanderbilts doin' for the people like your pa does."

Alix smiled as she smoothed out the lace

overdress of the ballgown that was spread out on the coverlet of her wildly elaborate canopied bed.

"You'd say it even if it wasn't so, Mattie. You're sweet on Pa. I wonder if you'd like him so well when he was young, the way he had to go mucking down in the Virginia City mines."

"I would, miss. I truly would. Now, don't you go tearin' that fancy lace. You want to look right pretty for your handsome young lord. He come clear across the ocean to get engaged to you."

The idea was romantic; His Lordship looked romantic, in a kind of melancholy way, but Alix couldn't get it out of her head that Lord David Miravel would rather be hunkered down in Pa's big library chair reading the books Pa had bought by the yard. Alix had laughed to hear Tiger Royle's order: "Send me along enough books — fancy bindings in leather stamped with gold — to fill a wall twenty feet long and twelve feet high."

That was Pa, Alix thought with more tender amusement than reproof. Mama, dead so long ago, had left Alix her own legacy from the days of her painful girlhood during the Civil War: "Learn from books, honey, but also from people. You can learn a lot from your dear papa, even without books."

Mattie smoothed out the layers of sky blue satin that Pa and Mattie swore were the colour of Alix's eyes. Alix only wished they were right. Her eyes looked grey-blue when they studied her thoughtfully from the long, oval mirror in the dressing-room but she pretended to accept the compliment. Maybe Lord David would agree with Pa and not with Alix's more candid appraisal.

Mattie lost interest in the eager women from those slums that huddled behind the great, grey mansion of the Comstock Midas, "Tiger" Royle. His tenacity and power had earned him the name of Tiger so long ago he could scarcely remember that he was born plain Dan Royle.

"Looka them pearls, will ya?" Mattie touched a loop of them on the skirt in a gingerly way. "No wonder that Lordship fella wants to marry you."

For Pa's fortune.

Alix flushed but there was no use in taking offence. She knew all of New York would be saying it after tonight's announcement of the engagement.

There were too many ropes of pearls looped diagonally across the layered skirts of the gown, but it would hurt Pa to mention it. Anyway, she could admit with just a little

11

vanity that her throat and shoulders, covered by fragile lace, would show well with this neckline and nobody had yet found fault with her slender form. She hardly needed to wear a corset except, of course, that it was expected of a lady and it pushed up her breasts nicely.

Some activity in the alley below caught her attention and she opened her window. A heavy-faced dark female, wearing a fringed shawl from the Old Country, had been pushed by the flank of a policeman's mount and screamed as she fell.

The policeman backed his horse away and tried to dismount. It hadn't been his fault. The crowd's movements were responsible.

Alix cried out at the mêlée. "Can't we help? Isn't there anything — ?"

Young Mattie was completely matter-of-fact. "She's right as a trivet. Mustn't let them folks ruin your evening, miss. They'd no business bein' here in the first place. There. See? She's out of the crowd, goin' home."

"Limping."

Mattie shrugged. "That's the way of it when you get into a mob. Busted my Uncle Feeney's leg, it did. Snapped it like that. He was out where he shouldn't be. Some kind of thing he had agin' poor Mr Parnell."

12

Alix closed the window. "We should send her something. Money for a doctor."

"Her?" Mattie scoffed. "She don't know no doctor. And where'd ya find her? World's full of 'em. Gotta keep to your feet. That's all."

The late winter afternoon reflections had faded from the East River and the slums behind the Royle mansion, but the crowd, mostly female, hadn't yet drifted away.

Alix looked back out the closed window once more, made uneasy by a sudden thought: "Mattie, in all our lives, we'll never again see another afternoon like this."

" 'Cause you'll soon be Lady Alexandra Miravel?"

Alix shook her newly coiffed head with its light, sand-coloured hair arranged to show off the diamond crescent Pa had given Mama on her last birthday before the typhoid took her.

"No. It's because we can never live in the nineteenth century again. Tonight at midnight it will all be gone."

This was too deep for Mattie. "Well, miss, we'll just have to get used to the twentieth century. It might be even nicer."

Alix laughed. "I like your philosophy, Mattie."

There was no more time to be philosophical.

Mattie was listening. "Voices. I think your noble lord's been fetched up from the docks. I'll bet he was mighty pleased to ride in your pa's new horseless carriage. It's the sharpest thing in New York, so it is."

She went to the heavy oak door and looked out in a conspiratorial way. Ten feet below the balustrade on the right side of the hall she could see glimpses of the impressive second floor at the top of the great marble staircase. From this third floor the servants often watched the names called out by the pompous butler as the great of New York mounted that staircase to the second-floor ballroom and formal dining salon.

Mattie closed the door gently, but her eyes were shining with mischief.

"Long as that fancy dressmaker from Paris ain't here yet, maybe we could watch His Lordship on the staircase. He'd ought to look mighty proper."

Alix started to giggle but stopped herself. She knew it annoyed Lord David if she giggled. In that Montreux ballroom he had said jokingly, she hoped, "Only kitchen maids giggle."

"Let's go."

"I'll go first. You'll look more ladylike."

Alix was happy to follow Mattie Fogarty out into the hall whose new electric lights,

14

carefully dimmed by their fringed shades, gave the third-floor landing and panelled walls a richly sombre look. Alix wished it might be less rich and more cheerful.

But Mattie was motioning to her. She joined the maid, crouching against the elaborately carved balustrade where she could see and hear the conversation of the three men at the foot of the marble staircase. The younger pair had just separated from their host, Tiger Royle, who waved them up the staircase behind McMurtry, the butler.

The Tiger looked strong and fit but a trifle odd in a duster and a cap and goggles, all necessities for his new Daimler automobile. Some Europeans called it a "Mercedes" but Pa said that was too sissified for his beautiful white and polished metal horseless carriage.

By the time Lord David Miravel and his companion were halfway up the stairs Tiger Royle was gone. The young lord shook his head and smiled. "A trifle uncouth, but he means well."

Alix bristled but Mattie put a hand on her arm and she subsided.

Unexpectedly, Lord Miravel's companion spoke up. "Not a bad sort. I've found you can count on them when you need it. Comrades-in-arms, you might say. In my country they have highest priority."

15

His defence of her father caught Alix's fancy. He was probably Prince Kuragin, David Miravel's best man, a cousin of some kind and a prince without a country. Alix was surprised because he seemed so unlike David to be related by blood. It was David, her gentle, hazel-eyed fiancé who looked like a fairy-tale prince.

Franz Kuragin was bronze as an Arab. He looked up, attracted by something on the second floor, perhaps one of the portraits belonging to her mother's family. She could see his teeth flash beneath a narrow moustache as dark as his eyes. After the drive in the open automobile his hair was unruly, whereas David's light hair was neat and straight.

"Lovely . . . lovely," the dark prince remarked, still looking at something on the second floor wall.

David glanced up, his face suddenly bright with excitement. "I've never seen a finer range of pillars. One might as well be in Pompeii before the eruption. As you say, 'lovely', indeed."

His cousin, the prince, seemed to find this amusing. "Not the pillars, Dave. The portrait. There is an unusual quality about it. Not European in the least."

This time David understood and laughed. "Take care, Cousin. That happens to be my

16

future wife, if the details have been arranged. My mother assures me they have."

The gypsy-faced man said, "Knowing Cousin Phoebe, I'm sure they have."

It seemed to Alix that this remark was tinged with sarcasm. Perhaps he didn't realise that all social marriages were arranged this way. At least, Pa had assured her of the fact. If she had balked like a young colt at the prospect, he would certainly not have insisted.

But who could balk at marrying a real, true lord who was as handsome and gentle as David Miravel? Marrying a strange man like Prince Kuragin would have taken much more thought. He looked capable of anything.

Mattie shared Alix's thought as she and Alix scampered to her dressing-room. Once the bedroom door was closed, she rolled her eyes.

"Don't you be thinking anything about what you heard, miss. That prince person probably beats his wives."

"I wouldn't be surprised."

Nevertheless, the little conversation she had overheard took away some of Alix's excitement over the evening. It would have been much more romantic if David had agreed with the prince instead of referring to tiresome old Roman pillars.

It had been different near Montreux where she met Lord Miravel two months ago. She was twirling her parasol after sketching Lake Geneva. She had rather hoped he would praise her work. People always liked her ridiculous comic sketches of people. It was only her artistic subjects like lakes, mountains and cities that nobody except Pa's friends liked. Lord David had been lukewarm about her "Lake Geneva". But by coincidence he had just come from a meeting with Pa and several Swiss businessmen. It was Pa who told him where to find Alix and His Lordship seemed to be taken by Alix at once. Only a little more than three weeks later, she overheard the word "marriage" mentioned between David and Pa. She was enchanted. Nothing so flattering had ever happened to her in all her sixteen (now nearly seventeen) years. It was easy to love David Miravel. At twenty-four he was a perfect gentleman, tender and kind to her, even though he was an aristocrat. He always made her feel elegant and never tried to do anything Pa wouldn't permit, like make passionate love to her.

That was only for novels. She ought to know. She had read a good deal during her two years at the Virginia Academy for Young Ladies. At first, it had seemed disappointing that so much was made of the financial settlement between Lord David and Tiger Royle. But Pa said it was very proper. The Vanderbilts and the Astors and the Jeromes did it all the time.

Besides, David hadn't made the arrangements. They were between David's mother, Lady Phoebe Miravel and Alix's father. All very proper.

But like Englishmen in books David was romantically reserved. He kept his feelings to himself. She knew he couldn't hold out against her warmth and love if she persisted. He might even be like Mr Rochester in *Jane Eyre*, the book she had read by candlelight so many times during her girlhood.

He had secret sorrows. That explained the romantic melancholy that seemed to be a strong part of his character. She must be patient, yet loving.

Someone rapped on the door and Mattie wrinkled her nose. "That'll be the French dressmaker from Worth's."

"Don't let her hear you call her a dressmaker. She is much fancier, I'll have you know. Too elegant for you and me."

"Ha!" Mattie expressed herself just before she opened the heavy oak door.

The little Frenchwoman swept into the room, giving a contemptuous sniff as her eyes flicked over the furnishings, especially

19

the absurdly regal bed with its tester and curtains of heavy blue velvet, and the huge mahogany armoire that required four footmen to move it.

Alix always remembered her mother's wise and gentle comment: "Such small things as furnishings are easy enough to live with, and think how happy it makes my darling when he gives them to us."

The longer she lived with them the more Alix tried to enjoy their beauty. It wasn't easy. She had never liked gaudy, over-decorated things. But she shared her mother's feeling that Tiger Royle was exempt from the usual standards.

The sharp-faced little woman from the great House of Worth in Paris looked Alix up and down, one gloved finger tapping her teeth. She seemed to regard her task as discouraging but necessary.

"I am here, *mademoiselle*. Let us proceed with what can be done." Behind her Mattie imitated her a trifle clumsily. Whatever else the little woman from Worth's might be she carried herself with dignity.

Alix stood very straight, trying to do justice to the Frenchwoman and the House of Worth, still the greatest name in couture. This was a mistake, as a poke of the woman's elbow in the small of her back reminded her.

"Attend, mademoiselle. The posterior must be out. To replace the bustle which is — *hélas!* — out of the new style. One regrets these changes, but *c'est la mode.*"

Alix was one person who didn't regret the bustle's departure. Her figure was far thinner than that of other Fifth Avenue heiresses and there was nothing she could do about it, certainly not by standing in the swayback way that was now so popular.

"When I am Lady Miravel I intend to stand straight if I choose," she announced rather daringly.

"What absurdity! Like all true ladies, *madame* will be dressed in the fashion."

That might be, but there were two people on her side: Mattie, who chuckled at her declaration of independence, and the gypsy prince on the staircase who had called her full-length portrait "lovely". Twice.

The dreadful business was finished at last, almost to the satisfaction of the Frenchwoman. She paused, considered what she saw in the long mirror, moved into the dressing-room, and pinched the narrow bridge of her nose thoughtfully.

"Well then, it is not entirely bad. No. *Mademoiselle* is as well gowned as one would expect of an inexperienced *belle.*"

It was as near to a compliment as Alix

could expect and she was grateful. She gave *mademoiselle* an effusive "thank you" which was received with a shrug.

But Mattie made up for it. "It's a rare beauty you are, miss. Who'd have thought it?"

Alix smiled but trembled a little. This was the first time she had been the centre of attention at a ball and when Mattie offered her the exquisitely mirrored fan which was her father's latest gift, Alix dropped it once but luckily did not break the cut-glass panels and carefully opened it as she had been taught.

Tiger Royle must have been reading her mind. He knocked on the hall door and called out in excellent humour, "Time to walk the plank, Alix honey."

Alix took a long breath that seemed to cut her ribs. "I'm ready, Pa."

"She'll do," Mattie told *mademoiselle* as she opened the door for what she hoped would be Alix's triumphant entrance into both society and betrothal.

CHAPTER TWO

"It drives like a thoroughbred," Tiger Royle informed his daughter as he offered his arm.

He was looking like a thoroughbred himself in his formal black and white topped by his snowy crest of grizzled hair. His lean, rough skin might not look soft or smooth, but he had always appealed to women, and no wonder, Alix thought. He could act the gentleman but he was a man first.

Slightly confused by his remark, Alix had to shift her centre of interest.

"Oh, really? Your carriage? How nice!"

"Nice, my girl! I'll have you know automobiles don't behave *nice*. They're like they had wings, just float along. Mine, anyway."

She contradicted him mischievously. "Not when you gave me a ride the other day, Pa. It chugged all the way to Wall Street."

He shrugged that off. "Well, you've got to allow for it being unused to you, honey. Bucked and kicked a little. But you wait." He looked down at her. "You know, you're turning into a real, grown-up lady. Your mama would be right proud of you . . . That young fellow you're aiming to marry, I just hope he's worthy of you. Kind of bloodless, seems to me. Sure you really want him?"

"Of course, I do. He was so tender and sweet at Montreux and Geneva. And you ought to see how graceful he is when he plays lawn tennis." She sighed contentedly at the thought.

"I guess that makes him perfect husband material. Got to look graceful when you play lawn tennis."

She was a little worried. It would be calamitous if Pa found something wrong with Lord David at this stage. Her only real problem was how to convince her future husband that she was no longer a child. During their brief acquaintance in Switzerland he was good to her in every way but quite as autocratic as Pa. Much as she adored the Tiger, she wanted her husband to see her as a woman, not a child. It was almost as if he had never been around young ladies very much.

But Pa was teasing. "I reckon he'll do. He spoke mighty carefully about you. His second cousin, the prince, or whatever he is, he's more the type I get on with. Not that I'd trust any daughter of mine to him. They threw his old man out of his country years ago. Calls itself Lichtenbourg. Just about so big. I've had him looked up. Afraid he lived off the Miravels, but it seems to be tother way around, thanks to the inheritance from his mother. She was Lady Miravel's cousin. Anyway, he's got a kid. Little boy he's fond of. Wife died back in '94. Some hanky-panky there. But anyway, he's got the kid. The wife came from some Balkan dynasty."

Alix felt self-conscious, remembering how she had been gratified to hear Prince Kuragin praise her portrait. It seemed like treachery against her fiancé now.

Wanting to change the subject, Alix heard the chatter and looked down over the balustrade to the ground floor two storeys below. The first-comers, divested of cloaks, coats and other wraps, and having examined the marble pillars that lined the ground floor like chilly ghosts, sauntered towards the conservatory that seemed to grow out of the south walls. Other early arrivals were being ushered in through the large reception hall with its heavy marble decor.

"We aren't a minute too early," Alix reminded her father. "If we aren't careful, the Astors or the Vanderbilts will be marching in, and they'd never forgive us if they were on deck before we were."

25

He grinned. "Don't worry. When they need old Tiger's influence on Pacific Ventures, they'll forgive us."

"You forget, Pa, Mrs Vanderbilt's daughter married the Duke of Marlborough. Not just a plain, hereditary 'lord'."

"Hold your head high, honey. Nobody'll ever know the difference."

She laughed, feeling much better.

With his daughter's arm in his, Tiger Royle strolled the length of the third-floor hall to the west staircase and on down to the impressive second floor which was the summit for all those who mounted the great marble staircase. Lines had begun to form, everyone trying to look as if he or she were not in a line at all but casually waiting to mount the stairs. At the top, in solitary splendour, Tiger Royle, the Comstock Midas, waited to receive them in the company of his somewhat overdressed, sixteen-year-old daughter.

The heavily corseted ladies puffing their way up in the height of swayback fashion studied the daughter of the Midas. It was all very well for their husbands to insist on their making an appearance in this vulgar house that looked like a railway station, but they claimed their right to express an opinion of the highly decorated hostess by an exchange of side-glances.

Alix found her face aching after all her endless smiles, but there was a new excitement when Lord David Miravel mounted the stairs with his cousin, the prince without a country. His Lordship received some attention from other guests in the reception line but Alix was resentful for his sake when his companion, the prince, seemed to attract more interest.

It was a pity other people couldn't appreciate Lord David's flawless manners, his stunning looks and that oddly sad smile. All the same, his approach added to her nerves. Her own smile flickered when he reached her and bowed.

"Dear child, how charming you look!"

Child. Well . . .

Giving him her gloved hand, she said something about welcoming him and a minute later found herself staring up into the black, amused eyes of the man David introduced as his second cousin, "His Serene Highness, Prince Franz Kuragin".

"Welcome again, to you both," Tiger Royle greeted them. "Any problems with your quarters? Just slip the word to McMurtry and he'll fix you up."

Was the gypsy-like prince laughing at her and her father? The intriguing pinpoints of light in his eyes made her think so. And he wasn't even a real prince. Tiger Royle had more solid reality in his little fingers than this so-called prince had in his entire body. And he didn't dress a bit better than Pa.

She was sure his show-off behaviour had been meant to impress the other guests. She smiled mechanically and drew her hand back, only to offer it to one of the Vanderbilt females, of whom New York seemed to have more than its share.

By the time Tiger nudged her she was thoroughly relieved. She had never shunted off physical labour and was still willing to run the endless errands of a miner's boy for her father, if necessary, but playing the perfect lady and greeting several hundred people, practically strangers, was the hardest work she had ever tried.

What would her life be like in England, with all its regal formality, such as meeting Her Majesty, or that *bon vivant,* the Prince of Wales, and curtsying exactly right, and standing until given permission to sit . . . Somebody had told her permission was never given!

For the first time she felt severe qualms.

Luckily, Lord David joined her protectively as she and Tiger were separated by two male acquaintances from the San Francisco-Comstock Bank. The young Englishman balanced two brimming glasses of champagne, offering one to Alix with the thoughtful admonition, "You must be very careful, my dear, and drink it slowly. I don't like you at this sort of an affair, with the drinking and vulgarity."

Astonished, she could only stare at him. "But how else could we get engaged?"

He dismissed this nonsense with his gentle and very adult reminder, "Luckily, my child, you have a devoted teacher who will always be at your side to see that you become the future *châtelaine* of Miravel Hall. My mother was once an enchanting child like you. You will recognise the charming resemblance in several portraits at the hall. She will set your course. Don't be afraid."

"But I'm not — That is — "

"I know. I will always understand. You may be sure of that. I wonder if you will be so kind, my dear, as to show me around the conservatory. The servants told me that my own Miss Royle herself would be my best guide."

She winced at the formality of "Miss Royle" but evidently this formality was expected.

"If you want. I'd be happy to."

"I caught a glimpse of it when we arrived, but I should very much like to examine the architraves. I am told they are most unusual

29

for this sort of enclosure."

What on earth was an architrave?

She tried not to look too blank and decided on the instant that she would let the architraves fall where they might. She would simply follow his lead and try to look intelligent about it.

Even one glass of champagne had an excellent effect on her. She was so glad to be free of the receiving line and to know Lord David better that she felt confident about showing him how grown up she really was. Meanwhile, he was so kind and protective she knew she was sure she would fall in love with him, passionately, as she had hoped to do, in no time.

There had been a few nights, studying the ceiling in her bedroom, when she wondered why Lord David Miravel had chosen to make himself available to her as a husband. Surely, every heiress in New York would like to marry him.

He took her arm now and they went down the marble staircase together, making their way through the little tangle of guests towards the conservatory on the ground floor. As they started across the reception hall to the glass-enclosed room she saw Prince Kuragin in the clutches of an Astor heiress with her fingers firmly pinching his sleeve. Alix was amused to see how bored he looked, but she was embarrassed when he looked over the girl's head at David and Alix with a wry smile.

David waved his fingers at his besieged friend in a flippant farewell and disappeared with Alix into the conservatory whose arched ceiling showed them the first faint glimmer of stars.

He was very enthusiastic about the exotic flowers as well as the architecture. "Very well organised, Miss Royle. The tropical blooms just where they catch both warmth and moisture, I note. I must congratulate your father."

She wondered when he would consider the intimacy of calling her "Alix" or even "Alexandra". But she was surprised at his admiration of something so foreign to the Royles themselves and was nothing if not frank.

"That's all the gardener's doing. One in particular. He is from the Orient. He sometimes makes voyages to the Hawaiian islands and brings those flowers back, along with some other very strange ones. Hawaii is ours now, you know."

The Englishman examined the fragile white flower with its yellow heart. The flowery scent was vivid, yet not offensive to Alix, but His Lordship released it quickly, remarking, "You Yankees are rapidly forming an empire of your own. Actually, I have met the native woman who called herself queen before you Yankees annexed the islands. A woman of great dignity."

Alix felt the sting in that. "I believe it was a revolution or something, and Pa says Queen Liliuokulani couldn't get along with the American sugar interests."

"So it would seem."

If he was somehow criticising Pa, she was ready for him. "I reckon you'd say our folks acted with her like your folks are acting with the Dutch Boers in South Africa."

He did not see the connection and raised his tawny eyebrows, gently scolding her. "My brother Bayard gave his life in South Africa nearly a year ago, and at this very minute our people are under seige, perhaps starving, in enclaves there." He added gently, "My dear, are we to have our first quarrel over politics? Surely not."

Appalled at such a thought, tonight of all nights, she was quick to deny any such intention. He seemed much more pleased by her apology.

"Well, well, we'll say no more about it. I must admit, I have been impressed by the magnificent marble columns your father has gathered for this house. I find the Ionic far more appropriate than the more ornate and decadent style."

"Yes, indeed." What on earth was he talking about? She would certainly have to do some studying.

"You will find Miravel very pleasing to the eye," he went on. "As you are obviously interested in flowers." She had said she and her father were not particularly interested, but no matter. He added, "The Miravel water gardens are famous in our part of the world."

She decided she must become interested in horticulture at once. "I've always tried to assist Pa in various ways. I know I can be useful around your lovely estate."

His laughter was light, as if he reasoned with a child. "I don't think you need concern your pretty head with such matters. My mother may be in delicate health but she has managed Miravel since she was a bride. And after my brother Bayard came into the title he asked Mother to remain in control. She has handled the task beautifully. She is perfect. You will adore her. Bayard was like her in every way." He broke off. There was a catch in his voice and Alix realised how deeply David had been attached to his late brother.

She tried to think of something soothing

to say. "I wish I might have known him." She added frankly, hoping for a denial, "But then, there would be no need to marry me, would there?"

Heavens! It sounded awful, blurted out like that. He did not answer but released her arm in order to examine some tiny orchids on long stems.

She was greatly relieved when McMurtry came to warn her and His Lordship, "Mr Royle suggests you may wish to join the others in the ballroom."

For the announcement, she thought nervously.

. . . *Do I look all right? Will I behave properly, not say something wrong as I just did? Is His Lordship angry with me?* . . .

He didn't seem to be. He took her arm and very sweetly broke off one of the tiny mauve orchids, offering it to her. She was touched and enormously relieved. Perhaps, after all, he was as sweet and kind as his mother, or his beloved late brother. Holding the little flower in one fist, she raised her head and walked back up the great marble steps with Lord David, anxious to have the announcement settled. Then would come the toasts and the dancing and she could hold her head high when she thought of her ability in that field. Everybody said she danced very well. One young guest recently had told her she was light as a thistle. Whatever that meant. But she liked it.

When they reached the crowded, noisy ballroom on the second floor Alix saw her father on the little musicians' stand talking to a trim, dark man who proved to be Prince Kuragin. She wondered what on earth he and Pa had to talk about with such interest. Alix whispered to His Lordship, "How very odd! You don't think they are talking about us?"

David frowned ever so slightly. "I shouldn't think it would be any concern of Franz's. Everything has been settled. My mother assured me of that as she saw me off on the *Kaiser Wilhelm*. Fine ship, the *Wilhelm*. A pity it took the Blue Riband. We rather hoped to regain it for one of ours. What the devil — ? I beg your pardon, but what can they have their heads together about?"

By the time they made their way through the tangle of guests sparkling like diamond-studded pouter pigeons, Alix heard her father discussing, of all things, the prince's successors as rulers of Lichtenbourg. Pa had never discussed it with her and she couldn't imagine him being interested in such a little country. Not even a country. A principality, they called it.

"I don't hold much with those cousins of yours, or whoever they are. Everybody knows they were sponsored by the Austrians. On the other hand, I don't reckon you'd want to be sponsored by the kaiser, either. Germans sure are hot against Britain in South Africa."

"They are pro-Boer, I know." The prince shrugged. "Perhaps I would be myself if Her Majesty's government hadn't permitted me to settle in England. Ah! Here are the romantic pair. I leave them to you, sir."

He bowed to Tiger Royle and stepped neatly backward, off the little dais.

He really is rather graceful, Alix admitted to herself, but she thought the guests around him were overdoing it a bit.

Many of them inclined their heads to him as though he were still, like his distant uncle, the present Prince Royal of Lichtenbourg. It wasn't very democratic. The older women were even more obvious, curtsying with great difficulty in spite of their tightly corseted flesh.

For Lord David's sake Alix resented all this attention, but she saw with surprise that he did not share her resentment. She considered this very generous of him. It showed what a kind nature David had. This was far more important than a gypsy prince without a throne. David turned to her now, with the soft, melancholy smile that made her long to comfort him for whatever sorrow ate at him. He was just what her teachers had always told her was a correct gentleman, and he wanted to marry a silly western girl hardly removed from her tomboy days.

No matter how many gypsy princes with fascinating black eyes kept watching her, she must never forget that David Miravel was their superior in every way.

CHAPTER THREE

Her father motioned to her and His Lordship. David handed her up on to the dais where she would be standing between her father and His Lordship. She felt stiff with nervousness before all these eyes staring up at her but, as usual, her father was in full control.

"Folks — Ladies and Gentlemen — here we come to the real purpose of this hullabaloo. It is my pleasure to announce the engagement of my dear and only daughter, Alexandra Victoria, to His Lordship, David Alistair Miravel of Miravel Hall, Devonshire."

"Shropshire," David reminded him, *sotto voce*.

Tiger Royle laughed. "How about that, folks? Made my first mistake already. It's Miravel Hall in Shropshire . . . Well, this calls for refills of the champagne. Get busy there, fellows. We don't want a dry throat in this room."

Proudly, Alix glanced at her fiancé. To her astonishment, David was staring at the caryatids that ornamented the corners of the ceiling and seemed to fight with the great crystal chandeliers. Embarrassed, she lowered her gaze, only to meet that of Prince Kuragin. He was looking up at her and, surprisingly, he seemed a trifle concerned as if he had guessed her reaction to her fiancé's indifference. She didn't want anyone pitying her because her future husband was more interested in architecture than in her. Probably David found her lacking in grown-up appeal. She would have to do something to make herself more attractive.

She smiled at the prince with all the confidence she could summon. She could not fault his returning smile. Perhaps she had found a friend in this group of comparative strangers. It would be nice to know there was someone at the wedding besides David and Pa who approved of her. She must stop criticising him, even if it was only in silence.

She found a glass of champagne, still bubbling, stuck into her hand. Since Pa usually watched her closely when there was liquor around, she felt a strong inclination to look at him now but refrained. David received his glass and many of the guests were balancing two glasses plus fancy crackers with caviar or pâté de foie gras, anything that suggested money, none of which tasted anywhere nearly as good as the crab and shrimp and lobster she used to get on the docks of San Francisco. These fancy people didn't know what good food was, no matter how they held up their noses at Pa and Alix.

Raising his glass, Pa announced, "Looks like there's a toast due along about now, but I don't go around giving away daughters every day, so I'll just turn it all over to the best man. Prince, will you do the honours?"

Somebody tittered but it wasn't Prince Kuragin. He said, "Thank you, sir. An honour." He took a few long strides, bringing him to within a yard or so of the prospective bride and groom, and raised his glass.

"May I ask all these friends of Miss Alexandra Royle and Lord Miravel to share my very good wishes for their long and happy future."

Several British voices shouted, "Hear, hear!" and others joined in. Alix was happy to see that everyone drank, even those who had looked her up and down in the reception line, as though she had somehow got into this company by mistake.

David turned to Alix and locked her arm in his. She had always envied girls who drank in this fashion, from the glass of a sweetheart. It seemed terribly romantic. She drank as she had seen others do, and sighed with pleasure, almost forgetting to be uneasy amid all this elegance.

Behind her, Tiger Royle gave a signal to the musicians who were climbing back on to the dais. "All right, boys. Strike up!"

The crowd shuffled backwards, leaving the centre of the floor empty under the crystal lustres of the largest chandelier. Alix waited nervously for one of the couples to sweep out into a Viennese waltz. She loved dancing but was too unsure of herself socially to be an exhibitionist.

It was her new fiancé who put an arm around her slight waist and led her out on to the floor. Everyone was looking at her and David. There was nothing for it but to fit her first tentative steps to his. David was very careful and precise. It was difficult at first to move with such deliberation, but David knew what was proper and it was up to her to follow.

With relief she noticed that after she and David had circled the room in David's decorous way, her father chose one of the Astor women, perhaps "the" Mrs Astor, and they whirled out on to the floor. Prince Kuragin followed with a mature lady who seemed flustered but not displeased.

When the waltz ended, with a great deal of sweeping and circling, some of the newly

41

hired footmen were once again busy with trays of hors d'oeuvres and champagne. Alix watched His Lordship turn away to summon the footmen. Seconds later, Alix stared at her gloved hands in astonishment. One held a fresh glass of champagne and the other a pair of toast points with caviar, carefully nestled in a double damask napkin.

She looked up into Prince Kuragin's face. It was impossible to ignore his lively eyes. On the other hand, she resented what she considered was his attempt to overshadow her future husband. She handed him the napkin and the champagne, explaining in her most grown-up voice, "His Lordship has my champagne, thank you."

"Of course. Forgive me." He accepted the rejected gifts and, somewhat to her surprise, drank the champagne to its dregs while watching her over the rim of the glass. He had just finished the champagne when David returned with a glass and a Royal Doulton plate of what appeared to be tiny sardines.

She wasn't sure they appealed to her but Prince Kuragin was already eating the caviar; so she took up one sardine in its stiff little napkin and ate it, washing down the oily taste with her wine. This gave her the courage to boast, "You see, Your Highness? My future husband will always attend to my needs."

It sounded very sophisticated to her own ears but she was somewhat put out when David laughed at her effort, and turning to his friend said, "What's this, Franz? I suppose you thought I had deserted my bride. Certainly not the night we arrive, old fellow."

He sounded carefree, almost flippant, and Alix decided the champagne was relaxing him. She told herself she was pleased.

The prince inclined his head courteously. "I can see that. If you will excuse me, I believe I am summoned."

Alix's attention followed him as Prince Kuragin crossed the ballroom to the tall, beckoning brunette who gave him a dazzling smile.

Effusive, Alix thought. These New York *belles* needn't give themselves airs over girls I've known. At least, we are *ladies*.

It gave her an obscure satisfaction to tell herself this. She reached for another glass on a passing footman's tray and drank rapidly while fanning herself. Her cheeks looked uncommonly pink in the mirrored fan. No matter. Everyone else looked much the same way.

David seemed to be in great spirits, whether due to the wine or just a feeling of relief that the first formalities of the engagement were over, she couldn't be sure. Not that she blamed him.

She knew she must be very kind and understanding to him. Nobody kept secret from her the fact that he had to marry well to restore his estates and his home — her home too, when it came to that.

A San Francisco banker caught David's attention and began to extol the merits of investing in possible new discoveries in the Nevada desert.

"Can't be sure, Your Lordship, but somebody's already named it Goldfield. Sounds promising."

Alix suspected her fiancé was bored. She also suspected he didn't have the backing for a stake in the explorations, but her father's arrival relieved her. Surely he would distract the banker's attention.

He didn't, though. He asked Alix to dance, thus disappointing half a dozen young ladies who had been eyeing him hopefully.

"But there's no music, Pa."

"We'll soon fix that." He raised an arm, snapped his fingers at the violinist-leader of the scattered orchestra and in no time they were back at their places, scraping away in preparation for a fast two-step.

"Now, Lady Alexandra Victoria, may a humble admirer have this dance?"

44

"Pa, you were never humble in all your born days. And it's bad luck to call me by Lord Miravel's title before the wedding."

"No such thing. Here, let's show these fancy dudes how it's done."

They were soon joined by other dancers. Tonight was a triple celebration, an engagement, a new year and, much greater, a new century. It was obvious to Alix that almost everyone took advantage of the free-flowing champagne to celebrate. She herself was no exception, as her father noted with a frown.

"I hope you aren't overdoing the champagne, honey. Remember, you aren't allowed to drink heavy liquor very often."

Alix laughed and tapped his broad back with her fan. "This isn't often, Pa. How often does a girl get engaged?"

He looked doubtful but then agreed in his dear and caring way. "I hope only once, honey. Are you happy?"

"Awfully. Awfully."

He broke into a grin. "Then it's all right."

"Besides, I still have to drink to the new century."

"New century . . . Seems kind of a dangerous notion. I don't like to think of my girl wandering around the twentieth century without her old dad to hold her hand when she needs it. I got used to the old century.

45

There were times when I thought it was pretty wonderful. It gave me your mom. And she gave me a real special present. My girl."

She felt a burning sensation of tears behind her eyes and blinked. She didn't like the way this conversation was going.

"Pa, don't you ever dare leave me, like Mama did. Promise?"

He cleared his throat but said easily, "I sure do promise. We may have an ocean between us, but as long as a ship sails, or its engines kick over ready for the crossing, we'll be seeing each other. And I'll send you a scribble or two whenever I can get one of them mail ships to hustle off with it."

She hugged him. As the music stopped with a flourish, they halted near a pair of panelled doors thrown open to reveal the wide portrait gallery and marble staircase beyond.

A very important-looking McMurtry strutted in from the gallery. With hardly a sketch of a bow he whispered in Tiger Royle's ear. Tiger rolled his eyes.

"Might have figured that," he explained to Alix. "A pair of latecomers. Had too much to drink somewhere else, so they want to end the night here. All right, Mac, you lead

46

the way. I'll be all shock and dignity."

"Pa, be careful."

"What?" He pretended to be hurt. "You think your old pa has lost his punch? I can still outswing O'Halloran at Spider Kelly's place on the Barbary Coast."

She shook her head but was smiling when she watched him go down the staircase and along the reception hall to the equally elaborate front doors.

Some poorly trained footman or waiter had left a tray of partially filled champagne glasses on the milord chair near the credenza and Alix crossed the hall to remove it.

"May I help you?"

She was beginning to know that voice with its faint, attractive accent and it made her uneasy. She was not used to feeling uneasy among the males she had known in the west. Either they regarded her as a young tomboy friend or they were afraid of her father.

This man, maybe because he had been a prince, didn't seem to be intimidated by anything, and if he felt like a flirtation with his friend's fiancée he did not hesitate. She felt that she understood him perfectly. He was like a good-looking actor who played the Piper Opera House in Virginia City and had all the miners' women in love with him. But in the end he had left Nevada with a

47

banker's wife and later deserted her in Colorado.

Most of all, she felt uneasy about Franz Kuragin because, by his mere presence, he caused her to think too much about him.

She said with cool politeness, "Never mind, Your Highness. I'll ring for a waiter. Meanwhile, I think I've lost my fiancé."

Obediently, he set the tray back down on the leather cushion of the chair but his attention was caught by a series of little sketches mounted above the credenza.

Alix reached the ballroom doors before she looked back and caught him studying her sketches. She wanted to point out the portrait of her mother that she was so proud of and which Pa claimed was the prize of his collection, but two arms suddenly embraced her and she swung around to find David Miravel smiling into her face.

"Here is my little girl, looking prettier than ever. Come along. Our dance.'

He swung her into the ballroom. The floor was crowded with dancers, all whirling to a Strauss waltz. She forgot Prince Kuragin, the sketches and everything else. This was the romantic David Miravel she had dreamed of. Maybe the champagne had brought David out of his melancholy self. He had certainly drunk more since she had seen him half an hour ago, but he danced in a much more lively way, laughingly swung her around the turns, and whispered comments in her ear about various guests that made her giggle and sometimes laugh aloud.

"When we are married, little one," he murmured, "we'll spend every evening dancing like this. We'll even get Franz to teach us the infernal Hungarian dances."

They swung past two dancers and, to Alix's embarrassment, bumped into Prince Kuragin who dismissed the accident with a laugh and an apology to his brunette partner.

Alix was annoyed to hear the woman assure him, "Oh, but it was not the fault of Your Highness."

David only held Alix more tightly and soon whirled into another pair of dancers. Laughing as she was expected to, Alix told herself she had never been so happy.

Already, outside the windows on the Avenue side of the building the noise of the new year's crowd could be heard. The blur of shouts, screams and an occasional pistol shot into the night air reminded Alix of what lay ahead. Not one new year but a hundred, all the way to 1999. What would that be like? Different in so many ways, but, surely, something of this dear old tired century would remain.

Meanwhile, in June of the new century she would be Lady Alexandra Victoria Miravel and they might dance like this every night, though not, she hoped, quite so recklessly.

The waltz came to a flourishing close and Tiger Royle leaped up on to the little musicians' platform. The dancers, still paired off, made a wide U-shape around the platform.

Tiger called out, "The wedding party, right here, where I can say 'Bless you, my children.' Yes, that means you too, Prince."

Everybody laughed, as he meant them to do, though the brunette complained lightly, "You may have him. His Highness has been horrid. He refuses to teach me the csárdás."

The prince did not seem to hear her. He stepped forward to join the engagement party.

There was no maid of honour for Alix, who had intended to make a final choice during the next few days, but Alix and David obeyed Tiger's orders, as did Prince Kuragin. They formed the little group beneath the overpowering figure of Tiger Royle.

The noise outside was reaching a crescendo. In the ballroom one of the musicians began a drum roll. Tiger spread his arms so that his hands touched the shoulders of the two men while Alix, between them, was directly

50

in front of her father. The countdown from ten began.

"Happy New Year to all of you," Tiger called, his voice audible even over the drum roll.

The drum roll stopped at "one".

Tiger raised his arms as if he were conducting an opera. "And now, folks, happy twentieth century."

His next words, drowned by the shouts of the crowd, were for the three below him. "Kiss each other, damn it!"

David turned, his mouth brushing Alix's cheek gently. A minute later, she was aware of Prince Kuragin's lips, warm upon her left temple.

If the new century began with 1900 as everyone said, then her old life was now gone for ever. She felt shaken inside, not sure she was ready for the twentieth century.

CHAPTER FOUR

Since the wedding was planned for the end of June the Royles missed the enormous celebrations, first after news came of the lifting of the seige at Mafeking and, second, the early June occupation of Pretoria which brought the beginning of the end to the war in South Africa.

Alix's introduction to the Miravel estate had not been arranged especially for her benefit, but the last day of June seemed a fortunate choice for the wedding. Mattie Fogarty had predicted it would be so, but Mattie had a good start on grandeur herself. Today she was given a horse and buggy and the second Miravel coachman at the little Miravel railroad station and had already arrived at the hall, accompanied by the Royle steamer trunks.

Half an hour later, riding in stately fashion in an open carriage behind a four-horse team, Alix and Tiger Royle caught their first sight of the estate on an unusually bright afternoon in late June of 1900.

Facing them, David Miravel quietly revelled in their surprise. He had made the rail trip to London, meeting them at the Savoy Hotel, in order to share this moment with them. He was not disappointed by their reactions.

The wooded fields below them were covered by endless gardens and by low, rolling areas alive with bluebells shadowed by slender trees she did not recognise. In the distance, on a slight ridge above a lily pond, was Miravel Hall, three storeys high, with two wings and a warm, pink brick façade. Its many windows relieved Alix of the sneaking fear that it might be dark, gloomy and medieval. It faced the south-west and appeared to get some sunlight most of the year. But Alix decided she would wait and see proof of this before she believed implicitly in what appeared to her at first sight. It was almost too lovely to be true.

It was not so in her meeting last night with David. She had seen him for the first time since he and Prince Kuragin left New York five months ago and he was looking his very handsomest, there in the elegant lobby of the Savoy Hotel. He greeted Alix with an embrace and a kiss, just the way he had parted with her on the docks of New York in January. She felt now as she had then that his kiss was genuine and his welcoming smile touched her.

Alix was a little surprised that he didn't appear in the Savoy lobby with the prince but, as she had remarked later to Mattie Fogarty, "It was a great relief."

Luckily for everyone, Prince Kuragin had kept very much to himself during the two weeks David spent with the Royles in New York. David was not surprised. He had explained, "Franz has family friends and followers in New York. They would like to see him back on the throne his father was forced to abdicate about twenty years ago, thanks to pressure from the German and Austro-Hungarian empires. Lichtenbourg is rather crushed between the major powers. But Franz keeps up with the politics in his country. He's very democratic. Our government would like to see him on the throne again. So would the French. With us, it's partly because his mother, Princess Adelaide, was English. My mother's first cousin."

Tiger Royle agreed with David's view. He and the prince got on very well and on two occasions, at Tiger's suggestion, the prince had taken him to those political meetings with his countrymen. Of course, it might have been Tiger's way of escaping a night at the opera with Alix and David. It seemed that only Alix felt uneasy in Franz Kuragin's company.

Perhaps without intending to, the prince was a disturbing man; yet he had never shown her any special attention since that unforgettable eve of the new century, and she was determined not to think of him.

Here in the Savoy lobby David had shaken hands with Tiger, who complained to Alix later that "the boy needs a stronger grip. Might have to teach him the trick of it."

Aghast at the idea, Alix pleaded with her father not to do any such thing. Tiger had laughed and agreed, but she wasn't sure she believed him.

In the carriage David leaned forward now, reaching for Alix's hand in its cream-coloured kid glove. "My dear Alix . . . I think I may now call you Alix . . . how do you like your future home?"

"It's breathtaking," she told him frankly. "I never saw anything so beautiful. Is it all yours, all that land?"

"As far as you can see in three directions. To the north we are cut off from the Welsh border by that ridge. Miravel has been in the family since the fifteenth century. Staunch Yorkists, you know. Wore the white rose and all that."

"The War of the Roses, Pa," Alix explained.

Tiger ignored that but agreed that it was "damned impressive". He gave the estate his thoughtful consideration. "Must be worth a lot of money, especially if you subdivided it, built up a whole community."

Alix shuddered and closed her eyes while she pulled herself together after this appalling suggestion. David managed to retain his usual good manners but his voice was distinctly chilly.

"I'm afraid that would be quite impossible. My mother and I regard the estate as our sacred trust left to us by my late brother."

"Pa was making a silly joke," Alix put in quickly. "Weren't you, Pa?"

Tiger read the message in her flashing grey eyes and chuckled. "Oh, sure. Didn't mean to get your dander up. Nice little piece of property. I'll say that for it."

David ignored him and concentrated on Alix's fingers to change the subject. "These look as though you might play the violin. I should have asked you in New York. Mother used to play for Bayard, my brother. Not since he died last year. Incredible that she can do so much, considering her fragility. You will adore her. Everyone does."

"How wonderful! I envy her." Alix hoped her voice sounded as bright and sincere as she meant it to, but she caught the look

56

Tiger gave her. It was hard to fool him.

David sat up straight, dusting himself off, obviously hoping to look his best. He repeated what he had explained at least a dozen times.

"Mother had thoroughly intended to meet you in London, but I'm afraid her strength is not up to her intentions. Everything, and everyone, depends upon her. God knows I do. But she has made the effort. She will welcome us to Miravel herself, you may be sure."

Alix sighed. It must be wonderful to be so perfect, so indispensable. She wondered if she would ever reach that supreme height. Probably not. Difficulties had a habit of cropping up in her life, just when she wanted everything perfect.

The horses certainly recognised the familiar road home. They began the descent of a gentle hill like thoroughbreds on the home stretch. Tiger enjoyed the kicking up of dust and leaned forward, clenching and unclenching his hands as if they were about to take the reins.

David's eyes shone with feeling as he stared ahead at the north-west corner of the hall, partially visible on its slope above the pond. So many bright flowers rimmed the waterway, combined with the lightly wooded area that it was now difficult to see the house.

But this fact only added to Alix's admiration of the hall. She understood David's obvious passion for it and made up her mind to share his feelings. This wonderful estate would be her home with David, her home with their children, and if life permitted, their children's children. How far away that seemed!

She felt as excited as David appeared to be, but far more nervous. The sight of Miravel Hall told her very clearly that David's advice about her bridesmaids was logical, although unpleasant to her.

All the way across the Atlantic in the White Star liner *Oceanic* Alix had discussed the matter with Mattie. She wouldn't ask some fancy society girl in New York whom she didn't know or like. On the other hand, as Mattie pointed out, neither her seminary friends from Virginia, nor the girls of Nevada and Leadville, Colorado would feel at home in this lavish setting. None of her real friends had been abroad and there would be the problem of getting about in strange places, among total strangers. Tiger was happy to pay. But it would be like showing off, and David had suggested that they might feel "out of place". It was surprising that his notions should agree with Mattie's, but since Alix herself felt "out of place" she no longer had any doubt about Dulcy Fuller of Lead-ville, Colorado or even Ginevra Meiggs of Tidewater, Virginia.

During David's two-week stay in New York he had given Alix a sweet note from his mother, Lady Phoebe Miravel, welcoming her and her father to the hall. Very gently, Lady Phoebe had promised that she would be honoured to attend to the details of the ceremony, including the wedding party "which should be private in view of your tender age", as she put it. "No tiresome procession, dashing bridesmaids et cetera try-ing to outshine the bride." She had closed by calling Alix "my dear child".

Alix did not feel, at the age of sixteen, that she could contradict this great lady, even with her seventeenth birthday not too far away. But until this minute she had been undecided. Seeing Miravel Hall before her, she found her own knees shaking.

She looked down, discovered to her relief that her new grass green taffeta suit revealed none of her panic, although close examination would certainly call attention to the flutter of the cream lace at her wrists. She clasped her hands, then remembered the elegant Mary Queen of Scots hat perched on her high, fashionable pompadour. One of these sudden little gusts of wind might leave her hatless.

She concentrated on the effectiveness of her hatpins.

Lady Phoebe, and Mattie Fogarty and David had all been right. She knew that when she looked out at the splendour of Miravel Hall. She was astonished that Alexandra Victoria Royle would one day be the mistress of this palatial estate.

The aged coachman, with picturesque white whiskers and an old-fashioned imperial, swung his team over on to a narrow estate road. The horses were less impressed than Alix by what they saw before them. Trotting along just short of a gallop, they cared only for their rewards at home.

The drive crossed in front of the hall, past the west entrance and disappeared around the east wing of the building, probably to the stables.

The coachman brought the team to a halt before a set of steps that ran that length of the building's south front, between the two wings. The main portal had once been a heavy oaken door but was now reduced to a modest size whose present graceful lines were accentuated by a fanlight above.

Alix was thankful for the improvement. The present door was ajar and she would have felt like a prisoner entering New York's famous "Tombs" if the original door had been standing open like a giant mouth, waiting to swallow all who entered.

Promptly, as the carriage came to a halt at the foot of the steps, David offered his arm to Alix. She accepted his help but was hardly aware of it. All her attention had been captured by the drama in the doorway. A stout male in green and gold livery, probably the butler, had thrown the door wide open and stood as if he were on the parade ground, looking back into what must be a formal hall. He held his arm out solicitously and Alix did not need David's glow of pride to know that her future mother-in-law was about to make her appearance.

Interestingly enough, the lady, or at any rate the doorway itself, had all the benefit of the afternoon sun's rays. The theatrical effect annoyed Alix, but she saw that her father was properly impressed. He started up the steps in his exuberant way, ready to introduce himself and, undoubtedly, his daughter.

David's grasp tightened on Alix's arm.

Alix wasn't quite sure how she and Tiger should act. She knew that women curtsied to Queen Victoria and the royal family, but Lady Miravel was far from royalty. She had an awful feeling that Pa wasn't sure how to act either. She cleared her throat and called

61

to him but her voice was drowned out by the butler's careful announcement. As she had feared, it would do justice to a court presentation, at least.

"Your Ladyship, Lord Miravel has arrived with the — er — young lady."

A pale, dainty hand accepted his offered support and Lady Phoebe Miravel stepped out into the sunlight, blinking. She looked a great deal like David, still light and slender, with a soft, sensitive mouth and the smile of one who bravely conceals pain.

Alix wondered what her illness was, precisely. David had been vague about it, stressing only her courage in overcoming the tragedies of her life. Alix had supposed the death of her elder son in South Africa affected her mentally.

"My dear child." Her Ladyship took one step down towards Alix and her son. "Here you are at last. What a joy to meet you. David, you did not tell me how pretty she is. I am David's mother."

The flattery was pleasant to hear but Alix was touched by the simplicity of Lady Miravel's reference to herself, not with her title but as David's mother.

Alix's first impulse was to hurry up the steps and offer her hand, but she let David guide her while Tiger stood watching them.

Wisely, for once, he waited to see what the etiquette was in this situation.

David led his fiancée to the step just below his mother as he warned Her Ladyship anxiously, "Dearest, don't exert yourself. We'll come to you. Here she is. Our own Alexandra. Welcome to your future home, dear Alix . . . She likes to be called Alix, Mother."

He kissed Her Ladyship's cheek. She made no reference to his remark about Alix's name but gave her hand to Alix accompanied by the sweet smile with which she favoured Tiger Royle behind his daughter.

"And you need not present this gentleman to me. I have seen Mr Royle pictured in our press. We are delighted to welcome so distinguished an American to Miravel, sir."

To Alix's relief Lady Miravel and Tiger seemed highly pleased with each other and when Tiger, of all things, took the Englishwoman's hand in his, he bent his head and kissed the slight fingers.

David's eyes widened but his mother blushed faintly like fragile china and ordered David, "Be a good boy and escort my new daughter into her home. I will do the honours for her famous father."

Alix didn't know who was the more surprised, David or herself. Tiger didn't seem the least out of place. As he and his hostess entered the stately old house he pointed out to Lady Miravel all the architectural marvels of the construction, plus the wisdom of her family in remodelling from the fifteenth to the nineteenth century.

Alix wondered whether Her Ladyship cared about such technical matters and thought she might have found a motive when Lady Phoebe remarked sadly, "We had wished to make so many changes, for the comfort of the next generation, you understand, but I'm afraid such hopes were dashed when my boy Bayard — " She broke off, adding brokenly, "I believe you know our tragedy. First my husband, the late Lord Miravel, was thrown in a hunting accident. He died instantly, I am told. It is my only consolation. And now, dear David's elder brother, in whom all our hopes rested — "

"I know just how you feel, ma'am." Tiger's voice held the pain of his own unforgotten loss. "My sainted wife. I never forgot. Never will."

Lady Miravel touched his tough hand. "How beautifully you put it. Your sainted wife. I often feel that about my own boy, Bayard. You missed the country's celebration when they saved Mafeking. They went quite mad. All those desperate, starving people waiting to be relieved by our armies. The people went quite, quite mad. But to this house it brought sad memories. My poor boy died for the queen, we say. And for what? They are talking of peace now. Still, I feel it very deeply when the bands play 'Soldiers of the Queen'."

"A fine march, ma'am. Does honour to you folks. We just finished a little war with Spain. Picked up a couple of nice pieces of property out of it."

Alix gasped, but Her Ladyship subtly evaded this bit of blatant money talk. Even David pretended he hadn't heard it; so she turned her attention to the various wonders her father was extolling. Having little interest in architecture but a strong preference for the romantic, Alix was depressed by the reception hall with its severely classical Empire furniture — what there was of it!

She was stricken with awe at the sight of the broad staircase at the far end of the reception hall. The staircase ran up singly to the Miravel portrait gallery at the right and left on the second floor. Here it split off to much steeper and more forbidding stairs with iron balustrades. They ran upward past a resplendent crystal chandelier that hung from a domed ceiling high above.

"I suppose I can get used to it," she murmured.

David was touching in his anxiety. "Don't you like it? You see the right-hand stairs above the portrait gallery? I tried sliding down one time. I'd seen Bayard do it, so, of course, I had to try it."

She was horrified. "You might have been killed."

"Not quite. Though I did smash my leg in three places. When I recovered my father thrashed me. I never tried that again."

"I hope not." She clutched his arm, whether to protect him or herself she wasn't sure, but she intended to have children who played in this house and she certainly didn't want them breaking their legs, or their necks, on those horrid, high stairs above the main staircase.

David was pleased by her concern, covering her hand with his own.

As she might have expected, Pa liked the main staircase and the double stairs above. He talked about "hanging stairs". Hanging over thin air, she thought.

They were moving up the first flight of stairs very slowly, behind Tiger and Lady Miravel, when a little man with the face of a lively but clean-shaven monkey hurried up the stairs and pinched David's arm.

"Sir? Sir?"

David stopped. "Yes, Cornbury. Control

66

yourself." He turned to Alix. "My valet, Cornbury. Well, what is it? I thought we were winding down the war with the damn Boers."

"No, sir. Worse. Prince Kuragin is riding down the estate road. Looks in a bit of a hurry."

David borrowed some of Cornbury's panic. "Oh, Lord! That is bad." He released Alix's arm. "Franz hoped to delay Bertie's visit until after the wedding." He sighed and added to his mother who had come to a dead halt, "Well, Mama, it appears we're for it now."

Alix was impressed, not to say surprised, by Her Ladyship's rapid recovery and her instant command of the situation.

Was it possible that the "Bertie" who caused all this panic was actually Queen Victoria's son, the Prince of Wales? She knew she would be presented to him some day, but not until she was better acquainted with these elegant aristocrats who were her new family.

Prince Kuragin had a gift for upsetting her, but this was the worst yet.

CHAPTER FIVE

Lady Miravel removed her arm from Tiger's firm grasp and excused herself.

"What a pity! I had so wanted to show you our charming Alexandra's suite. Only until the ceremony, of course. Her maid thoroughly approves. Of good, Irish stock, by the way. Well suited to service."

"Mother," David interrupted hesitantly, "hadn't I better handle the matter with Franz? You mustn't exert yourself. Bertie will only be here overnight, after all. He and his party should be returning to Amesbury House when the ceremony is over."

Lady Miravel laughed, a careful, precise little sound, without opening her mouth. "No one else can attend to this matter. Alexandra my dear, and dear Mr Royle, you really must forgive me. We cannot have royalty arriving on our doorstep when we are totally unprepared. We will never hear the end of it. You see, he wasn't to have come until after the wedding."

Even Tiger was impressed. "Well, I'll be — Are you trying to tell me somebody connected with Queen Vic, I mean the queen, wants to meet my girl? Bertie. Isn't that what they call the Prince of Wales?"

Alix groaned. She despised herself for being ashamed of her father. "Pa, Her Ladyship has things to do. Leave her alone."

"Not at all," Her Ladyship contradicted sweetly. "I am most grateful that Mr Royle has been of such help so far. As you may have heard, I am something of an invalid. But one must rise to an occasion like this. There is certain protocol. One might say, certain training. You do understand, Mr Royle? You seem a very understanding person, with all your vast experience."

David and Alix looked at each other. They were much more surprised at the lady's friendly manner towards Tiger than the Tiger himself was.

Seeing that he had made a conquest, he suggested with solicitude, "Suppose I give you a hand, as you might say. I'll wait around here, just in case."

"Please do." Lady Phoebe touched the sleeve of his coat before turning and walking down the stairs. "I shall probably be in need of a little assistance after Prince Kuragin and I discuss this difficulty. David, show our Alix to her rooms. Her maid will take over the matter from there."

Frowning, David took Alix's hand and they went on up to the picture gallery together while David confided, "Dearest, you have quite won her over."

At any rate, someone has, Alix thought wryly but she thanked him for his compliment.

They left Tiger on the staircase leaning back against the iron stair-rail with his hands in his pockets. He was looking down, watching Lady Miravel move deliberately along the reception hall to the double doors that the liveried butler opened for her. She was probably heading through a salon towards the stables to the north-east of the house.

Mattie Fogarty had been waiting for Alix in the doorway of a daintily furnished room at the end of the south-east wing. However, the activities below the east windows attracted her and before Alix could greet her, she pointed out, "There's that good-looking prince. The one that kept running out on us in New York."

Alix dismissed the matter but followed her pointing finger with curiosity. "Never mind him. We probably bored him. I'll bet he was looking for a flirtation. Or a rich New York heiress."

"Hmph." Mattie kept watching the scene below as Lady Miravel crossed the herb garden to the distant stables. "There goes Her Ladyship. I see she's — " She saw David behind Alix and added brightly, "Wears clothes real nice."

Alix relaxed. "Yes, indeed. David, it's lovely. I never saw a room so light and pretty."

David reached around her waist and hugged her to him.

"Don't become too attached, dearest. It is only temporary. Our real apartments are on the west side where you will always see the sunlight through the beech trees on the hillside. You can see the estate road coming downhill on the edge of the woods. I love that view."

"Then I will too." She admitted now, to herself, that she had always been afraid to show her affection for him, a handicap which had troubled her from the moment of their engagement. She wanted to love him and to express that love physically, but it was hard when she kept wondering if he felt anywhere near the same feeling for her. She had felt that his reserved nature might reject her, but now, she began to believe with warm relief that he really cared for her.

The worst of her fear seemed to have

vanished: the idea that love had nothing to do with his choice of her as a wife, that the financial settlement was everything.

Today it was like the days back in Switzerland, walking by the lake, twirling her frilled parasol, and warmly flattered by the gentle attentions of a handsome and very real "lord".

She reminded herself how lucky she had been that he was not the violent, sensual hero out of those novels she and the girls of the Virginia Academy had secretly devoured by candlelight. She could still fancy she smelled the fudge candies the girls made, also secretly, to be eaten while they turned the pages with sticky fingers.

Mattie Fogarty had put her new wardrobe safely in place and carefully covered her trousseau in the oaken wardrobe; so Alix was free to go along the gallery with David to see their post-wedding apartments.

Alix was more oppressed than impressed by the many dark, gloomy portraits lining the walls. There not a woman among them, no lavish gown of a past age to add a little interest where badly needed.

She was about to say so when David saw her interest and told her proudly, "There you see them, the fourteen Lord Miravels."

"How nice, having them all where you

can see them! Did no one ever get above a lord?"

He looked startled. "I beg your pardon?"

She knew she had done something embarrassing and floundered for an explanation. "I mean, there are usually a few dukes and earls and things scattered among lords."

He smiled at her innocence. "Not in the Miravels. We are very proud of that. We have never permitted our family to be seduced by titles into serving Tudors or Stuarts, or Hanovers. Perhaps some may think us absurd sticklers for the honour of the Miravels. But there it is. When King Richard the Third died, the man whose family had lifted the Miravels from yeomanry, the first Lord Miravel took a solemn oath never to permit the family to serve any usurper."

"Never?" It seemed to her if her history was correct that this must have been over four hundred years!

"Of course," he reflected thoughtfully, "the family has made an exception with the present reign. As you heard just now, His Royal Highness is occasionally our guest. And Mama is very pleased with Queen Victoria."

Glancing at the stern, humourless faces of the Miravel ancestors again, Alix muttered, "How nice for her!" but when David failed to hear her and asked what she had said, she was wise enough to answer, "Nothing."

They crossed the gallery at the top of the main staircase and Alix looked somewhat uneasily at the two narrower staircases that curved upwards on either side of the centre stairwell. The third floor, the dome with its sunny light and the glittering chandelier, made up for the shortcomings of those stiff ancestors.

Below, on the ground floor which looked a long way off from where she stood, Alix could see a tiny garden with two stone benches and a statue of a medieval knight with his helmet carried in a businesslike fashion under one arm. The arrangement made the small area look like a sanctuary. The marble statue was surprisingly new and shining. In Alix's experience such places were old, dusty and unused.

David saw her interest in the area as she leaned over the wrought-iron rail but he made no explanation and she was too intimidated to ask for any. He held out one hand to her and she took it, answering his gentle smile with what she felt was probably juvenile enthusiasm. But it was very warm, very welcoming to know he wanted her close by him.

The apartment he referred to as their post-marital haven was fully as delightful as he had promised. It seemed feminine and he apologised for that, though it suited her very well.

David watched her reaction to the bright gold decor, including the tester and coverlet of the four-poster bed.

"This was Mama's suite. I swear to you, I didn't do more than hint, but Mama is very sharp. After a minute or two she understood and said we must have it. See the view? Those flowers under the trees marching up that hill are bluebells."

In the doorway behind them Lady Miravel was standing with His Serene Highness, Prince Kuragin. She said to him brightly, "You asked if she had arrived, Franz. Well, do greet my prospective daughter-in-law."

Alix was strongly conscious of him as always but tried to be nonchalant, knowing that even her private feelings would be a betrayal of her future husband. The prince took her hand. His lips touched the circle of flesh below the glove button. Once again, she was aware of a delightful tingling sensation in the way his touch affected her. She wished she had been shocked, but truth compelled her to admit to herself that she wasn't. When he raised his head and stared at her with those gypsy eyes, she lowered her own gaze uneasily.

Fortunately Lady Miravel did not notice this little byplay. She was too interested in the arrival of Tiger Royle.

"I was explaining why I am so happy to give David and your charming daughter the suite in which David's father and I were once so happy. I feel it only suitable. Alexandra, your father has graciously told me he thinks you will be very happy at Miravel. We are getting on famously. Your father has such interest in the estate. We are so well attuned. He has even suggested certain changes which would never have occurred to me. He has such a good eye for these masculine matters."

Somehow, Alix had never thought Pa would get on so well with a great lady like David's mother. It seemed strange. But maybe, being very female, Her Ladyship was captivated by his masculinity. It wouldn't be the first time such a thing had happened.

Alix said hurriedly, "But ma'am, I wouldn't dream of putting you out of your very own bedroom this way."

"How very good of the dear child!" She motioned to the prince and Tiger who were watching this scene between the two women. Tiger grinned, highly satisfied, but Alix found Prince Kuragin's expression odd. Surprised? Or something else? He had suddenly turned all his attention to Lady Miravel.

He was puzzled by something about her. That was it. Maybe he didn't credit her generosity.

The idea did not reassure Alix. Everything about His Serene Highness made her nervous. Whatever it was that troubled him about his mother's cousin, it seemed ungrateful after Her Ladyship's generous welcome and even if there was some insincerity in Lady Miravel's gesture, Alix preferred not to know it.

Her Ladyship made a graceful, apologetic gesture. "Of course, I am not settled into the centre suite yet, but we do have almost a week in which to prepare. Bertie — His Highness — insists on bringing the Amesbury party the night before the wedding; so it will require endless preparations and some long rehearsals. You have never met royalty, have you, my dear?"

Wasn't Prince Kuragin royalty? No matter. Worse was to come.

"No, ma'am."

"A pity." Her Ladyship sighed. "So much to do in so short a time. Fortunately, the honeymoon can be delayed — and must be — until Her Majesty is feeling more herself and Wales can be permitted to appear at some presentations. He handles them delightfully, and with his enchanting wife."

What? No honeymoon? Alix was about to protest but Tiger was ahead of her. He roared, "My girl isn't to have a honeymoon? Even a kitchen slavey gets a honeymoon."

Lady Miravel's soothing voice took command. "But my dear friend, you would not have your daughter marrying a Miravel and yet ignored at court. It would be a most shocking affair. I can promise you that."

"Well . . ." He looked sheepishly at Alix. "If my girl says she's willing — "

"I understand, ma'am." Alix hoped the slight hurt she felt and her embarrassment in front of a genuine prince did not show in the coolness of her voice.

Her ladyship did not notice. She began busily to recount the many things Alix must learn. She was just about to give Tiger his instructions when he gave everyone a mock salute.

"I'll let you folks do your playacting. Meanwhile, if it's all the same to you, I'll be giving the estate a good look. Nice little place you've got here, Lady Phoebe."

Alix wanted to laugh at Her Ladyship's open-mouthed surprise. Probably no one in her entire life had ever referred to the Miravel estate as "a nice little place" and compounded this by walking out on her. But she managed to remind him gently when he was already on the stairs, "I do hope you will not find it too shabby. Some day, perhaps. So many things need doing. You must give us your excellent advice. Do not hesitate to speak your mind, Mr Royle."

He looked up from the staircase with his natural assurance. "You can be sure of that, ma'am. Then we'll see what we can do to fix things up."

Alix caught the prince's eye and looked away quickly, beginning to understand. He must realise, as she did belatedly, that there was method in Her Ladyship's surprising acceptance of Tiger Royle despite his "western" manners. Large as the marriage settlement had been, she was looking for more.

It was painful, the way her insinuation about Alix's manners had hurt, but at that moment David asked eagerly, "You do think you will be happy here, dearest?"

"Of course I will." She squeezed his hand, grateful that at least he was sincere.

"Good. Now, I'll show you over the rest of the house. You must choose a room for your very own, for music, or reading, or entertaining the ladies. Similar to my study. All very private. Just for you and your own enjoyment."

Similar to my study. Very private.

She took the hint. This must be the way it was among aristocrats.

Lady Miravel patted her gently on the shoulder. "Dear child. How well you and David suit each other. You might have been created for each other."

Before Alix could give her the thanks she expected, Tiger called up the stairs from the reception hall below.

"Prince? You coming? I've got some ideas about loosening your uncle's bony fingers from those Lichtenbourg taxes. There is the matter of the state bonds, too. My informants tell me they are ripe for the plucking. That gang is bleeding your people dry."

Prince Kuragin turned to his hostess. "Is there something I may do for you, Cousin Phoebe?"

Her Ladyship clasped her hands with excitement. "No, Franz. Certainly not. Run along to Mr Royle. How thrilled your dear mother would be if there were even the faintest possibility of an overthrow. The princess and I used to discuss it so often when you children were in school in Switzerland. Do go now."

She was certainly unselfish in her treatment of Prince Kuragin, Alix thought, glad to find as many good qualities as possible in her future mother-in-law. She only hoped the prince wouldn't take advantage of Pa, maybe get money from him.

"Come, dearest," David whispered. "I want to show you my study. Then we may plan your own little *aerie,* as the poets say."

After David kissed his mother's cheek lightly, thanking her for the sacrifice of her bedroom, he and Alix went off to enjoy her rare privilege of entering his study.

CHAPTER SIX

Alix tried to make a joke of nearly three hours spent going up and down those curving stairs, peering into elegant rooms with faded furnishings, and actually being invited into the little study sacred to her future husband.

"I loved it all," she told David in answer to his anxious question. She added, "Even your Chamber of Horrors." She couldn't get over the fact that he carried a key to his study and locked the door carefully as they left.

David was clearly offended. "I'm sorry. I thought the way I spent my hours might be of some interest to you."

"And it was. It was."

The room had been very small, no bigger than a child's sleeping quarters, which he explained with some kind of perverse pride as "Bayard's bedroom when he was a boy. Then, when I arrived, Bayard took a larger room on the west front, and I inherited this room. I have spent many a happy day here. My bed used to be over under the window, but there were always books to remind me that if I tried very hard, I would one day be like Bayard. He read books too, but they were what you might call 'daring-do'. Very heroic. I'm not that sort, of course. But I try, in my own field."

She longed to say, "Of course, you are as good as your brother." But she was sure he would resent her praise of him. His hero-worship was too deeply ingrained.

The room itself was made smaller by its heavy furnishings, a leather-cushioned arm-chair and an equally heavy oaken desk, and three walls lined to the ceiling with richly bound but ageing books. She noted that, like the statue in the stairwell, the books were kept dusted. It was not a task she envied the upstairs maid.

There was a ladder on wheels. Out of curiosity, she stared up at the shelf just behind the top rung of the ladder. Three books were missing. Probably the three on his desk. One book was open, with a fringed tapestry bookmark in place, revealing a full-page sketch of a Greek pediment.

Beside the open book was a sheaf of paper, each page covered by careful, inked notes. The inkwell itself looked serviceable, not ornamental. The few other furnishings, in-cluding a small window opening outwards, gave on water gardens as far as she could see, bright and flashing between the summer foliage.

"You see," David pointed out, "it is my study because I study. Most so-called studious men of our class acquire all these properties of the student but they are backdrops, like furniture on a stage. What are you looking at?"

"That long column there on the page, beside your lamp. It's so plain. I like pillars with a little curl. You know. Circular."

David smiled at her naïveté. "Of course you do. That's because you are young. Lord! How young! But you will change. As I told you, I like the severity of this column. Bayard and Mother had my thesis published on the subject. Your favourite curly columns did not fare very well against the Doric and Ionic."

"The — " It sounded vaguely familiar.

"Never mind, little one. We've seen it all. Shall we go?"

She scowled at the "little one" but he was right. Nothing else seemed interesting and she was ashamed of her own ignorance.

At the door he looked back longingly. "If only we had electricity, what a blessing it would be."

She made up her mind to speak to Pa about it.

He locked the door carefully, pocketed the key in his waistcoat, and they went on to examine the rest of the third floor which was given over to guest bedrooms and, on the north face of the building, to some of the upper servants' quarters.

Alix was relieved when David recovered from his pique at the Chamber of Horrors remark. Just before sunset they joined the others at tea in a small salon opening on to the herb garden. It was a lovely room furnished in the delicate formality of the Regency style, although Lady Miravel pointed out that she preferred "the Empire" reference.

"More respectable, I always think."

David corrected his mother for the first time. "Mama, the empire, if you refer to the Napoleonic, was every ounce as shocking as the doings of our late-lamented Prince Regent."

"Not according to my grandmother, dear boy. She attended both courts. She insisted that the emperor would never have permitted such doings."

It was obvious to Alix that her future husband held one thing sacred, the attraction of design. He was even willing to do battle with his adored mother.

As for Alix herself, she wondered if she would ever, in all the years to come, be able to manage such a place with its endless rooms, plus servants, and responsibilities. But of course there would be her mother-in-law to oversee the estate. In spite of Lady Miravel's fragile appearance Alix was beginning to suspect she would be around for a long time.

Both Tiger and Lady Miravel wanted to know how Alix had enjoyed her tour of the hall's interior and she gave them a glowing endorsement, though she surreptitiously rubbed her ankle where she had kicked the bone against a wrought-iron stair-rail.

"She hasn't seen the formal salons yet," David reminded them. "Mother, will there be time to do a little refurbishing before Wales arrives? You know how he notices things."

Lady Miravel looked reproachful. "My dear, we do not discuss our personal problems in company."

"Oh, I'm not company," Tiger reminded her. "Just family, as you might say."

Lady Miravel was seated in a gold brocade-covered armchair with a high back. The brocade was somewhat faded, but the silver tea-service on the stand within her reach was highly polished and looked like an heirloom.

Tiger leaned on the top of her chair back.

She glanced up at him with one of her smiling apologies.

"We will do very well, I am sure. You must not think, Mr Royle, that we are unable to entertain properly . . . May I offer you more tea? Or those currant biscuits to your right? Our cook is an adept with sweet buns."

"Thanks, ma'am, some other time." Tiger straightened up. "I don't reckon you'd have any Kentucky Bourbon in your larder?"

Her fine eyebrows went up and she glanced at her son in a doubtful way.

Alix lost patience with her father. "Really, Pa. This is England."

"Well, good G — Lord, it isn't Scotland, so why should I drink — Never mind."

Alix was grateful to Prince Kuragin who seemed amused and saved the day.

"I've acquired a taste for it myself. If you will excuse us, I'll take Tiger to my room for a finger of bourbon. Isn't that what you call it? It is said to be a good brand."

Tiger grinned. "Well, *fingers* is more like it. Say two fingers and I'll take up your offer, Frank. Excuse us, ladies? Dave, how about you tagging along?"

Alix thought, What next? Evidently, Pa and the prince were now Tiger and Frank. If Pa insisted on being so familiar he ought at least to get their names right. Ever since she had heard David call Prince Kuragin by his first name she thought "Franz" sounded rather romantic.

But Dave refused the offer and remained to "entertain the ladies", as he put it. For some reason, perhaps because Alix felt uneasy around Lady Miravel, she was very sorry to see the other men leave. The little gathering for "tea" lacked a certain excitement; even Pa's outspoken conduct would have helped.

Her Ladyship, however, seemed happy with this arrangement and Alix soon understood why.

"What an opportunity, my dear child, for you to learn a few of the important little aspects of entertaining. Let us say I am Her Royal Highness, the Princess of Wales. Enchanting creature, Princess Alexandra."

"I was named for her," Alix put in, happy to find she had done something to please her future mother-in-law, even if Alix herself was not responsible for the royal names.

"How fortunate! Now, you will advance towards me and curtsy."

Alix set her teacup down and rose to her feet, aware that her knees were shaky as they had been in the Miravel carriage. It was absurd to feel this way. She had met President McKinley and merely inclined her head in respect. Pa had introduced her to Vice-President "Teddy" Roosevelt who didn't wait for bows and curtsies but shoved his hand out and clasped her fingers in a grip that almost rivalled Tiger's.

Well then, if she could stand up to such famous men, she felt quite capable of meeting the beautiful Princess of Wales. She stepped forward, nodded, smiled and bobbed a brief curtsy.

Lady Miravel took a long, deep breath. "Exactly like an upstairs maid." She looked over at David. Thank goodness, he didn't appear shocked.

He came to Alix, murmured in his kindly way, "Well done for a first try. Perhaps if we rehearse together?"

It was sweet and understanding of him. It also told her that his reserve might well be plain shyness. He did speak up when it seemed necessary. Dear David. She tried to let him know by her eagerness how very much she valued his support.

"Again," Her Ladyship commanded. "Not a bow, Alexandra. A curtsy. Remember. You are a lady, not some wretched miner's child."

Furious, Alix raised her chin. "But, madam, I am a miner's child, wretched or not."

David said, "Really, Mother," but his remonstrance was not needed.

Her Ladyship realised her mistake and corrected herself. "My dear, how stupid of me! I do beg your pardon. I would not have offended your father for the world. He is a splendid example of the self-made tycoon. You do well to be proud of him. Now, let us begin again . . . You will sink gently without letting any part of your person except your feet touch the floor. David, you will bow, naturally."

Alix had found it easy to make a curtsy at the Virginia Academy, but she knew her handicap here was Lady Miravel. The woman thought she was clumsy, and she felt clumsy. Luckily, David was kind and generous. He insisted on praising her, even when, at one ghastly moment, Alix lost her balance and sat down, still under the stare of Her Ladyship.

Eyebrows were lifted. No question of the lady's contempt. But just when David was helping Alix to her feet, the scene was interrupted by Horwich, the butler, to Alix's relief.

Lady Miravel had bitten her lip to avoid saying something she would regret. She snapped now, "What is it, Horwich? Please do not sneak about so. Say what you have to say."

"Yes, My Lady." The butler didn't seem the least upset by her tone. "The young person from the village would like to speak to you. In Cook's parlour."

"Young person? What young — Ah, yes. Very well. Probably about the charity bazaar. Give me your hand, Horwich."

But it was David who helped her out of her chair.

"Mother, don't exert yourself. Let Horwich see to this fellow."

Watching this, Alix was puzzled by the amount of silence between mother and son as she stared up at him. Then he shrugged.

"But you know best. Horwich, escort Her Ladyship to Cook's room. And Mother, Alix will do very well. Her manners were considered unexceptionable in New York."

"Yes, yes. Horwich, your arm. Forgive me, children. Domestic matters are always calling me away from pleasure." She left the salon on the butler's arm, sweeping up the train of her tea-gown with the other hand.

Pleasure? Alix asked herself, forcing a dutiful smile for David's sake.

When Tiger and Prince Kuragin returned matters brightened.

Dinner in the formal white and gold dining salon was excellent, the mutton succulent, the vegetables not overcooked but in what

Lady Miravel explained was the French style, and several other French innovations, like a delicious citrus ice between courses, soothed Alix's depressed feelings.

"Our cook was a present from Franz," David explained. "Old MacGaffrey died last Christmas. A bit too much of the season's cheer, I believe . . . Anyway, this one used to be in the royal family in Lichtenbourg. Franz pays his wages. But that's not unusual."

His mother frowned at her son before explaining to Tiger, "He absolutely insists, dear boy. If we could only persuade our Franz to make his home with us permanently, he might take more advantage of his gift. He has been so good to us since my dear Adelaide was taken from us. We were very close, you know."

"Not at all, Cousin Phoebe. I can never forget the way you have always welcomed my boy and me. Dave, you were going to introduce me to your new foal tomorrow."

"Tomorrow? My pleasure. Tiger Royle might enjoy the little creature, too. All legs at this stage, of course."

Tiger was just about to accept with enthusiasm when Lady Miravel interrupted.

"What a pity it must be tomorrow, David. It seems there is a somewhat delayed baptism in the village and I gave my word I would make an appearance. Rather as a moral gesture, I fancy. I should so like to have shown Mr Royle a few of our small achievements on the estate. Naturally, everywhere one looks there are things that must be done, but all in good time."

David studied his plate, trailing a bit of mutton around on his fork.

"If you must go, you must, I suppose." He apologised to Alix. "One of our local duties, you understand. They expect it from the lady of Miravel Hall."

Alix was pleased. "I think it's nice. I'd love to go."

This simple remark brought a pause, a moment when she could feel she had said something wrong and failed to understand why.

Then Lady Miravel murmured, "A generous thought, my dear. But I'm afraid it would not do. They are a proud people and they haven't been presented to you yet." She sighed. "I will go. You see, there is the embarrassment of the boy's age. To be baptised at the age of four — Well, one knows what to think. But I will allow that the creature was recently married and her husband feels that the boy should be given his name and legitimised, so to speak."

"Who is the mother of the child being

93

baptised?" Prince Kuragin asked.

David waved away the question. "No one you would know."

Lady Miravel took him to task immediately. "Don't be absurd, my dear. It is a local girl. Glynnis Chance, since her marriage. You remember her very well, Franz. You danced with her several years ago at the Midsummer Bazaar. Her child, Nick, is being baptised."

The prince said, "Ah, that girl. Four — No. Five years ago. I remember the young lady. She wanted to know if I would one day be a real live king. I said the best I could hope for was to be Prince Royal, the title my father had held."

"And a noble man your father was," Lady Miravel told him, adding to Tiger with emphasis, "We still hold high hopes that our dear Franz will regain his throne. The Romanoffs would like to see it, Franz. But you must have thought already of Russian cooperation."

"I don't entirely blame my relations for overthrowing Father. There was a great deal of meddling by the Hapsburgs. Not to mention German Willy."

"So the young lady of the bazaar has finally married someone else?" Alix asked the prince.

"So it would seem. I'm afraid she was disappointed in a mere prince. So is Max.

My son is absolutely determined to be the future 'king' of Lichtenbourg . . . But who has the young lady chosen as the boy's father? I'll be highly offended if he is anything less than an emperor."

"Some Welshman from over the border," Her Ladyship explained. "Mature, but of a better class. I attended the wedding as a favour to our vicar. He confided to me this spring at the time of the wedding that it was a trifle tardy, her fatherless boy being over four."

"Mother! Good Lord! Not before Alexandra."

Alix laughed, forgetting to look modest and shocked. Tiger waved away all this careful shelter of his daughter's morals.

"Don't worry, folks. She's a plucky little girl, my kid. Not much she can't face, and that includes boys getting fathers when they're past four. Puts me in mind of that preacher's daughter in Virginia City. Remember, honey? What a doing that was! But no harm to the kid, far as I know."

His "plucky little girl" winced but Lady Miravel, unruffled, gave her opinion as the final one.

"It is sometimes necessary to know the facts of life when one is a Miravel."

I wonder if I will ever be so pompous,

Alix thought and decided confidently that such a thing would never happen to her!

In spite of the interesting talk about girls having illegitimate children, Alix was relieved when dinner was over and with it, the better part of the evening. She wanted to be sure Mattie had seen to her clothes, especially the newest ones, and she was also anxious to be relieved of Lady Miravel's careful surveillance. No one seemed to think she might be curious about the prince's own seven-year-old son, or about the prince's wife. Maybe that explained why the prince seemed to wander around unattached. He was certainly attractive enough to have found another "princess" by this time.

She would ask David about him when she got the chance.

She was surprised when Her Ladyship, who said she had estate business to discuss with David and the estate agent, invited Tiger Royle to join them. "It might interest you to learn more about estate matters than the mere dropping of a foal. It is nothing to compare with your vast acreage in the west, I understand, but you may be curious."

"My pleasure, ma'am. I might be out of my depth but on the other hand, I could possibly have a few suggestions to offer. Not meant to intrude, of course."

"My dear sir, you would never intrude. Besides, as you put it so kindly, you are one of the Miravels now."

"One of the family, that is."

She corrected herself with a charming little blush. "One of the family. Alexandra, I hope you will forgive my snatching your papa and my David away so soon. But you must have things to do. I am sure you will wish to rearrange your rooms and to rest after such a strenuous day. Just have your maid summon our housekeeper, Mrs Skinner, and she will show you to the bathroom for a good bathe, or see to any errands you wish performed."

So this great house had "the" bathroom. Alix had heard of great houses in Europe with one bathroom, but she hadn't expected to share one with four or five other people. At home, Pa saw to it that there were several baths.

Lady Miravel was saying, "We will study our court manners tomorrow, before I leave for the village. You will be available, Alexandra?"

Alix doubted if she had a choice. "I will be available."

"Excellent. Franz, would you be so good as to escort Alexandra to her apartments?"

"A pleasure, ma'am." The prince had already got to his feet and seemed genuinely pleased, though he was cheated of the after-dinner port that the other two men were sure to be offered.

Alix would like to have warned Tiger about the "estate business". She suspected that such matters might further Her Ladyship's hints about repairs and refurbishing. Apparently the Miravels needed even more than the settlement of something over a million dollars that Pa had made to them.

It seems to cost a lot of money to get rid of a daughter, she told herself ruefully.

When the men stood up at her dismissal and a young footman in livery arrived from nowhere to pull her chair out the prince offered her his arm. There was a light-hearted gallantry about the gesture that raised her spirits a trifle.

But she had always kissed her father good-night and he was waiting with arms outstretched for a hug.

"Excuse me." She left the prince and went around the long, delicate, Adam table to Tiger. "Good night, Pa."

He hugged her with rib-threatening strength, looking over her head to make his boast, "Reckon you won't find a more devoted little puss than my Alix. Warm-hearted, just like her ma was. Now, you go pay your respects to Her Ladyship and His Lordship."

Embarrassed, she curtsied to Lady Miravel with limbs trembling but back straight.

Her Ladyship patted Alix's carefully dressed hair. "Dear child."

David kissed her forehead, murmuring, "I do hope you are going to be happy here, dearest Alix."

She was touched by the sincerity in his voice and left the room in the prince's care, feeling a little less depressed for the moment.

Outside the dining salon the big house looked dark, as if unoccupied. The prince took up an oil lamp with a pink globe from a hall side-table and noticed the look she gave to her surroundings.

"You were expecting electricity. But don't you find this glow much friendlier?"

She nodded because it occurred to her that she was almost drained of feeling at a moment when she ought to be thrilled and excited.

Maybe he understood. He said nothing while they were on their way to the portrait gallery and her bedroom. Just as they turned the corner from the great staircase to the hall she noted a portrait she hadn't seen before. Smaller than the Miravel family portraits, it revealed three painted figures, a man, a woman and a baby.

The woman was not unattractive but

seemed sullen, as though she resented this entire business of portraits. She had masses of dark hair and large, gloomy eyes. Without the circlet of stones, probably diamonds, in her hair, she might have been a stage performer.

Curiously enough, the child leaned toward the male figure, with one small hand on his "father's" sleeve. Alix studied the male figure and was suddenly intrigued.

"Is it Your Highness's family?"

He was studying the portrait. "It was. My wife, Princess Sophie Obrenovic of Serbia. And Maximilian, our son. My wife died six years ago. A carriage accident in Paris."

Alix realised she must have brought back a painful memory and he was the last person she would willingly hurt.

"I'm so sorry. I didn't know."

The princess was not a happy-looking woman, or maybe she was just in a bad mood during the sittings, but the baby's conduct was strange to Alix. It lacked the normal closeness of feeling towards his mother. There must be even more painful feelings here than she had supposed.

"My boy is at school, as you know." He smiled without humour. "Max is not yet eight but he knows the family history. Two years ago I visited schools in Britain with

Max. The Prince of Wales was most kind to us in that regard. But Max wasn't happy. He preferred the Swiss school. It was on the continent. He thought it might be closer to home."

"And you couldn't be with him, sir?"

"I know. I am far from a perfect father. Politically, it is necessary for me to travel a great deal." His fingers touched the child's small hand in the painting and lingered momentarily.

"My son Max is not the only member of the family with ambitions. I owe it to our principality. The present Prince Royal, his Chamber of Deputies and the chancellor have been disastrous to Lichtenbourg. Riots and enormous tax burdens. With private banking accounts set up in Berlin and Viennese banks. In March petitioners for tax relief were murdered by 'unknown parties'. These parties were said to be military in bearing and appeared to be under orders. They took a notion to enter the homes of a score of citizens and beat them to death. But 'unknown' assassins? I think not."

"How terrible!"

She began to realise that this man who seemed to be nothing more than a Miravel dependant, might be seriously engaged in trying to save his small country.

He turned away from the portrait.

There was tenderness and understanding in his voice. "You must be very tired after your busy day, with this new life surrounding you." He added, obviously seeing her so sympathetic, "I hope you will meet Max soon. He is a fine boy. Politically as ambitious as his father, but if you forgive that, you will like him."

"I know I will." She held out her hand. "You have my word."

For a few seconds there was something between them as they stared at each other, an electricity that Alix had never felt before. The next instant he had taken her hand and drawn her to him. The violence of his kiss made her stagger but did not shock her as much as her response. She felt a shame she had never known before. At the same time she never wanted to be free of his lean strength or the strange passion of his mouth. She returned his kiss without quite understanding herself. Then he let her go. With that release the heat and the unfamiliar passion she had felt were gone.

"I am sorry," he murmured a trifle hoarsely. "I never meant to . . . It was despicable of me."

It hadn't felt despicable to her. For that one breathtaking minute she had wondered if she was marrying the wrong man. Apparently not.

The prince walked her to the end of the hall.

The door of Alix's bedroom was opened by Mattie Fogarty holding up an oil lamp.

"This place is dark as the Con-Virginia Mine."

After a glance over her shoulder Alix corrected her. "Not at all, Mattie. The glow of an oil lamp is friendlier."

In spite of the way her moment with Prince Kuragin had ended, she had learned something that surprised her. Royalty could be very human. Even sympathetic. And unforgettably romantic.

She asked the prince as he was leaving, "Shall we see you tomorrow at the stables?"

"I am afraid not. I have a curiosity to see Mrs Chance's child at his baptism."

It was odd, almost rude, the way he had apparently cancelled his meeting with Tiger. She wondered why a baptism was important to him. Maybe he recalled the young Glynnis Chance more than he pretended to.

As for herself, Alix determined not to dream about princes who kissed and then said the act was despicable.

CHAPTER SEVEN

Down.

Curtsy.

Up.

Do not speak to royalty. Reply only.

On first being presented: "Your Royal Highness".

At any later conversation broached by the great man, address him as "sir."

Do not initiate subjects.

"Nothing to it," as Tiger Royle told Alix when she complained. "You're as good as they are, damn it!"

She groaned. "Please, Pa. That's the very attitude they sneer at in Americans. They're not going to sneer at me, I'll tell you that."

Her tiresome hours of practice and memorising took up most of the five days before the wedding, including the two hours during which Lady Miravel attended the baptism of young Nicholas Chance. In her sweet, tired voice Her Ladyship had suggested that while she was in the village at the baptism David should demonstrate the conduct ex-

104

pected of the family during the visit of the Prince of Wales.

Tiger was amused and pretended to agree, although Alix doubted if he would change an iota of his usual conduct.

Learning to cope with the Wales party didn't take all of her time. It was several days before she found her way around the hall. For her first breakfast which she preferred to "have at the table rather than in bed as if I had an ague", she walked into the little dining-room shared by the stout, good-natured housekeeper, Mrs Skinner, Horwich the butler, and David's valet.

They were a good deal surprised to see her and she didn't miss their exchange of glances. Obviously she had done something very gauche. But while the housekeeper was giving her directions, the little valet leaped to his feet in his agile, monkey-like way and escorted her to the family breakfast parlour.

"His Ludship's at breakfast now, miss. I'm bound to say, he'll be mighty pleased to see you, him being left to dine alone mostly, on account of his mama's being took sick so often."

"Just what is Her Ladyship's complaint?" Alix asked and then, feeling that she hadn't phrased this carefully, she added, "Poor lady.

It must be terrible to lose both her husband and her son in a short time."

Cornbury seemed to skip along as they turned a corner of the shabby but carefully cleaned and dusted hall.

"Lord Bayard now, he was the shock. She had great plans for him. 'Might have provided Miravel with an heir before going off to be a hero,' she used to say. But all's well. Master David will do his duty, beggin' your pardon, miss."

What a strange talk to be having with a man she scarcely knew!

But he was confident. "No question now. Don't mind telling you it was touch-and-go there for a time. Him being so bookish. She thought he'd never take an interest in — " He broke off, coughed and explained. "When Master Bayard was alive, I used to think maybe Master David would become one of them recluses you hear about. His grandpapa was like that. But no danger now. Thanks to you, miss."

They reached the pretty yellow and white breakfast parlour with its cheerful sunlight and David's gentle pleasure at her arrival made her feel wanted. He got up and, to her surprise, embraced her.

"You look so lovely, dearest. I know I've said that before but it's true, none the less."

His actions went far to wipe out the memory of some disturbing dreams last night in which Prince Kuragin played too vivid a role.

Still with an arm around her David led her over to the long sideboard. She was touched by his unexpected attention and satisfied with the thought that she had not taken his cousin's attentions too seriously. It would have been a dreadful thing to do to her future husband.

He pointed to an assortment of covered dishes on the sideboard, indicating what he thought she might prefer, and explaining, "Mama hoped you wouldn't take offence. She suffers from a weakness of the heart, so we don't encourage her to appear before she is entirely ready. She has that tiresome baptism to attend, and all the social duties."

"It was kind of her to think of me."

As a matter of fact, she was relieved. Being on her good behaviour at all times was wearing on the nerves. She had raised a polished silver cover and dropped it with a ringing bang.

"Heavens! What's this leathery, fishy thing?"

She had surprised him but he was too polite to laugh.

"Kippers, dear. You'll learn to love them. We all do."

"Not me. Ugh." She went on to take scrambled eggs, a slice of York ham and one of cold, well-done beef. There didn't seem to be anything rare. Poor Pa. He must have really suffered. She looked for potatoes but they seemed to be missing. So was the coffee. She wondered what kind of breakfast actually had sustained Pa.

The tea was there. A young man, hardly more than a boy, and not in livery at this hour, poured some steaming liquid into her cup. It was so dark she hoped it might be coffee.

Watching her with some apprehension and a very little smile, David said, "I'm afraid it's tea."

She swallowed hard and got it down. "Yes. I guessed that."

"You see, we like it so strong you may stand a spoon in it."

It was an old joke but she felt that she had to be sporting. David tried to please her. She stretched her hand out to him across the table but there was still considerable space between them.

He saw the problem and asked plaintively, "Do you think you could be happy here? It probably isn't anything like those romantic things females dream of, but it really can be quite nice if we apply ourselves. I want you to know we'll do whatever we can to make you feel at home here."

"Just be your very own self. You've already made me feel like we belong together."

"My dear . . . my dear."

A little uncomfortable at his solemnity she changed the subject, hoping to lighten this breakfast table conversation.

"Wasn't that funny how Prince Kuragin seems so interested in the baptism of that half-grown boy today?"

He signalled for more tea and drank, then peered into the cup as if he hoped to tell his fortune from the leaves. Suddenly aware that she was waiting for an answer, he shrugged.

"Oh, well, that's Franz for you. I was surprised that he remembered the girl so well. Rather a pushy sort. Out for what I believe you call 'the main chance'. I saw that years ago at the bazaar. The Welshman may have taken on a bit of a handful."

His mood had returned to the melancholy. It was something of a disappointment.

After that, the lessons in manners began. David was obliging, Tiger was amused, and Alix tried hard to live up to Miravel expectations.

It was obvious that Lady Miravel did not expect her to behave well before visitors among the country aristocracy in the neighbourhood. She had been prevented from attending the baptism of young Nicholas Chance and she was expected to be too busy to visit Miravel village.

Looking back at those first days in Miravel Hall, she was almost pleased to face her nerve-racking wedding day and the coming change in her position when she became Lady Miravel. The present title-holder would be relegated to the less prestigious "Dowager Lady Miravel".

Surely then she could rule her own household and go where she was needed or where she herself chose to go.

She had not yet heard any particulars about the Chance boy's baptism or why Prince Kuragin had said in that firm voice, "I have a curiosity to see Mrs Chance's baby."

The Royle-Miravel wedding would take place between rows of azaleas on the path to the pond, weather permitting. The hour would be exactly noon. The Prince of Wales had insisted that he and his party could easily arrive "sometime in the morning and be there in the water gardens promptly before the hour".

With this reprieve in mind Alix prepared

for bed the night before the ceremony, breathing a little easier. Mrs Skinner had supervised her bath and Mattie Fogarty set out her favourite Coty beauty cream to make her feel very glamorous while Alix undressed.

"When you're in the bath," Mattie suggested, "drink this. It's hot and it'll calm you. Sort of what we call a chicken broth. I'll be back with your night clothes when you've had a good long soak."

That was all very well and she thanked Mattie, but all day, as the hours had moved forward inexorably, she had begun to feel that the enormous future creeping up on her was too much. It made such a radical change in her. Alix Royle was being devoured by something she knew she didn't understand, a total stranger named Alexandra Victoria Miravel. It was all very well to tell herself that one day she would rule her own life. As what? A stranger?

No one, not even Mattie or Tiger understood. They thought her transformation would be glorious. If only there were one friendly face, one person who understood her deepest fears, that she would lose her real self. Prince Kuragin was sympathetic considering that he was a stranger. Lord knew he was charming and democratic to her, but he had been born a prince.

Buried deep in the huge, shining tub with its soothing water lapping at her slim young body, she wondered about the two maids who had brought the water in buckets to fill the tub. She had no right to complain about her own lot in life. They would gladly change places with her.

She examined her body with great care. After all, David would expect to find her as perfect as possible. He was a fastidious man and would be sure to notice blemishes. She had a freckle on her upper thigh. She couldn't imagine how it had got there. But he would be interested in her groin. That was where the Miravel heir would come from. It would be fantastically exciting, according to several of her knowing friends at the Virginia Academy.

She lay back, aware that her head was almost under the water, but not caring at the moment. The long strands of her hair were skewered on top of her head and the ends hung down in little ringlets.

Somewhere below her window the coachman or his aides must be noisily exercising the teams. There was a good deal of commotion. But she drank the bouillon and told herself that she would soon feel at home here and, looking back, wonder how she could ever have doubted.

It was still not time for Mattie to come and escort her back but she felt reasonably sleepy and she was curious to find out what the noise outside was about. After drying herself on the towels warmed by the little oil heater, she saw Phoebe Miravel's initials inside a circle in gold thread on the linen.

Meanwhile, what on earth was happening out on the estate road that dipped downward towards the drive in front of the hall?

She wished Mattie would come back with her nightgown and robe. Mattie had dropped Alix's chemise when she left with her clothes. It was something, anyway. She slipped on the delicate bit of silk and lace which barely came to her hips, and opened the door carefully.

There were only two lights to worry about if anyone was around. A lamp had been left on the credenza by her door at the far end of the hall, and the candles in the chandelier above the staircases glowed softly. They cast a romantic glow over the area of the portrait gallery.

It wouldn't be far to her rooms. She could always run. She grabbed a towel to warm her shoulders and hurried along the hall. Just as she was approaching the light from the chandelier high above the main staircase, she heard footsteps on the stairs. Someone

113

was speaking and she recognised at once the voice of Prince Kuragin. This was bad enough, but it was followed by another, not so pleasant in tone, though the voice sounded jovial, like someone's good-natured uncle.

She swung around but it was too late to turn back. Already, her lengthened shadow was cast on the wall of the stairwell and the big, neatly bearded man in the lead was on the top stair and had seen her. Worse, though her shoulders and breasts were partially concealed by the towel and straps of her chemise, the chandelier's light glowed upon the cool, smooth flesh of her limbs from the hips down.

Prince Kuragin recognised her at once. She heard him catch his breath. He almost smiled. She sensed the burning brightness she often saw in his eyes. She could have killed him. But at least he said nothing.

The bearded man broke off whatever he was saying and inclined his head to Alix in the most friendly way, accompanied by a grin that relieved some of her horror. She knew him as the next king-emperor, Edward Albert, Prince of Wales.

"Good evening, little lady. Did we startle you? Quite unintentional. Run along now, before you take a chill."

Though her limbs were stiff with shock and cold, she bobbed a curtsy and bowed her head, hoping he would not see and remember her face.

He chuckled as she scurried by and she heard him say to Prince Kuragin, "New at her post, I fancy. Must have frightened the poor creature out of her wits. Probably thought I would eat her. Remarkably fine limbs."

Little did he guess that her real fright was reserved for quite different matters, Prince Kuragin's opinion of her, and Lady Miravel's probable reaction when she heard about these scandalous doings.

Alix threw her sitting-room door open, slammed it, and seeing Mattie Fogarty at the window, joined her there, demanding, "Where were you?"

Mattie jumped guiltily. "I meant to come and fetch you, miss, but they're raisin' Cain down there and I just took a peek out to see what's goin' on."

"What is it?"

Mattie whispered, "Look at them furs on the females. He's come with a party, like he promised. Prince of Wales, I mean. And about twelve hours too soon. I seen him. He's already gone in."

"That I could have told you." Recovering

from her fright, Alix was feeling cross with the world.

Mattie turned away from the window.

"You saw His Nibs? When?"

"Not five minutes ago." Alix shook her hair out of its confines. Big tortoise-shell pins scattered over the carpet, but she ignored them. She dug her fingers into her scalp and massaged it along with the thick lengths of her hair.

Mattie stared. "And you lookin' like that?"

"Exactly like that. Except my hair was charmingly screwed up on top of my head."

"Oh, me Gawd . . . Me Gawd!"

Mattie looked so stricken Alix had to laugh.

"Never mind. He thinks I'm a new servant at the hall."

Mattie shook her head at the possibilities ahead. "Wait till he sees the bride tomorrow. And what d'ye suppose the old lady will say when she hears about it?"

Would Prince Kuragin tell her? Surely not. He wasn't the tale-bearing type. Would His Royal Highness himself tell her, thinking it an amusing story?

"Who cares?" Alix lied. "I'm going to bed. If I don't, tomorrow will be here before we know it."

"Glory be! If you can get through tomorrow, Miss Alix, you'll be a *'lady'* and nobody

116

can do nothing to you, including the old woman."

Alix was growing cynical. "I wish I had your confidence."

CHAPTER EIGHT

Like a veritable Cassandra, Mattie announced, "It's raining," as she opened the drapes, their pink and gold threads somewhat faded.

"Who cares?" Alix turned over and yawned. Suddenly, as the ghastly truth registered, she sat straight up in the ancient canopied bed. "Well, there goes the wedding. I don't suppose they would let it be put off because of rain, like lawn tennis."

"Not likely. The old lady's captured an almost-king under her roof. She's not going to let the show go by. Wonder where he slept last night?"

"I heard there are important married ladies not far from his suite." Alix laughed wryly. "I don't reckon he's going to visit a new upstairs maid. He said I was a 'frightened creature'."

"Don't you pay him no mind. When he sees you today he's going to get his eyes opened. Wide."

Alix got up with a groan, muttering that

fate was against her. Since this was supposed to be her special day, she rang for a hip-bath in her room and felt a little more optimistic when Mattie had fastened her into her petticoats and stockings, turned back the tea-tray and requested coffee.

No coffee being available at the moment, she settled upon chocolate which was rich, foamy and satisfying. She was still licking chocolate off her lips when Lady Miravel knocked gently and came in before Mattie could get to the door.

Alix watched her uneasily but she didn't seem to have heard about "The Prince and the Upstairs Maid". She was surprisingly calm in dealing with the rain.

"I know you must be troubled, my dear, but don't give the weather a thought. We are planning for both indoors and out of doors. His Royal Highness suggested that. Such an amiable person."

Alix was all innocence. "Then he has arrived? I did hear some sort of commotion last night."

"The wretched man came down upon us completely without notice, bringing the entire house party from the Amesburys. My consolation is that he and the Amesbury party will leave after the ceremony."

Apparently His Royal Highness could be

both amiable and "a wretched man" at the same time.

"Good old Bertie," Alix murmured.

Her Ladyship was vexed at this ill-timed humour. "Not that, if you please. Never, where anyone may hear you. After all, with Her Majesty so frail, he may be our king any day."

She gave Alix a careful examination.

"Dear me, I am afraid something must be done about your hair. It is all very well in the ordinary course of the day — I don't mean to offend you, Fogarty — but I believe I will send Pyncheon to arrange it especially for the veil and wreath. She never fails me. Spent her childhood in Paris, you know."

Pyncheon was Her Ladyship's maid, a tall, gangling, severe woman who certainly did wonders for Phoebe Miravel, so Alix had no objection. Anything to make her unlike the "frightened creature" His Royal Highness had seen last night.

Her Ladyship inspected Alix's wedding gown where it hung in all its splendour, from the top of the clothes press, its veil flying out behind the gown in a cloud of tulle.

"A pity," she murmured.

Alix and Mattie exchanged grimaces. Alix thought, Might as well brave the lioness in her den, and asked aloud, with an edgy voice, "In what way is it a pity, madam?"

Caught as much by her tone as by the words, Lady Miravel was recalled to her present position. "I mean, what a pity I could not have been present when the pattern was chosen. I see the bride in a sheath of satin with a medieval headdress from which the train was suspended."

Mattie barely suppressed a giggle but Alix managed to remain outwardly sober. "Really? Yes. I imagine that might be suitable. To an older bride."

Her Ladyship pursed her lips, gave a hint of a cold smile, and went away "to see to His Royal Highness's comfort".

"Poor man," Alix remarked after she had gone.

"You'll be havin' trouble with that female yet, mark my words."

"Only until noon. After that, Alexandra Victoria is going to run this barn of a house. Don't forget, Pa used to listen to me about a lot of things when it came to the house."

Mattie cheered her on. "That's the spirit, miss. You show 'em who's boss. Too bad there's to be no bridesmaids. I don't hold with Her Ladyship's notion of a 'private wedding'. You'd think, with two princes lookin' on — well, no matter. I think she wanted to save money."

"I wouldn't be surprised. She kept reminding me that with a private wedding, it was unbecoming. I wouldn't have them anyway. If my own friends can't be here, I don't want a pack of strangers lording it over me."

There was a good deal of bravado in Alix's outward attitude. What lay before her, except making a home and family for a kindly man like David, was a formidable challenge. David himself was the least of her worries.

From the time Pa left the mines he had pictured her future as the wife of a great and titled gentleman. No one was too good for his daughter. "Except the Prince of Wales. He's already been nabbed." The picture was alluring as a fairy tale, but frightening, too. Suppose her husband had proved to be gross, intemperate, and given to beating his wife.

One sunny day on the shores of Lake Geneva she had twirled her parasol and suddenly seen this vision, the gentle, remote man who, by wonderful coincidence, looked like the fairy-tale prince of her dreams.

This should be the happiest day of her life. Why must she be so nervous and secretly unsure of her future? It was certainly too late now to change her mind.

All the same, she kept putting off the

fateful event from moment to moment.

"Is it raining? If it is, they are bound to put off the ceremony. For an hour or so, anyway."

Mattie looked out the front window. "Seems to have let up. Bright spots here and there. It's real pretty, miss. There's an arch of flowers and leaves and stuff that you walk under. Real classy."

What with one thing and another, Mattie persuaded the curiously reluctant bride to sit still, first for her hair to be coiffed ready for the lily of the valley wreath and the flowing chiffon veil, then to stand up for the shapely silk and satin gown. As everyone else did, she had the skirt lined with taffeta which would produce a satisfying swish of sound as she walked down the still-damp path. The gown was caught at the hips by lilies of the valley and, having outlined her slender figure, it then draped her hips and limbs to the floor in many folds. The leg-of-mutton sleeves were too tight below the elbow but they accentuated her throat and bosom, especially the diamond necklace of small, dainty stones given her by her father.

It was the first thing he noticed that morning as he came in to "sneak a look at his gorgeous daughter".

Unfortunately Lady Miravel arrived shortly

after to make a final inspection. There was an immediate collision on the subject of Alix's diamond necklace and the diamond in her lily of the valley wreath crowning her elaborate coiffure.

Having acknowledged Tiger's presence by accepting his hand and placing her own small left hand on top of his, Lady Miravel said, "How proud you must be of this dear child."

"Always was. Always will be. You are looking mighty pert and sassy, ma'am. That blue hat's about as fetching as you'll find on Fifth Avenue."

Somewhat taken aback, Her Ladyship acknowledged the compliment with thanks. "It was made especially for me. Eight yards of butterfly blue veiling. But we are here to do honour to our charming Alexandra. You look quite correct, my dear."

"Thank you, ma'am."

Then Her Ladyship caught sight of the necklace flashing in the shafts of watery sunlight and closed her eyes at the painful sight.

"My dear child! My dear — really! It is totally unsuited to your age and condition."

"Condition!" Tiger thundered. "What's the meaning of that? What condition? You won't find anybody in this damned island that's more decent than my girl."

While Alix stared at herself in the mirror,

Her Ladyship's hands fluttered in her explanation.

"No-no-no. I mean to say, an unmarried young lady, a virgin — if you will pardon the term — does not wear vulgar diamonds. Not, at least, until she is Lady Miravel."

Alix caught Mattie's eye. The two girls found this whole *contretemps* delightful. Alix, in particular, was so amused she forgot to be frightened at the approaching ceremony. Not to mention her presentation to His Royal Highness.

Tiger calmed down. "So that's the idea. I'm mighty sorry, Your Ladyship. You may know best. But she's got to have something around her neck. I hate these high, tight collars all the females wear. They need some decoration or other."

Lady Miravel was nothing if not gracious. "I understand perfectly, sir. Perhaps, in the interest of time, I can save the day." She reached behind her own neck to unfasten her three strands of pearls. "These should be quite correct. Let them be my wedding present to my new daughter-in-law."

The gesture pleased Tiger. "That's real nice of you, ma'am. Fogarty, the diamonds go off. The pearls go on."

This transfer having been made, Tiger was left with the little diamond necklace Mattie

125

dropped into his hand. He turned to Her Ladyship, bowing gallantly. "And my girl's present to you, ma'am, if I may be so bold."

Lady Miravel blushed prettily. "How typically generous you are, my friend. I should not accept. It is so very — "

"Rubbish. Here. Let me fasten them around your neck, ma'am. Mighty handsome, if I do say so. Brings out the sparkle in your eyes."

"Really, sir . . . Too generous. Far too . . ."
But she accepted the diamonds.

It was less than half an hour until noon when Franz Kuragin appeared, looking in every way a prince in what Alix assumed to be his dress uniform of royal blue and red, with insignia and decorations unknown to her. Alix noted with secret admiration how his dark eyes lighted as they looked her up and down. There was no denying his pleasure at the sight, but he did not mention the fact. He was correct and circumspect, addressing Her Ladyship.

"His Royal Highness is taking his place near the pond and the orchestra has been seated. The Amesbury group are finding their places. I'll join Dave at once."

"Oh, dear. And not even noon yet. But we cannot keep Bertie waiting." Her Ladyship was always at her best when in command.

"I shall join His Royal Highness and as we rehearsed, the bride and Mr Royle will begin their walk upon the rendition of the march." To Alix she added, "Don't forget your curtsy, my dear." Then she swept out of the room, upon the prince's arm, her free hand fingering her necklace.

Tiger grumbled, "A fine how de do when an old fogey not even connected with the wedding can tell my daughter when to get married. Just on account of being a prince. We licked them Limeys twice. Don't they remember?"

Mattie laughed but Alix was not in a humorous mood. She looked around nervously.

"Pa, please. You're talking about the greatest empire on earth."

"Ha! Are you ready? How's she look, Fogarty? Anything undone?"

"Nothing, sir. You're both just about perfect. I'll be pretty close, miss, to let your veil float out behind you when you start your walk."

"Thank you, dear Mattie." Alix was shaken but she hugged the Irish girl, and took her father's arm.

As they reached the top of the broad staircase the whole enormous future loomed up before her and she laughed nervously. "Sure is a long walk, Pa. And how it'll end, I only wish I knew."

He patted her cold knuckles. He looked a bit tense himself but she thought he had never appeared more handsome in her eyes.

"It'll end with my girl's happiness."

They walked down the stairs together. She wondered if he was thinking that after this hour her future would be devoted to English David Miravel, not to her American father far across the vast Atlantic.

In their uneasiness they were a minute too early for the orchestra when they reached the open south doors. They waited, both of them taking deep breaths until the music hit the precise note they had rehearsed. They moved forward, Tiger trying for a shorter step, Alix for a longer one, and came out almost perfectly together.

Ahead of them, down the path which had been covered by a slightly moist crimson carpet, Alix saw Prince Kuragin first. He was somewhat taller than David and, of course, considerably darker. She told herself that he stood out. That was all. But she was conscious of his gaze which seemed to her much more penetrating than that of anyone else. He did not smile. His expression was sombre; yet even the portly Prince of Wales, with his fine bearing and a genuine smile, did not seem so impressive. What a magnificent Prince Royal Franz Kuragin would make if he could only win back the throne that was rightly his! She was ashamed that the thought should come into her head at such a moment.

She shifted her gaze to David, standing beside his friend and staring at her and Tiger, as everyone was. David looked wistful as usual, poor man. Very likely he was as nervous about the future as she was.

She looked at him tenderly, hoping to make him understand the affection that would go with the future they must share. Over David's beautifully composed features a faint smile flickered. He understood.

In spite of the crimson carpet, the water from the night's shower seeped through. She began to feel the sogginess in her white satin slippers. It would certainly stain her lovely silk stockings. She almost stumbled in trying to avoid a puddle but Tiger's heavy hand under her arm kept her from disaster.

"Doing fine, honey," he murmured, almost between his teeth.

Among the more than a dozen guests from the Amesbury house party there was no mistaking the Prince of Wales. He looked so genial, so friendly, he could not have recognised her as the "frightened maidservant of last night".

She and Tiger had almost reached the small vicar in front of the pool, with David and Prince Kuragin on his left and the Prince of Wales on his right. Now was the moment she had dreaded.

She whispered, "Here goes, Pa," and curtsied to His Royal Highness at the precise second that Tiger bowed more gracefully than at the rehearsal. She knew the beautifully embroidered satin hem of her gown had dipped in rainwater but too much was happening for her to care.

The Prince of Wales acknowledged her curtsy with the friendly smile she remembered from last night. She only hoped his memory was not so vivid. Then Tiger gave her over to David and when the vicar had cleared his throat a couple of times, the service began.

The weather had turned chilly after the night's rain, but Alix was too nervous among these elegant strangers to feel it. David's arm pressed close to hers as they stood before the vicar and Alix sensed that he shared her feelings, but he was sensitive enough to give her a gentle look that seemed to understand and she felt better for a minute or two.

The service itself had been rehearsed and Alix was prepared for her own vows. Nevertheless, her imagination ran wild when she

130

heard the Reverend Pittridge command: "I require and charge you both . . . that if either of you know any impediment . . ." She recalled those fateful words in one of her favourite novels, *Jane Eyre*, and waited anxiously during the few seconds the vicar allowed for a reply which none but Alix expected.

No voice was raised against the marriage, and Alix was intensely relieved when Prince Kuragin handed the ring to David who carefully eased the simple gold band on to her finger. Her engagement ring, temporarily on her other hand, did not overshadow the plain band by its blinding emerald-cut diamond in a frame (a trifle gaudy) of less ostentatious diamonds. She had always suspected the engagement ring was actually Tiger's contribution, in part, at least. It was far too "vulgar" to have been David's choice. Alix felt David's lips brush her cheek, followed by a warm embrace. She returned his hug almost too enthusiastically, in order to show her relief that the ceremony had gone off without a hitch.

She and David were both embarrassed when the Prince of Wales ordered David in his jovial fashion, "Kiss her, lad. It is quite legal, you know."

Everyone laughed dutifully, the younger

women tittering, although it was obvious that His Royal Highness's attentions were directed in general towards more buxom and mature ladies.

But David kissed Alix again, this time on the lips. His kiss meant less to her than his whispered words, "I do love you, my dearest. I can't imagine anyone else, ever."

She felt flushed and happy. He cared for her. He had practically said so.

The others came after. His Royal Highness had obviously assumed he would be the next to kiss the bride but Tiger Royle elbowed his way forward, kissed her brusquely on the forehead, and then squeezed her so tight she laughed and cried out at the same time.

The Prince of Wales had gallantly stepped aside but now claimed his turn. Alix wondered if she should curtsy but he was too quick for her, kissing her just beside the lips and tickling her with his beard. She had a dreadful inclination to sneeze but luckily controlled herself.

How nice that David was clean-shaven!

The Prince of Wales was just making way for the next man to salute the bride with a kiss when he must have recognised her. He blinked and then grinned knowingly at her. She felt sure he wouldn't tell Her Ladyship or David about last night. She gave His Royal

Highness her best smile in gratitude.

Others poured forward and Wales moved back, enjoying a spectacle in which, for once, he was not the leading figure.

Lady Miravel presented Alix to Sir Humphrey Amesbury and Lady Amesbury, without whose house party Alix thought the whole affair would have been pleasantly intimate.

The stout Sir Humphrey seemed friendly, even flirtatious.

Lady Amesbury had very "speaking" eyebrows. They spent some of the time looking surprised. She was polite though, and ignored Lady Miravel's frown when Alix made the mistake of curtsying to her.

Then one of the guests unknown to Alix called, "Lady Miravel?"

Alix heard Lady Phoebe answer, "Yes? Who called me?"

There was an awkward laugh and a pretty, yellow-haired female who had called out to her said, "You mean ter say I'm the first to wish the new Lady Miravel good luck and a deal of happiness?"

Several people laughed to cover the moment and Lady Phoebe's stiff reply.

"Of course. How stupid of me! You mean my daughter-in-law." Then she turned her back pointedly on the blonde.

The crowd parted and Alix got a good look at the yellow-haired girl who was fussily overdressed in a *Lapin* fur coat and a small-crowned hat trimmed with a profusion of artificial flowers. The girl nudged her way forward. Her voice slurred a little.

"So you're the lucky Yankee. S'a privilege, Yer La-ship. Me, I'm Glynnis Chance. 'Spected I might see you at my lad's bap-bap — naming day, but I reckon you'd better things to do."

"I'm sorry. I wanted to come, but — "

Glynnis gave the Dowager Lady Miravel a side-glance. "Sure now, I could've guessed it. 'Scuse the in'erruption. Got to get at the champagne 'fore it runs out. See you, Yer La'ship."

She sounded as if she had been at the champagne for some time.

Alix saw Prince Kuragin take her arm and lead her away. She wondered what was between them, or was he simply doing the rest of the company a favour? She watched while he got the girl a glass not quite full of champagne. Then he talked to her in what seemed to be a friendly way.

He had not kissed the bride.

CHAPTER NINE

The Prince of Wales proposed the toast.

"Dear old fellow, and the enchanting Lady Alexandra, may you know a century of happiness."

Everyone responded with enthusiasm. Alix looked up at David, just as he was gazing at her.

He seemed to come out of a spell. "My dearest, may I take this perfect moment to tell you I am the luckiest man alive?"

She was too touched to do anything but brush his lips with her kiss. It sounded to her as though everyone cheered. With his arms around her and her head back against his cheek she looked at the guests. On the outskirts of the laughing, joking crowd Franz Kuragin stood alone, watching the bride and groom. He seemed to have forgotten the champagne glass in his own hand. It was still full.

As she stared at him, wondering, he raised the glass and did not stop until he had drunk the champagne to its dregs. She felt the moment so intensely she was afraid he might throw the glass down and break it like a character in a bad melodrama, but he merely set it on a rock bordering the pond and, with a laugh, responded to something Glynnis Chance said to him.

Was it possible, even remotely so, that Prince Kuragin was the father of Glynnis Chance's child? The idea revolted Alix. It couldn't be true. But why not? She suspected he would be quite capable of it. He was too attractive for his own good.

The Dowager Lady Miravel, who had been exchanging chit-chat with the Prince of Wales came up to the bride and groom.

"I think you may throw your bouquet, my dear. David, take our Alexandra to the steps. The rest of the ladies will gather on the driveway below."

Alix hated to give away her bridal bouquet with the long trail of tiny lilies of the valley and the exquisite white satin ribbons, but it was certainly expected, as her mother-in-law had sweetly reminded her.

She nodded and David began to lead her up along the now soggy red carpet to the long south-west front of the hall. On the way there were jokes and good wishes from the Prince of Wales surrounded by the usual chattering group of "courtiers".

Alix dropped a dignified curtsy of which she was rather proud but the effect was spoiled by His Highness's knowing grin. He hadn't forgotten their embarrassing encounter in the portrait gallery last night. Alix's respectable effort was ruined by her quick, answering smile in response to his grin.

She passed her father who blew her a kiss which she returned with devotion shining in her eyes.

Reaching the steps Alix turned her back upon the guests so she wouldn't show favourites. She tossed the bouquet. As usual, she had a very poor aim. Lady Miravel was prominently in front of the noisy group. At the last minute a giggling Glynnis Chance made the catch with an athletic leap into the air. She was immediately pursued by the laughing Amesbury ladies who claimed forfeit because she had already captured her man. Glynnis held the delicate *muguet* to her nose and looked up into Alix's eyes.

Alix ignored her, searching through the crowd for her father. She saw Wales. He was exchanging a few words with Prince Kuragin. He began to clear his way among the chattering women towards Alix and David.

Alix wondered what his conversation with Prince Kuragin had been about, but it was good to know that a man of Wales's future power was willing to wield it in the cause of a man like Franz Kuragin. She glanced over at Kuragin. He bowed to her. She nodded, giving him her pleasant, impersonal smile, and saved her warmth for His Royal Highness.

"How good it was of you to come, sir."

"Most rewarding, I assure you. I had the pleasure of a few words with your father some minutes ago. Admirable man. How fortunate you are to have a father who cares so much for you. I am a father and I know how little of our children we see. I was explaining this to His Serene Highness who may be making the mistakes so many of us do. He is forced by circumstance to place his child second to the rescue of his country. Then it is necessary to purchase a child's affection with expensive gifts. But we love those children all the same."

"I never doubted it, sir, and I know His Highness feels very deeply about his son. But it is true that my father never had to buy my love. I was always with him, except when I was at the Ladies' Academy."

She was surprised by the edge to his rough voice.

"Then you are both fortunate. An understanding parent is a pearl beyond price, and as rare to find."

He peered up into the sky where black clouds scudded across the blue, threatening a downpour.

"I think it best if we all leave you and young Miravel to the joys of your honeymoon. The sky looks very forbidding and Amesbury is quite a distance."

She told him earnestly, "I'm sorry. It was a pleasure to meet you. We will miss you. Really."

She thought he was going to smile at that spontaneous addition, but he only added, taking her fingers briefly, "You are a good child. You will make a handsome woman. Miravel has chosen wisely."

She curtsied, tongue-tied for the moment.

Shortly after, the guests, plus a coterie of valets and ladies' maids, had loaded carriage-boots with their overnight properties — enough to keep them a month, Alix thought, and one by one, each carriage and each horse-man departed.

Those in closed carriages were lucky. The more hardy adventurers rode off, buffeted by wind and rain, but with many a good wish for the bride and groom.

The Dowager Lady Miravel accepted all such wishes in her usual gracious manner, leaving Alix speechless, though perfectly willing to reply.

She was nervous enough to let the matter rest for the time being. This would be a ghastly time to quarrel.

The servants ran about in the rain, clearing up the debris left by the guests who had dropped double damask napkins and various hors d'oeuvres wherever they happened to be when the Prince of Wales decided on their departure.

Instinctively, Alix started to help them but this produced alarming symptoms of impending palpitations in the dowager who gave her son an unmistakable signal. It was time for him to get better acquainted with his bride, preferably in a bedchamber.

Alix accepted David's escort and they went on up to the suite reserved for her the night she arrived. Here they met Mattie Fogarty who sighed over the raindrops on the white satin of her wedding gown.

Alix looked out the front window and was astonished to see her father and the dark prince working in the rain. The prince's damp hair made him look more like a gypsy than ever. The two men had organised the cleaning-up of the garden and the azalea walk. At this minute they were busy rolling up the red carpet.

Alix muttered, "Well, I never! A prince cleaning up, and in the rain."

David looked casually over her head. "Oh, that is nothing to Franz. He enjoys being active."

Mattie interrupted whatever thoughts were circulating in Alix's head. She wasn't quite sure herself. She was still nervous over behaving "correctly" when David made love to her tonight.

"You best get out of that outfit or it'll never be good for anything. Just look at that hem. Must've dragged it in the mud."

Alix reminded her flippantly, "I don't see how I'd have got to the preacher — I mean vicar — without dragging it in the mud. It wasn't my fault."

Mattie glanced over at David who was beginning to act as if he wished he was anywhere else. Watching young ladies disrobe was not, apparently, a common practice with him.

"Your Lordship might be unhooking Her Ladyship tonight. Reckon you don't want to be all thumbs, sir."

His fine skin flushed at her frankness and Alix laughed, but he came back hesitantly, with an embarrassed attempt at a knowing grin. He fumbled with the satin and lace at her neck. Alix leaned her cheek lovingly against his knuckles.

This inspired him to kiss her hair which

141

was still windblown and slightly damp.

She was pleased and touched. If only she could teach him to kiss her like Franz Kuragin.

No. Banish the thought.

Suddenly, Mattie reached around to a shelf of the open clothes press and Alix found herself showered with little rosettes made of the satin left over from the wedding gown.

"Thought somebody'd ought to treat you like a bride, miss."

It was so dear of her that Alix hugged her.

David said pleasantly, "Fogarty, would you go down to the kitchen and see if Lady Alexandra's afternoon tea-tray is ready?"

Mattie went off on a run. When she had gone David squeezed Alix's hand to soften his quiet criticism.

"Dearest, we don't treat ladies' maids as family . . . But there. How could you know? You mustn't ever mind asking Mother or me if you are in doubt."

"Oh, I will, I'll just do that."

He was satisfied, reading nothing but eagerness and a dutiful, wifely respect.

This was no day to show annoyance, so she tried to dismiss the feeling of resentment he had aroused in her by saying with a teasing manner she hoped would break down his reserve, "I mean to change for tea, David. Maybe you can help me unfasten the rest of this gown. It seems to have me locked in."

"Yes. Of course." He tried to make a little joke. "Glad to be of service, madam." For good measure he added, "How very charming you looked today. And now too, naturally."

It seemed to be an afterthought but he did his duty, so far as the wedding gown was concerned. All the same, he was relieved when Mattie returned with her tray.

Alix had thought he would join her at tea, especially since she was looking quite seductive in her apricot lounging gown with its layers of fragile, opaque chiffon floating around her. She was just as uncertain about the marital aspects of their relationship as he could be, but she had trusted to his gentle concern and hoped he would lead the way in teaching her.

Instead, he seemed pleased that she was so comfortably seated on her *chaise-longue* and he could leave her to Fogarty's attentions.

"I really must see to matters in the garden. These temporary hired servants are so impossible. In Father's day we had an adequate staff. But we also had Father. An incurable gambler." He shrugged. "Dearest, this can't be interesting to you. I'll leave you to chatter away with Fogarty."

She was so annoyed she said with cutting brightness, "Yes. Do." When the door had closed she asked Mattie, "Is this what marriage is all about?"

"Now, miss, don't you be downhearted. His Lordship's shy. That's the straight and truth of it. Men's shy, just like women. Maybe you're his first."

It's Pa's money, Alix thought. And that's all it amounts to.

She threw off the seductive pose which she had borrowed from her favourite romantic novels and got to her feet. She crossed the room trailing a cloud of apricot chiffon and began to scramble through some of her possessions temporarily stored in her cedar chest.

"What on earth?" Mattie asked.

"I'm going to read a book. That, at least, should be exciting."

"Now, miss."

"Now, miss, nothing. I'd rather read *Quo Vadis* than beg my husband to love me."

"*Quo* who? I don't hold with them Frenchie writers. Like as not, they're full of nasty sex."

"The writer is Polish and the sex is confined to Nero. Ah. Here it is. I'll bet Nero could teach David a few things."

Mattie rolled her eyes. "Wouldn't doubt it, miss." She began to put away the pieces of Alix's wedding regalia which were not water-stained.

While she folded and laid aside these items of lingerie and petticoats to be put into another chest, Alix threw her book aside and got up.

"I'll take the tray down."

"What? You'd never. Her Ladyship will be all hoity-toity."

Alix grinned, her eyes sparkling with battle signs. "You forget who's Lady Miravel now. Remember that girl from the village, that Mrs Chance? She was the first to call me that. I'm afraid Her Ladyship was confused by it. Probably forgot."

"Well, I never."

Alix stripped off the chiffon, had Mattie fasten her into yesterday's tea-gown, and went out with the untouched tea-tray. She met no one on her way down the servants' stairs but managed to startle a thin, wide-eyed scullery girl as she appeared in the kitchen.

"Yes, Maud, it's me," she told the girl cheerfully. "I just wanted some exercise. Where is everybody?"

Maud had as bad a time as Alix with her curtsy while she confided, after looking around furtively, "Her Ladyship — I mean

145

the other Ladyship, scolded the prince, the handsome one, a bit ago."

"Scolded? About what?"

Maud was non-committal. "Dunno, ma'am. But I fetched in the whisky as ordered, all the household being busy in the gardens."

Alix, who had been leaving, found this puzzling news. She stopped to ask, "And is Lord — I mean my husband, drinking too?"

"I'd say so. I brung the whisky to the small salon. That prince looked downright cross. Maybe he don't drink."

"Maybe." But he had certainly managed his share of the champagne at the wedding.

A trifle late, Maud recalled, "Your good father, ma'am, he said give you this when you wasn't busy. Is now the right time?"

"Yes. Certainly." Alix took the sheet of notepaper and unfolded it. What was Pa saying that he couldn't tell her himself?

She understood when she made out his familiar, rough hand which was always difficult to decipher.

Honey,
Didn't want to interfere with the honeymooners. I'm up to London to get you and my new son a nice little surprise. God knows you need it. I asked Frank K. to come with me, kind of lend me

his ideas on the make and all, but Her Ladyship had a conip — [This was crossed out] conniption fit, said she needed him at the hall, so I'm off. While I'm at it I'll tend to some bank business.

Love,
Tiger

Dear Pa. He probably thought she was divinely happy.

The references, both by Tiger and by the girl Maud were puzzling and Alix returned to her suite wondering what had brought on this odd behaviour between the dowager and Prince Kuragin.

Not that it mattered. Alix's steps were slower than usual as she walked up the servants' stairs. She felt tired and painfully disillusioned. The events of her wedding were nothing like the way she had dreamed they would be. She wished now that she had never met handsome, sad-eyed David Miravel on the shores of Lake Geneva, or anywhere else.

She had just reached the door of her suite in the gloom of a rain-threatened afternoon when two hands went over her eyes and she was trapped in someone's arms. It was the sort of thing she had dreamed, once or twice, of Prince Kuragin doing, but he would scarcely try anything like this today, of all days. She struggled, angry that her own mood should be so carelessly taken for granted.

"Let me go. I don't like being pawed."

David's voice murmured in her ear, "I wouldn't paw you for worlds, sweetheart. But you are so delightfully young, so adorable, what can you expect?" He kissed her ear. It was an abrupt gesture but pleasing to her pride and her downcast mood. He went on murmuring in her ear, saying things that should have offended her, but they didn't. She knew he was trying desperately hard to be the lover she expected.

"Everyone envies me. Did you know that? Come, be kind to me. Remember, this is our wedding day. We only have one in our whole lives."

She laughed. It was slightly hysterical, but he mistook it for gaiety.

"That's my dearest girl. Come. Let's celebrate. I sent Fogarty off. We have a perfect right, you know. Josiah Pittridge said so."

"Josiah Pittridge? What has he to say about our lives?"

"The vicar. Good Lord! It's perfectly legitimate." He broke off, adding with a sudden rush of painful doubt, "You could learn to love me, couldn't you? Dearest, you've been so kind, I know I could love you. I suppose you've guessed by now that I'm not precisely

148

a Don Juan. Bayard did all of that sort of thing. I envied him a little, but it was easier just to be myself, with my books and my quiet life."

Something lost and hopeless in his voice touched her more deeply than she had imagined. Whatever his reasons for neglecting her, he wanted to make up for it now, and she turned to him smiling. Her eyes lighted again as she hoped to excite his own feelings for her.

Having gone this far, he reached over her shoulder, pushed the door open, and then, having inhaled deeply, picked her up in his arms and carried her into her bedroom.

After a first clumsy second or two he managed very well. She was thrilled by his romantic gesture. Nobody but her father had ever picked her up before, and of course, in Tiger's case, he picked her up when she fell down flat on her face in the middle of "C" Street in Virginia City. Still, being practical, she felt that she was lucky to weigh so little.

Before David set her down on the high, four-poster bed she began to smell the heavy liquor fumes on his breath and remembered how it had taken liquor to make him dance so recklessly on the night of their engagement party. They were not pleasant fumes, but she understood. He must have tried in every other way to gird his loins, literally, in order to make this a romantic wedding day.

She held out her arms to him and he went into them, his face close over hers, excited by his great success in having aroused his innocent bride. He bent closer until his mouth touched hers, his flesh surprisingly warm, for David. She found herself unexpectedly aroused. When he kissed her in a way that suggested "sampling" to her perverse humour, she remembered the hot passion of Prince Kuragin's kiss and responded to her husband with all the pent-up emotions that had been suppressed all day.

She was excited by the success of their combined efforts. His hands had gripped her shoulders but now he began to fumble with her chiffon gown, trying to slip it off her shoulders. She made no attempt to undress him or herself but lay quiet under his exploring hands, her pulses rising with her desire. She wondered if he had ever undressed a girl before.

Practice . . . Practice . . . she told herself, and wanted to laugh but luckily did not.

His fingers moved over the lacy top of her tea-gown, found the buttons at the back and slipped the high neck down until he reached the first buttons of her bodice. Whispering words that were half lewd, half apology, he bared her bodice and camisole, covering her pale flesh with kisses.

She knew by what the girls at the Young Ladies' School had told her, that his hardness meant he was about ready to come. She reached out, trying to remove his tight trousers. He drew back, his light features red with mingled embarrassment and desire, and removed the trousers as well as his underwear. His flesh was almost as white as hers.

He had calmed a little but the sight of her well-developed breasts gleaming pink and white in the late day made him shudder with what she hoped was desire. He tore away the lovely pleated skirt of her gown, then the petticoats, and suddenly, forced his way painfully into her body.

She cried out, though she had expected it. That too she had heard about. But she felt sorry for David who desperately clung to her, yet whispered repeated apologies. He was sweating and breathing hard.

In spite of everything, she felt that he might learn to love her. He certainly seemed more assured now. She put her arms around his neck and urged by the faint but delicious thrill of his body joined to hers in spite of the first pain, she let her fingers trail sensitively over the back of his neck.

Her effort must have pleased him. He whispered endearments even as he retreated, shaking with the strenuous and unaccustomed emotions he had released.

He sat up, pulling himself together, very much the conquering, generous male.

"You see, dearest? We belong together, just as Mother said." As if a slight doubt had occurred to him, he went on, "It will be better next time."

She told him stoutly, "You were wonderful this time."

He leaned over her again and hugged her. "Sweetheart."

She had two thoughts: it was bound to be better with experience, and these stained sheets must be put to soak at once.

CHAPTER TEN

Ten days later Tiger Royle made an entrance on to the estate drive which not only attracted the gardener, the coachman and several housemaids but most of the small wildlife of the neighbourhood. The chugging, rattling noise he made as he drove along the pebbled drive startled Alix and Lady Phoebe who were finishing breakfast. Lady Phoebe was not surprised, however. Apparently, Tiger had taken her into his secret, or, quite possibly, the idea had been hers in the first place.

Prince Kuragin had come around from the stables and stood on the south steps to welcome Tiger with his new toy.

"How'd you like it, Prince?" Tiger called out as he leaped out of the two-seater open Renault. "Got a great deal. Easy to handle. Quiet."

Alix, coming to the doorway with Lady Phoebe and Horwich, the butler, frowned when the prince contradicted her father.

"I would not say, precisely, quiet. Otherwise, very handsome. So you drove all the way from London."

He was at the little car now, examining the big wheels and while Tiger pointed out the advantages of this particular horseless carriage Lady Phoebe fluttered down the steps to join the two men.

"What a charmer it is, dear friend! You said you would bring back the finest of all, and so you have. How thrilled David will be. And Alexandra. I can hardly wait to try it myself."

Alix did not doubt that the addition of her own name was an afterthought. She went down the steps and over to the little automobile. Prince Kuragin made way for her, watching her in a way that made her very much aware of him. They had exchanged only casual amenities since her wedding night, but then, they hadn't seen each other very much. She had a feeling he was avoiding her.

She shook her head over the expensive "toy" and scolded her father. "Pa, you have been far too generous, and I certainly don't appreciate the way you are behaving like a Santa Claus with poor relations."

"My dear!" Lady Phoebe gasped. "What a dreadful thought. I certainly hope David would not be guilty of such a remark."

"Now, now, little girl, if I didn't spend it on you, who would I spend it on? Answer me that."

It was difficult to scold him in company and when he was so very pleased with himself, so anxious to share his wealth. He lifted her off the ground and swung her around in a way that made her scold him again.

"Pa, for heaven's sake! People will think we are barbarians."

"Not at all, my dear friend," Lady Phoebe assured Tiger. "I only envy Alexandra a father who cares so much for his daughter. I am sure I wish mine had been half so kind."

Tiger dropped Alix and Prince Kuragin caught her around the waist, helping her to stand on her two feet while Tiger pretended to pursue Lady Phoebe.

"So you want a father like old Tiger. Shall I oblige her, folks?"

He reached out, making a pretence of following through, all of which dumb-show brought on a shriek and some delighted laughter on Lady Phoebe's part as she ran from him.

The prince and Alix exchanged the understanding glances of adults watching children at play.

Alix said, "I had better get David. He will want to thank my father and probably

155

take a ride in the machine."

The prince agreed. "It might be wise. I have a feeling Cousin Phoebe may get entirely the wrong idea about your father. Unless, of course, you wish to inherit a new mother as well as a mother-in-law."

"Good God, no!"

He laughed at her frankness. "Just so."

She lowered her voice. "I'm sorry. I didn't mean that. She's been awfully kind to me. They both are. I mean Lord — I mean my husband."

"Yes. I guessed that," he said gravely, but his dark eyes were amused as he looked at her. "Do you want me to get him down? He is probably in his sanctum."

"I'll go. He showed it to me the day we arrived."

Nevertheless, as she started indoors past Horwich who had eyes only for the horseless carriage, Prince Kuragin was beside her. She would have lied to herself if she hadn't enjoyed his nearness.

Behind them Tiger was leaning on his palm with his elbow propped against the car's headlight, looking into Lady Phoebe's face.

"You're a mighty taking female," he was telling her. "I saw that first thing. Not many I've seen hereabouts that could stand up to you."

Alix heard that, but try as she would she could not hear her mother-in-law's response.

"I hope he doesn't offend her," she whispered.

"I can think of many things that might offend Cousin Phoebe, but compliments from your father are not among them."

She was amused and also relieved by Kuragin's cynical view of his cousin. She didn't want him to think she was being catty, especially when she was.

He took her arm when they went up the main staircase and she thought, not for the first time, how dangerously different his effect on her was from that of her husband. She must be very careful.

At the top of the main staircase, as they were about to pass the spot where she had seen his portrait with his family, he stopped.

He looked at Alix for several seconds without speaking. She tried to avoid the intimacy of that look by staring at the portrait of the broken family.

Then he asked gently, "Are you happy, Alix?" It was the first time he had called her by what she considered her "real" name.

"Wonderfully."

Why not? She and David had made love every night and David was much more confident. If he lacked the passionate ability to

157

excite her, it was probably her own fault.

"I'm glad. Dave is a good fellow. He never was much for passionate involvements. He is deeply devoted to his mother and he admired his brother Bayard, probably more than anyone in his life. Certainly more than the late Lord Miravel who managed to gamble away anything left of the family fortune. Too bookish, Bayard and his father claimed. But I always felt that Bayard wasn't quite fair to him."

"Personally, I think his precious Bayard was badly spoiled by everyone. I know David looks to him as a model. It isn't fair to David."

"I know." He touched the tiny hand of his son in the portrait. "I hope I don't make that mistake."

Studying the portrait, she couldn't help remarking, "The princess doesn't look happy."

His voice was grim. "She wasn't. I'm afraid her desire for a son, and for me, as a matter of fact, was based upon a miscalculation. I failed to become the ruler of Lichtenbourg and she found comfort elsewhere. An Austrian musician, for one. They died together on a visit to Paris."

Feeling she had pried too much, she could only say like a child, "Oh."

He smiled. "Don't be sad on my account. We were totally mismatched. We found that out almost at once." He added lightly, "Shall we venture up the next flight?"

"I'll chance it if you will. David told me about his childhood fall."

He looked up at the top of the stairs, apparently thinking of David's very private study.

"He does like to be alone. You mustn't mind."

"I don't." She knew she was speaking too rapidly. "He's given me a sanctum, as you call it. It's around on the west side in the wing. Awfully nice."

He boosted her around the twisted iron-work balustrade of the upper floor. "You don't seem like a person who spends a lifetime alone. You enjoy people too well."

"You may be right. I never thought much about it."

He had taken her arm again, then seemed to recall what he was doing and removed his hand.

"I hope you won't be lonely. You are Lady Miravel now, you know. It is your right to choose any rooms you prefer." He hesitated. "Poor Phoebe. She likes to pretend the estate is still hers."

She raised her chin. "I don't want to disappoint her. Or you. But I am no longer a little girl, in spite of what my father says. And I don't intend to be pulled about and given orders for ever."

"Certainly not. I'm sure no one wishes you to remain a child. Forgive me. I have no right to discuss the matter. Here we are. Shall I knock?"

"Please."

He knocked and called David's name.

The answer was not reassuring. David sounded grumpy.

"I'm in the midst of my calculations, Franz. The approximate dimensions of the Colossus of Rhodes. I'll be down to luncheon soon. You needn't wait."

Alix had heard somewhere that the Colossus of Rhodes had fallen down in ancient times and she didn't know whether to laugh or frown.

The prince called to David again. "Lady Miravel is waiting. Tiger Royle has brought back a magnificent present. Her Ladyship has been promised a ride. Come along."

"You be a good fellow and take Mother yourself, won't you, old chap?"

The prince looked at Alix. Like her, he was between laughter and annoyance.

Alix raised her voice. "It's Lady Alexandra. You remember her."

160

That brought him to unbolt the door. He looked his usual kindly self but his mind was on his project.

"Good Lord, dearest, you should have spoken up!" As if he wanted to demonstrate his possessiveness, he put an arm around her ostentatiously while he addressed his cousin. "What's the excitement?"

"A Renault for you and your wife. Is that excitement enough?"

David received this with a certain vagueness.

"And what is a — Oh, one of those horseless carriages. Good of him. Generous." He squeezed Alix's shoulders. "A great man, your father. I always said so. A Renault, eh? That should be something to see. I'll tell you what. Why don't you and I take a little drive later in the day, dearest? Around the estate."

The prince was turning away without comment but stopped when Alix demanded, "Why not now? And to the village. I haven't been there yet."

David looked back over his shoulder at his room. The oil lamp was burning on his crowded desk, though the sun shone outside, beyond the closed shutters.

"Give me just a few hours, and I'll be done with my calculations for this project.

Franz, I'm into my next book. It's to be the creation of Six Wonders of the World."

"Why not Seven?" The prince's question sounded sarcastic to Alix but David obviously took it at face value.

"Everyone knows about the Pyramids."

"Of course. I'd never have thought of that."

Prince Kuragin started away again just as Alix asked, "Then you can't come down now and thank Pa?" She had been trying to call him "Father" lately, but under certain emotions she forgot.

"Not this minute. Later, dearest. We'll give it a whirl around the estate before dinner. Shouldn't be very hard to drive it."

She nodded and walked away, following Prince Kuragin.

David called after her, "Be sure to thank dear old Tiger."

"I wouldn't miss it for worlds." This remark, she knew, was sarcastic, but David had already closed the door.

Dejected at her own childish disappointment, she felt even worse to think that Prince Kuragin was witness to her husband's indifference to her. She had heard that this was a commonplace among aristocrats who married American heiresses.

"Pa will be awfully disappointed," she explained to Franz. "He's just like a child when he gives people things. He wants a little appreciation."

"I certainly don't blame him. What do you intend to do now?"

There was a little pause between them that struck Alix as portentous. She hadn't intended to make her proud boast so like a declaration of independence, but she had done this often enough with her father, so the Miravels had better get used to it. Pa had laughed and called her "spoiled". She wanted her way, he said, and she would get it.

But obviously, English husbands were not at all anxious to spoil her. She said, "I didn't mean to sound as though I always got my way. I don't, actually."

His mouth looked hard and set. He was angry, but not, oddly enough, at her. "I don't think this has anything to do with a young bride getting her own way. It is a matter of common courtesy. Would you think I was beneath contempt if I drove you into the village and back?"

Like the tomboy of the Comstock, she blurted out, "No. I'd love it."

That made him laugh and she went back down the stairs with him feeling infinitely lighter in spirit than she had felt a minute before.

CHAPTER ELEVEN

When they reached the south steps it was clear that neither Tiger nor Lady Phoebe had missed them at all. Tiger was still leaning his elbow on the headlight of the car and talking with great animation. It was Lady Phoebe who surprised Alix. She seemed fascinated by his conversation.

"Good God!" the prince muttered to Alix. "If ever I saw Othello enthralling Desdemona." He felt Alix stiffen beside him and reminded her, "Your father is a charmer. He must have had this effect on women before."

"Oh, heavens, yes. Women always flock around him. I'm used to that."

He smiled. "Then we only have Cousin Phoebe to worry about."

"How true." Though she relaxed outwardly, her concern was not entirely jealousy. In the case of Lady Phoebe, there was always a possibility that Pa's money excited her more than his life history.

Interrupted in the midst of a tale that had

Lady Phoebe wide-eyed and thrilled, Tiger looked around as if Alix and Prince Kuragin were hiding David.

"Where's my son-in-law? Here she is, hot to the touch and raring to go."

Lady Phoebe gasped and Alix could hardly keep from laughing.

It was Franz Kuragin who managed to suggest, while carefully stifling his own amusement, "You are referring to that beauty of an auto, I take it."

"Really, Franz!" His cousin pretended to look shocked but Tiger was so busy apologising to her that she enjoyed the misunderstanding and assured him, "I understand perfectly, my dear friend. I may almost say, we understand each other, being the senior members of the party, so to speak."

"David wanted to come," Alix explained. "And he will, very soon, but he was in the most touchy part of his book. He's writing a book, you know. And the figures and dimensions are awfully important."

Lady Phoebe, trying hard not to call attention to her son's ingratitude, said quickly, "I don't believe David understood. He has wanted an auto-car this age. I must go and tell him. It will be a great thrill."

Alix tried to soften the moment. "He wanted me to tell Pa how very much he

165

appreciates this lovely automobile. He said to tell you it was far too generous of you and you shouldn't have done it." After a hurried thought or two, she added, "But he's terribly glad you did."

Lady Phoebe hesitated. "But of course he is anxious to take you riding, my dear. You misunderstood entirely." She glanced nervously at Tiger who laughed at her concern.

"The boy is ambitious. I like that. Don't interrupt him. If I wasn't so damned tired after that drive — beg your pardon, ma'am — I'd take my girl for a drive myself. Maybe later."

Before the prince could say anything Alix waved away Tiger's concern. "That's not necessary at all, Pa. You see, Franz has very kindly agreed to take me for a drive." It was the first time she had ever called the prince by his given name and felt a little daring, but that suited her mood and her annoyance with David.

The prince gave her an odd look. She wondered what it meant and if he disapproved of such familiarity. Well, he must learn to see her for what she was, Tiger Royle's daughter.

Tiger spread his hands. "You see how easy it all turns out? Great. You do that, Frank, but don't keep my girl out too late. You might give Dave a jealous twinge or two."

"But David will be here any minute," his mother insisted. No one paid any attention to her and she started towards the house with an uncharacteristically rapid step.

The prince said, "I'll get coats in the event of rain, and Alexandra will need a scarf."

Alix wondered what David would say when he discovered that his cousin had taken his place and driven the car belonging to David and his wife, but perhaps this little jaunt would waken David to his responsibilities. His ingratitude still astonished Alix. She had seen even David, on several occasions, react to his mother's hints and her greed; yet he accepted everything Tiger did for him as though it were his special right.

Maybe it was always that way wherever this sort of marriage took place. There were all sorts of gossip items about the treatment of women like Consuelo Vanderbilt after she became the regal Duchess of Marlborough, not to mention Jennie Jerome who became Jennie Churchill. Unluckily for them, they weren't married to anyone like David who usually treated Alix very well indeed.

The prince brought out a scarf and one of Alix's velvet evening coats which had apparently been the first wrap he could find. He himself wore a tight-fitting and exceedingly attractive belted jacket which he had worn once or twice before when off on some business or other. He looked as though he might put her coat around her shoulders but Tiger took it and pushed Alix's arms into the sleeves as if she were five years old. He was impatient, but jolly, as usual.

Lady Phoebe hadn't returned yet. Alix was boosted into the auto's single seat by her father and the prince swung up beside her. The two men discussed starting the car and Tiger came around to the front, giving Franz a few last words of advice. Franz Kuragin obviously knew how to handle an auto and they started off past the stables, towards the country road and the village on the other side of the hills that also hid distant Wales from their sight.

Alix looked back just before the rutted road curved around over the hill and vanished from Tiger's view.

"Do you think we shocked them?" she asked.

"Would you mind?"

"Not at all." She thought that over and amended her careless and lying statement. "I mean, I would care, but it did make me so angry that David and his mother should accept everything and still expect more."

He was busy with the car for a few minutes.

It certainly made noises that were more frightening than a horse's neigh. But when they were travelling along very nicely with only a few chugs and puffs, he said, "You must accept my cousin for what he is, you know. He is kindness itself, but not always thoughtful. He would never offend your father deliberately."

Money, she thought. I can't talk to this man about it, but David has no regard for it whatever and Lady Phoebe thinks of it too often. How could she tell their friend and relative such a suspicion? Instead, she laughed and talked about the brisk noonday scene around them. It was a pleasant, gracious countryside. Not at all spectacular like the views of western America where she had grown up, but she liked it for the change it provided. She hadn't yet reminded herself that this view was to be her entire life.

Would she ever learn to feel a great passion for David?

She thought of her wedding night again and of the puzzling gossip related by Maud, the scullery maid. Did she dare to mention it? Why not? Franz knew everything about the family anyway. Was it Franz who got David drunk that night? And was that why Lady Phoebe quarrelled with him?

"Does David drink very often?" she asked abruptly.

The question certainly took him by surprise and, she suspected, it was unwelcome, too.

He examined the headlight nearest him, evading the question, she thought. "I wonder if Tiger made these scratches on the drive down from London. However, not much harm done." He turned his head and studied her. "David scarcely ever drinks."

So it must have been Franz who caused David to get drunk on his wedding night.

The wind had come up and she felt wisps of her hair flying out around her scarf. She began to push them out of sight but was made more deeply aware of his emotional power over her when he put one hand out and slapped her hand away from her head lightly.

"Don't. I like it that way."

Perhaps because he had turned into the gypsy prince before her eyes, with that black hair windblown and untidy. She pretended to take the moment more easily than she felt.

"I don't know about myself, but you look just like a gypsy. Do you know that?"

He grinned at her, his eyes black, and yet with that pinpoint of light in them that she had noticed so often.

"I've been told so. One of the Kuragins, I expect. I can't help it, you know."

Greatly daring, she said, "I like it."

Fortunately, he had enough good sense and perhaps loyalty not to respond to that imprudent remark.

Apropos of nothing, he began to point out the various rooftops and objects of interest in Miravel village which lay below them at the foot of the road they had taken over the hill. When he mentioned the church and its little stone tower with crenellations on the top, she was reminded of one mystery that had puzzled her.

"That must be where Mrs Chance's boy was baptised. Do she and her husband live here?"

"Good God, no! Chance and his wife live in Cardiff. He is Welsh, you know."

He was certainly emphatic about it.

"Why do you suppose Lady Phoebe has shown such interest in the boy?"

He was non-committal. "Phoebe has the interests of the villagers very much at heart. The name of the village probably suggests to her some sort of feudal ownership, though, of course, she doesn't say so."

"It certainly surprised me."

"And me." It was so abrupt he caught himself and added, "But I should not be

171

surprised. She has attended other baptisms and is a good churchwoman. Well, here we are. The pub to your left. The lace and home goods shop to your right. You will find excellent woollen bargains there. Before the church is a little town square that once was a graveyard."

"Graveyard? How horrible!"

He disagreed. "If I were there, I should like to know that living beings, children, old people, the vigorous young, would cross paths over my grave. It seems to add a note of — what?"

His thought seemed reasonable. "Eternity." She promised him laughingly, "If you ever die, you shall be buried where people can cross paths over your grave. Shall we put it in writing?"

He laughed. "I accept your word for it."

It was a pretty village, quite small, but, as Franz said about the graveyard, full of life. There were a number of shops and a half-timbered bed and breakfast house of two storeys that probably had been immortalised in a painting at some time or other.

The little Renault aroused a great deal of interest. Business stopped in the streets and before the shops while people stared at the peculiar little horseless carriage. A woman in a pony-cart was passing when the car began to make some of its odd noises, like a snort. The pony reared up. The woman screamed, and the prince brought the car to a sudden, coughing stop. He swung over the side of the machine and reached for the reins that had gone flying out of the woman's hands.

He got the pony under control and offered the reins to the woman whose yellow hair looked all too familiar. Glynnis Chance was not in Cardiff, no matter where her husband might be.

It wasn't until Franz offered the reins to her that he noticed Mrs Chance. Alix wished she could see his face but it was turned away from her. She didn't think he was too happy about the meeting and turned away while the woman was thanking him. Alix heard her voice with its sly, knowing lilt.

"And how's the pretty new family, Your Highness?"

"Attending its own business as always." He got into the automobile looking angry, his cheekbones looking hard and, Alix thought, rather ruthless. She wondered what kind of a ruler he would be if he ever found himself in that unenviable position. But when he turned to Alix he had softened to a whimsical apology.

"Sorry. The woman seems determined to

drive her way into the Miravel family."

Glynnis Chance waited, obviously hoping for more to come, but she waited in vain. Franz started the car and they drove on at a sudden speed of over ten miles an hour.

Alix put out her hand to stop him. His own hand met hers by accident and then held it, turned the palm up and to her astonishment, raised it. She thought he might touch it to his lips and breathed a little faster with anticipation. But he set it down in her lap and slapped it instead. When she opened her eyes wide, almost indignant, she saw that he was smiling. It was a gentle smile and she was painfully aware that gentleness from this gypsy man was far more exciting than her own husband's perennial kindness. She was ashamed, but did not like it the less.

"We both know better than this, don't we?" he reminded her, trying to make the question lighthearted.

The terrible part was that he had seen something in her eyes which she hoped was hidden. She returned whatever feeling he had for her. She became stiff and proper while he took a tree-lined lane out to the edge of the village, past the church.

"I don't know what you mean, Your Highness," she managed after pulling herself together mentally.

She was humiliated, but honest enough to realise she had given him every reason to believe she was attracted to him. Worse, he stopped the car beyond a grove of wind-breaking trees, leaned over her and with one hand grasping her shoulder, held her while he kissed her. She tried to draw away. She had been a respectable girl who went to Sunday School in the far reaches of the mining country. She had been taught that adultery was one of the cardinal sins, and here she had been inviting the attentions of the gypsy prince.

The heat of his mouth and his hard fingers did not make it easier for her. She had never wanted David as she wanted Franz Kuragin, and it was all wrong. The worst wrong was in her mind. While he held her she dreamed of lying with him as she had lain with her husband; yet so differently. Those same acts that made them briefly one body rather than two were a sin she had never thought she would be capable of committing. But then, she hadn't known Prince Kuragin.

"Please, don't," she managed finally when she could free herself. "It is so wrong. Terribly wrong."

"I know." He sounded hoarse, unlike him-

self. "You belong to him. I belong to — "
He pulled back, avoided her eyes, staring
ahead at the winding, bumpy lane. "I have
what I owe to my people, my parents. The
people of my country. Dave told me how
you two met at Lake Geneva." He started
the car again. Its little protests and "chuffing"
noise did not drown out his words. "If I
had met you at Geneva . . . if I had been
strolling along that day . . ."

She scarcely dared hope he would confess
he really felt something deep for her, not
just the flirtation of a carefree prince.

"Yes? If you had?"

"You know the answer to that. We might
have married and thumbed our noses to the
world. Our world. I felt it the evening of
your engagement when I saw your portrait
as we came up those monumental stairs of
your father's palace."

She wanted to cry, but had sense enough
not to. He was right, of course. She might
not feel that she "belonged" to David, but
she had no right to betray him. It wasn't
even as if he had betrayed her with another
woman.

Feeling very adult, a heroine in a tragic
play, she saw him glance at her and smile,
a very little smile, gentle and understanding.
He must think her terribly childish. But this

was her first love affair and she felt all the pangs of loss when he took her tense fingers in his free hand and kissed the knuckles. He kept her hand in his as they drove on but he looked ahead at the bumpy wagon-rutted lane.

"I've made my home with the Miravels since the old lord died. It was my mother's wish that we see to their interests. They were left in such a bad way Bayard and Phoebe talked of selling off part of the estate. Whenever I have discussed leaving, she has always been afraid the Kuragin backing would go with me. It isn't true, but with a mentality like Phoebe's it is natural that she should think so. Then you came along and I knew I had to leave. But here I've stayed. You can see how desperate the situation could become."

So he supported the Miravels, and when he was gone, it was obvious that Tiger Royle would be expected to take his place as the banking house for the family.

"I see." She wondered what Pa would think when he found out. Even he could be driven too far in his generosity.

"No. I don't think you do see," the prince said. "Tiger and I have discussed this. There are funds drawing interest that I expect to leave in proper hands for the Miravel estate.

Tiger knows the bankers and has been in London to arrange matters. He is far from a fool, you know, in spite of his generosity. He believes you are happy with David, as God knows, I do, and he doesn't want you worried about financial matters."

"And my mother-in-law?" she asked on a note of irony.

His smile told her that she too had been discussed between Tiger and himself. He added, "Let her imagine what she likes. In any case, she will not be left penniless, nor will David. Tiger enjoys doing things for people, but I doubt very much if he can be fooled."

She felt that this was true. "Thank you. I should have known that you were aware of what was going on, long before today."

"You must remember, I have known my cousins since I was born, and David is probably the best of them. Perhaps he should have been a monk or some other reclusive scholar. But Bayard's death made that impossible and you were chosen for him." He shook her hand in an angry way. "I wish to God you had not, but it is too late now."

She knew that his honour as well as his deep ties to the Miravel family made any legitimate relationship between them deeply wrong. If he could be strong about this, she

178

was not going to be a wishful coward, or especially a woman like her mother-in-law who expected everything to come her way if she simply wished for it. She started to release her hand from his clasp but failed.

He raised her fingers to his lips and held them there as though his thoughts were far away. Probably they were. She looked at him, feeling a tenderness she had never dared to show him before.

Suddenly, as though all her fears had come to life, she heard hoofbeats in the lane behind them and glanced over her shoulder to see her husband riding towards them, very close, so close he must have seen his cousin's gesture. Had he been deliberately ambling along to surprise them? He had certainly made an effort to be silent.

Because she was so very much in the wrong, she immediately took the offensive. "Well, David, I see you were able to come after all."

He looked hurt, as well he might have been and drew up alongside the automobile, his mare rearing a little at the close proximity. "I beg your pardon, Alexandra, but you know how very important this project is to me. However, I have a message for Franz."

Franz had stopped the car and slowly released Alix's hand. She was sure he did not wish to behave furtively in front of his cousin. "That was good of you." She was surprised at his cool response. From the way David was breathing hard, the message must be important. Unless, of course, and most unlikely, David was jealous over what he had witnessed. At least it would show spirit in him.

David said in a clipped voice, "A message from the King and Queen of Serbia. There may be war with the Turkish empire and King Alexander would like you at his right hand."

"I see." The prince reached out, touched Alix's coat where it covered her knees, and then quickly got down from the car. "Will you continue the drive? Lady Alix hasn't seen much of the countryside. She might enjoy the country air."

"Of course. I intended to." David dismounted, gave his cousin the reins which the mare permitted in a docile fashion and Franz mounted.

When Alix got up enough nerve to look at him without revealing any of her deep disappointment, he was still staring at her. She didn't know what that look meant, but by the way his black eyebrows frowned in a peculiar way, she felt that this was his goodbye, a very small message to her. She tried to smile but it was an effort and here was David, getting up beside her, looking over the wheel and the big headlights, sizing up the situation for a novice driver.

Before he could start the car and move along in fits and starts, Prince Kuragin was riding back behind them, through the village. Sick inside, Alix wondered if she would ever see him again. People were killed in wars. Anything could happen, but why was Franz so important to the King of Serbia, a small Balkan country many miles and a whole continent away, not to mention the English Channel.

After trying to start the car David got back in, too busy to answer her, but she asked as crisply as she could make it, "Why does the King of Serbia want the prince in the Serbian army? The prince isn't Serbian."

David was busy manoeuvring the car over the wagon ruts but after a minute or so he reached out and put his arm around her. "There. Isn't that better? Windy this afternoon. I'm surprised Franz was willing to take you out in this weather. I thought he had more sense. But I suppose he wanted to make me jealous."

"Are you?"

"No, dearest. I know my wife too well; don't I?"

She wondered if he was thinking of the nights when he felt so very manly, so in command after a few whiskies.

She was too depressed to show any emotion beyond a subdued, "Yes, David."

Happy now, he explained as they jaunted along in reasonable style, "They are all cousins in the Balkans. Franz's wife was related to Queen Draga of Serbia. The queen stood up with Franz's wife at their wedding and she was Max's godmother."

"Is there any real danger?"

David shrugged. "He has handled diplomatic affairs before this with the Sublime Porte as the Turks call it. If all the Balkans go to war, and they usually do, it might be dangerous. I certainly hope not. We've practically run out of cousins. But nothing holds Franz here except the contingency plans he has discussed with Bertie. The British government wants to see him back on the Lichtenbourg throne." He leaned over and kissed her ear, to her surprise. "Dearest, your soft heart does you credit."

She gave him a smile that was more of a grimace. It was the best she could do at this moment. Seeing Glynnis Chance coming out of the woollen shop carrying several packages she pointed out the woman to David.

David avoided the young woman.

"Grasping creature."

He noticed Alix looking back at Mrs Chance and returning her wave. "Best not encourage her. She can be a great bore."

"Do you know her well?"

He shook his head. "She was more Franz's type. Years ago he took a fancy to her until she made a nuisance of herself. He is a great man for the ladies, you know."

Alix had not known so directly. She stopped waving back at the woman and faced forward again like a good wife.

CHAPTER TWELVE

The family saw Prince Kuragin off at the little station dignified by the ancient Miravel name. To Alix his departure was much simpler than that of most royalty she had read about.

Several villagers shuffled about on the station platform but beyond touching two fingers to their caps in respectful salute they paid little attention to the prince or the Miravels. Evidently he had been a familiar and democratic figure in the village.

Perhaps during visits to Glynnis Chance before her marriage?

The thought chilled Alix and she banished it quickly.

It had long ago ceased to puzzle Alix that so many people of all stations in life liked her father, even before they knew he was rich. But to prove the rule, here was Tiger Royle, deep in conversation with Prince Kuragin. More surprising, here was Tiger listening to the younger man's opinion as if he valued it. He also went so far as to reassure

Kuragin about something or other.

"Don't you give it a thought, Frank. Leave all that stuff to me. Forget the folks back home. The thing you have to do is to knock those Balkan heads together and remind them how expensive a war can be."

"I would love to do exactly that," the prince assured him. As he talked with Tiger he had his back to David and Alix, giving her a chance to study his figure in the royal blue jacket with some kind of red military insignia. His peaked blue cap was under his arm and he looked like the dashing villain of a musical comedy.

All the same she was not surprised when two young village girls came to the station platform with ancient carpetbags and spent most of their time staring at him and giggling behind their hands.

Tiger pulled out his card case and wrote something on it with the pencil that he always used, though it still bore the tooth marks of his baby daughter at the age of eight months.

"If you get to Constantinople and have an interview with the sultan or his advisers, try to deal with this man. He's a power behind the throne and he knows me through one of our banking sources. He doesn't want war any more than you and I do."

"Thank you. I won't forget this, sir."

Tiger laughed and stuck a fist in his ribs. "I'll remember that when you're back on the throne in that toy country of yours."

The prince refused to be disturbed by this insult to Lichtenbourg.

"Just so, Tiger. We must make some special award to you on that happy occasion. Shall we steal a note from your Mark Twain and say 'You and your heirs will for ever be permitted to sit in our presence'?"

"Sounds perfect. I don't like all what they call 'standing on ceremony'."

This time the prince did laugh and threw an arm around his new-found mentor. "You couldn't have expressed it better."

Lady Phoebe joined the amusement, clearly wanting to be part of the good time.

The distant rumble of the London train brought everyone to attention. They all moved to the edge of the platform and Alix wondered if Franz would actually leave without saying goodbye.

The train puffed into the station and with a hiss of steam halted before Prince Kuragin. The prince stepped aside, bowing to the two young village girls and boosting their carpetbags up into the carriage beside them. While the villagers called out their own farewells to the girls, he turned to Tiger Royle and the Miravels.

David shook hands with him, wishing him success, and Tiger took the prince's hand, talking to him as if he were Alix's age.

"Remember now, you get in trouble, you let me know by hook or by crook."

"Thank you, my friend." The prince clasped Tiger's hand between both of his own. "I'll not forget your support and advice."

Lady Phoebe murmured, "And I suppose I may expect you to forget your old cousin."

"I see no 'old cousin'. Here is my payment to you, dear Phoebe."

He kissed Lady Phoebe's forehead, then moved to Alix. "And to my new cousin."

Alix felt his gloved hands rough on her cheeks and remembered painfully that she might never see him again. Holding her face between his hands, he kissed her mouth. His lips were warm. He whispered, "Think of me sometimes."

The train made such a racket Alix did not think anyone heard him.

A minute later he swung up into a carriage and was gone.

As the others moved away, David said casually, "I'll wager twenty pounds he knows those two young women before that train is out of sight."

Tiger laughed but both Lady Phoebe and Alix ignored the remark.

The family returned home in the carriage although Lady Phoebe, greatly daring, had made the coy, joking suggestion, "I could almost wish I were driving home excitingly in David's new horseless carriage."

Tiger said, "Capital idea some day before I leave."

Alix said nothing. The thought of his departure, perhaps for as long a time as Prince Kuragin expected to be away, only made her depression worse. But she need not have concerned herself with worrying about his departure. Lady Phoebe was shocked.

"But my dear friend, how are we to get on without your excellent advice? I feel so helpless these days without a man's strong presence."

"But that's just the thing, ma'am. You've got a splendid replacement in your son."

"Oh," Lady Phoebe objected without thinking. "But you see, my boy is absolutely untrained. It isn't as though he were someone like Bayard who always knew exactly how to handle estate matters."

"Now, Your Ladyship," Tiger began, only to be outtalked for once by his daughter.

"How can you say that, ma'am? David is just as able to conduct the affairs of this estate as your precious Bayard ever was."

David's hand tightened under her arm. He raised his head and Alix almost felt his jaws firm up. She was delighted.

"Well, I wouldn't quite put it that way," he began. "After all, there was only one Bayard. But — " He looked at his wife with a gratitude she had never seen in him. "If my wife thinks I'm capable, that is enough for me." He kissed the crown of her head, despite the interference of a feathered hat.

"Bravo," Tiger cried. "That's the spirit. Wouldn't you say so, friend Phoebe?"

"Friend Phoebe" had been so wounded she found it difficult to speak, but Tiger Royle was waiting so expectantly she managed a faintly smiling agreement.

"I'm sure you are right, my dear — Tiger, if I may be so bold. And we are all relieved that David's wife feels so very defensive about the matter. But I assure you, it has never entered my mind that David would not eventually be able to take over all such problems. So long as he has the excellent advice of a man like you."

David felt that he could afford to be generous. He was red with the excitement of having been praised by two people as important to his mother as the Royles.

"Dearest," he said to Alix, "we should

plan to go up to London this autumn or during the Christmas season and the new year. Remember how we spent last new year?"

She was thinking of the two men she remembered at her engagement party but she said staunchly, "It would be wonderful, and highly appropriate. We are an old established married couple now, and last year this time, we didn't even know each other."

"Come along."

She accepted his arm and they walked up the south steps, past the interested eyes of the housekeeper, Mrs Skinner, and the always observant Cornbury, David's valet. Alix hoped he would understand that her husband loved her and was willing to demonstrate as much in front of the entire household. She would forget Prince Franz Kuragin for ever. It was her duty, and she owed David that.

Much as Alix dreaded the thought of her father's departure, she could see that he was growing bored by the commonplace country life of two women, always bickering politely, and an intellectual young man with whom he had nothing whatever in common.

He was for ever going up to London on business, some of which he admitted was connected with the Lichtenbourg matter.

"I don't understand, sir," David said at

dinner one day when Lady Phoebe had already read to them a note from their cousin Prince Kuragin. "Isn't Franz down in Serbia or Romania or some such place, trying to make terms the Ottoman empire will understand?"

Tiger announced proudly, "Our friend Frank has also managed to prove a leader for his people. According to my correspondent in Constantinople, a regiment of good fellows have arrived in Athens, ready to back good old Frank in any move he cares to make."

"Not a revolution, I hope. I don't hold with that."

"Nonsense, David." His mother was nothing if not warlike. "I have always felt that Lichtenbourg needs a thoroughgoing revolution."

But Tiger waved away such talk. "He refuses to make a move that can be from the outside, he says. It's got to come through free elections. A pretty daring idea, but I must say, I admire his notions. I'm doing a little here and there to hurry things along. It wouldn't hurt at all if Lichtenbourg could get some handy loans and what-not."

"Pa," Alix raised her voice, not for the first time, at the table. "I was never more proud of you."

"And of Franz," David put in without looking at her.

"Yes. Of His Highness too."

With the coming of autumn and Tiger's imminent departure, Alix had hoped they might all go up to London to say goodbye, but Tiger discouraged the idea, since he would still have to take a boat-train to board the new, speed demon *Deutschland,* of which the German kaiser was so proud. Pa had also hoped that Alix was "in the family way", as he said in an embarrassed and uncharacteristically low voice. She wasn't pregnant, as a matter of fact, a matter that upset everyone, even herself.

Heaven knew it had become a matter mentioned to Alix in frequent hints from the expectant grandmother. Lady Phoebe went so far as to send up a "tonic" for the newlyweds which David, in particular, was supposed to take before bedtime. The dose involved a crystal glass of something that smelled suspiciously like whisky, Scotch, of course.

The results, as on his wedding night, were vigorous, if not romantic, to the bride. It was this that kept the family hope when Alix would very much have enjoyed a visit to London with, perhaps, a royal audience. She didn't have thoughts of being presented to the old queen. But it was highly possible that the delightful Prince of Wales would receive them.

The "tonic" before bedtime had become a custom now, not a goblet of liquor but at least, something that would stimulate David, give him more confidence and perhaps most of all, more desire.

Alix was beginning to appreciate the beauty of the Miravel estates, but beyond their borders she saw things she hadn't noticed before. She made frequent trips into the village, usually walking. The almshouse, that ancient hall with its leaking roof which was divided into partitions for the ill and indigent, troubled her most. She wanted to help but wasn't sure how, except with money. Pa had settled so much on the Miravels, there must be something of the estate money that could be used to repair the roof of the Elder Home and give the aged inhabitants something to look forward to.

But none of this was as immediately important as saying goodbye to Tiger. Even for the Miravels this was the hardest task that autumn.

Afterwards, Alix visited the village more often, trying to make friends with the villagers, but she could never get beyond their polite courtesy.

At Ewen Chance's order Glynnis Chance had moved to Cardiff with her son, a fact that should have made Alix's trips easier. From the beginning Alix had been uneasy about the girl and now felt she had reason to suspect that Franz Kuragin was once her lover.

But there was worse.

As the autumn went by, Alix felt further removed from the prince's activities, his devotion to his people, the things that reminded her of the man she had so briefly known. She was sure now that Franz Kuragin was the "romantic prince" she had thought she was marrying when she became engaged to Lord David Miravel a year ago.

She had lost love twice. She saw David's weaknesses, now his total lack of strength, his selfishness . . . And Franz Kuragin who had kissed her, made her love him, and all the time he was very likely the father of young Nick Chance.

That was the keenest hurt.

By early November when Americans were talking about the celebration of Thanksgiving, she proposed that Miravel Hall celebrate by inviting the village to a feast on the American holiday, at which time the Miravels could supply much of the money needed by the almshouse and, certainly, the crippled veterans of recent wars: the African battles against the Ashanti, the Zulus, the Mahdi's Fanatics, the Whirling Dervishes, and there were still those long-forgotten heroes of the Crimean War. Not to mention India's Sepoy Rebellion and, of course, the Boer War which was not yet ended.

The household was not enthusiastic. To her astonishment Lady Phoebe did not use poverty as an excuse, in which case Alix was prepared with the reminder of Pa's generosity. Instead, she objected, "The Miravels have given enough. When we gave Bayard, we gave all."

Without looking directly at him, Alix felt David flinch as if he had been slapped. That night Alix was specially kind to him.

She mentioned something of her troubles in a letter to her father but did not speak of the money problem. She knew him too well and she refused to let him spend more money on something that would never benefit him. He deserved to spend his profits on anything that made him contented, like the deals in foreign markets, foreign banks, foreign adventures, if he enjoyed them. And she knew he did. Considering all that he had poured into the Miravel coffers because he thought his daughter should be happy, she could never repay him except with the love and devotion she felt for him.

His answer was as good as a smack on her seat when she got too big for her britches in her young days.

Honey,
I always knew you were some punkins and a lot better than any old English lord and lady, but it ain't real modest to say so when these poor folks — yep, poor, have kind of lost the "snap" we Yankees have.

That seems to be high praise from the Prince of Wales and he told me American girls, and specially you, had lots of snap.

Well, if our Miravel family don't have snap, then we'll just have to love them for what they do have. Like honour and good manners and courage and that kind of stuff.

Love and hugs from your Pa,
Tiger Royle

His words, so like his dear, rough self, made her grow up a little.

David himself was working hard. His book on Wonders of the Ancient World had suddenly found an interested ancient history professor in Edinburgh. David's head was in the clouds these early winter days. He had actually been invited to Scotland to meet the reclusive professor and work with him on the final stages of the book. It was understood that the Miravels would finance the publication, after which time David was assured that the tome would be a standard work on the subject throughout the English-speaking world.

Cornbury had packed for David and was ready to leave with him in two days. No mention was made of either his wife or his mother accompanying them. It was automatically assumed by all parties that this was "man's work".

David was still in a state of understandable ecstasy which he tried without success to play down with his wife and Lady Phoebe.

"It may mean nothing at all. Professor MacLeod has only read the first three — "

"First three?"

"Wonders."

"Ah."

But his enthusiasm escaped. "Well, consider." He offered the many-times folded and slightly soiled letter which Alix pretended to read. It was her fourth reading but she wanted him to know her pride in him and in his accomplishments even when he added, "I shall be firm about returning for Christmas. I know how excited you will be over our

British Christmas. But if we should be caught in the midst of our technical data — No! I refuse to contemplate it."

"Dear, I know you will be a great success."

Still it was a lonely idea, to share Christmas with no one but her mother-in-law. Alix knew she had to make herself useful. It was the only answer.

She visited the chunky little vicar in the village, the Reverend Josiah Pittridge, to explain her difficulties. She had not thought too much about him since he performed the marriage ceremony competently, but once she had been received in his little stone vicarage and invited to share tea with him she found him excellent company.

Maybe it was his lanky cook-housekeeper, Mrs Tether, who broke the ice. She was a superb cook who brought out all manner of sweet biscuits, novelties like lemon curd and a very drinkable tea unsweetened as Alix preferred it. Mrs Tether also had what the vicar warned Alix was an incurable habit of eavesdropping.

Alix had no sooner brought up the subject of her difficulties about trying to help out than Mrs Tether stuck her head around the half-open study door. Her iron grey hair was piled high on the very crown of her head and skewered there with all manner of hairpins, most of which appeared to be slipping out.

"Got to be a mite careful, My Lady. Don't listen to the Reverend here, saving your grace." That was a remark thrown to her employer. "He's as like to give the shoes off his feet to put 'em on a beggar."

"Now, Tether — " the vicar began, taking all this in his stride. "You'll have me blushing." He confessed to Alix, "It's not true of course, Your Ladyship. I'm one of the selfish ones of the world. I might give my shoes, or my clogs, the ones I wear when it's all over muddy. But I won't give my reading and study hours. That's true selfishness. To be a good Christian one must sacrifice what he himself loves most."

"Oh, tosh!" Mrs Tether said and went out of the room, having conveniently left the door ajar.

The little man grinned. "A dear woman. And a true Christian. Did you hear that, Tether?"

Silence reigned in the hall.

Alix laughed and explained her problem.

"I want to do something to help," she ended, "but nothing seems right. At least, Lady Phoebe has given me the idea that it's wrong, that I'm interfering."

Pittridge put his fingers together with the

middle fingers propping up his sturdy chin.

"In a sense, I'd be inclined to agree. That is to say, your purpose is commendable, but these are proud country people and though some are sick, some elderly and many crippled or otherwise incapacitated, they are proud. They would starve without food and be taken off very rapidly without good warm clothing, but if it could be offered, if I may say so, in an appetising manner, you understand what I mean?"

Alix nibbled thoughtfully on a delicious, buttery scone. "Not precisely."

"Mrs Tether and I try to make things right with them. She bakes and cooks each week for the needy. But so much is wasted when they cannot eat food because of its presentation."

The rasp of Mrs Tether's voice called out, "Just think how you'd like to receive food gifts, ma'am. If you do play the Yankee Lady Bountiful, don't throw it at us. There's been too much of that these past years."

Offended at this lack of gratitude for her good intentions, Alix looked at the vicar and saw that he was nodding agreement with his housekeeper. He saw that he had hurt Alix's feelings by not expressing himself carefully enough, and raised one hand.

"Please, Lady Miravel, don't misunderstand. Your intention is to be applauded. It is only in the delivery of it that we might make a few suggestions. I tried to speak of this very matter to Her Ladyship, that is, the Dowager Lady Miravel, but I am afraid she did not feel well enough to hear me out. She has palpitations, I believe."

"I know about Her Ladyship's health. What is it she does that could be improved? Tell me. Maybe I can do something about it."

"Now, there's something like it," Mrs Tether bellowed, sticking her head around the door again. "You ever seen the food left over from the gentry and the servants at the hall?"

"Is it sour? Or rotting?" The idea revolted Alix.

"No. Certainly not. Her Ladyship isn't a heathen. Neither is the housekeeper, that Skinner female. Good folk. Well-meaning. But it's been the habit since time out of mind. Everywhere in the shires."

Still confused, Alix looked to the vicar for an explanation.

He provided it, apologetically. "In the kitchens of the great folk, they scrape together all foods, beef, turnips, mutton, fish stew, plum pudding, hog trotters, minced meat pies and sometimes the dregs of tea. Then they toss them all in a pot and have them carried to the old and sick. Even if the foods are appetising, it is impossible to separate them for the toothless and the sick."

Alix found this picture almost as bad as the thought of rotting food. "But that's awful. I can't believe it."

"Try eating that mixed-up slop sometime, ma'am. You'll see."

"Hush, Tether," the Reverend Pittridge ordered Mrs Tether, but he added to Alix, "Not but what it's all too true, Your Ladyship. You name any great house and I'll tell you where it's done."

"Not at Miravel Hall. Not any more."

Mrs Tether slapped the door with enthusiasm. "There's a lady for action."

The vicar smiled. "I am inclined to agree. Your Ladyship will have the earnest prayers and thanks of our people. And no talk of charity."

"It doesn't seem like very much."

"We can't all be saints, Lady Miravel. Sometimes it is much more comfortable merely to be good neighbours, as you Yankees might say."

It was true. Alix laughed, realising just how true it was. Simple, decent thought for a neighbour was very like the philosophy she had seen, and heard, preached in the mines.

At the end of her visit with the Reverend Pittridge, not to forget the omnipresent Mrs Tether, Alix felt that she had girded up her courage and was able to argue against any objections made by her mother-in-law. She walked home over the hillside road by which she had come once, and only once, with Prince Kuragin. A rainy weekend recently had left muddy ruts but this sort of exposure to the elements had never troubled her. She was surprised, however, when she saw David driving over the hilltop and heading toward her in Tiger Royle's present, the little Renault.

He brought it to a grinding halt as she ran towards him. She knew at a glance that something was terribly wrong. He looked stunned, his pale features rigid.

Not Pa. Please, don't let it be Pa.

"What is it? Is it Pa?"

"No, dearest. That's one blessing."

He got down, helped her up into the seat and took her hand which was chilled, even beneath her glove.

"Alexandra, I know you were fond of my cousin. God knows we all were. Poor Mother is prostrate."

Her lips were dry. She moistened them. It couldn't be possible. She had barely got to know Franz. In spite of her suspicions about him and Mrs Chance, he was always in her thoughts.

"Something has happened to Prince Kuragin?"

"I wasn't very kind to him at the last. I didn't mean to let him go off that way without any genuine good wishes. I was just envious, I suppose. Franz was all the things I've wanted to be, since Bayard went."

"What happened?"

"They had some sort of political upheaval in Constantinople. The new minister swears Franz was a Balkan spy. He was condemned in a secret trial. Our Foreign Office has been informed."

"Is he — ?" She tried again. "Was he killed?"

"The sentence was death. London heard about it and half the continent is buzzing. They think the Prince Royal of Lichtenbourg has something to do with it. Afraid of old Franz's popularity. The theory is that the Lichtenbourg government did some forging of information. Something of that sort. Wales himself had a message sent to us. Poor Mother. She read it first. We are fortunate the news didn't affect her heart. She was so very attached to Franz."

Alix heard a low voice that must be her own repeating, "It can't be. It can't."

Hurt that she could not believe him, David demanded, "Why not? The sultan is capable of anything. Our Foreign Office calls him 'The Damned'. Even his own people want to be rid of him. He tortures prisoners for the fun of it."

He felt her body shudder and softened.

"Poor little thing. I shouldn't have told you like that. It's not the kind of news for a female."

When she said nothing he reminded her, "There is Max, that poor child left an orphan if this news is accurate. I wonder what the child's political future will be?" He took a long breath. "Strange. Not an hour ago I was so damnably happy. Cornbury was completely packed for us. He thinks of everything."

Her mind was tangled with horrors. "Everything? But not this."

CHAPTER THIRTEEN

Whatever the gloomy prospects for Christmas, Alix felt David's unhappiness and disappointment. It seemed cruel to play the martyr with him. He could do nothing at home to cheer them up, and in Edinburgh he'd be doing what he loved best in the world.

A week after the news about Prince Kuragin's probable fate had swept Europe, David welcomed Alix's agreement that he was needed in Scotland. He was humble about it and couldn't stop thanking her. She was glad for him.

She herself was grateful for work, anything to take her mind off the incessant public speculation on the continent and in the British press. She began to carry out the plan formulated by the vicar and Mrs Tether. Whenever Alix's haunting fears for Prince Kuragin's safety returned and it was growing more and more difficult to sustain her hope, she was grateful for the new tasks suggested by the vicar.

She knew the reputation of those "go-getter" American girls who married into the British aristocracy and tried to change centuries-old customs in a month, so she was careful how she made her suggestions about the household. A few ideas worked, such as visiting those villagers who were in bed with pneumonia or the prevalent galloping consumption. Those who were recovering liked her to read to them, and better yet, sketch absurd and exaggerated pictures of their neighbours. They never saw resemblances to themselves, but the special look of their neighbours that she caught proved a delight to them. The Reverend Pittridge reported her growing popularity with great satisfaction.

But ideas for improvement at Miravel Hall were another matter. The plan to separate the various foods delivered to the almshouse and the Elder Home was simply ignored. No one flatly refused to listen. There was politeness on all sides. But nothing happened. Alix suspected her mother-in-law was behind this stubborn refusal to make things easier for the less fortunate. Lady Phoebe considered herself extremely unfortunate.

Lady Phoebe was especially crushed by the news David expressed regretfully and yet with a certain understandable pride. He and his mentor would not be quite finished with the last Wonder until January of the new year.

"January at the latest should see me home in the bosom of my family," he said. Then, for fear his mother and wife would worry about his own lonely Christmas far from home and loved ones, he informed them that Professor MacLeod had kindly invited him to the MacLeod home in the Highlands for the holidays. "Mrs MacLeod will have a goose and some Scottish cheer for the occasion. We will continue our work, of course, during these ten days."

For Alix, at least, one hope loomed on the horizon. Pa was trying to gain support for a rescue, if Prince Kuragin was still alive.

Pa had taken the fastest liner, the *Deutschland,* across the Atlantic to the continent and was now using his considerable influence in every European capital, beginning with republican France whose democratic sympathies were all with Prince Kuragin against the suspected conspiracy of Lichtenbourg's present, aged ruler.

During her more hopeful moments Alix smiled at the stories that drifted back about Tiger Royle replying to the Tsar of All the Russians with "Sure thing, sir."

For years the Slavic Russian empire had

been anxious to bring the Kuragins back to rule Lichtenbourg, thus tweaking the noses of the Teutonic kaiser and the sprawling Austro-Hungarian empire. It was easy to forgive the "Friendly Savage, Tiger Royle" who laid out money so lavishly, money which could be used to support Slavic causes in the Balkans. As in his dealings with Serbia, Montenegro, Bulgaria, Albania, Romania and all the enemies of the Ottoman empire, their sympathies were with the Once And Future Prince of Lichtenbourg.

The people of the prince's own principality were divided between Teutonic elements in the north, Hungarian influence in the centre and Slavic sympathies in the south. The Balkans were, for the most part, of Slavic sympathy, which put them on the side of the Kuragin family, rather than the Germanic von Elsbachs now in power.

In spite of the sympathetic letter of condolence to Lady Phoebe from Sandringham in the name of the Prince of Wales regarding the rumoured death of Prince Kuragin, Alix took a small but passionate hope from her father's activities.

The continental newspapers were also encouraging. The *Paris Herald* correspondent in Constantinople relayed the latest rumour, that His Highness was not dead but very much alive. He had been "seen" in one of the sultan's more noisome oubliettes.

In the Balkans Queen Draga of Serbia, related to his late wife, boasted that though Prince Kuragin had failed in one escape he would succeed on the next attempt.

But no one was certain. Europe waited breathlessly for proof, none more so than Prince Friedrich the Third of Lichtenbourg who may or may not have provided the forged documents that condemned Kuragin as a spy. A man of eighty-six, he did not have many years left to contemplate the glamorous aura that he had helped to create around his enemy and possible successor.

Alix wanted desperately to believe that Franz Kuragin was alive and would be safe very shortly, but meanwhile, there was his unfortunate little boy, perhaps orphaned so short a time before Christmas. She had written to the Zurich school to ask if Prince Kuragin's son could spend the holidays with his cousins in rural England. She and her mother-in-law signed the letter but no reply was received until a week before Christmas when the answer came, a curious one to Alix.

My dear Lady Miravel,
Your invitation to His Serene Highness,

Maximilian Ernst Rudolf Kuragin, is most opportune.

The boy shall be delivered safely to your family whom I know by sight. The rendezvous, as you suggest, will be the Pas de Calais, my son-in-law's old inn on the Calais waterfront. We will await Your Ladyship and Lord Miravel on the Channel ferry the evening of 21 December.

If you please, there will be no change in the above plan, as I am urgently needed in Zurich at Christmas.

(signed)
Wilhelmina Vogt,
Headmistress

Alix was astonished.

"You signed that letter to Fran Vogt, ma'am. I never mentioned any Pas de Calais. As a matter of fact, I've never heard of it."

"It belongs to her daughter's husband. Quite pleasant, for a Frenchman."

"Then you approve of our meeting them in Calais?"

"If you like, my dear. Use your own judgment."

"But she specially asks for David, or perhaps you. Someone she knows by sight."

Lady Phoebe took this into consideration. It was clear that she didn't like what would

211

be Alix's next suggestion.

"Young Max should be with those he knows at school. Or perhaps David will go over with you, as the woman requests. Yes. We must send for David. Heavens! What plans, all to give the boy a holiday. One might as well be appearing at Covent Garden."

Her complacency was enough to drive Alix mad. "And just how are we to notify David?"

"You must send him the message by telegraph in the village."

"We can't very well send a telegraph message to 'somewhere in the Highlands'. Besides, we haven't the time. We must leave for London tomorrow. The following afternoon we are expected in France. What would our port be for Calais?"

"Dover, I should think." Lady Phoebe threw up her fragile, beringed fingers. "I wash my hands of it. The poor child will be better where he is. I'm sure Franz would approve if he knew the full truth."

"You can see by this letter that there is something urgent about it. 'No change in the plan,' she says. You and I will have to go over and bring him back. Franz — Prince Kuragin would expect it of us."

"My dear, I have fully as great an affection for dear Franz as anyone. But to travel up to London at a moment's notice, then to some wretched little town like Dover, and after that, to cross the Channel, would require an enormous effort on my part."

Alix, who was beginning to understand the dowager's motivations, said casually, "If you were in London, I suppose Bertie — I mean His Royal Highness, would want to receive you. But he has no notion of what it would cost you. It would be exceedingly thoughtless of him."

Lady Phoebe set down her teacup. Her pale eyes looked considerably harder as they fixed on Alix. Alix was always surprised at the quiet menace that could creep into her mother-in-law's voice and her eyes when she felt she had been tricked. It amused Alix to arouse that spirit, even if it was directed against her.

"Just what do you mean by that, young lady?"

"I, ma'am? I care for your health. That should be our prime concern, shouldn't it? Pa says so."

"Indeed." The dowager picked up her cup and looked over its rim at Alix. She began to sparkle a little. "How dear of your papa! But he has always been a pet of mine. I must admit that in spite of everything, there are times when no sacrifice is too great if family loyalty is involved. And poor Franz deserves all my exertions."

Enormously relieved, Alix said, "How good of you! I know the prince will appreciate it."

"If he is alive. The prince. Yes. I must simply make the effort. Several new gowns will be absolutely necessary. I refuse to let his mistress, that odious Keppel woman, outdo me."

"But ma'am, the schoolmistress expects us the day after tomorrow."

Obviously Lady Phoebe's mind had not been on the same prince. Chagrined, she dismissed her mistake. "Quite true. I was referring to a short stay in London before we bring the child home. Perhaps a small Christmas foray. Shopping and visits to old friends at such a delightful time."

"Charming," Alix agreed, forcing her best smile.

She went up to the room she and David still used, Lady Phoebe having somehow failed to depart from her old suite. "Mattie, pack something for me to go to France and back in one or two days. And a gown for London, in case Her Ladyship decides to invade Bertie's dominion."

Mattie stared as if she hadn't heard correctly. "Holy saints, miss! It's Christmas coming right along. And you're going off to some heathen place across the waters? And with Her Ladyship, and all?"

"We must. It's important."

Mattie shrugged. "If you say so. But I'll be telling you this. It's a sight easier packing for you than for Her Majesty the Dowager. I sure don't wish I was in Pyncheon's boots."

Nevertheless, she went at her work with a will.

When Alix went down to dinner she and Mattie had decided on Alix's wardrobe of a violet silk dinner gown she had worn but once, a dove blue street dress with a high lace collar, and her favourite blue-grey overcoat, tight-fitting to the waist, with leg-of-mutton sleeves. It looked warm enough to take her across the Channel which was bound to be bitterly cold on a December day.

She met Pyncheon on the way down and saw her ordering the young second coachman as he dragged a steamer trunk over the carpeted hall to the west suite that had been promised to the newlyweds months ago.

"I must do something about that suite," she reminded herself, but at the moment it was less important than the fact that Lady Phoebe apparently intended to take an entire wardrobe to France for an eighteen-hour visit.

She pointed to the trunk. "We can't take it, Pyncheon. We could never manage it on board, or in a hansom cab."

"You may trust me, ma'am."

"Yes, but — "

"I'm to accompany you and Her Ladyship, ma'am. I've handled these matters before."

Alix studied her face and thought she read a trace of humour in those vinegary features. She was doubtful but also relieved.

"Thank you, Pyncheon. I'll leave it with you."

It always surprised Alix to see how Pyncheon, with her abrupt and unfriendly manner, could manage her mistress, but once they set out for London on the train the next day, Alix breathed more freely. When she first tricked Lady Phoebe into accompanying her she had been afraid the responsibility might make a definite breach between them.

Luckily, the bad moments were handled by Pyncheon, totally indifferent to her mistress's tiresome complaints and the long, changing catalogue of her ailments. She provided a spoonful of a tonic when Lady Phoebe moaned that watching the winter scenery rush by gave her a headache. The tonic was equally effective in London at the elegant Savoy Hotel on the Thames Embankment.

While dining in great style, Lady Phoebe became jolly and talkative after two glasses of champagne, even to repeating a naughty joke Lady Amesbury had told her about Bertie and his mistress, Mrs Keppel.

Most of the dining-room was discussing Queen Victoria and her future, if any. Over tall glasses of good German wine, almost all of them were interested in what kind of a king Bertie would make.

"No more German wine, I dare say," one of the male gossipers at a nearby table added after loudly toasting the birthday of one of the beauties at his table.

"You're right there," someone else agreed. "Thanks to Bertie the Francophile, we'll all sound like a head waiter with our Frenchie talk."

The toasted beauty rolled her eyes.

"At least, it should help that good-looking Prince Kuragin, if he's still alive. The papers were full of the fellow's dashing exploits. That's what they called them, at any rate."

One of the men added, "They say Bertie has been annoying the Foreign Office about him. Wait till the old queen finds out he's meddling in politics. She'll probably have his head."

Lady Phoebe raised her beaded fan and used it vigorously. "How crude! Just because the Prince of Wales prefers Franz to that dreadful Friedrich the Third. Everyone says he's behind all that evidence against Franz in Turkey."

With difficulty Alix pretended not to hear the remark at the next table about the "good-looking Prince Kuragin".

Similar gossip about the Prince of Wales had spread over the room, as though he were already king. Much as the average citizen revered the old queen, Alix noted that to the aristocracy Victoria seemed merely a relic of the previous century. She would not like to have thought of her own mother in that light; yet she had belonged to the nineteenth century.

Lady Phoebe played with the elaborate cake and pudding on her plate. "Now, I shall never get to sleep tonight, remembering all the excitement tomorrow. I must remind Pyncheon to give me a dose of that syrup. It is the only thing in the world that makes me sleep when I'm so highly strung."

Alix wondered if there would be trouble ahead. She must check the matter with Pyncheon. It would be calamitous if Lady Phoebe had to be carried aboard the Channel ferry still asleep.

She need not have worried. When she spoke of her fears to Pyncheon, that flinty female dismissed the idea with one of her grim smiles.

"Don't be troubling yourself, ma'am. It'll be syrup of cherries and sugar water."

Pyncheon had an answer for everything. Lady Phoebe slept reasonably well and told Alix the next morning that it was all due to Pyncheon's tonic. She rode down through the stark, foggy countryside to Dover and went aboard the plump ferry with almost no difficulty. It was only after the ferry had nudged its way into a Channel suddenly blue under a crisp golden sky that Lady Phoebe remembered to ask, "Where on earth is my trunk? Pyncheon! Where did they put it?"

Alix waited with both interest and suspense. Mentally, she placed her bets on Pyncheon.

"But madam, the trunk is safe at the hotel. Your Ladyship wouldn't wish all your lovely things stolen by some foreigner tonight in France. We could never replace that brown georgette with all those shimmering jet beads. It suits your form so divinely."

Alix smiled and walked to the rail as the discussion shifted Pyncheon's way. In spite of the winter sun she was glad of her grey kid gloves and the warmth of her high fur collar. Once outside the harbour protection the ferry cut into the waves, bringing with it a distinctly unpleasant feeling that made Alix queasy. She hadn't been seasick once on the Atlantic but this was another matter entirely.

It wasn't something she could confess to. There was a disgraceful and humorous aspect to the idea. She pulled herself together and stopped looking down at the dark blue waters.

The ships they passed were far more interesting. Many of them were square-rigged, deep-water ships, brigs or barkentines with all the masts catching the wind. The schooners, smaller and less stately, with their fore-and-aft rigging, cut across the stern of the ferry, making for local harbours.

When Lady Phoebe decided she must have tea or die of the cold, it was a welcome suggestion to Alix. They went into what Pyncheon called a lounge, which was crowded, chiefly with commercial travellers. There were few women of Lady Phoebe's class but any number of European women who looked like peasants and were herding many lively children.

In America, as Alix knew very well, people took their places and fiercely held them against all onslaughts. Here, she was surprised to see how people made way for Lady Phoebe in particular, but even Alix and Pyncheon were regarded as rulers of the earth, with prior rights to the tea and various muffins and tarts.

Off the French coast the ferry caught cross-currents and wallowed briefly but recovered, to Alix's relief. This gave her a chance to enjoy the thrill of pulling into the picturesque Calais harbour which had played such an important part in one of her favourite Alexandre Dumas novels when she was a girl.

The arrival of the ferry had attracted a small crowd, though the sun had already set over the Channel, leaving a winter afterglow in the westerly direction. Alix did not know what to expect or who would meet them, if anyone, on the wharf and she was shaken by hope when Lady Phoebe whispered to Pyncheon, "Good heavens! Isn't that Franz? The tall man in the greatcoat."

Alix stood on tiptoe trying to believe in the identity of the man whose face was partially hidden by a peaked military cap, part of a European army uniform. The man's upper torso was concealed by the capes of his heavy coat. He was either unshaven or had a close-cropped beard.

It would be too much to hope for, a Christmas miracle, to think Prince Kuragin had survived and was here before them. But as the women made their way to the wharf in the swarm of passengers, the man approached them through the crowd, bowed to Lady Phoebe, and picked up their two suitcases. He was a stranger to Alix.

But not to Lady Phoebe or Pyncheon. The dowager fell upon him as upon a rock of salvation. "My dear Monsieur Benoit, you cannot imagine what we have endured on this wretched journey."

Pyncheon explained to Alix, "Frau Vogt's son-in-law, Monsieur Jean Benoit. He will see us to his inn."

This close view showed Alix an attractive moustached man, unshaven for some reason, but looking not unlike Franz Kuragin. He seemed very alert.

Was something wrong, just as Alix had first suspected?

When he was presented to Alix he set one of the cases down, removed his cap, held it under his arm, and bowed to her. He turned a little, looking around over her head as if surveying the crowd. Several people glanced at him. He must be wondering where David was.

Alix apologised for her husband's absence. "I'm afraid we couldn't reach David in time. He is in the Scottish Highlands on a research project."

"A pity, Madame de Miravel. It is always

well to have an extra man in case of difficulties."

While Alix digested this with a frown, Lady Phoebe added mournfully, "So necessary indeed. The difficulties we have endured. The crowds, the jolting, and the freezing weather. But there you have my poor son. It was so different with my Bayard. His mama always came first with him."

Watching him, Alix was convinced that the difficulties he mentioned had nothing to do with the discomforts of an elderly lady. He remained there looking around. It was almost as if he wanted to be seen. Curious behaviour, more like an actor than an innkeeper.

He replaced his peaked cap which shaded the upper half of his face, and then offered the dowager his free arm.

He led the three women across the wharf to a cobbled side-street where they could see ahead of them an ancient Norman inn with a wooden sign reading PAS DE CALAIS. On the door itself above the latch, a hand-printed paper, flapping in the wind, said: "FERME POUR UN MARIAGE".

The inn, with its timbered two-storey interior, was right out of a novel to Alix's eyes. Probably the wedding mentioned was an excuse to keep out the customers. Whatever this journey meant, Alix felt relieved that at least the mystery would soon be over.

They were expected. The door opened almost before the women and their host reached the worn stoop. No one came out but once they were in the dark little passage smelling of wood smoke, two women came to meet them.

The younger, Madame Benoit, was pretty and plainly dressed in black. She greeted them but Alix thought she sounded frightened. Her glance kept shifting from her husband, Jean Benoit, to her mother, the stately and formidable Frau Wilhelmina Vogt. The latter also wore black, but her gown was a satin redingote over the straight, high-necked gown. Her hair, swept back to a bun, was steel grey, matching her eyes.

The schoolmistress made rapid introductions in English which Lady Phoebe received with a chatty description of their ordeal aboard the ferry. She ended, "You may imagine my exhaustion after that. I certainly look forward to a night's sleep."

Frau Vogt and her daughter looked uneasily at each other. Alix caught the exchange. Had something gone wrong?

Young Madame Benoit began, "We regret your discomfort on the voyage, *madame*, but I'm afraid — "

She got no further. Lady Phoebe cut in. "Yes, yes. I appreciate your concern. Meanwhile, I really must retire at once. Of course, Pyncheon will bring me a light supper and you may send Prince Kuragin's little boy to me for a visit. Then I will try to rest."

Jean Benoit had no patience with this chitchat. "The government wishes the prince all safety while he is on French soil. We are sympathetic to the Kuragin cause, as you probably know. There will be protection from an agent of the Sûreté and myself on the return crossing tonight."

Lady Phoebe was appalled. "Return crossing! My dear man, do not even think of it. I could never survive another of those dreadful crossings without at least one night's rest."

Benoit did not wait for her agreement but strode down the hall that opened off the period taproom. Alix watched him suspiciously. What was he up to?

He took a key from the pocket of his greatcoat and unlocked a door at the back of the hall and went in.

Meanwhile, Frau Vogt managed Lady Phoebe. "There is no alternative, Your Ladyship. It is for the safety of those concerned. I will show you to a warm room where you may take your leisure for the next hour. Your maid, of course, will be with you. Perhaps you may rest on the Channel ferry tonight."

Still protesting, and with the powerful addition of tears, Lady Phoebe left the old inn's taproom leaning heavily on Pyncheon's bony shoulder.

Mrs Benoit took the two women into a room off the hall and went in with them, passing her husband who nodded to her.

The innkeeper then returned to the taproom. "It is well," he remarked to Frau Vogt in French. Then he turned to Alix. "If Your Ladyship will come with me."

It was not so much a request as an order. She obeyed.

Meanwhile, where on earth was the young Prince Maximilian? Possibly waiting in the room set aside for his cousin Phoebe. Alix's imagination was at the peak. She wondered if she was safe, having been separated from Lady Phoebe. Not that her mother-in-law would be much protection, but at least they would be together. And it would always be well to have the strong-minded Pyncheon close at hand.

Getting up nerve as they passed the room to which the dowager had been taken, she said, "I expected to be with my mother-in-law. Is there some reason for separating us?"

"Yes, *madame.* There were most particular

instructions for Lord Miravel. It is unfortunate that His Lordship could not make the crossing but I am told Your Ladyship will be an excellent substitute."

She said firmly, half believing it, "I am."

He said nothing to that. He stopped again at the back of the hall, unlocking the door.

The back parlour they entered was lighted only by a low-burning fire on the hearth. Benoit said, "As Your Highness requested." He inclined his head respectfully, then turned and left the room, closing the door behind him.

The title and the innkeeper's bow were not lost on Alix. She thought Prince Kuragin must be in this room with her but in spite of their last meetings she must remember that Benoit's respect signalled her own behaviour.

She was also confused by the half darkness with its flashes of crimson and blue as the wood crackled. Then she made out the man standing just beyond the fitful light of the fire. He had one arm raised, bent at the elbow. She could not recognise his features; yet she had little doubt of his identity.

Franz Kuragin's voice told her all she wanted to know. He was alive, and he was here before her. There was in his voice that faint note of humour and laughter he seemed to have retained throughout whatever his ordeal had been.

"A fine greeting. Don't you know me, little one?"

In her excitement she was afraid she would cry, and that would be disastrous. He didn't need a sobbing woman on his hands. She wanted to go to him but hesitated. He had not asked her to come. All she could say was, "You are alive. Really. Truly."

"Really, truly. How pretty you look, all windblown and red-cheeked. I see David decided discretion was wisdom."

"He is in the Scottish Highlands, writing a book. Can I come nearer? I promise not to throw my arms around you and make a fool of myself."

He said lightly, "You could never do that." He was silent for a long minute. When he spoke again she heard the troubled doubt in his voice, in spite of his laugh. "Are you afraid of me? If you are, I have no hope at all of the others. I'm not a pretty sight."

"Don't say things like that. Don't ever. Not to me."

Still in the shadows beyond the fire, he kept up the light pretence. "You see, I am a bit scratched up at the moment, and Cousin Phoebe is certain to give the game away."

CHAPTER FOURTEEN

As an inducement he challenged, "My boy Max took the sight of me very well." He added on his usual ironic note, "But I rather think he was a trifle disappointed by my resurrection. He likes to think of himself as Maximilian the Second, the Prince Royal. That is, if we get rid of my Great-Uncle Friedrich."

She could not let him think she was re-pulsed by whatever "scratches" he had undergone. She forced herself to remind him in his own light manner, "Your Highness forgets I am a miner's daughter. Have you ever seen men brought up after an explosion hundreds of feet below the surface?"

"Fortunately, I have not. You make me feel quite lucky." He added on a lighter note, "If I asked you to kiss me, for old times' sake, would you oblige? I am a bit handicapped, but not for ever, I devoutly hope."

He held out one arm and she reached for his hand quickly, touching her lips to the raw flesh that was like a bloody bracelet around his wrist.

She felt him kiss her hair as she bent over his hand. She raised her head. A charred log on the fire rolled down the grate and illuminated the raw wound on his left temple. It was still enflamed and perilously close to his eye. She had been captivated by his eyes from their first meeting, and she loved them even more now. She swallowed hard before reminding him as casually as she found possible, "You should have that covered. It may bleed again."

"Too easy to see. The cap shaded my face but a bandage would be easier noticed."

She did not ask why his left hand and arm were in a sling. As if she discussed simple political gossip, she remarked, "I guess the Turks did that."

"No. These were souvenirs of the sultan's police. As a matter of fact, two Turkish guards made my second attempt at an escape possible. The Turkish people have very little love for Abdul the Damned. I might add the evidence against me was provided by Friedrich the Third of Lichtenbourg."

She gasped. "Horrible."

"Not at all." His free hand caressed her fingers, so much smoother than his injured flesh. "Western Europe is about to read the story, along with two pieces of evidence provided by my Turkish friends. They hope to involve their sultan in the bloody business, of course. Now!" He shook her hand. "I must get back to London and Friedrich's men know it. I am to act as your escort. As a matter of fact, I will take the good Benoit's place. It was Mina Vogt's notion. She is a loyal friend. No one more so."

Alix had never thought she would be jealous of the stern and rigid schoolmistress, but she managed to keep to the matter at hand. "Everyone on the docks saw Mr Benoit's face, so they won't look too closely at you when you take his place. As Lady Phoebe says, it's like a play."

"Ah, Phoebe. The one fly in our ointment. I certainly didn't expect her when Mina Vogt wrote to you. I had contacted her from Belgrade and worked out this tentative arrangement. I did count on you and David."

"He didn't know. We couldn't get him. Otherwise, I know he would have done whatever he could."

She began to wrestle with the problem of one fewer man than he had counted on but was distracted when he drew her against his body with his right hand and she felt the warm flesh of his lips transfer its heat to her own trembling, anxious mouth.

There was long pent-up emotion in his kiss but she was better able to answer it now than in that dark upper hall the night she arrived at Miravel. Stimulated by her own hunger for him, a hunger that had increased with her dreams and the painful realisation that David was a poor substitute for the man she had learned to love, she returned his kiss. She was only aware of his mouth taking hers, the heat of his body, and her own passionate response when the door opened across the room and Jean Benoit said, like cold water on a hot coal, "The night ferry leaves within the hour. Your son reminds me that you must hurry."

The innkeeper carried his many-caped coat over one arm and his cap in two fingers.

"I know," Prince Kuragin said impatiently. "It is all arranged."

As he let Alix go, trading her for the peaked cap low over his left eye, she was embarrassed by what Jean Benoit had seen, but she still felt throughout her body the delicious aura left by that embrace.

The prince could not manage the coat but when she saw Benoit reach out to help him she was careful not to offer her own help. He winced as he threw off the sling from his left shoulder and, together with the inn-keeper, managed to get his arm into the left shoulder of the coat. The heavy cape-collars served to disguise the stiffness of his shoulder.

He grinned at Alix as Benoit studied him. "Satisfactory?"

"Stunning." She tried to be as casual as the men were.

"You see? I told you. You may count upon her," the prince told Benoit, who nodded without further opinion.

The prince then gave Alix what she thought of as her marching orders. "Our greatest problem is Phoebe. Max is with her now but he knows better than to mention me until we are aboard the ferry. It is British and two of the crew are Scotland Yard. So Inspector Gallien must escort Phoebe and Max aboard the ferry. I will follow immediately behind them in Jean Benoit's coat and cap with you and Phoebe's maid. As we go aboard the British will take over for Gallien."

"But she may recognise you before we are on the ferry. Then, there will be cries and moans and all the rest."

He took her hand. "Trust Max. My boy has orders to keep poor Phoebe so occupied she won't have time to look behind her."

Say what he would, the whole scheme was alarming to Alix, but she could only shrug and say, "I hope you are right."

His smile was grim. "Believe me, so do I. Benoit, take Cousin Alexandra to Lady Phoebe. They have about forty-five minutes more to finish dinner. Then we will meet in that dark street outside your tavern, as we planned."

"Very good, Your Highness. The inspector has just arrived. I know him. There will be no trouble there."

When Benoit was about to leave the room with Alix Prince Kuragin turned the nervous palm of her hand up and kissed her wrist. She must hold to that giddy delight for a long time, perhaps even for ever. There was David to consider, and in Franz Kuragin's case, there was a kingdom to win. She knew she was only secondary to that, if, indeed, he had any permanent feeling for her.

By the time she arrived at the reception parlour of the Pas de Calais the rest of the party was already waiting for her. Lady Phoebe had apparently been complaining for some time, objecting to this change in their itinerary.

"Only an hour or two in France. Heavens! Scarcely enough time for that wretched sour wine and oyster stew. Those *were* oysters, I trust. Take Max here. Aren't you hungry? Little boys always have large appetites."

For the first time Alix saw Franz's boy

who must be eight years old by now. He was seated in a regal way against the timbered wall. Nothing could have been more suited to his manner than the high-backed armchair of heavy oak, its leather cushions worn by many bodies.

Exceedingly handsome, with brown eyes and his father's finely sculptured nose, he looked as if he might already be enthroned in Lichtenbourg City. At the same time, despite his grace and elegance, Alix thought there was a certain weakness about him that she had never seen in his father.

He studied Alix with interest, then motioned to Lady Phoebe. "You may present Cousin David's wife to me."

Obviously, he expected Alix to bow or curtsy, or grovel in some way, which she had no intention of doing. Besides, all this excitement had tightened her stomach as if she were seasick again.

"How do you do? I imagine you must be Prince Kuragin's boy." Before he could do more than open his mouth in surprise, she asked Benoit, "May I have some broth? Salty."

"No more than that, Your Ladyship?"

"I don't want to get seasick."

"Very true. Tea might help, as well."

She shrugged. It didn't matter. Her appetite

was gone. Too much had happened and was about to happen, and she wasn't at all sure whether they would all come through it alive.

The broth was excellent. More than a simple broth, in fact. There were delicate bits of vegetables in it and to her surprise, she found her appetite returning briefly. While Lady Phoebe dozed in her chair across the room, Alix's dinner tray acted as a magnet for Prince Max. He wandered to the old-fashioned tapster's bar to stare at the contents of her tray.

"Is it good? I had thick potage and oysters in the shell."

"Mine is very good, but I have to eat fast, so we won't miss the ferry."

He smiled, a winning smile that warmed her. "Then I'll order some cake. That will give you more time."

"But I don't want the ferry to leave Your Highness behind either."

"Oh, they won't dare to do that," he assured her airily. "They know who I am."

"You mean because you are Prince Kuragin's son?"

He swept this aside indignantly. "Of course not. It's who I am."

"And who are you?"

He was astonished by such naïveté. "I am almost the Prince Royal of Lichtenbourg.

When Friedrich the Third dies, and he's an awfully old man, and we get back the throne, I'll be like the Prince of Wales."

For a child he was mighty ambitious. She reminded him, "There are a great many 'ifs' in that plan."

His smooth young brow wrinkled with his confusion. "Don't you want me to rule Lichtenbourg?"

"I think you should wait until your brave papa is safe on the throne."

Madame Benoit had come over to the tapster's bar in answer to the boy's imperious summons. He gave Alix's reminder a little thought, then dismissed Madame Benoit.

"I'd better not have cake. They might not wait for us."

Alix commended him, "You are a very wise boy. You learn fast."

Max raised his chin and gave the others in the room a look compounded of pride and benevolence. To Alix he confided, "I intend to be a good prince. Not like that old Friedrich. He tried to have Papa murdered. I hate him. If I ever get hold of him I'll have his head cut off."

"They don't cut people's head off any more in your country."

"What do they do?"

"I believe they bring them before a firing

squad if they have royal blood. Otherwise, they hang them."

He was still considering these alternatives when Frau Vogt came in from the back of the passage, probably the room in which Alix had seen Prince Kuragin all too briefly.

"*Mesdames,* I am afraid it is time."

Seeing that Lady Phoebe was blissfully dreaming, Alix addressed Pyncheon who had been sitting on a straight chair nearby, staring patiently at the opposite wall. Pyncheon got up now.

"Yes, madam." In her quiet, competent way she aroused her sleep-dazed mistress, helped her into her voluminous, fur-trimmed coat, then put on her own plain coat and felt hat. She looked over at Prince Max. "Will Your Highness need help?"

The young prince started to speak, looked at Alix, and dismissed the maid's assistance. "Of course not. I'm no baby."

He sounded so childish and yet so adult that Alix wanted to smile but luckily did not.

They were all ready in less than five minutes and headed for the street door just as a stocky, fortyish man with a beaver hat lowered the latch and came in. Over the heads of the women and the boy Inspector Gallien spoke to Frau Vogt.

"Is all in order?"

"In order."

"Good. I will accompany you and the child, My Lady."

Next to Alix she felt Prince Max bristle at the derogatory word "child" but he relaxed at once, squared his shoulders, and got into his own fur-collared jacket.

About this time, while the little party was ranging itself in groups of three and three, Alix began to feel that now-familiar prickle of terror. A male figure moved to her right side but did not take her arm. It had to be Franz whose injured left shoulder was nearest her. She was afraid to glance at him. Did Franz look enough like Jean Benoit in figure and manner?

Thus far, he had fooled Lady Phoebe who was still sleepy and yawned several times before they were out of the little side-street. Nearing the wharf she began to fuss, making objections, addressing them first to Inspector Gallien in the tightly buttoned coat and beaver hat, looking like a baker dressed as a Paris boulevardier.

"I should have Pyncheon beside me," Lady Phoebe insisted. "I need her. She carries my smelling salts. Where is she? Pyncheon, come here at once. I can't see in this cursed darkness. I thought Paris was the City of Light.

239

Where are all the gaslights?"

"We aren't in Paris, Cousin Phoebe," Prince Max reminded her. She started to look behind her and Alix stiffened. Pyncheon, on Alix's other side, likewise guessed the problem and looked anxiously at the disguised Prince Kuragin. But young Max chattered on merrily as he had been ordered to do.

"I know I'll like Christmas in England. They say they have carollers and yule logs and presents too. We have German Christmas in Frau Vogt's school, with real Christmas trees and candles and berries."

The street was now busy with Channel passengers carrying or dragging their luggage through the gaslit darkness to the Channel wharf with its many lights, its noise and activity.

Inspector Gallien had just reached the wharf with his two charges, looking around at the crowd every sixty seconds or so, and Alix, behind them, breathed a sigh of relief, when Lady Phoebe turned her ankle on a cobblestone. She screamed and started to go down. With Max trying to hold her up, Prince Kuragin reached for her with his good arm and then with both hands just as Inspector Gallien swung around again, elbowed the prince out of the way and produced from nowhere a heavy pistol. He fired over Alix's head into the crowd behind them.

Panic followed. The running, shoving mob left in its wake a small, harmless-looking man who writhed in his own blood. Alix paid little attention to the would-be assassin. She knew that Prince Kuragin must also be in deep pain, having put so much pressure on his injured shoulder. She left the inspector's victim to Gallien and the imperturbable Miss Pyncheon while she helped get Lady Phoebe on her feet.

"Are you all right, ma'am?"

The dowager waved Alix away. She was too busy staring at Prince Kuragin.

"Good heavens, Franz! Is that you? It's so dark I can hardly see you. I thought you were that French innkeeper."

Before she could get a close look at the raw wound on the prince's temple which would be illuminated by the ferry's bright light, Alix hustled her into the ferry. Here they were almost knocked down by two running sailors. One of them flourished a pistol which caused more consternation among the crowd. The other British sailor stopped in front of Prince Kuragin, bowed and said something quietly. The prince argued, nodded towards the crowd around the wounded man, but the sailor took his good arm firmly and ushered him on to the deck of the ferry.

Obviously, Alix decided, the two sailors were sent to protect His Highness. She saw that the prince's face looked pale and drawn in the deck lights. She was not surprised. He must have suffered using that injured shoulder. His son was now beside him, looking more proud and imperious than ever.

Alix wanted desperately to go to Franz but was afraid of the dowager's reaction when she saw his battle scars. Pyncheon came aboard with the last passengers and her report to her mistress.

"Inspector Gallien and the French police will take the injured man away. Your fall was a lucky one, madam — "

Lady Phoebe was appalled at this insensitivity. "Lucky! I should not call it precisely lucky. I very nearly fell on the wretched wharf before half of France. What was that running all about?"

"The man the inspector wounded was about to shoot His Highness. The police hope to discover who hired him. I am told it will be excellent for the Kuragin cause."

Only a little mollified, Lady Phoebe accepted this good news. "I'm sure I wish them well. Do you realise that assassin almost shot me?"

Pyncheon said, "Very true, madam. We

must be grateful that he was only aiming at His Highness."

Both amused and annoyed, Alix remembered someone's advice about seasickness and, after excusing herself to Lady Phoebe, went out on the bitter cold afterdeck to inhale some fresh air. The danger to all of them, and especially Prince Kuragin, had not helped her stomach. She began to feel the motion of all those Channel currents as soon as the ferry was out of the harbour.

Hearing a footstep behind her she turned around, startled, still half expecting some assassin with a gun or, almost as terrifying, one of the highly efficient policemen, also with guns.

It was Prince Kuragin. Even in the starlight she could see the warmth of his smile and shuddered inwardly at the thought that he might easily have been murdered only half an hour ago. She must have shown something of this in her own face, because he joined her at the rail and said softly, "We are on our way home, and we are safe. You must remember that."

"Thank God. I was just about thanking God when you came up, though I don't think I was conscious of it then."

He put his good hand on hers. She scarcely saw the ugly, raw wound that circled his wrist. His hand itself was warm and strong.

"Are you going back to him?"

She avoided his eyes. "I don't want to."

He looked out at the stars which did little to lighten the enormous dark of the sea. "I am partly responsible for it."

"You? You had nothing to do with our meeting in Geneva. Or the idiocy that made me marry him even after I met you."

He raised her hand. She felt his lips upon her cold knuckles. "My darling, thank you for that. It was something else I was talking about. Some day I will tell you. Unless, of course, he loves you? Or you love him."

"I know now that it was something he was forced to do, to produce an heir for Miravel. He has been very kind to me. But — poor man — he doesn't love me. He loves his books and his intellectual toys."

He gave her hand back to her and kept staring at the distant, unattainable lights in the dark sky.

"I am no boy of fourteen in love with a dream. If I were, I would tell you what you will never believe."

She looked at him.

He said quietly, "I loved you that first evening at your house in New York. We were coming up the stairs and I saw a full-length portrait of you on the wall above us.

I loved you then. I think I said something of the sort to Dave. He laughed, accused me of seducing his future wife. God knows, I wanted to."

She remembered all too well. "And he said he was going to marry me because Pa and Lady Phoebe had arranged the settlement. Pa was buying me a husband. A fancy one with a real title. Not as big as yours, but quite respectable."

Then she realised the other barrier and reminded him, "When the people of Lichtenbourg call you home to be their ruler, and they certainly ought to after they hear about that awful man's latest crimes, you will be forced to marry some princess."

He laughed tenderly. "You have Lichtenbourg confused with a Graustark novel, my darling. I married a princess once. I have an heir." He hesitated. "If the obstacles were in my own way, they would have to choose, my wife, my son and me. Or nothing from the Kuragins."

She was appalled and yet thrilled that he should be willing to make such a sacrifice. "You can't mean that."

"I know what I want in my life from now on. I've had some weeks of the sultan's hospitality to think about it."

She shuddered and he reminded her, "That

is all in the past. The problem is yours, and you are at the beginning of your life."

"I do know how I feel and what I want. But there is David and what the scandal would do to him."

He hesitated. "I'm sorry. David and I were once good friends. I wish we might have remained so. But there are other things between David and me. Lies. Or the implication of lies. Even Phoebe has joined him in — "

They both heard Lady Phoebe's breathless voice across the windswept deck.

"Ah! There you are. We thought you had deserted us, got off in mid-Channel. Maximilian thinks you don't like him, Alexandra. Do reassure the poor child."

Young Max carefully led his Cousin Phoebe to his father and Alix. Pyncheon stayed behind saying nothing, as usual.

Deeply disappointed at the interruption, Alix managed to smile at the boy. "Of course, I like Your Highness. I just think young princes should know American manners as well as European ones."

Max looked doubtful. "Is your boy going to be European or American?"

"My boy? What boy? I have no sons yet."

"But you were sick," Max insisted. "Like ladies when they are going to have a son. Or maybe a daughter. One of our teachers felt like that and she went away and had a son."

Alix saw so little of David that the possible cause of her "seasickness" hadn't seemed likely. She was never seasick. She had been proud of what she boasted to Mattie Fogarty was her cast-iron stomach. But it explained so much of her illness today. She was stunned at the possibility.

Coyly, Lady Phoebe scolded the young prince. "Max, you know you were not supposed to talk about it."

"Why not?" Max demanded. "Pyncheon says you must be going to have a baby. You were sick all the way to Calais, and I saw you when you ate dinner. You weren't feeling good then. Pyncheon says that's a good sign; isn't it?"

Prince Kuragin cut in sharply, "There are other explanations. I had just explained all the dangers ahead, and Cousin Alexandra has already done quite enough to help us."

"Now, now," Lady Phoebe chided them all, "one would think this wonderful news was not welcome. Nothing could be further from the truth. We are all delighted, are we not, Franz?"

"I am sure you are," Prince Kuragin said in a distant voice as cold as the rail behind them. "That was always your aim, wasn't

247

it, dear Phoebe?"

Alix felt his hand near hers on the rail. His fingers searched for hers. After a long moment she drew her fingers away. But his touch remained on her fingers as in her memory. She told herself desperately that David's child would never come between her and the man she loved.

CHAPTER FIFTEEN

The old queen died on 22 January of the new year, surrounded by the many members of her family, and in the arms of her nephew, the German kaiser.

In ordinary circumstances Lady Phoebe would have been outraged at not witnessing the historic splendour of the great queen-empress's funeral procession. All of the world, even democratic United States and the Republic of France, agreed that never since Roman days had there been so many of the world's anointed heads present in one place.

To cap it all, David was fond of reminding one and all that his good friend Bertie was now the king-emperor of the greatest empire in the world's history. Still, even David had more interesting matters awaiting him at home.

As Lady Phoebe explained incessantly to half the population of Shropshire and dozens of her most intimate friends in London, "The Miravel dynasty calls me home. Yes. My son David will soon welcome the next Lord

Miravel. I am very naughty in confiding this to you, but one of Her Late Majesty's own accoucheurs has assured us, in private, that we may be prepared for a male heir. You may imagine how important that is."

Of her daughter-in-law the dowager had less to say, though she complained to Pyncheon, "One would think Alexandra had never heard of babies before. Imagine. She has been in the most depressed state ever since we received the delightful news. I'm sure she will never again do anything so creditable, but she seems totally unaware of what it means to bring into the world the next Miravel heir. A pity these Yankee women have no sense of history."

"Takes after her father, no doubt," Pyncheon remarked.

Lady Phoebe blushed at the mention of Tiger Royle. "I won't have any aspersions cast at that dear man. He would be here now if it weren't for Cousin Franz and his wretched political affairs, so inconvenient at this time."

Everyone had already heard how Tiger rode out around the neighbourhood in David's automobile with Phoebe, as if they were young sweethearts. Who knew what this little attention from Tiger Royle might lead to? No need in telling those who saw them together that he had rushed home to Miravel apparently to be certain that his daughter was in good health. He hadn't been satisfied, but Alix assured him there was nothing he could do. He would have to wait. About seven more months, to be almost precise.

In the dowager's opinion young people like Alexandra just didn't have the stamina of the pregnant wives in Phoebe Miravel's day. Of course, many of them had died in childbirth, but at least they did their duty first. Not like Alexandra who had been warned by those absurd London doctors that she must remain off her feet during most of her pregnancy. She was too thin across the hips, they said, and she was certainly unwell.

The only thing that seemed to excite Alix was the way Pa told her about the influence being used by Russia, France, and most of the Balkans to permit the prince's return to Lichtenbourg. This was long overdue and there should be no way to prevent it, now that the truth of Prince Kuragin's detention by the Sublime Porte had been spread to all the newspapers of the sympathetic powers.

The first news of his torture at the hands of the sultan's police was mentioned two days after his return from France and in the following month, when the kaiser came to visit his dying grandmother, Queen Victoria, he was greeted with cries, shouts, placards and some wet vegetables, along with demands that he stay out of Lichtenbourg's internal affairs. It was now widely known that the German empire and its ally, the Austro-Hungarian Hapsburgs, were all that kept old Friedrich the Third in power.

"I never was a kingmaker," Tiger explained to Alix. "But there's always a first time, and I'm game."

But Alix's thoughts were elsewhere. Franz had wanted to speak to her alone in London before she was bundled up and hustled home to Miravel, but she knew this would only increase the pain of her unfulfilled relationship with him. She could face an ugly divorce and the charge of adultery, but not where her child and David's was concerned, nor where such a charge would destroy Prince Kuragin's future and perhaps the future of the little country he loved.

So she had refused to see him alone after the physicians' considered report.

On the morning of the Miravels' departure for home Lady Phoebe offered her own invaluable Pyncheon to help Alix do her final packing. It was an offer Alix refused. She was as depressed as she had been the moment she learned that there would never be a future for her with the man she loved, and she didn't want the hawk-eyed Pyncheon reading all the signals in Alix's manner and her eyes.

Shortly after she had politely turned down Phoebe's offer, someone knocked on the door of her small, corner suite in the Savoy Hotel. This would be Pyncheon, of course, Phoebe having refused to take "no" for an answer.

Alix went to the door and opened it with a friendly but firm refusal on her lips only to find herself staring up at Prince Kuragin. There was a light in his gypsy eyes as there was so often when he looked at her. She was conscious of the slight, coagulated blood below the healing wound on his left temple. She longed to be in his arms. She was more drawn to him now than she had been months ago when his olive flesh was unscarred and she had considered him fascinating.

Her hand remained on the door, ready to close it, but with her first movement he laid his hand over hers. It was a hard, muscular grip.

"We must talk."

She managed to say, "Please. Phoebe is leaving for the station at noon."

She shifted her gaze to his hand but still felt deeply aware of his eyes. Creatures in the forest must feel like this, mesmerised by the very danger they knew they should avoid.

Firmly, he pushed the door open and she fell back, protesting, "I can't betray him. Not now. David has done nothing to deserve this."

"My cousin David deserves — " He broke off, and closed the door behind him. The click told her it locked. She had not often seen him looking so angry. His voice was harsh, unlike himself.

"You were so young. I wanted you to realise what you were doing before I spoke. But you married him. I did worse. I tried to make that marriage work for you on your wedding night. I let him drink, deliberately."

She remembered the scullery maid with her story of a quarrel between Lady Phoebe and Prince Kuragin. Something about whisky. Had he wanted to get David drunk on his wedding night? He had succeeded. And David consummated the marriage.

It was this night, and others like it that made any future love between Alix and Franz Kuragin impossible.

She reminded him, "David is innocent in all this. He should have his child. Don't you see? It's the reason he married me. I didn't go into the marriage blindly. He told me all about it. It isn't a secret."

For some reason this astonished him.

"*He told you all about it?* And still you went through with this farce? Are you so ambitious?"

She said stiffly, "If I were ambitious I would have tried to become Princess Royal of Lichtenbourg." In her anxiety to make him understand what she owed to her husband, the father of her child, she found herself brushing away tears in a maddeningly childish way. "But I didn't, did I? Even though I love you."

Instead of being angry, he was softened by the breakdown of her firm resolve and raised his hands to cup her face between his palms. He touched the tear-stained cheeks gently with his lips and his thumbs. Then, closing his lips over hers he took possession of her mouth, exciting her to sensations that seemed to rack her body with waves of delight.

A knock on the door with sharp knuckles ended for Alix the single most passionate moments of her young life. Her body still felt the reverberation of what had begun as a gentle kiss.

She pulled away, caught a glimpse of his face, whimsical, but with a heightened colour. Even to him it had not been a simple kiss.

Alix raised her voice. "Yes. What is it?"

255

She sounded hoarse but didn't care.

"It's Pyncheon, ma'am. Her Ladyship asks if you will meet us in the lobby. His Highness, Prince Maximilian, has gone to find his father."

Alix glanced at Prince Kuragin, then said more firmly to the woman beyond the door, "Send a bellman to me. I'll meet you in the lobby. Thank you."

The woman's footsteps receded.

The prince took Alix's hands in his. He was as gentle as she had ever seen him.

"I do understand, my love. I want you to know only one thing. It is all-important. You must believe it."

She nodded, looking into his eyes, too lost and embittered to cry. "I'll believe."

He shook her hands playfully. "I have made it clear to those who believe in our cause. I will marry only in my own time and my own choice. My wife must be accepted with me or I will abdicate and serve on a regency for Maximilian. Do you understand what I am saying?"

She knew he meant it at this moment and under these emotions. But even at a remote time in the future, if it should be possible for her to marry him, she knew it would destroy Franz and perhaps his country. Charming young Max might never be the man his father was. He and his country could easily be gobbled up by Lichtenbourg's powerful neighbours.

Nevertheless, she lied and said, "I do understand."

"My love."

She smiled. "I do understand, my love."

Then he was gone.

A part of her felt as though it had died when she said her goodbyes to him in London, in the presence of Lady Phoebe, Pyncheon, and the Prince Maximilian. When the boy hugged his father and Franz bent to kiss him goodbye he looked over Max's curly head, directly at Alix. In these moments he must understand what the fulfilment of their love would mean to their children.

Even now, with Tiger Royle in and out on missions between Miravel and the prince in London or on the continent, it was impossible to soften her parting memory of Franz.

Tiger Royle returned to Miravel briefly in January from his business on the continent, and no one was more glad to see him than Alix. She had never known a time in her active young life when she found herself doing nothing day after day.

She insisted on going into the village to help the vicar and Mrs Tether with the Midwinter Bazaar and organised the May Day Children's Party between her work, at the vicar's suggestion, on behalf of the new Shelters for the Elderly. She was intensely grateful to him for finding her something to keep her busy, as Lady Phoebe was always carping at her when she tried to make some revisions in the ancient ritual of household affairs at Miravel Hall.

Lady Phoebe constantly claimed that "the boy" must be guarded from harm and the disaster of his mother's lack of exercise. Alix's condition gave the dowager the excuse she needed, at least until the famous heir was born. Most annoying was the knowledge that Lady Phoebe insisted on spreading news that her daughter-in-law simply would not exert herself.

One summer day when Alix pretended she was asleep to avoid the dowager's persistent chatter about past Miravels, she overheard Lady Phoebe gossiping with Lady Amesbury. The latter was remarking that it had been a pity when "young Lady Miravel" was forced to discontinue her work on the Midsummer Fair several weeks ago and retire to Mrs Tether's rooms, gasping with pain.

The dowager shook her head. "She simply refuses to think of our heir. There is so much to do on an estate of this size, as no one knows better than you, and she could be useful in a quiet sort of way. The dear baby should have exercise."

Lady Amesbury, as peacemaker, reminded Phoebe, "I do think there may be exercise in her time at the Elder Home. All that work in persuading them to take up woollen crafts, relearning all those beautiful things their ancestors took pleasure in, the carding and spinning and whatever else they do, knitting, of course, but it may produce a few shillings for the poor creatures."

Phoebe brought her guest sharply back to the subject at hand: "My daughter-in-law's illness at the bazaar was embarrassing, you will allow. Now I, for example, suffered excruciatingly when I was carrying David, but I managed to be on my feet as much as possible. Strangely enough, I had no trouble at all with Bayard. What a love he was! Why is life so cruel? He was mischievous, naturally. He had some of his father's liveliness. But what of that? So clever. I must say, poor David will never be what his brother was."

From her *chaise-longue* Alix spoke, startling both women. "Let's hope my baby has sense enough to ignore rivals."

"Rivals?" Lady Phoebe repeated. "What can you mean? David was never my Bayard's rival in any way."

Alix persisted, to the quiet satisfaction of Lady Amesbury. "Maybe the boy will be twins. Then who will be Lord Miravel? Who is to say which is the true heir? Just like the Dumas story about the man in the iron mask. He tried to murder his twin brother."

"Heavens!" Lady Phoebe fanned herself with her lace handkerchief. She ignored her daughter-in-law and complained to Lady Amesbury, "One wonders where these young people find their reading matter. Now that the prince's boy is on our hands I devoutly hope he will not be encouraged to read French literature. There must be a limit somewhere."

"The prince's boy" came in at that minute, rolling a hoop with a broken tree limb. He grinned at Alix and then deliberately behaved as he knew would annoy her.

"How do you do, Cousin Phoebe? Have I met this lady formally?" He dropped the hoop and held out one smooth hand to Lady Amesbury. "You may take my hand if you like. We are not formal here, you know."

Alix was more annoyed at her mother-in-law than at the boy. She suggested, "In a formal gathering, of course, one is expected to curtsy to His Highness. But perhaps merely touching his hand with one's fingertips would be satisfactory at such a time as this."

Max looked at her with his eyes wide, but he played her game without knowing why.

Much embarrassed, Lady Phoebe tried to patch things with her guest who did not know whether she had committed a social error or been the object of someone's peculiar sense of humour.

"If Your Highness has no objection," Lady Amesbury said finally, "I will assume we are already old friends."

Alix approved. "Well done, My Lady."

The woman looked at her, then frowned and smiled at the same time. "I understand. I have reared children myself."

Having come off worst from this encounter, Lady Phoebe found an excuse to leave the room.

"We have a new bust of my boy in the shrine behind the staircase. Really exceptional, made from a portrait painted when he was seventeen."

Both women arose with a rustle of silk. Lady Amesbury gave Alix a curious, understanding little smile, as though they shared an opinion before she asked Lady Phoebe, "Your boy Bayard, of course?"

"Of course." The dowager's tone carried only surprise at the question.

Lady Amesbury took Alix's hand, wished her well, and followed her hostess out to the hall.

There being no one left to express herself to except Max, Alix muttered, "No child of mine is going to feel unloved because his brother or sister is too much loved. That I'll swear to kingdom come."

"I'll remember, Cousin Alix," Max said gravely.

Alix appreciated the young prince's company. She then convinced her mother-in-law that "the old methods you mentioned to Lady Amesbury are best. You understand these things so well. Prince Maximilian will go with me. He has offered to do so."

Lady Phoebe flew into a panic. "But you know what the doctors say. It can be dangerous."

"I prefer to believe what you told Lady Amesbury. Mattie! I want to go walking. Find me something light. My voile and then the green cape to wear over it. And a parasol, too. Against the sun. Be sure and tell David where he may find me. He is always saying I conceal myself from him."

Mattie and Lady Phoebe exchanged glances but before the maid could utter a protest, Alix repeated, "Mattie? Did you hear?"

"Yes, ma'am. I'm coming. But so's the

rain. You best stay inside where it's dry. You know them summer showers."

In the end Alix got her way and with the hood of her cape pulled far forward, over her head, she went down the south steps to the pond escorted by Prince Max, very proud of his new and responsible role.

"I heard from Father today," he told her importantly. "He said I was to look out for you."

"He mentioned me? By name?"

"Well, he called you Alix. May I call you Alix? Alexandra makes me think of the new queen. Father presented me to her last month. She didn't hear me when I told her she was very pretty. She doesn't hear, you know."

"I've never met Queen Alexandra but they say she is lovely. And very kind. So is her husband Bertie — " She caught herself. "I mean King Edward."

"Maybe you will get to meet the queen after your baby comes. I hope it's a girl. If it's a boy it might be like Cousin David and you might like it better than me. I hate Cousin David."

"Max! What a thing to say! Your Cousin David is extremely kind to you. He lets you stay here in his own house. You eat his food."

Max stunned her. He scuffed the pebbles

on the path and contradicted her in a low voice.

"I heard the servants talking. I do what you asked me to, Cousin Alix. I see that the food is separated for the poor and the old people."

"And very kind of you. Some day, when you are the future Prince Royal, you are going to be glad you learned how to be kind to those less fortunate. But this is Lord Miravel's estate. That's David."

He shook his head stubbornly. "Cook sees the statements when they are paid. And the butler — he's awfully pompous, but he's not a bad sort. I heard him say it was your father's money and my father's money that pays for everything on this land. Even the food."

She recovered and issued the stern warning, "Don't you ever let me catch you talking such silly gossip again. Someone had better see to the servants. I suppose it's up to me."

He scratched his head. "I can, if you like. I'll just tell them they are liars and if they don't stop, when I get to be Prince Royal, I'll have them shot." She caught her breath with a hissing sound and he retracted. "Oh, I forgot. You said that was wrong."

"Wrong indeed. Good Lord!"

"Yes. They're commoners; so I could have them hanged."

"Max!"

He helped her across the rocks of the little stream below the pond, reminding her with gentle reproof, "I'm really Prince Max, or Your Highness, but I don't mind if you call me Max."

"You should be more democratic, like your father."

But this went against all his training. "Father shouldn't do that. You have to have your own proper place when you're like us. People ought to look up to you. If they don't, you'll lose your throne."

She saw David hurrying towards them across the grass on the other side of the meandering stream. He was waving a package at them; so she had to say quickly, "I don't like you criticising your father. Except for my Pa, His Highness is the finest man I know . . . Hello, David. What's the rush?"

He shouted across the stream, "It's come!"

She had never seen him so animated and guessed at once that the parcel he waved was the first copy of his book on the Wonders of the Ancient World. He must feel as a woman might feel over her first-born. In his case he was justifiably proud to show her his second-born, tearing off the paper wrapping with hands that trembled in his haste.

She could see the marbled covers and linings and was duly impressed. A great deal of work had obviously gone into it. She was even more impressed when she riffled through the heavy pages.

Meanwhile, David was prompting her anxiously. "Well? Well?"

"It's wonderful. I'm so proud of you, dear." She kissed his cheek which made him flush with pride.

Max watched all this furor over a dull book with very few sketches. Then he looked around Alix's arm to be sure he hadn't missed anything in the book.

While Alix exclaimed over the excellent quality of the work and David put his free arm around her, hugging her shoulders, Max got to more important matters.

"What did they pay you for it, Cousin David?"

Both David and Alix looked astonished at such a naïve question. David said, "This isn't one of those cheap, trashy romances that parlourmaids read. When you're grown up you are going to find this book in the library of every important house. Not to mention the universities. In the United States and wherever people care about history they will have this book."

"Yes, I know. But what do they pay you?"

Seeing that David was losing patience, as well he might, Alix explained with a frown, "Books like this are paid for by the author for the use of humanity."

"Then Cousin David paid for it?" The young prince gave Alix a look she understood better than she wanted to and walked away, skipping from stone to stone in the stream. He called back over his shoulder, "My father wouldn't go and do a silly thing like that."

Alix felt that the sensitive author had been put through enough from this badly brought up little princeling. "Your father isn't a scholar, young man. If he were, you might be a more intelligent boy."

"My dearest," David murmured, deeply appreciative.

Max stopped with his back to her, stood there for a few seconds straddling two stones in the stream. Then he hopped onward, his head down as if he wanted to be sure he did not miss a stepping stone.

As she and David walked back to the house Alix decided, "We must have a real tutor for Max if he is to stay here until his father is settled. That nice fellow in the village is too intimidated by the boy."

"I can understand that," David admitted.

"But if you say so. Though why he must stay here at all is a mystery to me."

She considered that the Miravels would not have had an estate without their cousin, Prince Kuragin, and she was almost tempted to repeat Max's remark about the money that had kept David, his mother, and their precious Bayard with a roof over their heads. Luckily she refrained, though she wondered more than once why Bayard the Beloved had not taken some responsibility for the family. Maybe he had been too much like his gambling father.

Alix claimed that the walk had been good for her. She may have been right except for her relationship with young Max who remained aloof the rest of the day.

Things brightened that evening when Tiger Royle, always a favourite with children, arrived for a visit. He carried a message for Max from his father and Max felt in duty bound to let Alix know that his father "spent more time asking about how you felt than he did about how I felt. Isn't that funny, Cousin Alix? He thinks you are really sick. I've been taught to write very good letters. I'll tell him you are perfectly well but the baby is being naughty. He might think that was funny. Do you think he might?"

"Of course, he will. And he will think

you are very clever for saying so."

"But you told Cousin David I was stupid."

"I was wrong, dear. There. You have a grown-up apology. Not many people your age get that."

Satisfied, he confided that Tiger was going to take him for a ride tonight. "Even though it's dark. I think it's exciting, don't you?"

"As long as nothing happens to you. What is his new car like?"

"Cousin Phoebe says there is room for both her and me. But lucky for me, Tiger says I would only annoy her; so he is taking me alone. I don't mind if Tiger says that. I like him."

Tiger had borrowed the Daimler from a friend in London. From what she had been told, it had front and back seats and even a partial top. It would have been ideal for Lady Phoebe, as she assured Alix.

"So truly elegant. No one hereabouts has anything like it. And to think of his rewarding that wretched boy for his bad behaviour is really too much."

Alix sighed. "What has he done now?"

Lady Phoebe enumerated his crimes but as one of them was Max's persistent excursions into the kitchen to supervise the leftover food for the "poor", Alix dismissed his other misdemeanours.

She was in considerable pain and didn't know whether this heralded the arrival of Miravel's celebrated heir, or not. She hoped not. The ponderous authority recommended by one of Queen Alexandra's ladies-in-waiting would have to be summoned and even Pa's Daimler wouldn't get him to Miravel before morning.

This fact brought an explosion from Tiger who demanded that Miravel have a telephone put in. Lady Phoebe argued with him for the first time.

"What? And have all that noise, bells ringing, people you can't see bothering you at all hours? Disgusting. No privacy whatever."

But they all knew that what Tiger Royle wanted, Tiger Royle would get.

By the time Tiger and Prince Max had returned to the house from their ride there was little doubt of Alix's condition. Cold sweat in the middle of a warm August evening was nearly as indicative as the excruciating pains that began immediately after.

Lady Phoebe panicked at the thought of calling in the local physician from Miravel village. "He is nothing but a dreadful miner from Wales. Worked his way up from the collieries to attend any village girl who gets herself in the family way, married or not."

"From the collieries, eh?" Tiger was suddenly interested. "Are those healthy deliveries?" He was already putting his coat on again.

Lady Phoebe had insisted that the first of what was generally expected to be the male heirs should be born where all the other Miravel heirs were born, in her spacious pink bedroom. Dr William Evans, a breezy, confident young man, therefore arrived in the custody of a violently nervous Tiger Royle at a little before midnight.

Dr Evans introduced himself to Alix before Tiger could do so, with the jolly and gratuitous addition: "*Evans*, ma'am. A long 'e'. Now that we've got my name right, let's see what can be done to get the rest of this business right and tight."

Alix couldn't have agreed with him more.

The following hours were vague horrors which racked her body until she realised in her delirium that this purgatory might endure for ever.

Dr Evans seemed to feel it was entirely her fault that she was so thin. "Would have made it simpler if you were nicely upholstered, ma'am. However, we'll manage with what we have to work with."

Jolly nice of you, she thought in one of her lucid intervals.

Almost exactly as the August sun broke

271

over the easterly horizon, promising a glorious summer day, a baby daughter, with perfect features and a wistful smile, arrived upon the scene. She was practically bald.

When the adult members of the family were let in to see the Miravel wonder Lady Phoebe was soon mollified over its sex. There would be other children, she promised optimistically.

"As for her hair, or lack of it, don't trouble about that. I am told I was born without hair and in a few months I was doing very well."

Everyone immediately assured her that if the child had her hair she would be lucky indeed. A fact with which Alix could heartily agree when she looked at that lustrous reddish auburn hair, which was the dowager's greatest beauty asset.

She considered the girl thoughtfully. "Rather like Bayard when he was born."

"No, he isn't. Not in the least," Alix insisted, though she hadn't the faintest idea what Bayard looked like as a baby. "I expect her to be an earthshaker like Pa, but it'll be her looks that open doors for her."

Lady Phoebe started to protest, but Tiger Royle could always win her over. His tawny eyebrows raised as he told her in his most ingratiating manner, "She's a real beauty.

272

Naturally, the little tike should be named for you. She sure is the prettiest thing."

Phoebe melted. "How very generous of you, my dear friend. Yes. Another Phoebe Miravel. How pleased I shall be! We will worry about a male next time."

Alix scowled at the thought of that name. She also saw David standing by the door, having been more or less accidentally elbowed aside by the proud grandfather. He was hurt by their possessiveness over his child, as if he weren't there at all. And thus far, not a single person had mentioned *The Wonders of the World* by David Alistair Miravel, which lay prominently displayed down on the credenza in the reception hall where all who entered the house could see it.

Alix cut into the naming discussion with all the strength she could summon up. "The girl will be Garnett Phoebe Alexandra, for my mother, David's mother, and me. How's that?"

When they all praised little Garnett's looks no one was prouder than David. He pushed his way to her bedside and kissed Alix gently on her forehead which Mattie had just dampened with rose water.

The two grandparents looked at each other. Lady Phoebe held both her hands out to Tiger.

"We are united in a sense, my friend. Like — "

"Brother and sister, as it were." Tiger took her small hands in his great ones. "Sister Phoebe."

"Brother Tiger. How strange that sounds, dear friend."

After taking another look at the little girl who was crying, perhaps for her baldness, the happy grandparents went out. David said, "It wouldn't surprise me if Tiger treated my mother to a tot of brandy."

"It wouldn't surprise me if she accepted it."

They laughed and set about examining this remarkable little living creature who belonged to them. David seemed especially taken with little Garnett.

"Poor little thing. She will have hair some day, won't she? If it wasn't for that, I'd agree with Tiger. She's the prettiest little baby I ever saw."

"Of course she'll have hair. You heard your mother, and you must admit she has soft, lovely hair."

"Very true." He brightened.

Alix was still amazed over the miraculous arrival of a living and lively human being after the hell of the night before. Garnett Phoebe Alexandra gave both her parents a seductive look from beneath long eyelashes.

"An enchantress," David said and bent his head to kiss his daughter's tiny, grasping fingers. She pulled them away from him, perhaps playfully, and made an impudent *moue* with her lovely mouth.

"She doesn't look nearly as bad as most newborn babies," Alix decided with satisfaction.

Prince Max might not share the family's enthusiasm but his critical instincts came to the fore a day later when he was allowed to look into but not touch the cradle that had rocked the heirs of Miravel for over four hundred years. The oaken exterior was harder than ever and seemed oddly inappropriate for its dainty cargo. Max scoffed at babies in general but admitted after a careful scrutiny, "The little girl has a pretty face, prettier than yours, Cousin Alix."

"Thank you, dear, for Nettie."

He wrinkled his nose. "You shouldn't call her Nettie. That's common. Like a peasant or something. Her name is Garnett. I like that."

Alix studied the girl. She murmured, "Here she is, born at the very beginning of the century. What will her life be like? Will she be happy and loved, or unhappy and wildly turbulent? Maybe both. I wish I could predict

. . . No. I don't. I don't want to know."

Max looked at her, surprised by the sudden passion in her voice. "I'd like to know, Cousin Alix. I'd like to know if I'm going to be the Prince Royal of Lichtenbourg some day." He added thoughtfully, "I don't see why not."

PART TWO

CHAPTER SIXTEEN

Prince Max and young Garnett between them managed to do what all Alix's hard work and charitable efforts had failed to do. They almost made Miravel village accept Lady Miravel, that Yankee, as one of them.

Most of the females, old and young, in the village fell in love with Max the first time they met him, or were presented to him, as he put it. The males never quite came under the spell of his potent charm. They were much more willing to accept Franz Kuragin as one of them.

After Alix and Prince Kuragin parted in London that cold January day in 1901, she intended to see him only during family gatherings of a day or two, either when the prince delivered Max to Miravel for his summer vacation or over the two-day celebration at Christmas time. His feeling for Alix may have faded into nothing more than a family loyalty in the years since their parting.

Correspondence was not to be thought of as far as Alix was concerned, yet she was passionately grateful to him during those infrequent family meetings when the touch of his hand, or a long, wordless look between them carried for her a warmth that remained with her for many days.

Garnett's coming had made clear to Alix the necessity of remaining faithful to Garnett's father as he was faithful to her. It shouldn't matter how deep or how shallow Franz Kuragin's affection for her might be.

There were moments in the night when she turned over in bed or reached out, still half dreaming, to touch Franz and found David instead, asleep and breathing heavily as a result of "one extra whisky"

She admitted now, at least to herself, that his only interest in sleeping with her came from his mother's constant harping on the necessity of a "future Lord Miravel to succeed him". The estate was not entailed, but in the dowager's eyes there could be no one but a male to carry on. Otherwise, the ancient title would die out.

For a long time Alix guiltily assumed the blame for her failure to produce the Miravel male heir. Despite the difficulties of her first pregnancy, she knew she would have undergone anything to have Franz Kuragin's child. Therefore, she was mentally unfaithful to David. She became as passionate as humanly possible in her attempts at seducing him into her arms.

She even took her mother-in-law's advice and saw to it that a couple of whiskies were nearby at night for David, to inspire his own passion, but more than three years after Garnett's birth Alix had almost exhausted her dubious qualities as a siren.

She remembered her suspicions of Franz and Glynnis Chance at a time that must have been an eternity ago. He seemed to have no feeling of guilt or remorse about the growing boy, Nick Chance. Her own guilty thoughts made her edgy; yet, with each of Garnett's birthdays Alix found herself more shaken by her realisation of how rapidly and pointlessly life was passing.

Garnett shared this fear with her mother, though not for the same reason. Garnett was afraid too many years would have to pass before she won her heart's desire and wore a real crown as Princess Royal of Lichtenbourg.

She had got everything else she asked for. Having passed her fourth birthday surrounded by far too many presents, Garnett had only one immediate wish for the Christmas of 1905, the arrival of young Max Kuragin to help her celebrate. And above all, he must make her his usual gold paper crown and describe to her in detail how he would one day be Prince Royal and she would be his princess.

It had started out as an effort to stop her crying when she was two years old and stumbled over a broken branch in the copse where the bluebells grew.

After that, whenever Max stayed at Miravel in summer or at Christmas time, Garnett must have her gold paper crown. Max pretended boredom but he would not disappoint her. As he told Alix, "I feel responsible for her. After all, there aren't many people who saw her when she was one day old."

The only one who objected to this charade was David, who adored her. Alix guessed that no one in his entire, lonely life had ever loved him and respected and belonged to him as Garnett did. Alix had deep compassion for her husband, blaming his mother, and probably her beloved Bayard, for making David what he was.

It was very moving to see David with his daughter. Clearly, he thought her a miracle. She could do no wrong in his eyes. So it was up to Alix and the outspoken Mrs Tether, Alix's greatest find, to correct Garnett when the child's bewitching ways took her too far.

Alix considered the Miravels lucky when

Mrs Tether volunteered to take the post of Garnett's nurse and her gruff but good-hearted disciplinarian when she wasn't preparing one meal daily for the Reverend Pittridge or cleaning the parsonage once weekly.

As the vicar confessed to Alix when he suggested Mrs Tether for the post, "The dear woman is my right hand, but I do admit, in confidence, that during her absence I accomplish a great deal more. Let us say, I am always a trifle relieved when that blessed lady is elsewhere. I hope this doesn't sound unChristian."

Alix assured him it was a Christian impulse on both his part and Mrs Tether's that permitted her to move into her own quarters in the south-east wing at Miravel with the nursery between her two pleasant rooms and the bedroom shared by Alix and David when David wasn't working in solitary happiness upstairs. No one could handle Garnett like Mrs Tether, except, of course, Prince Kuragin's son Max.

David's quiet revenge in his jealousy was to demonstrate, especially in front of young Max, that Garnett's favourite was her "Papa". Even at the age of three Garnett had seen through this and constantly played David against Max. She was in a fair way to being spoiled, and when Alix tried to correct her or punish her with the loss of a toy she had thrown into a corner unused, Garnett cried for "Papa".

It was a problem. But luckily Garnett's general disposition was friendly and confiding. She held no grudge.

Alix might not have considered Max his father's equal when it came to running a country, but during his summer and Christmas visits to Miravel she realized how fond of him she had grown.

Max conversed with Alix very much like a grown-up. One of the reasons for the close relationship between them seemed to be her treatment of him as a grown-up. She felt far easier with him during these visits than with his father whom she saw so seldom but with whom she was still passionately in love. Yet she was sure she knew him less and less.

It was being rapidly shown to her through Max's gossip that no matter what she might feel for Franz Kuragin, he was a future ruler, a member of Europe's royalty.

On his last visit while Franz asked David how his new book on Hadrian's Roman Wall was proceeding, Max confided to Alix, "I can marry any princess I want, because the Council of State is going to recommend Papa for the next Prince Royal of Lichtenbourg.

Course the princesses, they'd rather marry Papa right now."

His father said, "Max, you talk too much. We are not running a matrimonial bureau."

David thought this was funny and was still laughing when Max sank lower in his chair beside Garnett, muttering, "No, sir." He spoke more softly to Alix but was still audible to everyone in the newly renovated gold salon.

"The chancellor says old Friedrich will have to name Papa to rule after him if Papa marries old Friedrich's granddaughter. She's quite pretty. She has yellow hair. The kaiser thinks that would be good, because her mother's from Saxony. That's in Germany."

"The kaiser is not ruling Lichtenbourg yet," Prince Kuragin had said crisply. He looked at Alix but she couldn't read any warmth or personal feeling in that look. What had been between them the day they separated in London seemed to have faded a little more with each of his quick, one-night visits to Miravel. She had only one symbol to cling to. When he wrote briefly to the family he still sent his love in the way he had described to her almost jokingly on the 1903 visit. "All my love to you" had been meant for her. Did it still have any significance?

Max raised his voice, leaning toward Garnett but addressing Alix. "Princess Ilsa von Elsbach. That's her name. She's almost Papa's age. If she wasn't so old I might marry her. But there's plenty of princesses for me."

Garnett's face had clouded and her lower lip began to tremble. "You promised."

Alix reached over and squeezed her small fingers. "Don't you worry, honey. Max will change his mind."

At the same time Prince Kuragin caressed the child's flyaway deep auburn hair and then restored her to happiness by his promise. "Never mind, Princess Garnett. If my son doesn't appreciate you now, wait a few years. All the princes will be at your feet."

She giggled and was pleased.

Alix settled back, only half hearing the mischievous chatter of her daughter and Max who said, "If I can marry anybody I want, I might choose Garnett after all. I can't promise, of course."

Alix was deep in her own dismal thoughts. His father could marry any princess he wanted, and he would be expected to do so. It was all exactly as she had predicted.

On that visit Alix had been glad to end this conversation.

On a crisp, sunny day in late autumn of 1905 Alix met Mrs Tether at the vicarage to walk home with her. Both had business in the village, this being Mrs Tether's weekly cleaning day, and Alix was highly satisfied with developments at the Elder Home near the Old Post Road. The "elder women", mostly widows and spinsters, had discovered a new interest in life when their long-forgotten skills suddenly began to bring them a little money and a great deal of praise. Alix's idea about the importance of wool in the shire had opened up possibilities.

The women were now relearning old tasks, carding and spinning the shire's own wool. Their first creations of mufflers and socks and warm vests had been decorated with embroidery, some appliquéd, and presented to Tiger Royle while Alix pointed out to him how many would welcome such genuine, hand-made items in the colder areas of the States. Whether there was a big profit or a little one, for himself or a friend, Tiger lived for the idea of creating success out of buried and forgotten materials. A number of speciality shops were already beginning to carry what the women of the Elder Home and the village itself voted to call "Miravel Woollens".

Some very simple designs and work sold at lower prices. Others, with more complicated patterns and embroidery, found their way on to wide winter collars then in style, and even on cape collars, bright and pretty enough to lend cheer on snowy winter days.

Thus far, profits were small but Alix hounded Tiger to see that all bills were paid to Miravel Woollens within a reasonable period, and when the latest objects, mittens and gloves, became popular in several shops, no one was more proud of every earned shilling than Miravel village.

The Reverend Pittridge presided over the little business, including its small but growing profits and its legal ramifications. Alix obtained markets and new business with Tiger's overseas help. She had never felt more useful. Each time the women and some men of Miravel received a small but growing share of profits on their work, Alix felt fully as gratified as they did. Many of the newer members of Miravel Woollens took to spinning in their small cottages as their ancestors had done until the Industrial Revolution destroyed cottage industry a century ago.

As usual, Mrs Tether was right at the forefront of knowledge on every matter concerning the Miravels as well as the village.

"I read that the prince, young Max's father, was chosen to take over that little country when the old devil dies."

"The Royal Council of State chose him

but the male citizens who vote in the plebiscite haven't completed the voting. Prince
Kuragin is in Lichtenbourg City now with
representatives from France, the Romanoffs,
and the Hapsburgs, to see that no harm
comes to the voters. I hope to God there
are no riots."

Mrs Tether gave her a side-glance. "You
like Prince Kuragin, don't you, ma'am?"

"We certainly do. His mother was Lady
Phoebe's first cousin. They were very close."

"Hmph. Wonder how you and the family
will like it when little Garnett becomes the
— whatever they call them. Princess Royal.
I can see it coming."

"Heaven forbid. Garnett is much too friv-
olous."

"I'd wager five pounds love will find a
way." When Alix did not answer, Mrs Tether
moved to less controversial matters. "Old
Sarah Reed, Glynnis Chance's mother, set a
new pattern yesterday. Did she show you?"

Alix smiled at the idea. "Not Sarah. She
scampers off and hides behind the door when
she sees me coming. But she has real talent.
We are lucky to have her."

"Her daughter's got a different kind of
talent if you ask me. Poor Ewen. Died last
month in one of those tin mine inspections.
I always thought he deserved better than

that yellow-haired hussy. So she will be back in Miravel, I'll wager. She has a little money from Ewen, but she's got big ambitions for that boy of hers, Sarah says."

So long as the Chances lived in Cardiff it had been easier to forget that Nick Chance existed. Would the boy be foisted upon Prince Kuragin next time he visited Miravel? Alix felt a chill. If the child was his, could she go on loving Franz when he showed no responsibility for Nick Chance? She changed the subject quickly.

"I must stop in and pick up the mail. Do you mind waiting?"

Mrs Tether brushed this aside. "You do that, ma'am. Young Mr Mortmain told me there was mail for you. Might be important." She was better than an ancient town crier when it came to her knowledge of everyone's business and she certainly wanted to know what that "important" mail might be.

Two gentlemen were in the doorway of the post office and tobacconist's shop. One was Mr Humphries, the innkeeper, who acknowledged Alix's greeting with great respect, nodded to Mrs Tether, and asked if he might present "a countryman of yours, Lady Miravel".

It was a strange sensation to hear the once familiar broad speech of the western United

States and to feel that he was "foreign" to her. Like most of his countrymen in California and Nevada with whom she had grown up, he was friendly and far more familiar than the English and Welsh whom she now regarded as her own people, neighbours and friends.

"I guess you must get a real thrill out of reading about old Teddy Roosevelt running things these days, Your Ladyship. Sure keeps things hopping."

She had been recovering from Garnett's birth when the President of the United States, William McKinley, was shot, and only later came to realise how much more visible the new president, Theodore Roosevelt, was than his martyred predecessor. She had met and respected both men. It was impossible not to have a special feeling for the vigorous young Roosevelt, already well into his second term, but she couldn't help defending the dead president's quiet efforts towards peace.

"I admired President McKinley very much. I think he and the Spanish queen did all they could to keep us out of the war with Spain. But of course, that wouldn't win him any credit with my father, Tiger Royle, and other businessmen."

"No, ma'am. Mighty profitable, all around. I've personally got myself a lot of sugar holdings near Santiago de Cuba."

He sounded exactly like Pa.

She was surprised and a little saddened to realise that she was losing her American identity. She even thought the Californian gentleman was a trifle loud and more than a trifle self-confident.

Perhaps it was just as well. She had a husband who cared for her in his moderate way, faithful and making little trouble for her or Phoebe, both of whom ran the household in a reasonably unarmed truce. She had an adorable daughter who was definitely English. Alix knew she herself must break the last ties that bound her to her native country.

With Mrs Tether grinning behind her Alix excused herself, nodded to both gentlemen and went into the post office. Long, lanky young Mr Mortmain had been leaning back in his chair, with his feet propped up on the counter. Seeing the two ladies, he lowered his legs and bounded up, fishing for the coat with which he covered his shirt, braces and chokingly stiff collar while further ruffling his bushy red hair.

"Lady Miravel. It's a pleasure, ma'am. I was just telling Mrs Tether earlier today that there was mail for you. Let me fetch it in." While fussing around in the post office section of the little shop which reeked of pipe smoke, he asked the requisite questions about "His Lordship, Lady Phoebe, and the little princess".

"You see," Mrs Tether pointed out, "even Mortmain calls Miss Garnett the little princess. Makes it a deal harder to discipline the child."

"It certainly does," Alix agreed. "But whenever Max is here he encourages her, and she is a natural-born charmer. You can't help letting her dream, though it isn't a good thing."

Mrs Tether agreed absently. "Just so long as she isn't hurt by it." She was studying a Bristol newspaper on the counter as Alix took the mail from the flustered Mr Montague Mortmain.

The young man was well known to idolise Lady Miravel, a harmless emotion except that it caused him to drop things frequently in her presence and to spend a great deal of time vainly trying to smooth his hair.

He was eager to have her notice a foreign envelope addressed in a well-remembered hand, slanting and careless, the writing large as if poured out rapidly in his usual manner. The sight of that hand made her pulse beat faster even before she saw the Lichtenbourg coat of arms with its falcon profile.

The letter was addressed to "Lady Phoebe

Miravel and Lord and Lady Miravel", but she had known since one of his visits in 1903 that somewhere in the letter there would be a curious phrasing which would be a reminder to Alix that he thought of her.

She knew that both her husband and Lady Phoebe would expect to read the letter aloud, as they always had done. There was nothing for it but to go home with it still wondering about its contents.

She had always been afraid for him when he left Britain and returned to his country or to Paris where he had recently acted in conjunction with the Lichtenbourg embassy there. He would be in greater danger than ever just before his uncle died, and the old man was over ninety. Who knew whether Franz could trust the Royal Council of State that had already pronounced Franz his uncle's successor? The council's presiding figure was Count Sergius Waldstein who had been Friedrich the Third's supportive chancellor for almost twenty years.

"Well, that's that," Alix told Mrs Tether as easily as possible, considering her tension. "We had better start home or Phoebe will be moaning that tea is late."

Mrs Tether remarked drily, "She does have her moments. But on the whole, you manage her very well."

Alix gave Montague Mortmain her best smile and the two women started up the street on their way out of the village.

When they were beyond Mortmain's hearing Mrs Tether remarked, "Begging Your Ladyship's pardon but the Bristol press says practically every male voted in Lichtenbourg City yesterday and the countryside did well too. Their first election."

"Did he win?" Alix's voice sounded shaky even to herself.

"Results are all sealed up. Order of the old prince. The French and Russian observers are protesting. The kaiser and the Austrian member of the observers said it seemed fair to them. Not that they surprise me. Our Bertie always did say you couldn't trust his nephew. That kaiser's got to be in everything."

Alix was not the least bit interested in international affairs, except where they concerned those she loved. How would this affect Franz? The old prince might still have him murdered and set his granddaughter in the place of the Kuragin dynasty.

She was deep in these disturbing thoughts when Mrs Tether stopped suddenly, catching her breath. Alix looked up from the cobbled street.

"What is it?"

There was no need for Mrs Tether to explain. Directly in their path a youth about nine or ten had been batting a ball hard against the half-timbered wall of the Tudor inn with his palm. As the boy turned he was facing the two women. He stood there staring at them out of thoughtful hazel eyes.

Alix said, "Hello. Who are you?"

There was something wistful about him, she thought, and then changed her mind. Something either shy or furtive. The shape of his pale face, his soft mouth and smooth skin added to a resemblance that leaped to her thoughts.

She asked her companion, "Is it my imagination, or does he remind you of anyone?"

Mrs Tether looked a bit rattled. "Youngsters all look alike to me. This boy might resemble Garnett. Not his manner, of course. Garnett is much more volatile."

"But otherwise. Not in disposition. I don't know a thing about this boy's disposition. But I certainly know those eyes."

Garnett had David's eyes. Not as furtive as this boy, or as wistful as David's, but she was her father's daughter. No mistake about that.

And very little mistake about this boy's resemblance to Garnett.

"Does everyone in the village suspect his parentage?"

Mrs Tether hesitated, then blurted out, "Well now, more than suspect, actually. Lady Phoebe paid calls on that hussy Glynnis. Everyone knew Glynnis had money afterwards. There wasn't much doubt. They can count, you know. The night at the Midsummer Bazaar there'd been talk. Lord David being so drunk, and all. Not like himself."

"Why didn't his mother stop him?"

Mrs Tether moistened her lips as she stared at Alix. "Most of the village knew how important it was to the Miravels, even to the people hereabouts, that Master David be able to — "

"To make love?"

"You see, he was so reserved. And it was important to Her Ladyship that Master David knew women before he was married to a very young girl with — "

"Money."

"Money is mighty important, Your Ladyship. And it was even more important that he should know how to — to teach a young wife her marital duty. But who'd have thought one hour or so with that Glynnis would produce — him?"

This was bad enough, but to insinuate repeatedly that Franz was guilty, that seemed

297

despicable. What had David said when Alix mentioned Glynnis Chance and the boy who was being baptised? Something about his cousin Franz having the eye for the ladies. And Phoebe too had been careful to implicate Franz. Alix had believed it all. She loved Franz but she let herself believe the child might be his.

She looked down at the boy. "What is your name?"

His mouth now had an insolent twist that made him look older. "Nick Chance. What's yours?"

"I am Lady Miravel and I know your mother. Please give her my condolences on her loss." Had Ewen Chance known he was giving his name to David Miravel's child?

But Lady Phoebe's money must have paved that path.

The boy said nothing. Alix and Mrs Tether passed him and when Alix looked back he was staring after her, his eyes narrowed. He looked as if he might smile at any minute. It wouldn't be a pleasant smile.

Mrs Tether said, "Don't think about it. These things happen everywhere with aristocrats. It's been going on since the Middle Ages. And probably before."

"Not to me." How could she and Garnett go on living in a village in which everyone knew this boy was Garnett's brother? He was a bastard, but he should have been the Master of Miravel. In a moral sense, David had made a bastard of Garnett.

It seemed incredible to Alix that a man who performed so badly in bed with his wife should have enjoyed Glynnis Reed's favours long enough to produce a child. More than a child. The true, if illegitimate, male heir to Miravel.

She looked at Mrs Tether. "So everyone has known this for years. They must think I am a great fool."

"Not at all. They believe you are surprisingly sensible, for an American."

Sensible. Was it sensible that Alix's absurd pity for David made her deny Franz on the Channel ferry or in London?

Probably not. She had felt that her baby should have her biological father. Anything else would be unfair to him and to Garnett.

Mrs Tether put out a thin, rough-skinned hand and touched Alix's glove. "I hope you won't act in haste. Long, sober thought. That's what's needed."

"You are probably right."

She had never known anyone personally who was divorced. Indeed, with English law what it was, she probably couldn't divorce David without a monumental scandal that might ruin Garnett's future.

Alix was positive of one thing. She would never sleep with David again. Ironically, it would be no hardship for David. Had he been equally reticent with Glynnis Chance? Glynnis Reed, as she had been then. Knowing David, she thought, it must have been whisky. That poor child was conceived in whisky.

But so was Garnett.

She shuddered.

She said nothing else until they reached the estate drive as it wound down past the bluebell field, now dormant until spring. She saw the beautiful glowing pink brick of the west façade and told Mrs Tether, "I don't want anyone at home to know what we saw in the village. Not yet. I must think."

"Very wise."

They entered the house through the south-west door, opened in its silent, mysterious way by Horwich, and went their separate ways, Mrs Tether to have her "tea" with Garnett who was learning to pour tea like "a great lady, a princess".

"Princesses don't pour tea," Mrs Tether had explained but Garnett tossed her head with its soft mass of curls and said, "You'll see. They'll do what I say."

"They probably will, too," Alix had

laughed when she heard about it. But she worried because life had a way of dealing unpleasantly with pretty, spoiled little girls.

She went directly to her rooms, removing her hat, her gloves and her fitted coat with leg-of-mutton sleeves as she went. It really was late and she hoped she would not be the last to enter the little salon. She was forced to take tea in her walking dress, which would earn her a headshake from the ever-correct Phoebe, but there was no time to waste. She didn't want to have her features too closely studied by Phoebe's sharp eyes.

She wasn't at all sure what her future moves would be, except that David would be crushed by the loss of his daughter, and until she was sure of herself, it would be unwise to give Phoebe time to plan a counter-attack.

She came to the little salon only minutes after Phoebe arrived looking her imperious best, "fragile but indomitable", as the Reverend Pittridge had called her at her sixtieth birthday ball.

Seeing Alix, Lady Phoebe reprimanded her with a gentle "tsk-tsk". In spite of her age she had excellent teeth and her disapproval was all too evident. A new young footman who served as general indoor boy brought in the tea-tray while Maud, the one-time scullery maid, carried in a tray of tiny sandwiches, cucumber, watercress and fruit jellies from the new forcing house in the lower garden, along with cakes, scones and sweet biscuits fresh from the oven.

Alix looked at this miniature feast and wondered what she was doing here. To Phoebe's surprise, she laughed. It was a short, abrupt sound that startled her as much as Phoebe.

"Just think of it. Less than an hour ago I met an American in the village."

Phoebe's pale eyebrows raised. "They are not common here but one cannot avoid them sometimes."

"And I thought how much I had changed."

"For the better, my dear. You have done remarkably well, compared to some of the other Yankee brides, as they call them. Cousin Franz asked me only this summer if I thought you were happy. I was pleased to say you had never been happier . . . cream?"

Alix never drank cream in her tea but Phoebe had asked the same question for more than five years. Alix gave up now. How little it mattered! She took the delicate, translucent cup and explained, "But I haven't changed. And you can't possibly answer for me to Cousin Franz. I'm as American as ever, and I despise what — "

Something warned her not to say too much.

Not to let them know she guessed the truth about David and Glynnis. Or how Alix could take Garnett back to the States. David would never let her go if he knew.

Phoebe was still looking at her. "What on earth do you mean, dear? Has someone behaved badly to you? We cannot permit that. We are Miravels, after all."

Alix had dreaded her first reaction to the sight of David but she was relieved when he came in now with his forefinger marking his place in a *Dictionary of Roman Antiquities*. He leaned over his mother, kissed her cheek very lightly and followed the same procedure with Alix before taking a buttered scone and sitting down to eat it. He saw the envelope in Alix's hand and asked casually, "A letter from Franz? About Max's arrival, I expect. There may be some delay, what with old Friedrich dying. I only hope Garnett isn't too disappointed." He held out his hand for the letter.

She gave it to him but winced when his buttery fingerprint blurred the writing on the envelope.

My dear cousins,
It seems Max and I will not be able to join you for the holidays. Instead, in February, you will join me. As of this writing

303

the full developments have not been released to the continental press, but the Council of State under Chancellor Sergius Waldstein voted to override the Prince Royal's order. The first plebiscite of the citizens of Lichtenbourg has chosen the Kuragin dynasty as the successors to Friedrich the Third.

The result of the plebiscite reached His Serene Highness in his bath. The shock brought on an apoplexy. At seventeen hours forty-six minutes on this day, Friedrich the Third died.

I can express decent courtesy at the state funeral but no more.

I tried repeatedly to see that connections were made between Lichtenbourg and England to tell you these things by telephone, but it was necessary to ask assistance of Vienna, and His Majesty, the Emperor Franz-Josef, has refused. They are unlikely to perform favours for the Kuragins until the coronation.

The council suggests that the sooner the coronation occurs, the sooner our country will be secure from outside disruption. February has been chosen.

Need I tell you, Cousin Phoebe, to polish up your coronet, choose your most elegant gowns, and to see to it that the family jewels of Cousins Alexandra, Garnett and David are similarly rescued from their dark hiding places?

I will talk to you the moment we are able to make connections with Great Britain. Meanwhile, Max joins me as I send all my love to you. All.

Franz Rudolf Feodor Kuragin

"Grown rather formal, I see," David remarked. "Franz Rudolf Feodor. Plain old Franz was good enough when we were boys."

His mother heard none of this. Her teacup shook a little. She set it down. "Not since the first Miravel served King Richard the Third have we been so closely allied with a ruling monarch. How proud his mother, Princess Adelaide, would be! Oh, my dear Alexandra, the wardrobe we must have! And so quickly, too. Less than five months. But we are going to manage, somehow. I feel sure Tiger will help us. He will want to do the correct thing. And he is so fond of Franz, I mean to say, His Serene Highness."

David dropped the letter among the biscuits and scones.

Alix picked it up.

Franz had not forgotten the little code he joked about to her on Boxing Day in 1903. The words "all my love to you" were for

305

her. The last word, "all", was written as though to emphasise that he included them all.

No matter. The important sentence was for her.

And all for nothing. His high eminence now placed him further beyond her than the master of the house from a scullery maid.

Pa was sure to accompany them to the coronation. She and Garnett would go home to America with him afterwards.

CHAPTER SEVENTEEN

Alix stood Garnett up on her lap, ignoring Phoebe's "My dear, your lovely coat," and let the child look out the train window as the sleek, blue and gold Orient Express rolled into Lichtenbourg City on its way between stops in Vienna, Budapest, and the Balkans.

In her new ermine-trimmed coat and hat Garnett pressed her hands flat against the snow-flecked glass, whispering excitedly, "See the twinkly lights. And the crowns. They're hanging right in the middle of the tiny streets, Mama. And the funny way the folks are dressed. It must be cold. They look like fairies and trolls and wicked gnomes. Does Max like it here?"

"It's his home now. He must like it," David told her, leaning forward in case she might fall. "Take care, love."

Garnett murmured, "Poor Max. He'd like it better at home, where we live. But it's nice to look at, things all touched with snow."

Phoebe said staunchly, "I think it's beautiful. Quite the way dear Tiger described it.

Like a painting of a medieval city, late on a snowy winter day. I do believe it isn't snowing any more. How very thoughtful!"

"Probably all for us," David remarked with more bitterness than sarcasm.

But Alix agreed with Phoebe. The middle European city which the train had entered did look medieval with its steeples and crowded, narrow streets all bridged by lamps and coronets, and lined with banners of royal blue with red initials of the Kuragin dynasty encircled by a crown.

There was a carnival atmosphere but Alix remembered that only a few years ago some of those same people dancing in the streets would have assassinated Franz if given the order.

Tiger Royle had been impatiently walking up and down the corridor outside the compartments. He opened the door now and stuck his head in.

"Some celebration! I always knew these folks wanted the Kuragins back in power. Wouldn't be surprised to see that von Elsbach princess out there cheering. She's no fool. They say she's due to marry old Frank and unite the two dynasties. Pretty, too, judging by the picture I saw at the Council Chamber here in town last year."

I've got to accept things like this, Alix

reminded herself, but the sickened feeling did not go away. Of course he must marry, and by far the most suitable woman would be a member of the rival house in Lichtenbourg. For one thing, it would prevent future events like the overthrow of Franz Kuragin's father and the crimes the old Prince Royal had instigated against Franz.

Phoebe patted the cushion beside her. "Do come in, dear friend. You can see the reception committee better. I wonder whom dear Franz will send. I have always loved that boy. Nothing could be more delightful than his success here. He deserves it."

"He does that," Tiger agreed, sitting down beside Phoebe and picking up the tapestried handbag she had dropped.

Alix watched them, envying their curious simplicity. Phoebe might be devious in her plotting now and then. Tiger might playfully flirt with her and any other attractive women, and look at Franz Kuragin's future as one planned and practically eternal, but at heart, they seemed quite simple, almost innocent, to Alix. She wondered if they had any idea of her bitter feelings, the lost hope that she might get over Franz and make a lifetime home for David as well as their daughter.

They would see Franz here. She would feel the pain of his presence, the knowledge that he was gone from her for ever. Then she must break the news about her future and Garnett's to Tiger. During the months since her discovery of Nick Chance she had remained aloof towards both Phoebe and David. She knew it hurt David but she was too torn within to make a pretence.

She spent most of her time in the village with the Miravel Woollens groups, wondering how she could persuade Glynnis Chance to talk about either her son or the Miravels. For many reasons, all suspicious to Alix, the woman was friendly and talkative on every subject but the ones that interested Alix.

Since she had no definite plan of campaign and the danger of losing Garnett was always present, her companions still found her moody. Even last night when Alix tucked Garnett into the upper berth of the compartment she always insisted on, the child said plaintively, "You're so sad, Mama. I didn't mean to sit on Papa's lap for dinner. I'm too big. But Papa said I could sit near you next time."

"I'm not sad, honey. Not at you."

"Was Papa mean to you?"

"Of course not. He couldn't be mean to anybody."

It was true. He had never been "mean" to anyone that she knew about. Alix wondered how he had treated Glynnis Reed that Midsummer Night many years ago. But what would happen when she took Garnett from him? Was there a Mr Hyde beneath that bland, wistful Dr Jekyll nature of his?

One result of her secret break with David amused her more than she had thought it would. After she met young Nick Chance last autumn she had told David she would not sleep with him. Naïvely, she had been afraid he would be angry or threatening. She wasn't sure she could bring herself to tell him why; since he and Phoebe would know that in the circumstances she would leave him and take Garnett. She was very much afraid of his feelings on that subject.

In spite of her bitterness the old feeling, almost the only feeling about her husband, had come through. Pity.

His reaction had been strange and unexpected. He simply looked at her a long, uncomfortable time before saying in his gentle way, "We will probably both be more comfortable," and then, that poignant addition, "It won't be my first failure. I suppose Garnett is my only success in life."

Garnett and Nick Chance, she thought.

"Your books are a success," she reminded him, not mentioning the fact that was self-evident. Someone paid for the printing and distribution of those books. She felt guilty in spite of the circumstances. There were moments when she thought the marriage might survive if they continued to live separate but reasonably friendly lives.

He didn't brighten as she expected when she mentioned his books. Instead, he belaboured the point that he had not been "as much a husband as she might have expected". And then, the worst of all, "Bayard would never fail. He never failed at anything. Did you know that?"

She went to her own sitting-room, at which time she gave Mattie instructions to have David's things removed quietly to the bedroom on this floor that he occasionally used.

There were still troubling moments in which she felt that David took the estrangement harder than she had thought at first. He would look at her with reddened eyes, which she blamed at first on his intensive work. But then he would glance around the little salon, or the dining table wistfully, and she wondered if he was thinking of what it would be like without the "entire family" there.

Did he weep in private? She couldn't bear that. He had always been good to her in his way. Their sexual failure did not necessarily make him a failure as a pleasant, sometimes boring companion. She must be boring to him quite often.

For a week or two Phoebe hadn't heard about the rift between her son and his wife. When she did hear, through Pyncheon, she spent the next two months nagging sweetly about her daughter-in-law's marital duties. It was David who defended her and as was his habit, blamed himself. She couldn't permit that.

When Phoebe talked far too much about the coronation and the necessity of their presence in Lichtenbourg, Alix felt that this would be disastrous. It would only bring her close to the man she loved and make a comparison with David more painful. In the matter of the trip to Lichtenbourg, David was on her side, as though he guessed the problem.

The battle was enjoined when Garnett spoke up, or rather, "cried the matter up".

"Oh, Papa, you can't leave us home. Max promised. He promised. He said I could wear his crown-thing if I did it with just us to see. Papa, we've got to go. Please . . ."

In the end it was not Phoebe but Garnett who made the entire trip a necessity, and Phoebe was happy.

She became too busy with her coronation wardrobe to pursue the matter of her son's male heir. Alix felt that it would be a matter of keeping a tight rein on her own feelings. David was still her husband. He might always be her husband, at least in name. Unlike Solomon's decision, they could hardly divide up Garnett who loved them both as they adored her.

In their compartment Tiger had been flirting with Phoebe but his eyes were on his daughter sitting opposite him. As the great trans-European train moved slowly, majestically through the capital of Lichtenbourg, attracting its usual admiration and envy, Tiger slapped Alix's knees lightly with the folded newspaper he had picked up in Vienna.

"Come out in the hall, honey. I'm going to show you how you curtsy to a real, live Prince Royal."

She started to say, "I know how to curtsy," but shut her mouth and waited until they were alone in the corridor. Everyone else had rushed to the compartment windows to see what the centre of the city looked like with its decorations.

"Well, Pa, what is it? I've already bowed to the man who is our king-emperor in Britain. I shouldn't think it would be any worse to meet an old friend like Prince Kuragin."

He didn't contradict her. "Honey, never mind the bowing. That was just an excuse. Are you feeling all right? You look like something the cat dragged in." An idea occurred to him. "You aren't in the family way, are you?"

That made her laugh. "Impossible. Literally impossible."

He frowned. "I don't like the sound of that. Aren't you and that boy getting along?"

"I'll tell you when this fancy dress ball is over. I hear cheering. I think we're coming into the station. They say there are several royalties on board."

Phoebe tapped on the glass of the compartment door and Tiger and Alix joined her quickly. Alix's depression had turned to a nervous wondering about how much the prince had changed. David buttoned up Garnett's coat and since Tiger was doing the same for Phoebe, David would have obliged Alix.

However, she had left him nothing to do. She was wearing her best suit, a hip-length blue jacket which fitted her closely. Like her daughter's coat, it was trimmed with ermine around the tight collar and the hem over a skirt of Miravel wool.

She tilted her small, blue feather toque over one eye in the hope of looking as delighted to be here as all the other visitors were. Her smile might be forced but it was there for the occasion. The committee sent by Prince Kuragin to meet them would undoubtedly expect it.

The train rolled smoothly to a stop in the station under a high glass roof. The place was surprisingly large for such a small country, but being on the direct route of the Orient Express undoubtedly meant a great deal to Lichtenbourg. Looking out the window Phoebe was more and more impressed.

"Tiger, who is that very tall, gaunt man in the square-cut beard? He seems to be the head of a delegation. Is he waiting for us?"

Tiger looked out over her head. "That'll be Chancellor Waldstein. I saw a lot of him when old Frank was dickering about his place in the succession. The fellow used to be old Friedrich's man. But the prince's death put him in our Frank's pocket. He and the Guard of Honour around him are waiting for — Yep. There's the standard-bearer by the steps to the carriage in front of us. See that fierce-looking German double eagle? They're waiting for the German empress. She's representing the kaiser at the coronation."

A minute or two later the stoutish, somewhat forbidding Empress Viktoria-Auguste descended with her attendants. A band struck up the German anthem, trying to drown out the train engine.

"Yep. That's her," Tiger informed his ladies and the less impressed David who lived in a world of Ancient Roman emperors. "Old 'Dona' herself. That's what her family calls her."

Knowing Tiger so well, Alix said, "I hope you didn't call her that, Pa."

Tiger looked mischievous. "Well, I'm never at my best after champagne."

Minutes later the empress, having been supported out to a carriage and four-horse team by her escort, was whisked away, leaving room for a troop of horsemen who galloped into the station itself and across the platform.

"Heavens, how barbaric!" Phoebe gasped. "One might as well be on the steppes of Russia."

Alix tried to contain her own excitement but it was difficult. Her heart was beating too fast. There was no mistaking her one-time gypsy prince in the lead, on a stallion as dark as Prince Kuragin. Young Max rode beside him on a white mare. The boy sat ramrod straight and was dressed in immaculate white dress uniform theatrically adorned with what Alix assumed were campaign ribbons and a gold medal or two. It was difficult to think of what battles might have been led by a youth his age, but he was wonderfully handsome, quite a contrast to the genuine warlike appearance of his father.

Garnett began to jump up and down, to her father's consternation.

"It's Max. He's come. Max!" She raised her voice and rapped on the window, but the train was making far too much noise and Max was too busy controlling his mount to hear her.

Tiger grinned at the excitement of his females.

"Frank and his sprig are showing you who counts with them. The German empress gets old Waldstein and the civilian council, but you ladies — and David here — you get the mounted guard. Some of them were refugees until a couple of years ago. They may look primitive but at least they're loyal to the Kuragins."

A horseman in blue uniform with red facings rode through the crowd which was cheering madly, "Kuragin! Kuragin!" And "vivas" in several languages that Phoebe insisted were barbaric to her. The horseman dismounted, gave his horse over to a waiting equerry and went to Prince Kuragin. He knelt before the prince who swung off the black stallion and gave him the reins.

Nervous at all this adulation of the man she loved in secret, Alix asked nervously,

"Shall we go out and meet him? He might expect it."

She was too late. Much to the delight of Phoebe and Garnett, the new Prince Royal of Lichtenbourg strode towards their carriage with a firm step. Alix felt a surge of warmth and anticipation. He was really here. Not in a dream but very much in the flesh. Nothing could come of their meeting. She knew that when she saw him in his correct surroundings, not a prince without a country but a ruler, hailed and beloved by his people.

Just to be near him briefly, she thought, would feed her dreams for a long time.

His uniform was concealed by an olive drab, full-skirted greatcoat. As he neared the train she saw that his boots were dusty. He took off his cap and handed it to an aide. Alix realised for the first time that his windblown hair was greying slightly.

Everything about him seemed a trifle more marked and severe than it had in England. The old wound on his left temple was still plainly visible. It added to his authority and perhaps his cold efficiency. Alix decided he would have to look like this to face down his enemies in central Europe.

Tiger said, "The least I can do is go halfway. Matter of fact, one of the few lads I'd go halfway for."

He went out into the corridor leaving the compartment door wide open.

Prince Kuragin must have come aboard and into the vestibule of the carriage because Tiger had barely waved to him before the occupants of the compartment heard the prince's well-remembered voice, "So here you are, my friend. Here at last."

It was impossible for Alix not to feel intense pride for her father when the prince strode rapidly along the corridor, met Tiger, and the two men embraced, each slapping the other's back. Figures filled the corridor behind the two but Prince Kuragin ignored them. He was already pushing the compartment door open wide with both arms and stepping inside to greet the rest of the family.

He had always been very circumspect at Miravel since the day they said goodbye in London over four years ago, and Alix did not dare to expect anything different from him now. She stood back, knowing Phoebe and especially Garnett would want to greet him first.

The prince, seeing Phoebe in his way, embraced her and kissed her on each cheek, saying, "Welcome to our country, Cousin Phoebe. How pretty you look, all in pink."

She blushed with pleasure but Alix, standing behind Phoebe, received a thrill of her own, as the prince stared directly into her eyes. He did not look away while he spoke over Phoebe's head. The poignant question in that gaze told her he had not forgotten. He must still feel something for her; yet he undoubtedly knew his present position made anything further than their family affection impossible.

Having let his flattered Cousin Phoebe go, he shook hands with David, then kissed Garnett who won everyone's heart by curtsying low to him. By the time he held Alix in his embrace, whispering something incomprehensible in her ear, the compartment was noisy with the greeting between Garnett and Max. The boy began by pretending a dignified reserve and a salute, but Garnett soon broke that down by curtsying again as she had to his father. Max forgot the elegance of his new role and lifted her up, hugging her until she squealed.

Max and Garnett began to chatter about the Christmas they had missed two months ago while David admitted to Max, "She missed you right enough. Nobody could make a paper crown for her except you."

Alix thought it was generous of him to mention one of those attractions Max could offer that David couldn't better.

She felt that this noisy little scene gave

her a few seconds longer in Franz Kuragin's arms. He must have shared her emotion. He kept one arm tightly around her waist when he turned back to watch "the children".

She tried not to make too much of this. She thought wryly, Maybe he's forgotten where his arm is. But he looked at her again. No easy smile of greeting. Simply the long, unblinking gaze that seemed to carry a message, or a question.

CHAPTER EIGHTEEN

It would only make things worse if she told him eventually what she had discovered about David, and admitted that she was beginning to feel there was no future for her anywhere but with "her family".

Meanwhile, several members of the Lichtenbourg Royal Council had crowded into the corridor outside the compartment where they were confused to find themselves elbow to elbow with the occupants of the next compartment, Mattie Fogarty, Pyncheon and Cornbury.

Tiger was trying to make casual introductions by much pointing and waving of hands, which did little to clear up the confusion.

Prince Kuragin, looking impatient, murmured to Alix, "I think we need a little clarity here." As he turned from her to get into the fray, he removed his arm from her waist and in doing so, raised his hand to her face. For a matter of a second or two his fingers caressed her cheek.

Then he was gone, making introductions

in the corridor while one after another, either servant or council member, made a bow or, in the case of the two women, a bobbing curtsy. Dozens of the crowd were trying to look into the compartment from the platform. Most of them appeared to be citizens wearing streamers of blue and red in support of the Kuragin dynasty. Watching them and then the politely non-committal faces of the council, Alix wondered how much any of them could be trusted.

In the years since her birth Alix had heard about the assassination of one ruler after another. Crowns did not seem to be the safest professional tools. She had not been too interested in the beautiful Empress Elizabeth of Austria-Hungary, or young Max's relatives, Queen Draga and King Alexander of Serbia, all of whom had been murdered in the recent past, but she cared passionately about the life of Franz Kuragin whose name the mob outside was shouting now.

The train crew was getting restless. Alix saw a conductor in the chocolate-coloured wagon-lit uniform swing up the steps of their carriage.

He pushed his way through the crowd in the corridor and, with a deferential bow, whispered to Prince Kuragin. The prince laughed and with Tiger's help he herded the council and the Miravel attendants off the train. More cheers erupted when Pyncheon and Cornbury were mistaken for the prince's family.

While the prince was helping Phoebe and Alix to the platform and Tiger shook hands with the wagon-lit attendant, Max gallantly escorted Garnett off. Garnett received more cheers than the royal family and enjoyed herself thoroughly.

Within minutes the great train moved off towards the Hungarian and Balkan capitals.

Since all the royal guests, including the German empress, a Russian grand duke, the Archduke of Austria-Hungary, and the prince's family were to attend entertainments in the city, the Miravels were hurried off through the snow-powdered streets in the royal coach to the old City Palace where Friedrich the Third had died some five months ago.

The ancient stone building had been remodelled by the von Elsbachs to resemble the great, solid Hofburg of Vienna, so gloomy Alix half expected to find the tomb of the late Hapsburg heir, Prince Rudolf, who died a suicide, it was whispered.

Tiger tried to make light of it. "If you're lucky, you may see the Empress Dona prowling the halls looking for the — "

"Tiger . . ." the prince reminded him but he was grinning too. "No, we've put her in the north wing, so she can see Germany, and Kaiser Willie."

"Well, the new Austrian heir, Franz Ferdinand, then. His wife is quite a nice little woman," Tiger suggested to David. "She's not high-class enough for the Hapsburgs but he married her anyway. They make her take last place everywhere, but I say good for her and Ferdie. At least they love each other."

To this Prince Kuragin added, "She will be treated with every respect as long as she is in this principality." The sharpness of his voice startled them and Alix wondered if anyone noticed the glance he had given her. She looked down at her gloved hands quickly.

Phoebe was busy admiring the decorated streets and aside from her small hesitation before asking another question, Alix could not be sure she had seen or understood any of these cross-currents.

The Miravels had been assigned to the south wing of the fourth floor in the old palace. Unlike the stately suites assigned to royalty, these were less regal and cumbersome. Phoebe pronounced them cosy, with all their clutter of late Victorian furnishings. They were romantic in their four-poster beds with freshly cleaned velvet curtains and a clean tester overhead. A perfect setting for love. Or in Alix's case, a dream of what might have been.

Alix had expected an embarrassing time of it when she requested a bedroom separated from her husband by Garnett's bright, childish nursery, with a bed in the alcove for the young Swiss woman who had been Prince Max's nurse. No question was raised. She couldn't understand until she saw Pyncheon and Mattie Fogarty watching her. To her alarm, Mattie winked at her. Did she actually think Alix would commit adultery under their very noses?

One of them must have managed to inform Prince Kuragin's household of the arrangement. Alix was relieved but nervous. Would the prince think this was a private message to him? She felt that he would be gallant, and tell her he still loved her, but even his gallantry couldn't change the basic facts.

Their worlds were now hopelessly foreign to each other.

Prince Kuragin accompanied the housekeeper as they dropped the various members of the family at their rooms, one by one. Already, Garnett had decided that they were all going to see Punch and Judy in the park that evening. It was Max's idea, and no one liked to countermand the plans of the young prince who was enjoying himself so much. He claimed that if they all dressed for the snowy background they would find the park at its most beautiful.

By this time Alix's nervousness and uncertainty over the coming eruption with David over Garnett had given her what she referred to as a "migraine", and she regretfully refused the Punch and Judy show.

Only Phoebe disturbed her by the laughing remark, "Migraines are so handy, dear, when one is bored."

David would talk of nothing but his plans for Garnett and himself tomorrow, in the morning, before the coronation ceremony.

He had discovered that the ruins of a Roman encampment were buried under the parade ground of the palace and he intended to write a monograph on the subject. Luckily for the palace, as he said, the ruins did not interfere with the main building itself, or the office buildings close by.

"I'll take Garnett tomorrow. I'm sure it would only bore the rest of you."

Max made a face at Garnett and objected, "But Cousin David, Garnett is going for a ride in the state coach with me. She's anxious to go. She said so."

With the wisdom of Solomon Garnett decided, "I'll do both. Papa likes me to be with him when he discovers things."

It was a painful reminder to Alix. If she took Garnett away what would David do? He needed her so much.

Alix couldn't give up her only child. But there was always the shadow of Nick Chance hanging over Garnett at Miravel.

Alix went into her bedroom, dismissed the eager, chattering Mattie Fogarty, and sat down to rest her throbbing head for a few minutes.

Tiger came to take her with the others to dinner in what he called "the best rathskeller in Central Europe", but she was certainly not in the mood for heavy German food right now and she excused herself. Tiger watched her carefully, frowning.

"Whatever is wrong, honey? You've got a family to think of, so why don't you stop mooning and join us?"

"Later this evening."

Unsatisfied, he left her.

She turned the lamp down low, curled up on the worn but comfortable *chaise-longue* and tried to think of what was best for Garnett. After all, it was her future that would matter in the long run.

Some time later she opened her eyes, hearing Prince Kuragin's voice in the hall and then Mattie Fogarty's reply. She knew it would be better to pretend she had gone with the others. When he knocked, she made no sound.

Then she heard Mattie say, "I know she's there. I'll go around through Miss Garnett's room."

There was no way out. She had to explain to him what had happened at Miravel. There would be no other way to show him why she had been receptive to him today when every instinct told her that it was disastrous.

"I'm here, Mattie. Who is it?"

Mattie was gone when she opened the door. He stood there in his dress uniform, looking almost businesslike.

"We must talk."

"I don't think it would be wise," she began but he cut her off with one finger sealing her lips. This time he did smile.

"But I do. And you must listen. You are not in a London hotel now. You are home. With me."

"Not home. My home is Miravel." She heard her own voice with astonishment and with pain. What a stupid thing to say! Did she mean it?

"But my love, this is a perfectly honourable proposal."

"What!" Had he any conception of what that would mean?

"I would not sign the Decree of Accession without the proviso that I might marry whom I chose."

"But I am married."

"Not in my church. And there is the Chance boy. You know about him, don't you?"

He must be crazy. She was shaking and clasped her hands to calm them. "I discovered late last autumn. Since then — "

"You have lived apart. Your talkative friend Mattie has confided in me, after a little persuasion."

Mattie. Of course. Probably thought she was helping me, Alix decided. He saw her hands and took them in his. The warmth of his blood coursing through those lean, powerful hands excited her, but it changed nothing.

"How long have you known?"

"Since the day you arrived at Miravel. I knew my dear cousin Phoebe was up to something, especially when she kept talking about this Glynnis Reed, or Chance, whatever her name was, in connection with me. I, at least, was not drunk at the Midsummer Bazaar. I knew David had been with her, but there was nothing I could do when he accused me of meddling. Obviously, I didn't think it would go so far."

"You might have told me."

He had imprisoned her hands and she felt powerless in her passionate desire for him.

"You were so determined to marry him, I thought there must be some love between you. That day in London when you said you 'knew' about Dave, I thought you were talking about the Chance affair. You seemed to feel that it would not be honourable to leave him." He was very close now and she felt his hands move from her own to her arms.

"He needs Garnett. And he needs me. His family."

The prince's mouth set hard. She had angered him or perhaps he was angry with himself.

"I need you. Why am I excluded? I have done you no harm, no humiliation. Why are only the weak entitled to take from others?" He looked into her eyes, then kissed her. It was a gentle kiss, tentative. He looked at her again. "I can be as gentle as my cousin is. I am not one of those dashing ogres you women read about. I was married once. My wife betrayed me for someone much more dashing, I assure you. A Viennese musician in a café . . . But that may be my fault." He was hurting her arms as his fingers tightened.

"I did not love her. I've been in love

once. You may believe that, or you may not. I've loved a girl in a portrait in a house on Fifth Avenue. There have been other women, here and there. I am quite human. But in the last year or two I have been much too busy making plans for what I hoped you would recognise as our lives together. If you don't love me, for God's sake, say so!"

She found her voice hoarse and more passionate than she had intended to sound, but there were some things she could not hide.

"I do love you. I knew it the night I arrived, when you kissed me in that dark gallery at Miravel."

The truth was, she hadn't believed in that kiss.

She was in his arms and she knew, even while she welcomed his embrace with her own arms, that this would lead to disaster. She did not belong here. All his nonsense about signing accession papers would not change the fact that a divorced woman, a woman who might be accused of adultery, would ruin him.

Even if they loved each other only this one night in their lives, someone would know and ruin him as well as her family.

Sensitive to these dangers, she thought she

333

heard a sound in Garnett's room, but a minute or two later all was silent again. It had merely been the noise of celebrants out on the parade ground or in the park beyond.

Here, close in each other's embrace, they were meant to have this time together, no matter what her fears for the future.

There was a strange beauty about their lovemaking that she had never experienced with the only lover she had ever known, her husband. He did not pull at her clothes or try to take possession of her as if she were a complicated piece of field machinery that he could control by sheer force. She had never guessed, even in her dreams, that love could be like this, forceful, yet gentle, in command, and yet waiting with great care for her own reaction.

She closed her eyes at moments, trying to remember this night for ever. When she dreamed of him next she would dream of every detail that she experienced tonight on this absurd and far too sensuous couch. She remembered the attempts she had made to arouse David and tried to give Franz Kuragin these same pleasures.

This time all was right. The hot desire between them was greater because she too could serve him as he delighted her. She was embarrassed to murmur the words of love and sexual passion he whispered to her, but she felt them, even when she didn't understand some things spoken in another language.

After her experiences with David it was hard to believe anyone could mean all he said in his love for her. She knew she couldn't be that desirable. She hadn't been desirable to her husband, and he was not a man sated with the loves of many women. Even now it was hard to believe that Franz loved only Alix Royle Miravel, of all the women he must have known. But the touch of his fingers, long and sensuous, the way his mouth found the most erotic points of her flesh, her breasts, her thighs, the warm, throbbing and vulnerable area between her thighs . . .

She could not name them aloud but she let her lips touch the areas of his own body that brought him to a climax as she had begun to feel in herself. She would never love another human being in the same way that she loved this man who was so far from her in what the world called "life".

Later, they laughed together and talked in low tones, reliving what they had known together.

He completed dressing first so, as he explained, he could dress her. The thrill of this performance as his hands traced his initials (the Kuragin dynasty initials? she wondered) on her pale throat as he buttoned up the bosom of the blouse she had worn under the ermine-trimmed jacket. He stood back then, and smoothed her ankle-length skirt briskly, and pronounced her perfect.

But he was watching her carefully, her hands, her mouth and eyes. When he spoke again the delight she had loved in his own features was gone. He reminded her quietly, "I have never thought of you as anyone but my wife."

"A princess, in fact?" she asked with gentle irony.

"Why not? You are Tiger Royle's daughter, and royal to your fingertips."

"My darling, I am a miner's daughter. They grub in the earth, not in palaces of gold and silver. I am a sometime British citizen. What you need is someone to keep your country safe from bloodshed and family rivalries."

She rebuttoned the neck of her blouse where he had missed a button. She was trying to keep her fingers from revealing her anguish.

"The bastard princess, in fact. You cannot believe she is your equal. Alix . . . Alix . . . Dave has a bastard boy and you despise that helpless child. He doesn't even admit the boy to his house."

"It's not true. It's a filthy lie!" David cried hoarsely.

CHAPTER NINETEEN

In the doorway of Garnett's room David looked pallid and agitated.

Prince Kuragin must have been startled but he had been emotionally involved in putting forth his argument to Alix and was able to recover rapidly.

"Of course it is true, Dave. We've seen the boy. I talked with his mother the day of the child's christening."

"The brat is yours. Ask my mother. She always suspected the truth."

Embarrassed and guilty as Alix felt, she was also remembering not only the looks of the child — painfully like Garnett and her father — but the knowledge held by the whole village. Worst of all, David had shifted the blame to Franz when he spoke to Alix about it. It was a cowardice that doubled his original drunken act.

"Ask Mother," David repeated with a kind of desperate hope. "She told me so. She tried to protect Franz. She even paid that awful woman to marry some Welshman or other.

Alix, you wouldn't leave me. You said you wouldn't. You just told Franz. I heard you. You and my little Garnett are all I have."

She said, "I don't know. I can't forget what you did to others. The Chance woman. The boy. Even your own Cousin Franz."

"Dave," his cousin began in a voice that touched Alix with its gentleness, "are you in love with Alix? Were you ever in love with her, even at your engagement party in New York? I stayed away from her during those weeks because I knew I was beginning to care too much. Did you show her at any time what you felt for her?"

David was clearly puzzled. He insisted, "Of course, I love her. I promised to love her. It's in the vows. Just because I am not a great Don Juan like you, doesn't mean I'm not fond of my own wife. She belongs to me. By our vows."

"Have you ever known me to be a Don Juan? I swear to you we will never take your daughter from you. Some provision would be made for you both to share her custody. Isn't that true, Alix? I have always trusted my son to the family, Dave."

David shrugged, like a child who is trapped in a wild statement. "What difference does it make to me what you do with Max? He's always underfoot anyway. But I was wrong.

339

You couldn't be a Don Juan." He looked over at Alix in triumph. "He was too busy being a hero, getting tortured and made much of, and winning those countries nobody ever heard of. He's another Bayard. Don't you see? He's turned into the Bayard of my life."

He looked around as if he wanted to grasp at help somewhere. Alix saw the prince's expression and was relieved that he felt her own compassion. She knew quite well why David felt inferior to more active men who made their place in the world. He had tried to do so in his quiet way, writing books and knowing all the time that his worthy attempts were financed by others.

In a last attempt David played upon Alix's deep guilt. "If it did happen about that brat in the village, I wasn't myself and I wasn't married. You are both worse than I was. This is adultery." He pleaded suddenly, "If I can forgive, you certainly can, Alexandra. You owe it to me."

Nobody said anything for a long minute. Prince Kuragin looked at Alix but he must have known how this bitter and poignant scene would end. David no longer had any hope. He turned abruptly and rushed back into Garnett's room, slamming the door behind him like a desperate child.

Alix said dully, "He believes what he is

saying. He doesn't want to admit, even to himself, that any of this happened to him. Or to us. He thinks he loves me, because my presence gives him security against the world's customs and opinions."

Franz was frowning. "He is losing you. I think he must care more than he has ever shown you. I've never seen him quite like this before. I thought he didn't deserve you. But I blame others for what has been made of him. This whole Bayard business. How Phoebe and David's father worshipped Bayard! He was one of those to whom everything comes easily. He didn't think twice about seducing a village girl, or anyone else. I always found David more honest and oddly touching."

"He seems so deeply wounded. If I go to him, perhaps — "

Franz started towards Garnett's door and tried the brass latch but the door was locked. He swung around. Alix was startled by his uneasiness.

"He was like this. Once. After word came about Bayard's death. He tried to comfort Phoebe. She was weeping, of course, and she burst out with something that hurt him in the deadliest way. She said, 'Why wasn't it you?' "

"Oh, God!"

"He said nothing whatever. He simply walked away. I scoured the countryside for him. When I found him he had taken a sleeping drug in whisky and was curled up in the old dower house on the edge of the Miravel water gardens. The place was torn down shortly after. It had been used by Bayard to entertain various — friends."

He tried the door again, then went across the room to the door into the corridor. "I think I had better tell him — what?"

She swallowed hard. "Tell him I never intended to do anything but go home with him. Your Highness, you always knew that didn't you?"

"No, I did not," he said shortly. "And don't call me Your Highness. I thought we could be happy. I thought we deserved it. Apparently, we did not."

He went out to the hall door of Garnett's room. Anxious to make reparations for the hurt she had done David, she followed him nervously. He tried the door and said "Thank God!" when it opened under his hand.

The room was dark. The prince and Alix made their way towards the bed, Alix fearing the worst and praying, "Please let him be all right. Please let us make amends. Dear God, please!"

Franz found the oil lamp and turned it

up. David was huddled on his daughter's bed, clutching a glass that rolled off on to the floor when Franz shook him.

"Here, old fellow. Wake up. You are a lucky devil. Your wife loves you. Wake up." He looked over his shoulder at Alix. "Pull the bell cord. The high one. It is for emergencies."

She did as she was told and ran out into the hall to waylay anyone who came to their assistance. Emergencies? Probably for protection from assassins. Certainly not to rescue husbands who had been betrayed. The housekeeper appeared within minutes. Her severe, stout face and pale blue eyes clearly informed Alix that she could handle any emergencies. She was as good as her appearance promised. The royal physician arrived just as Franz had roused the drowsy David and was trying to reassure him. David seemed dazed when Alix leaned over him to add her own assurance.

"If I could know what the drug was?" the doctor murmured.

In a sudden flash of memory Alix recalled Pyncheon's little spoonful of a liquid that she had given Phoebe now and then. She said, "Laudanum, I think. Lady Phoebe Miravel takes it. We may find it around the room. He must know about it."

The remarkably useful housekeeper said in her firm way, "The gentleman spoke of wishing to retire and sleep. He must have taken too much. Laudanum is not always reliable."

"Not reliable, indeed," the doctor agreed. "The gentleman may owe his life to Your Serene Highness's quick action. He must be aroused. No sleeping. Then, a walk around the room. Afterwards, perhaps, the corridor. I will relieve Your Highness, with your permission. You will need all your rest for the long day before you."

The coronation, Alix thought. He must go through all that after what has happened here tonight . . . My darling, I love you more than ever for what you did, but the doctor is right. And we mustn't let David know he owes his life to you . . .

She told the doctor with a little of the housekeeper's stiff competence, "I will help in any way possible. He is my husband, Lord Miravel."

The doctor sent for his equipment, whatever that entailed, and when David looked around with a blurred view of the world he had almost given up, he saw Alix sitting on the side of the bed, trying to keep him warm under an extra coverlet that was decorated with baby chickens and rabbits.

The coverlet, obviously meant for his daughter, made him smile faintly but the sight of Alix seemed to stimulate him more.

"Have you been here all the time?"

"Certainly. I always want to be with those I love. If they want me." It occurred to her that the idea of his being a donor of forgiveness for a change might cheer him up. "Can you ever forgive me, dear?"

She had been right. He felt for her hand, tried to squeeze it but lacked the strength. Nevertheless, his colour looked better.

"I knew you wouldn't go. You or Garnett."

"David, what a thing to say! Do you really believe our daughter would desert you for anyone, even me?"

She had begun this little treatment, hoping to arouse him from his dreadful lethargy, because she owed it to him, but the thought of their friendly renewal of relations warmed her as it cheered him. There was much to forgive on both sides.

Franz Kuragin had been a dream from the first. Would he ever be anything else? She had one consolation. There was no one to destroy her dreams. She had survived on them before. She could do it again.

Meanwhile, there was the treatment of David to be completed, walking the poor man up and down, rousing him from that alarming comatose condition.

When the family returned from the Punch and Judy show they were not surprised over David's "excruciating headache". He had given it as his excuse for leaving them in the park. Whether he had known what he would find when he returned to the palace Alix did not know. He seemed determined to keep to this story when Alix gave him her word that she and Garnett would stay with him. She honoured him for that. But one in the merry crowd at the Punch and Judy show did not seem to have been fooled. Alix knew from the way Tiger looked at her that he had guessed, though he was careful to assure Phoebe about David's condition.

"Dear boy," Phoebe said of her son, "he was always a trifle weak." Everyone looked at her. She added, "In health, I mean to say. If he is quite restored, I will go with Pyncheon and get a much-needed rest. I'll see you all tomorrow. Ah, what a glorious day!"

Pyncheon took her away to her room after a brief glance at Alix and Prince Kuragin. Alix wondered what she would think when she found the drops missing from her little vial of laudanum.

Garnett had run to her father and hugged him, mourning his "nasty headache" and was sitting there with his arm around her when Tiger said quietly to Alix, "I take it things are sensibly settled and the coronation goes on without any more disastrous problems."

"I am returning home with David and Garnett immediately after the coronation," she told him, evading the whole story. "I would like to leave before, but — "

"You can't. You can't," Garnett cried. "We promised Max we would watch him. Papa, you won't let us go before, will you?"

David caressed his daughter's tangled hair tiredly. "Not if my little girl promised. We Miravels never break our word. Do we, Alix?" He couldn't have been more obvious in his reminder but he did not wait for her reply. "You see, Garnett, Mama agrees with us. So we will leave the minute the coronation is over."

Alix caught the searching look of His Serene Highness. His mouth twisted a little, as though he had started to say something and changed his mind.

Satisfied, David began to listen with sleepy pleasure while Garnett described the savage excitement of Punch and Judy.

Tiger suggested to the prince, "You could use some sleep, Frank . . . Your Highness. Need I remind you? Tomorrow is the biggest day of your life."

Franz said, "How good of you to remind me, my old friend."

There was a cutting edge to his voice. As if in defiance of Tiger's reminder, he took Alix's hand. "See me to the door."

She could not have said "no" if life depended on it.

The two of them had almost reached the door when David stirred and tried to sit up with an arm around his excited daughter. He called to Alix, "Don't be too long, Alix. Garnett wants to tell you about Punch and Judy. Don't you, sweetheart?"

Garnett giggled. "I'm Papa's sweetheart. Max'll be mad."

Alix felt the prince's hand tighten on hers but she promised, "I'll be back in a minute, honey."

Garnett reminded her father, "Mama called you honey. She hasn't done that for a long, long time."

Alix did not correct her. The prince closed the door behind them and they were alone in the old hall with its high, dark, medieval ceilings which must produce echoes along with dusty spider's webs, Alix thought.

"You are definitely going back with him?"

"With them."

He took a breath, staring down at her fingers, thin and slight in his grip.

"This isn't goodbye. You know that."

She was startled. She reminded him, "I can never again visit you here."

"Well then, you need not. I will find you instead. Our worlds are small. And this I promise you. Look at me." He raised her chin between thumb and forefinger, staring into her eyes as they widened under his gaze. "You may never know where or how we meet, but I will be there. I swear it. By this."

Without any conscious move of her own she was in his arms. As they kissed and the passion of his touch overwhelmed her, she raised her own arms, locking her body to his. They were gradually aware of each other's heartbeat and when they parted she laughed on a note that was half joy and half hysteria.

"I'll hold you to that promise."

"You may, my little love."

She broke away from his dangerous touch. "We shouldn't meet again before we leave, but we know what we feel."

"And with that you go home to his bed?"

"Never!" It was a vow.

He did not want to let her go and held her hands until she reminded him gently, "I must go."

She started to open the door to Garnett's

bedroom but looked back.

He was still there, watching her, his face and hands shadowed but his blue uniform with its red facings standing out ghostlike, as in her dreams.

Some day, she promised herself. In some way. Only not now. Not while I am needed at home. Miravel was still home.

It was this idea, so unlikely, yet so necessary to keep her dreams alive, that she clung to the next day during Lichtenbourg's proudest celebration.

She had thought David's condition might prove to be a problem but she had not counted on his daughter's influence. When David pleaded that he was tired and ached in every joint, Garnett was desolated.

"If you can't go, then we can't, Papa. We came clear over to this wonderful castle just to see Max crowned. And his Papa too. Oh, Papa, you can't stay in bed."

David excused his sudden decision to attend the coronation. "I don't want to lie about here until late in the afternoon when the train comes by. We'll all go."

Alix did not know whether she was glad or sorry. It would only hurt more to see Prince Franz Kuragin made a hereditary Prince Royal of his own country but it was better than not seeing him at all.

CHAPTER TWENTY

The Miravels were escorted to the old but highly renovated cathedral which had been rededicated to its original sponsor, the first Kuragin Prince Royal. They arrived before the royal visitors from the European royal families, but this was highly satisfactory. They were able to see and criticise most of the famed figures they had heard and read so much about. Tiger pointed them all out to Garnett for the benefit of David, Alix and Phoebe.

It seemed to the Miravels that these celebrated characters in the chessboard of Europe were dressed in regalia that had not been worn, or perhaps cleaned, for a very long time. Everything was heavy, and there was a thick odour of mothballs from some of the lesser nobility seated around the Miravels on one side of the nave down which the new Prince Royal would walk to his chair of state beneath the baldequin.

Garnett had been seated in the front row between her father who was "just recovering

351

from a painful migraine" and her grand-mother who had complained that to sit behind the front row would only exacerbate her rheumatism. The Royles, Tiger and Alix, were content to sit behind the Miravels, Alix because she did not want to stare at Prince Kuragin, in case anyone read her true feelings in that stare, and Tiger because he wanted to escort his daughter. Lady Phoebe had seen this as excessive attention. She thought that her son might very well be seated by his wife, behind her and Tiger. But it was not to be. For some reason which Phoebe could not in the least understand, Alix was being very attentive to her husband. It did not suit her previous aloof manner.

David had said almost nothing to Alix since he recovered from his close run with death the previous night, but he was overjoyed by the flutter of attention his daughter gave him.

There were few smiles from the members of royalty present. Clearly, they felt that Prince Kuragin's relations from Great Britain were of a somewhat lower order than their own illustrious backgrounds.

Garnett was the exception. The Russian grand duke was much taken by her. He had evidently drunk the usual Russian toasts to his kinsman, Prince Kuragin, and was quite willing to socialise with the talkative, enthusiastic Miss Garnett Miravel. The handsome, bearded grand duke informed Garnett's parents that he would be happy to adopt the enchanting Miss Miravel and take her back to St Petersburg where she could be moulded into a true "Kuragin".

Before the dumbfounded David and Alix could speak, Garnett refused prettily, announcing that it would be unfair to the man who was going to make her a future Princess Royal. The grand duke, not to be outdone, vowed to buy her from Prince Max. Garnett thought this was exciting and confided to David that she was going to ask Max to buy her instead.

The cathedral, with its long, narrow length and high gothic towers, now could afford two choirs, one above either end of the nave, and the magnificence of the Vienna-trained voices with their organ accompaniment thrilled Alix to the point of tears. Surely no one deserved such a glorious display more than the man she knew she would never forget, the Prince Royal, Franz Kuragin. Nevertheless, when David turned and looked back at her, she was grateful for his wistful smile. She wondered if perhaps he was sensitive to her feelings at this minute and she reached forward, clasping his shoulder in a comradely way.

Those in the crowded cathedral could not miss the arrival of His Serene Highness. Most of Lichtenbourg swarmed around the square in front of the cathedral, shouting the Kuragin name and pointing out that the "Square von Elsbach" was now, by order of the Council of State, renamed "Kuragin Square". When the object of this momentary adulation arrived in the state coach accompanied by his son and heir, Prince Maximilian, the noise grew deafening.

Everyone in the cathedral sat up stiffly, with all heads turned towards the two great doors which were opened suddenly, revealing a blinding sunlight beyond as it glittered on the melting snow from the previous day's snowfall. The trumpets almost drowned out the two choirs and the two organs. A curious and startling silence followed for a minute as the Prince Royal moved up the wide steps and stood momentarily in the doorway alone. Chancellor Waldstein and Prince Maximilian flanked him, a step or two behind.

With a rapidly beating heart Alix watched Franz step into the cathedral in blue uniform decorated by several small medals from other countries, given for "valour" in one war or other during the past five years. He wore a curious helmet which shone in the sunlight that surrounded him.

David was excited. He whispered to Garnett, "Roman, you see. A tribune's insignia. Look at the red plumes on top from front to back. Well chosen. It gives a man a look of power and strength."

For some reason Garnett sensed that her father might wish to wear such a helmet himself. To Alix's pleasure she whispered back, "You should wear one, Papa."

Looking at David now one would hardly have believed that last night he had almost died from a suicide attempt. Talking to his daughter, explaining in whispers all the background and reasons for the various uniforms as they approached, he had taken on more colour and a very real enthusiasm.

The Prince Royal moved along the way past his invited guests with a slightly faster pace than Alix and many of the others had expected. He had always seemed more commander than ruler to Alix and now he must feel that he had achieved all his goals, for which he had given so much, including his own blood.

Garnett was disappointed that he did not wear a long, heavy train, but in Alix's opinion, that would not have suited him. Behind him came Max in his white and gold with a smaller helmet and red feathers, then came the old chancellor in blue uniform with red facings and the Roman helmet. The young prince did not look Garnett's way and she was disappointed.

She whispered, "He doesn't like me any more. He won't look."

"He can't," Alix explained, leaning over her shoulder. "It's a very solemn moment."

Solemn or not, Prince Kuragin must have heard Garnett. As he passed, he moved his head slightly and thrilled Garnett by a wink which most of the crowd in the cathedral did not see. From Garnett his glance took in Alix. It was all done in a couple of seconds, but to Alix there was a message in that brief look. She felt warmed and refreshed. He had remembered her.

Like Garnett, she needed that refreshment amid so much solemnity.

She hugged to herself the thought that he had not given her up. He still loved her. It was cruel and unfair of her to let him know she loved him and then return to David. But he understood. One day . . . One day . . .

The rest of the ceremony was long and tiresome to Garnett. Most of it was in Latin which made it more incomprehensible than ever, but David's day was made for him. He was one of the few who understood what was being said and the sacredness of the promises made by Franz Rudolf Feodor Kuragin to "live for this sacred soil, under God, and to defend it and its people with the last drop of his blood".

Most of the Miravel group were affected by the solemn words of Maximilian to serve his liege lord, the Prince Royal, and to devote his life to this sacred soil. David was unimpressed. He whispered to his mother, "The boy will sell out at the first chance. He's not the man his father is."

Alix heard this and wondered if David had seen something in Max that she had missed. Of course, he was not perfect, and his self-importance was perhaps obvious, but he remained a delightful and charming young man, even worthy of Garnett, if that was their destiny.

There was one curious thing which came at the time the thin, gold coronet was set upon Franz Kuragin's black and still gypsy-like hair. Prince Max was crowned afterwards when he had sworn loyalty to his father, and he looked as if he were born to wear a crown. On the contrary, the crown was not Franz Kuragin's proper headgear at all.

Following the *Te Deum* praising God, the Lichtenbourg anthem was boomed out by the organs and the choirs. During these stirring minutes the procession began, led by the Cardinal of Lichtenbourg and the bishop of the Lichtenbourg diocese, with the now consecrated Prince Royal of Lichtenbourg alone, followed by Prince Maximilian and Chancellor Waldstein. Various notables came after them, most of these very much aware of their part in the ancient ceremony.

Prince Kuragin walked with the stride Alix remembered, always a step or two faster than the lesser dignitaries around him. He looked imposing, a leader, not a princely puppet dressed for a special occasion. He did not look towards the Miravels, although Alix was amused to note that Max tried to glance their way, or at least Garnett's way. He carried himself, and especially his neck, very stiffly. The coronet doubtless inhibited him.

As the great doors opened again, a slim, youngish blonde woman sparkling in white, jewelled satin and a flashing tiara, stepped out of the audience and gracefully curtsied to her new ruler.

"Who is she?" Alix asked her father.

Tiger was grimly amused. "She almost became the Princess Royal. Of course, if our boy Kuragin marries her, she may make it yet."

Ilsa von Elsbach. And alarmingly beautiful.

Tiger nudged Alix. "Great idea if he does marry her. Keep this little fly-speck of a country from all these revolutions."

Because the idea of that marriage sickened Alix, she was non-committal.

With the principals gone, already being hailed by the crowd in the square, the royal guests in the cathedral began to collect in the nave for their own departure, strictly by order of precedence. Tiger leaned over to discuss their own departure with David.

"Are you feeling all right, old fellow? I have things arranged. An American automobile out behind the cathedral, with all our luggage in it. We can get to the station in a few minutes."

Phoebe began to fuss. "I'm sure some of my things were left. I can't trust Pyncheon to remember everything."

"She did," Tiger said firmly. "She and the others are already waiting at the station. It shouldn't be too long a wait before the train gets here."

Alix thought her father was overdoing this business of separating her from Prince Kuragin, but there was no use in dragging out a painful goodbye.

David must have agreed. He said, "Good. If Cornbury has taken care of my things, I see nothing to hold us here."

Nothing to hold us . . .

It seemed to Alix that their entire world,

small as it was, had conspired to hold them apart. She made no objection.

For once, even Garnett's pleas failed to move her father. He put an arm around her, thus removing her from Alix's side, and promised, "You'll love the train ride. And when we are back home, I will let you ride on my lap when we drive the new car."

This persuaded Garnett, for the time being, at least. When the four grown-ups crowded into a two-cylinder touring car parked in front of a closed apothecary shop it was a close fit. After Phoebe and Alix had been helped into the back seat, with due allowance for Phoebe's train and her Siberian sable cape, David took his daughter on his lap in one of the front seats beside Tiger.

Phoebe was a little put out because it had seemed to her that her obvious place was with Tiger in one of the front seats, but Tiger said he didn't want anyone to imagine Lady Phoebe Miravel was not elegant enough for the back seat. Phoebe acknowledged that there was a great deal of truth in this.

"One must always show one's colours before the natives."

"How well you British express it!" Tiger complimented her, avoiding the sardonic glance Alix gave him.

They chugged their way out of the little

medieval street with its timber buildings tumbling towards each other to form almost a cave out of the street. The street itself was little more than an alley but once they got out into the decorated main boulevard, with the railway station looming at one end and the old palace at the other, they could better admire the city.

David was fascinated by the architecture and made some remarks about the interesting clash of periods shown here, which made Garnett sit up and look around.

His mother rolled her eyes and remarked in a low voice to Alix, "One would imagine there was something of more immediate interest to discuss."

"He isn't boring Garnett. She enjoys hearing him describe things."

"That's as may be. But we are not all children."

Garnett's mercurial interest switched from architecture to the railway station. She sat up with fresh enthusiasm. "Are we going to ride in a pretty train with shiny walls, like we did before?"

"Not until we get to Vienna," her father explained. "Then we ride all the way across Europe to Paris and the coast in our very own compartments. To England and home."

"To home."

"Yes, sweetheart. Won't you be glad to get back home?"

"Maybe my ducks will be born. You won't eat them, will you, Father?"

Alix listened for his reply. He sounded more like the endearing, well-meaning man she had met near Geneva as he promised Garnett indignantly, "Of course not. What do you take me for, a cannibal?"

Phoebe muttered, "Really, David," but Alix laughed. Tiger also chuckled and looked around, pleased that Alix's mood had become happier.

He pulled up at the depot, helped the women down and made a sign to the baggage attendant who strolled out of the station.

"His Serene Highness will have the car picked up. It's royal property. I hope nothing happens to it." Obviously, the baggage man did not understand English so Tiger repeated his warning in what Alix suspected was somewhat eccentric German. The man was shocked that any such possibility existed in this foreigner's mind.

"*Nein, nein, Meinherr.* Prince Kuragin. Understood."

They had been waiting with a few local passengers, carefully wearing their best finery, for some minutes before the Budapest train rolled along in a cloud of steam, noise

362

and cinders. Tiger was herding his little group into the coach when there were shouts from the stationmaster and the baggageman. Garnett had just been boosted up the steps from David to Alix when she started screaming for Max.

Tiger motioned to Max who had driven up in an overcrowded German touring car with two uniformed men. He ran on to the platform waving to the family with special attention to Garnett. He held out something that shone with a dull glow.

"For you. To remember me." It was a crown made of dull gold paper.

Alix was touched by the gesture but Garnett threw her arms up and hugged as high as she could reach, around the neck of his slightly dusty white uniform. He, having set the crown on Garnett's soft hair, dislodged her hands and stood off to be admired.

"How did you like me?"

Garnett breathed and sighed together. "So handsome. Better than anybody in the whole world."

Satisfied, Max set her crown more carefully on her head. Then he announced, "You may kiss my hand. It's the proper thing now."

With eyes as big as saucers Garnett took his gloved hand up and was about to follow his order when he pulled his hand away, lifted her up and kissed her on the nose. She giggled hysterically.

"I'll take her on board," he explained to David and Alix.

He passed them on the steps and escorted Garnett into the coach where several travellers stared at them with interest.

David followed them, calling out, "Don't detain the boy. We will be leaving any minute."

Alix stood on the top step in a kind of trance, reliving the events of twenty-four hours in this city. Max's two escorts, the men in stiff-billed caps, boots and military overcoats like the one Franz had worn, moved slightly, drawing Alix's attention.

She looked down at the foot of the steps. He was there, looking up at her. She started to rush down the steps but was stopped by Max who pushed past her down to the platform, and then by the train attendant who said something in Hungarian. It was the "all aboard!" signal.

She reached down, fumbling to touch Franz. Their fingertips met. Glove against glove. Not his dear flesh at all. He raised his voice against the noise around them.

"Remember." It was the least dangerous thing he could say, in case someone recognised him in spite of the billed cap and the coat. David and the world were so near.

His features looked strained, older. She must have matched his desperate look and the smile that was her last sight of him. The coach attendant pushed her, not ungently, into the coach. The train picked up speed.

The train whistle had a high, mournful shriek.

PART THREE

CHAPTER TWENTY-ONE

Garnett Miravel always considered that her "growing-up period" began with the fairy-tale visit to Max's country. She never saw herself as living anywhere else when she grew up. Of course, Max would be there.

But it had all been over so quickly because of Papa's illness. The air of Lichtenbourg wasn't good for him. He felt ever so much more cheerful when they had left Vienna and started home across Europe, as Papa put it. Eventually, even Mama felt ever so much better and became her old, lovely self. She wasn't terribly emotional, not like Papa whose feelings were so easily hurt. But you could tell she loved you. Sometimes she seemed like a very pretty version of dear Tether whose bark, as Grandpa Tiger said, "was worse than her bite".

It was lucky for the whole family that Mama was able to manage things nowadays. Grandmother Phoebe did nothing but talk about their being "special guests of the new Prince Royal. Our cousin, you know." She

369

even mentioned it like that to the king himself when he visited the Amesburys with a kind lady whom everyone gossiped about when the king couldn't hear them. But when Grandmother talked about being "special guests" Garnett caught the little, friendly smile the king gave to Mama.

He liked Mama a great deal. What a nice king!

And he didn't scare Garnett like the Prince Royal had done once or twice during their short visit. When he wasn't talking with the family, Garnett saw that everybody snapped up and obeyed him instantly. Maybe it was his eyes. Garnett had seen a band of gypsies from Hungary in the park the night Max took the family to see Punch and Judy. She thought the fierce, fiery gypsy people had eyes like Prince Kuragin. The first time Garnett said he had gypsy eyes she got a very odd look from Mama who probably was a bit afraid of him too.

He didn't look much like Max. Garnett was glad of that. If she married Prince Kuragin it wouldn't be like Max, at all. She couldn't twist him around her finger. Not at all. It was funny that Mama seemed able to do so.

Garnett caught herself occasionally being a little like Grandmother, boasting to the few children in the village that Father and Grandmother let her talk to after church on Sundays.

"We stayed in a real castle." She went on to describe it in detail.

Castles seemed so much more romantic than palaces. After all, their own King Edward lived in palaces. Anybody could if he was related to Grandmother Phoebe's friend Bertie. Garnett knew she wasn't supposed to call him by his nickname, but he had taken her on his lap once. He ought to have a castle, he was so kind.

The innkeeper's boy wanted to know if there were drawbridges. Moats fascinated Mirella Amesbury. And of course, the ceilings were all solid gold, Nick Chance teased, heavy with sarcasm.

It was funny about Nick Chance. Some of the villagers treated him like his family was as important as the Miravels. Others were rude to him. And none of the better families had much to do with Nick's mother.

Garnett knew a secret about Glynnis Chance. When Garnett and Mrs Tether were waiting for Alix near the post office one summer afternoon Garnett saw Glynnis Chance come sneaking out a side door of the Old Tudor Inn owned by Silas Putnay. She had her wide-brimmed straw hat pulled over her eyes and she looked around in a guilty way before stumbling up the street towards the big house she lived in with Nick. She acted like the Miravel chauffeur when he drank too much and Alix dismissed him. Garnett had never seen a lady drunk before.

Intrigued by her mysterious actions, Garnett remarked to Mrs Tether, "She was all dressed up in a silk dress just to see the innkeeper's wife."

The innkeeper's wife, Mary Putnay, was famous for her careless garments with their uneven hems and nasty stains under the arms.

"Rubbish!" Mrs Tether muttered. "More likely, Glynnis is after Silas. Never gets too much, that girl."

"Too much what?" Although Garnett had a suspicion.

"Never you mind." Shortly after, she cleared her throat, harrumped, and added, "None of our concern. Best you don't mention it at home."

"But Tether, I don't see — "

"They won't let you play in the Christmas pageant with the Chance boy."

"Oh." It was odd about Nick. She was afraid of him sometimes. He looked as if he hated her. But other times, he was clever and made jokes about people. She knew he didn't like her and she didn't really like him. Not at all the way she felt about her hero, Prince Max who was so much older and wiser. And so handsome.

But once during Christmas rehearsals at the inn she had caught Nick looking over her head in the glass frame of an old Amesbury portrait. He had said such an odd thing: "I could have been your brother. We look alike."

"We do not." She was offended. Some people said she was pretty. Nick Chance wasn't pretty at all. But she studied his features and hers in the glass frame, as much of them as she could make out. His eyes were a fox's eyes. A fox she and Papa had seen when they came upon the vixen's "earth". Papa didn't want to kill the furry little creatures and when she begged him not to, he shrugged, pretended he refrained because she asked him. But she knew it was because he really didn't want to kill the little family.

And Nick was like that fox, his eyes burning with some emotion she couldn't understand. The day they saw each other's face in the glass Nick had said, "Suppose I really was your brother. I'd be the heir to Miravel. Not you."

She had been so indignant she flounced out and missed the rehearsal. But oddly enough, later on she had more respect for him than before.

"There's your mama now," Mrs Tether said as Alix came out of the post office. Garnett waved and ran after her mother. Mrs Tether signalled to Alix over Garnett's head.

"Best take the hill path. She's hanging about up the street. Been at the gin with Silas, I expect."

Mama looked sorry. Was she thinking of Nick Chance or his mother?

"Oh, no. Has the boy seen her?"

"Don't see why not. He's helping her home."

Alix shook her head. It was all very strange. Maybe she wouldn't mind, after all, if Garnett tried to be Nick's friend. She thought of the odd way they looked alike. It would be comforting to have an older brother.

Then she saw Alix's mail, especially that one with the royal Lichtenbourg stamp that had Prince Kuragin's profile on it. Papa had said once, "Why doesn't he play it more subtly and send it through the diplomatic pouches? Or doesn't he know they now have an embassy in London?"

Alix's voice was calm but Garnett thought she was angry inside. "Because most of the Lichtenbourg mail is for Garnett. Would you care to read Max's latest to her?"

Maybe Alix was angry because Max hadn't been to Miravel for such a long time, and Prince Kuragin never came after the coronation. He must be very busy. Or maybe he thought he was too good for the Miravels now.

But on that day the letter really was from Max and Garnett was allowed to read it aloud. Papa didn't seem to like Max, and yet he was pleased when Garnett read the letter to the family. He didn't even object when Max sent his love to Garnett on her birthday and added, "Don't forget, sweet Garnett, I saw you when you were only one day old. You were very funny-looking. So no airs with me, your faithful cavalier."

Thus far, it was a wonderful letter, but a postscript was another matter. She hesitated. Papa was watching her.

"What else does he say?"

"Just that my grammar is terrible, and I don't spell very well." She shrugged, but read on, "If you are to be Princess Royal of Lichtenbourg, you must learn English, so you may one day learn German and Russian and Hungarian. Hungarian is even more difficult than English."

"So it is," Papa agreed.

Alix got up abruptly. "I had better talk

to Mrs Skinner about dinner. I'm very much afraid we are going to have mutton again today."

Garnett was surprised when her father called to Alix, "When Garnett writes to Lichtenbourg again, I wonder if you would have Franz send me as much material on those Roman ruins as his state librarian can find. I would appreciate it."

Garnett wasn't the only one who had been taken by surprise. Alix stopped in her tracks. She reddened a little, with pleasure.

"If you like, dear. I'm sure he — and the librarian — would be flattered by your interest. Garnett must also write about the letter of commendation you received from Edinburgh about your Highlands book."

To everyone's relief, David looked touched and pleased.

"It isn't a bad book, is it? Took a long time to finish, but it was worth it. The book on the Roman Wall might impress his librarian as well. That ought to be available before Christmas. We may even make a little profit on it."

"Absolutely, dear." Mother was really happy. Garnett could tell.

Prince Kuragin travelled everywhere except to Miravel. According to Grandpa Tiger who kept up with Lichtenbourg, it was the prince's negotiations that brought the latest border clashes between the Turkish empire and the Balkan States to an end.

During the trouble involving Serbia, a leader in the eternal quarrels with its old master, Turkey, Max Kuragin had been wounded and mentioned in dispatches. Garnett, like her grandmother, was careful to boast of Max to all Prince Kuragin's old friends in Miravel village. Luckily, Max had received only a superficial cut across his right forearm. But a "sabre cut" sounded frightful.

Anyway, it was good to know he loved only Garnett and not some nasty Balkan princess.

The next day Alix went to keep the accounts for the Reverend Pittridge's disbursement of Miravel Woollens' quarterly profits. She also wanted his advice about a proper tutor for Garnett to replace her newly married young governess from Bristol.

It was a matter of some importance to Garnett who had been reared on her father's romantic tales of history but was deficient in almost everything else. Even to Garnett it was clear that Max's criticism of her English was a serious matter.

Alix was not at all pleased by the vicar's suggestion.

He was friendly but quite sincere. "You

could do far worse than have your charming daughter tutored by a boy in the village. He is too intelligent to be wasted washing dishes and ale mugs for Silas Putnay."

"Who on earth — ?"

"Mrs Chance's boy. You must have seen him around the village. His age is against him. He's not quite fourteen, but he is extraordinarily bright. A very sharp boy in many ways."

"I should think so, indeed. Whenever he used to see me he would put out his tongue. Now, he merely glowers."

The vicar looked down at his bitten fingernails, then raised his eyes and asked directly, "Can you blame him, Lady Miravel? You know his story, I fancy. Some gossip has doubtless reached you."

"Then you know why I don't dare to have him near my family." She looked over at Garnett who was listening with great interest. "Garnett, dear, would you stop by the post office and see whether any letters from your grandfather have come?" She explained to the Reverend Pittridge, "He has been busy rebuilding his banking connections in California. He spends much of his time there since that terrible earthquake and fire in San Francisco three years ago. So many companies have been broken by their losses. He is very devoted to 'The City', as we call it."

Garnett would like to have heard more about the mysterious Nick Chance but if there was a possibility of hearing from Grandpapa Tiger, that came first. She gave the vicar a well-practised little curtsy and left them.

She was just closing the study door when she heard the vicar's kind remark, "What a beauty your daughter has become! The other doesn't resemble her in that way, certainly. But there is a noticeable resemblance in some ways."

Garnett didn't know whether to be glad or sorry that she might be related to the foxlike Nick Chance. Maybe Uncle Bayard had been Nick's father. She often looked at Bayard's portraits in the gallery at home and in the gold salon. Grandmother Phoebe talked of Uncle Bayard's wonders, but Garnett thought her father looked much kinder and more sensitive.

She went over to the post office but there was nothing from America.

She stopped to look at a paper pinned to the wall while the funny, youngish postmaster chattered away: "It was such an honour to see Her Ladyship yesterday. Please give her my humble greetings."

"Humble," Nick Chance repeated with

scorn as he came in, slamming the door. "What've we got to be humble about? We work harder than they ever did."

The postmaster turned purple with outrage. "A little more respect, if you please. This young lady happens to be Lady Miravel's daughter."

Garnett grinned sassily at the boy. At the age of nearly eight it was very nice to be called "a young lady." In her childhood they had just been words. They meant nothing.

Nick Chance did not react to her smile but he was obviously interested in what she saw on the wall. "I received a First in the Bristol Competition. That's the thesis that did it. Like it?"

Garnett read the first paragraph doubtfully. There certainly were big words in it. All about the dullest thing: "Laertes, True Hero of Hamlet." She'd heard of *Hamlet*. Seen it, in fact. And fallen asleep in it. But who Laertes might be was a mystery to her.

She didn't want to hurt his feelings, so she damned it with faint praise. "It must have been awfully hard work. I mean, so many big words."

The young postmaster snickered.

As for Nick Chance, he dismissed her with disgust. "You really are remarkably stupid, even for a Miravel. Must be your mother's influence." He held out his hand for the mail that went to the Old Tudor Inn and having received it from the astonished postmaster, stamped out the door, past Garnett.

She was shocked by his insult to her mother, of all people, and after a stunned silence she rushed out after him. She caught him before he reached the inn.

"At least my mother doesn't go wobbling up the street like she's drunk."

He swung around. "You bitch!" Raising the half-dozen pieces of mail and a small package he threw them all at her. They fell around her like rain. The package broke open and scattered tatting shuttles in the street.

Garnett was not physically touched, but her feelings were hurt. She wanted to be liked. It was upsetting to see such hatred directed at her. She turned and walked back to the vicarage, careful to keep her chin up proudly.

When she looked back he had picked up the letters and was chasing the small shuttles.

CHAPTER TWENTY-TWO

The Reverend Pittridge and Alix were just getting up.

"Then you will give the boy a trial, Your Ladyship? I can't tell you how grateful I am. The boy is wasted in that present atmosphere."

Alex said, "We will try. I can't promise you more." She took Garnett's hand. "You don't mind too much, do you, honey?" Not waiting for an answer, she shook hands with the beaming vicar as Garnett curtsied gracefully.

By the time they passed the end of the church and were crossing Miravel's only paved street, Alix saw Nick Chance picking up the last of the shuttles. She called to him while Garnett awaited Nick's reaction with interest. She knew what he would think, that she had tattled on him and now he was to get in trouble with her mother.

He looked towards the inn, as if for help, then braced himself for what was coming. Undoubtedly, it would be bad. Alix came to him with Garnett walking beside her as though she had nothing to do with this business.

Alix said, "I'd like a word with you and your mother."

Garnett was sure he looked uneasy. Maybe his mother was drunk. It wouldn't be the first time.

"She's busy. She can't see you."

Alix hesitated. "I suppose I should talk to you about it anyway. It's more your concern than hers."

"Is that what she told you?" He looked at Garnett but she avoided him, innocently studying a puff of cloud in the summery sky.

Alix was puzzled. "I've been told that you received a 'First' in your school work. We need someone to tutor my daughter." His eyelids flickered with his surprise. "It would only be a trial, but you never know. My daughter will be happy to improve her English and especially her spelling."

For the first time the boy revealed a flicker of a smile. Garnett shrugged. She felt he had been punished enough.

A little more at ease he felt able to make his own offer. "A copy of my paper on *Hamlet* is in the post office, if you would like to test my — my English and spelling."

He added after an anxious pause, "I would like the post. That is, if I suit."

Alix looked at her Lavalier watch. "Heavens! We won't have time now. We are late. His Lordship will be wanting his tea. Can you come to Miravel tomorrow in the forenoon? We might see how you and Garnett get on together. That is, if your present post permits you to take the time."

Nick Chance said, "I'll come."

Alix and Garnett walked home with little to say to each other. Garnett noticed that her mother looked very serious. After an uncomfortable silence Garnett asked, "Is it all right, Mother? I mean, about Nick Chance?"

"We won't know about that for a while yet, will we? I'm just wondering what your father will say."

Garnett thought about this. "I don't think Papa ever notices people." She smiled at a thought. "Not till they've been dead a thousand years."

That made Alix laugh and they walked the rest of the way in excellent spirits. Garnett wondered why her mother didn't mention the boy who was going to tutor her until they were all at dinner. Even then it was slipped into the conversation: "The vicar recommended a village boy to improve Garnett's writing and spelling and perhaps a few other shortcomings. It may not work out. We'll see. How was your day, dear?"

David began to describe with enthusiasm his first solid work on the Roman encampment under the old palace at Lichtenbourg City, but Phoebe interrupted him with news of the Amesbury spring ball in London.

"Bertie, I mean His Majesty, is expected to attend. They are hoping to capture our own Cousin Max, what with Franz being busy with those dreadful Balkan affairs."

In different ways this aroused the attention of the other three at the table.

Alix felt David looking at her and said quickly, "We will have to stop calling Max 'young'. He must be about sixteen now."

Garnett dropped her fork. "Oh, Papa, can't we go? Can't we? Please?"

Everyone looked at him. He reminded them, "The matter won't come up unless we are invited."

It was as close to a "maybe" as Phoebe, Alix and Garnett could get.

Garnett spent a restless and excited night. Close to dawn she heard the boards creak in the hall outside her room. Wondering who it could be at this hour, she got up in her bare feet and went to her door, opening it ever so quietly.

Of all things, it was Mama.

Alix walked to the west end of the hall, stood there looking out at the estate road, and then walked slowly past her own room. After a minute she started her slow walk back again.

How very curious!

In the morning Garnett had more important things to worry about. Nick Chance arrived at the path through the herb garden and was let in through the small salon by a properly imposing Horwich.

"You are to be taken to Miss Garnett's schoolroom, I believe."

Nick shrugged. Alix was waiting for him by the main staircase and Horwich, after indicating the boy to Alix, bowed himself out. Obviously he was not used to playing the guide for a village youth of dubious antecedents. Alix smiled. She was not too pleased with herself when she realised that she shared his feelings, though her dislike went deeper than that of the butler, and snobbery had little to do with it.

Nick had taken pains to look well groomed and in spite of the breeze outside his hair had been smoothed neatly. But his manner was just short of insolent. Alix was sure he wanted the people in this house to understand that he was in no way inferior. In fact, he belonged here. She could understand it, even while it frightened her a little.

He gave walls, carpeting, floors and the central chandelier a cursory inspection, as if he might buy the place if the price was right. His manner amused her. She couldn't help admiring it, even if his narrowed eyes were as unfriendly as a wild animal in his own domain.

She had left the schoolroom door ajar and went in to her own sitting-room which now adjoined it. She thought it wise to find out whether Nick Chance was mature enough for the job of teaching a friendly but not scholarly girl of Garnett's age.

It was soon evident to her that although Garnett might not be serious, Nick was here for one purpose, to succeed at his post. Every time Garnett said crossly, "Oh, bother! Who cares?" he dismissed her boredom with insults that taunted her to go on.

"You are stupid. I knew you were. Lazy, too."

"I am not lazy. Very well. Once more. And that's all. Max doesn't care. He likes me the way I am."

"A muddlehead. Probably ashamed of you."

There were no sounds for a few minutes. Then a rattle of her father's thick, engraved notepaper. Nick must have taken it to examine. He read it in a monotone. Alix could catch words here and there It was a letter from Garnett to Max. Gossipy and inconsequential, with talk of the Midsummer Bazaar, the Young Persons' Party given by the Reverend Pittridge, and her own birthday dance at which she waltzed twice with Keiron Amesbury.

Nick stopped in mid-sentence. Apparently at the spot where she had stopped writing.

"Well?" she probed him. "Was I better?"

Alix smiled at the boy's elderly and considered criticism.

"Better. That I'll allow. You've only misspelled eight — no, nine — words. Of course, you've bored him out of his mind."

Alix sat up with renewed interest.

Garnett cried, "You are horrid. Really horrid. I told him every single thing I could think of that I did this summer."

"And not a single thing about what he's doing. Or is this princeling doing nothing, like most princes?"

"How can you be so nasty? He almost got killed a few months ago. He's very brave."

"Does he know? You haven't said a thing about it. And you left out the 'o' in Lichtenbourg. These little dots on the map are sensitive about those things."

"Oh! I forgot. I'll copy it over."

Alix relaxed and smiled. He had obviously caught Garnett's sensitive spot. She wanted to please Max.

The letter got written and Garnett let her teacher read it aloud. This time she was rewarded by his grudging praise.

"Better. Not too bad for only a fourth attempt."

There was a sudden commotion in the schoolroom. The hall door slammed and Garnett cried out with pleasure.

"Papa! You ought to hear my letter. I wrote it myself. Show it to him, Nick."

"I heard the end of it. How did this fellow get in here?"

"But Papa, he made my spelling right. Max can't laugh at me now."

"Laugh at you? Certainly not. As for you — "

"Nick Chance."

"Nick Chance, sir!"

Alex was already on her way to the schoolroom door. David's harsh voice troubled her. He was usually controlled. Thank God, there had been no hysteria or suicide attempts since the Lichtenbourg coronation. Obviously the vicar's suggestion about Nick had been disastrous.

She pushed the door open wide just as the boy said with great care, "Nick Chance, sir." He was almost too polite, but she couldn't blame him. The fault was hers. This did not hide his faint smirk, however. She put her hand on David's arm.

He was startled by her touch but insisted, "I want him out of here. His family has caused the Miravels enough trouble with their filthy lies."

"But Papa, it's not fair. He's been helping me. And you'll like his paper in the post office. There isn't one mistake. He writes about old — I mean, about history and things. All about *Hamlet*."

"*Hamlet* is not history," David corrected his daughter.

Alix said, "The vicar speaks remarkably well of him."

"I want him out of here. And I don't ever want to see that slut of a mother in my house either."

Alix caught the boy's dark flush at the insult. "David, for heaven's sake!" But what disturbed her more was the narrowing of the boy's eyes and the glimmer of hate she read in them.

Then, almost at once, there was the soft, wistful smile again. For an instant that wistful look was like his father's smile. How could there be any doubt, except that, even at his angriest, David never had that hateful smirk.

"Father! You are horrid. I hate you."

Garnett slammed herself into her chair and kicked the chair legs once for emphasis.

David looked from Nick Chance to Alix and took a long breath. "You don't mean that, sweetheart. We'll talk about it later. Alexandra, I want this boy removed from the estate. I don't expect him back."

"Yes, sir." Nick Chance bowed like a well-trained boy, and started out between Alix and David. Here he stopped, pulled out his handkerchief, and wiped his hands. Alix wondered if he was wiping off the Miravel touch. Then he went into the hall.

Alix gave David a reproachful look and followed the boy. Along the hall, he stared at several of the gallery portraits of former Miravels. She wished she could see his face and guess just how much he hated them. She thought she understood him but she felt that he was no less dangerous for that.

Just as she reached the great staircase and he was going down, Garnett called out in the schoolroom doorway, "Nick, you dropped two papers here. With writing on them."

Nick Chance ignored this and walked on with dignity to the reception hall. He meant to leave through the south "guest" entrance. Though she feared him, Alix felt tempted to applaud him. She called his name.

He was determined not to hear her or Garnett. She could hardly run up the estate road in her French heels and gave up. She decided to discuss him with the vicar tomorrow. It would also be fortunate if they could arrange a post for him in some other town, something suitable to so intelligent a boy.

When she returned to the schoolroom Garnett was still in her chair scowling and David was standing over her, trying to make up the differences between them.

"Sweetheart, I don't mean to be harsh with the village lads, but this rascal — er — this young man, is too forward. I've seen him now and again in the village. He has been very insolent to me."

Garnett wound up two heavily written sheets of paper and then rolled them over the embroidered tablecloth as if she hadn't heard him. Her movements obviously upset David. He reached for the rolled sheets.

"What are they?"

"Nothing."

Alix stood in the doorway, wondering. The papers had originally been folded small and the writing on them was too mature for Garnett.

She realised that Nick Chance had dropped them when he took out his handkerchief.

Evidently he didn't want them. He had paid no attention to Garnett when she called to him about the papers.

After a little silence Garnett rolled the sheets across the table. They fell to the carpet again. Alix started forward.

"The boy must have dropped them, David."

"So I see." He picked up the sheets and walked over to Garnett's wooden waste-paper-basket with its frayed silk lining. He opened them up, intending to tear the sheets in two.

Alix did not want to provoke another quarrel. If the sheets were at all important she would rescue them after David left the room.

"Aren't you hungry, Garnett? It's nearly time for your lunch. The cook has something very nice for you. Some baked Eccles."

Garnett got up, somewhat cheered by the thought of this treat. "Cinnamon?"

"The very same."

Garnett brightened. "Are you coming, Papa? Real cinnamon Eccles."

"Just a moment, sweetheart. I'll be right with you."

Alix saw him pressing out the folds in the two sheets with the palm of his hand. She was surprised to see that he had begun to read them.

What on earth could Nick Chance write that would capture David's interest?

Another, less pleasant thought intruded.

Had the boy dropped the sheets deliberately?

CHAPTER TWENTY-THREE

There had been months, and finally years after her last sight of Franz Kuragin at the Lichtenbourg train station when she lived for the signs that he had not stopped loving her. She would not see him without David's permission, and that was not likely, but there was still the correspondence between Garnett and Max. This covered the cryptic notes between Alix and Franz which often contained but one letter, "R", for his final word to her at the station that day: "Remember."

There were dozens of ways in which the "R" appeared in Max's messages to Garnett. The sight of it was enough to keep Alix happy for months. She had no idea whether Max knew what it meant, or why it was so important that Franz should include it in his son's letters.

On those black occasions when the press and the European magazines were full of gossip about the Prince Royal's approaching engagement to this or that princess, a letter from Max was sure to come, jeering at the gossip. And there at the bottom of the letter would be the "R" in thick black ink which soothed her fears and made life bearable again.

It was childish of her, and of Franz, but they never failed to include the symbol.

Alix's work with Miravel Woollens and Reverend Pittridge's charities was a blessing. And David helped in his own selfish but kind way. She would catch him studying her sometimes and when she smiled at him he was relieved. He would be much more cheerful.

Tiger Royle kept them informed about the Kuragins' difficulties and their successes, dangerously situated as they were between their quarrelsome neighbours, the dual monarchy of Austria-Hungary, the Romanoff colossus in Russia, and that eternal meddler nearby, Kaiser Wilhelm the Second.

Tiger had his own problems at home, particularly in San Francisco, which was rising like a phoenix from the ashes of the great earthquake and fire.

Alix saw with tender amusement that his love for the city of his youth was almost as great as his love for his family in England.

She had a suspicion that his long flirtation with Phoebe Miravel was the one love and great thrill of that lady's life. She was glad for Phoebe's sake. They were often antagonists but more often comrades, when they found each other indispensable.

As for instance, Phoebe's anxiety to go to the Amesbury ball in London. It seemed to Alix that between her mother-in-law and Garnett, the Miravels might actually visit London at the same time one of the Kuragins was there.

It was almost too much to hope for. But miracles did happen. Even to see Max would be thrilling. And it was always possible that Max would carry some sort of symbol from Franz that proved to Alix his father was thinking of her.

The day after David dismissed Nick Chance with so little ceremony Alix was on her way to the Elder Home when she saw David go into the post office. It was surprising, because he disliked the village and seldom went near it if he could help it. He drove their new Buick to one of the cities he could reach in a couple of hours, and completely avoided Miravel. She wondered if he might be suspicious of something in Max's letter. It was unnerving.

She walked across the street and went in after him. To her astonishment he was standing there by the postmaster, ignoring the man, but reading a paper posted on the wall.

Some sort of manuscript or a lengthy letter. He was so engrossed he read the first page clear through and then held the sheet up with his left hand so he could read the second sheet underneath.

The postmaster-tobacconist, seeing Alix, suddenly sprang to attention. He always made her nervous with his twitching anxiety to please her.

"Lady Miravel. Just in time. His Lordship is here in this very shop."

Over his shoulder David called to her. "You should see this, dear. Quite remarkable for a lad like Chance, with a limited education."

Now he was a "lad". Tentatively, the "rascal" was gone. Alix read a few lines and was impressed, although why anyone should write two pages glorifying a minor character in *Hamlet* puzzled her.

"Very well done. Perhaps the vicar was right when he praised the boy."

"He should be." He added on a note of irony uncommon to him, "It was the worthy reverend who first schooled young Chance."

"He forgot to tell me that."

She was amused by the wily Reverend Pittridge who probably thought his partiality would prejudice her. But David's mention of the vicar was surprising. Except on Sundays and occasional children's festivals David

398

had very little contact with the Reverend Pittridge.

"I didn't know you were interested in Shakespeare. I take it that you've discussed the young man with the vicar."

He took her arm and walked out of the post office with her.

"That tobacconist-postal clerk is a great gossip. Yes. I will allow, I may have been too hasty about Chance. You will find those papers Chance left at Miravel yesterday were part of a composition on the subject of Aquae Sulis and the Roman discoveries that have recently been made there."

"Aquae Sulis?"

"The Roman City." He was never rude about her ignorance of ancient history. "It is their name for our own city of Bath. But his theories about what else may lie beneath Bath really whet one's appetite. He believes more effort should be made to uncover these ruins, no matter what is built on top."

"You mean, tear up that beautiful city?"

David was nothing if not reasonable. "Perhaps it sounds drastic, but eggs must be broken if one is to make an omelette."

She passed off this horrendous suggestion and returned to the original problem. It sounded more and more as if a great deal of Nick Chance's thought had gone into it since she offered him the post two days ago. If so, he was a remarkably clever boy, not to mention — devious.

"Then you think he can tutor Garnett?"

"I think he is remarkably knowing for his age. Garnett's letter to Max was quite satisfactory. I must ask Pittridge about the boy's honesty. Did you know, by the way, that the boy was learning to use a typewriting machine in Bristol when he had to return home?"

"Why did he return home?"

David said offhandedly, "That woman was ill. Pittridge didn't like to say but I take it she spends most of her money in the Old Tapster's bar at the inn."

She shuddered. "Horrible atmosphere for a boy like that."

"Great possibilities in him. A remarkable coincidence that his interests should be so perfect for the post."

Not at all remarkable, she thought but didn't say so.

As she might have predicted, the vicar's endorsement of Nick Chance was ringing and positive. He went further. "Nick is cleaning my windows today. I wonder if you would permit me to give him the good news. He will be so grateful."

Alix smiled. "But not surprised."

Her remark slipped by the two men. They were already heading towards Nick Chance who had finished the vicar's study windows. He was lowering the chandelier in the big double parlour which was used for entertainments of a more respectable sort than those offered at the Old Tudor Inn.

"No need to clean the prisms yet, my boy," the vicar told him. "Come and meet your benefactor."

"Sir?" Nick Chance asked, looking humbly from the vicar to David. "Do you mean I may have a trial, after all?"

David felt pleased. It wasn't often that he could be the centre of attention as Lord Bountiful.

"A trial. Precisely. Who knows? In my spare time I might dictate to you a few of my own ideas about Aquae Sulis."

"Oh, sir! That would be my dream, if you are sure I will suit. A year ago I began to save every penny. I hoped to walk to Bath. I mean Aquae Sulis, and buy some photographs. Perhaps see some of the excavation." He began absently to polish one of the glass prisms of the chandelier. "But Mother was taken ill."

"Hmph." The vicar patted his shoulder. "Never you mind. The village will help its own."

401

"Excellent idea," David agreed. "Perhaps, when the time is ripe, an auto trip to Bath. It would be rewarding."

Alix bit her lip. "David, one thing at a time." She caught a flicker of movement from Nick Chance.

He had flashed her a glance that was anything but humble, yet he agreed, "Her Ladyship is right, sir. I must prove I'm worthy."

"Good boy." The vicar was enormously pleased.

Even David started to shake hands with Nick who snatched his own dusty fingers back.

"No, sir. Excuse me. But I've got all this dirt on my hands."

David was impressed by these good manners. "Very well, Chance. Shall we say Monday next?" He nodded to the vicar, took Alix's arm again, and they left the vicarage.

David was clearly pleased that he had made so many people happy, including himself. "Withal, an excellent move, I believe."

"I hope so. It was very kind of you, dear. But you do have a good heart. Everyone knows that."

"Rubbish. I did it to please you. It opens endless possibilities. That business of the typing machine. I do hate having my manuscripts typed by strangers. They are sure to misspell the simplest words."

"Like Aquae Sulis?"

"Exactly. You've no notion how people cannot write, much less speak, competent Latin."

"How true!"

In his pleasant reverie of self-satisfaction he added, "I think Garnett will like my decision. She almost quarrelled with me when I dismissed the boy. She is very sensitive about such things. She seemed to know he would be of help to me in some way."

"Very likely."

He was right about Garnett who was delighted by the news and immediately took credit for her father's reversal.

Sometimes by accident, and in other cases, deliberately, she managed to let all the household know that she now had her very own tutor. She softened this braggadocio streak by ending it with the admission that she had been so stupid lately, the poor young man would probably be sorry he was asked to help her.

On Monday next Nick Chance arrived, neat and well behaved, neither too humble nor too arrogant. It was difficult for Alix to fault him in any way. His work with Garnett was confined to corrections of letters she wrote to various members of the staff and relatives.

Her grandmother Phoebe became indignant when Nick made his pupil rewrite her letter on the grounds that she had made two grammatical errors. Phoebe insisted to Alix that no granddaughter of hers was going to be reprimanded by the son of "that female".

She had never admitted that Nick Chance was in any way related to the Miravels. Alix did not press her on the point until Phoebe made the mistake of going too far.

By the beginning of Nick's second month as Garnett's tutor the household had begun to accept him in his role, and he himself retained his good manners, for the time, at least.

"I think Garnett shows a little improvement already," Alix admitted over tea that afternoon.

Phoebe gave it some thought. "It must be the Kuragin blood. Good blood will tell, you know."

Alix set her cup down with a tinkle of broken china.

Phoebe stared at her, shocked. "My dear, that is our best tea-service."

"Will you please stop this pretence that Franz is that boy's father?"

Phoebe was innocence itself. "But everyone

knew. Naturally, there are some things we don't discuss, but men are men. And princes are a trifle more — Well, you know."

"I do, indeed. All you have to do is look at the boy. He is so obviously his father's son. Though not as kind or trustworthy, I will admit."

Phoebe said huffily, "I'm sure I don't know what you mean."

"You do, but let's not discuss it again. I mean that."

Phoebe was stunned into silence for at least five minutes.

A shadow and a knock on the door to the herb garden made both women look up. It was Nick Chance with several packages under his arm. Alix went to the door accompanied by Phoebe's perennial warning: "Dear, far be it from me to interfere, but we do have servants for that purpose."

Nick thanked Alix with almost exaggerated courtesy. "I would never have returned this late in the day, ma'am, but Lord Miravel said he had some pages he would like to dictate to me if I could be free to return."

David came into the small salon at that minute, clearly expecting Nick.

"Ah, there you are. Come along. I am really very keen on this chapter and I'd like your opinion. I realise you are young, but you may have some interesting observations. You often do."

"Yes, sir. It will be a pleasure, sir."

It was too effusive and Alix looked at him. Nick caught that look and went on more rapidly, "I've been most awfully interested in your references on the new books, sir. I'm sure you will be thrilled by the Bath discoveries. I'd have given anything to be there. What excitement to be there, to actually see the Minerva head. And bits and pieces two thousand years old."

"Thrilling is the word, my boy. We'll have to make that trip to Bath one day."

"Ah!" Nick's sigh was full of regret.

Alix wondered if Nick Chance really was that excited over the Roman antiquities.

"This is not the best time to visit Bath, David. You still haven't got over that wretched cold you caught last week."

"No, indeed," his mother put in. "You would miss dear Alexandra's Christmas party for the children and the elders."

David was no match for two women. "Quite right. My wife has persuaded me, over-persuaded, I might say, to play one of the Wise Men who will deliver the presents."

"Really, sir?" Nick was staring at Alix. Then he seemed to recollect himself. "I'm sorry. I thought I might save your people a trip to the tobacco shop if I brought your mail." He took several books and letters out from under his arm.

Alix could see the two envelopes from Lichtenbourg. It was impossible to miss them. Her breath caught in her throat.

David said, "Good of you, Chance. I see my books have come. Excellent."

He had been about to lead Nick up to his study but held out his hand for the mail.

Alix remained motionless. Nick seemed to be caught in a dilemma. He held out the books and letters to David, then pulled them away.

"Sorry again, Lady Miravel. The mail is your department, I believe." He handed the books to David and with excellent manners, bowed and put the letters into Alix's palm.

Alix knew a performance when she saw one. Nevertheless, she smiled sweetly and thanked him, taking care not to separate the two Lichtenbourg letters. In her hand they appeared to be one and were partially disguised by London mail, including one from the Amesburys. No doubt the anxiously awaited invitations to the London spring ball, the one which might include His Majesty, the king, Max Kuragin, and some sort of surprise.

No matter. Only one meant the world to her.

David was already on his way out of the room with his books. Nick watched Alix as she thumbed the letters. The one from Lichtenbourg that meant the most had not been opened. She looked at Nick. He smiled. Then he joined David, remarking mournfully, "If only it could be possible to see and touch that Minerva head at Bath! Wouldn't that be exciting?"

"Quite right, my boy."

They left together.

Nick Chance had taken care to watch her as she thumbed the letters. He was waiting for that telltale nervous moment when she found the letter still sealed.

She suspected it had all been a threat, to show her his growing power. He might have given David her letter, but after threatening her he had carefully put it in her hands.

The price?

He expected her not to stand in his way when David talked of taking him on that little expedition to Bath. Who knew what the price would be next time?

I'll see him rot first, she told herself.

But it was obvious he wanted to make himself indispensable to David. Was it even possible that he had thought ahead to Garnett's inheritance and her place as the mistress of Miravel?

CHAPTER TWENTY-FOUR

After a late supper Alix delivered Max's innocuous letter to David, saying, "I know you will make Garnett happy with this."

He was pleased to be responsible for anything that would improve his relations with his daughter, and rewarded Alix with a light kiss upon the cheek before he went to his own bedroom to read himself to sleep.

Alix did much the same thing, taking her own letter with her to her bath and lying for some time with her body perfumed by lavender soap, her flesh warmed as much by the note from Franz as by the water itself.

It was none too subtle but it told her that he remembered, and even if David saw it, Alix thought it unlikely he would trouble to interpret it:

My dear cousins,
You may count upon Max at the Amesburys' spring ball.
He has just asked me to say, "My love,

remember." I trust you will deliver the message to its rightful owner.

Always, my own love to you. Cousins.
Your Cousin Franz

Absurd but a perfect way to remind her that he had not forgotten. Even the words themselves still linked them together. She could imagine him smiling as he wrote them. But there would be tenderness in that smile.

She thought about that note whenever life, and perhaps the weather, depressed her.

"My love, remember."

"Always, my own love to you."

Towards the time of the Christmas Achievement Social, held in the double parlour of the vicarage, she began to wonder if, just possibly, there was a chance that the Prince Royal of Lichtenbourg might be the "surprise" and accompany his son to the Amesbury ball.

It was too much to hope for and would mean that both she and Franz were breaking their word to David. Quite possibly, considering Nick Chance's rapid rise in David's literary life, Nick would do something to soil the prince's reputation and ruin Garnett's future by the hint of her mother's adulterous conduct. Certainly it would make Franz Kuragin's political life much more difficult if anything of their feelings for each other was bruited about among the press and the aristocracy, perhaps the greatest gossips of all.

It was decided between Mrs Tether and Alix, with an enthusiastic agreement by the Reverend Pittridge, that the awards to the children for scholastic or artistic achievement were to be given out by the females at the Elder Home. Each award for each child would be given by a different woman, and the women would be gowned for the occasion. Gowns they could keep and perhaps wear at the next Achievements awards.

The real surprise would occur at the end of the programme when the Elder ladies themselves were to receive a plaque for their home, stating their achievement in bringing back the woollen trade which benefited so much from Miravel Woollens.

The expense of this, with small medallions for each lady, proclaiming their noble task, was borne by the Miravels, the Amesburys and a sheep farmer who had profited considerably with his flocks.

Nick Chance had acted as though the affair were childish until he saw how touched David was to be appointed a Wise Man. Nick then "remembered reading somewhere" the important fact that Balthazar of Egypt, David's role in the pantomime, was by far the leading Wise Man.

In fact, "the wisest Wise Man".

Alix had not come across this detail of the Egyptian's life and place, but she was not foolish enough to deny it.

The biggest disappointment on Christmas Eve was that Garnett had eaten too many Banbury cakes that afternoon, a thoughtful gift from Nick Chance, and might have to stay home with Alix to keep her company.

At the last minute, when Alix was warmly wrapped in an old Miravel Woollens robe and preparing to reread the Christmas story with her, Garnett recovered and demanded to be taken to the village celebration.

When she did arrive with her parents, Alix having hastily changed from the robe to a grey crepe tunic over a pink underdress, Garnett was in her element. She wore lilac silk with a dozen ribbon flounces, not including the splendid braided ribbon flounce around her neckline.

As Garnett confided to David on the way to the village, "I couldn't just lie there with a stupid tummy-ache and not let anybody see my new dress."

"And looking like a princess," David reminded her. "Thank heaven, you are all right now." He reached over to the back seat and patted Alix's knee which was the nearest part of her he could reach. "You too, my dear."

Alix thanked him, forbearing to remind him that it was Nick Chance's "sweets" which had made Garnett sick in the first place.

With exquisite timing Garnett arrived after all the young people at the vicarage. She was surrounded at once by her village friends, among them Mirella Amesbury who announced in a perfectly audible whisper, "You'd have won a First for your drawing of the fox vixen if it hadn't been for *that* one with his essay."

Alix looked up at the posted winners. Truth to tell, Garnett's fox bore no comparison with the winner, the essay on "Laertes, True Hero of Hamlet". It might shock the Shakespearean purists but it was almost professional in its expression.

She saw Nick hanging about on the outskirts of the crowd, obviously not at home here, and she called to him, "Congratulations, Nick. It was exceedingly fine; wasn't it, David?"

David was so pleased he had to apologise to Garnett for his enthusiasm. As for Garnett, she was much too excited over the praise for her dress and had to be told why her father was apologising.

"Oh. That's all right. I was always stupid, my governesses said. I just want people to like my fox. The drawing doesn't matter."

The children's sector of the entertainment climaxed with the Christmas Eve pantomime including a live lamb and Mirella Amesbury's springer spaniel who became "the animals at the manger". It had been thought a villager's new baby would be the Christ child but this proved impractical during rehearsals and a bisque doll was substituted.

The vicar played Joseph like a born actor. The Wise Men were played by David in a false beard, Silas Putnay clean-shaven and just a trifle tipsy, plus the "Melchior" of the group, the generous sheep farmer who came equipped with his very own beard.

Alix enjoyed the genuine happiness, especially on the faces of the Elder ladies as they caressed the medallions prominently displayed on their bosoms.

Alix had forgotten Nick Chance entirely when she felt a gentle tap on her shoulder. She looked back and frowned at sight of him. She put one finger to her lips for silence. It did not seem to be enough. He motioned her back, out of the audience.

Wondering at his impertinence and not trusting him in the least, she followed him to the empty kitchen which still showed signs of the food preparations in the cake and biscuit department an hour ago.

"Well?"

He was very humble. "I wonder, ma'am, if I could ask a great favour of you. It would mean the world to me."

"Nothing to do with Banbury cakes, I hope."

His pale eyebrows went up but he pretended innocence. "No, no. I give you my word, ma'am. It was meant for a little Christmas present. I'm afraid I couldn't afford what I'd like to give, to show my gratitude."

"What is the favour?" But before she got the words out of her mouth she was sure she knew.

"You see, all my life I've wanted to study antiquities at close hand. I just thought next spring when His Lordship wouldn't take one of those miserable colds, if I could visit Bath as his secretary, and maybe his valet, just for the trip — "

"Cornbury would have something to say to that."

He waved aside trivialities.

"I could take a typewriter in the car. They are big, of course, but we could find room. I'm really very good with one of those machines."

"And why should I be interested in your typing future?"

The wistful smile spread over his lips.

"I leave that to Your Ladyship's good conscience." He felt around his jacket for something. "I meant to bring your mail with me tonight. Yours and His Lordship's, but he was so busy being Balthazar and all. Then I forgot it. Here it is. And I was afraid I lost it. I'd better give it to His Lordship when the pantomime ends. Unless — I'd really rather give it to you, ma'am."

"Why do you think I care?"

He pulled out the letter and looked at the Lichtenbourg stamp as if he had never seen it before. She had given orders that the Miravel mail should be picked up every day, either by herself, or Lord Miravel, or Horwich. This boy had managed, somehow.

"If you were going to London to the ball the Amesburys are giving, I could almost promise His Lordship would like the Roman ruins more. And you could both have a fine time."

"You are really disgusting." She did not take the letter.

"I come by it honestly, Your Ladyship."

He dropped the letter, bowed in a very grown-up way, and left her alone. She looked down. The letter was probably not dangerous. It was in Max's handwriting.

But it had been opened.

CHAPTER TWENTY-FIVE

In view of Nick Chance's blackmail attempt
Alix had no more to say about the Amesbury
ball. If she gave in now and theoretically
"paid" his price, there would be no stopping
him in his future efforts.

Garnett talked of nothing but seeing Prince
Max in the spring, and Phoebe was not far
behind her. She even sent Tiger Royle a
lacy valentine that stood up by itself, with
an assortment of forest animals waiting in a
glade for St Valentine. This carried the message in her round, careful hand. "Your friends
are still hoping to see you at the spring
ball."

As was so often the case in Alix's life,
Tiger Royle did more than promise to come.
He made the entire London ball possible for
the Miravel ladies by showing up beforehand
and discovering a part of the basic problem.

"Still the same passionate marriage, I see,"
he remarked one morning when David had
hurried up to his study after breakfast, ordering Horwich, "Send the boy up as soon

as he arrives. I want him to try out the new typing machine. Even I have managed to punch out my own name on it. Remarkable tool."

Alix said, "He was going to tutor Garnett this morning."

"Yes, naturally. But he can do that when I've finished these pages."

"Certainly, Your Lordship," Horwich agreed as if Alix had not spoken. He inclined his head faintly but with deep respect.

"What the devil is that all about?" Tiger demanded of Alix when David had gone. "Is that the lad who was taking down his golden words yesterday afternoon?"

Alix was succinct. "The same."

He looked at her and then at Phoebe who blushed a little. She was staring out the window at the one-time coach-house, now a garage for their touring car and David's old runabout. Phoebe made it a point never to look Nick Chance in the face or utter a word to him. When the boy spoke to her she ignored him.

Phoebe had developed a severe hearing loss where her son's new assistant was involved. Alix understood this attitude perfectly, but since she was sure Phoebe had been unintentionally responsible for Nick's presence on earth, she sometimes felt pity for the brilliant young scholar. His life would be far more balanced and fair if he had been acknowledged in some way at his birth.

She disliked and feared Nick Chance, but she thought she understood him, even when, as she soon discovered, he hated her. To him, Alexandra Royle had taken his mother's place and in the end, because she received all the benefits and recognition as Lord Miravel's wife, Nick's own mother had become a drunken disgrace.

Alix could read this in his eyes every once in a while when he accidentally betrayed his real feelings.

Tiger brought up the matter again when they were alone that day at the new Miravel Woollens shop and factory. This was the village's first skyscraper, a three-storey building remodelled from a rundown manor house on the Old Post Road. It was within sight of the Elder Home and many of the women walked to the building with their work for sale. Others, less ambulatory, were driven to and from their work.

The fact that they had their own place of business and that they could still work at home, like the spinners of the old days, gave them almost as much pride as the little silver medallions they wore. Old age no longer presented such a bleak face to them and the new chemist's shop was now handy for the doctor's home and the single surgeon of the district.

Having satisfied himself that the village looked all ship-shape and no one was taking advantage of "his" Elder females, Tiger broached the subject of Nick Chance.

"Have you really looked at that young man?"

"The resemblance?"

"No question about it. He might have been David's son."

"He is. Before we were married."

"Good God! And you have him in your house? What about the mother?"

"She drinks." She tried to be fair. "Nick is astonishingly capable for his age. And I will admit, since he's been assisting David, the work reads much better."

"Well, I'll be damned! I never knew old Dave had it in him to play fast and loose."

"Only once, before our engagement. She — I mean he wanted to be certain he was experienced before he was married. It was invariably done among some very high personages. The kings of France, for instance. Otherwise, there might be no heirs to the estate, you know. I take it Nick was an accident, not intended."

"I never thought I'd be talking so frankly

to my daughter."

With a glint of humour Alix asked, "Do I have any illegitimate brothers floating about the United States?"

Tiger took out his big handkerchief and wiped his moist brow. "I devoutly hope not."

Tiger broke off. They were entering the half-finished Miravel shop and factory at that moment and passed two Elder Home women also inspecting the work done on shop counters. They curtsied to Alix and gave Tiger their thrilled smiles. Almost every woman Alix had known since childhood succumbed post-haste to Tiger Royle. He, for his part, delighted in making people happy.

Money worked, but with the ladies, his grin was better.

"Now," he began when they were leaving the village, "what are we to do about David's by-blow? Good God! I hope Phoebe never finds out. This would kill her."

Alix muttered, "I doubt it."

"Does he make trouble? Is he dishonest? What kind of a reference would you give the boy?"

Leave it to Pa to get right on to the point. During their hour in the village he had probably been making all these plans.

"The highest references, so far as I can tell. I've never found him to be dishonest.

But David does appear to need him. For his books."

"What about a temporary job? You know. Tell Dave that the boy will be better trained, more useful to Dave when he returns to England."

She stared at him. "You mean, take him home with you? I mean, to the United States?"

"Why not? You say he's capable. We can always use a smart young fellow in our San Francisco and Comstock. Or in Virginia where your mother's old farm is going to rack and ruin. Far as I can see, it never did recover after the Civil War. Reckon I should call her place the Plantation. My sweet girl always did."

So he hadn't forgotten. Mother was still his sweet girl.

But she wondered. David was talking more than ever about some statue's head that had been dug up in Bath. Perhaps, if he was able to get enough facts on his new book about Aquae Sulis, he might be willing to give Nick his opportunity.

"Of course," Tiger added with a side-glance, "if David goes to Bath for a month or so, he's sure to miss that ball affair in London. And what's more important, you girls will miss it. Garnett's been chattering about it. Not to mention Phoebe."

"I know."

"Unless I am your escort."

"Pa!"

"Providing you don't run away with any old prince or other. I don't hold with divorce."

Alix reminded him coolly, "I'm not about to run away with any old prince. Besides, it's Max who will be there. Not Prince Kuragin."

"He loves you, by the way. He told me that long ago."

Her heart skipped a beat and within herself, she hugged the news.

There was a stern edge to his voice.

"In any other matter, you'd find me on Frank Kuragin's side every time. But this would bring too much disgrace to you and Garnett, and that fine prince, too. He's worthy to be any woman's husband. But not when it's adultery and all of that. You know what I mean."

She knew.

There was no use in telling him that Franz Kuragin had been willing to make the sacrifices such a romance would involve. He would only point out that this proved the prince's basic decency. And he was right.

The notion of actually spending a month

in his very own Aquae Sulis was immensely appealing to David whose selfish innocence did not permit him to think there might be ulterior motives in Tiger's gentle approach to the matter of Nick Chance.

Tiger read, or skimmed over, the work David had already done on the background of Bath's original Roman city, with special attention to its architecture. Following that, David had begun work on the discoveries themselves, and hoped to make the climax of the book the daily excitement of his personal visit to the antiquities.

"A pity," Tiger murmured, shaking his head as the family waited for his opinion of the book thus far.

David was shaken by this reaction. Nick Chance watched the scene suspiciously.

"Then you don't care for it?"

"Certainly, I do. How could I help it? In fact, it is far superior to anything I've read in the field."

This was very likely true. Ancient history was not Tiger's favourite reading.

"Then?"

Tiger gave it thought.

"I must say, your young assistant is apparently worth every pound you pay him. He is a fine addition to your staff."

A thread of a frown crossed Nick Chance's

sleek young forehead. It was clear to Alix that he suspected compliments from that quarter.

"As a matter of fact," David admitted, "young Chance is Garnett's tutor. The post doesn't — er — pay much, I'm afraid."

"But with training the young man could be of enormous help to you. I only wish we had a fellow like him in our New York office. Lazy and incompetent, all of them. Can't write or typewrite a single coherent sentence."

"You don't say. I had no idea."

Alix watched Nick Chance. His brow cleared and she surprised a little smile that quickly vanished.

"I couldn't consider leaving Lord Miravel's employ, sir. However . . ." Everyone looked at him. "It might be of great benefit to His Lordship if I had more training. Then, when I returned to his service I would be of genuine worth to him."

"All very well, my boy," David objected, unaware that the description "my boy", had aroused his mother's uneasy attention. "But in the meanwhile, there is Aquae Sulis. That must come first. I definitely need the boy for that. His typing machine, you know. And his fine, basic intelligence. You admitted that yourself."

"What a pity!" Tiger shook his head. "Such an intellect wasted when it might be yours to call upon." He roused himself suddenly. "I have it, by George! Why not make the Bath expedition in April or May? A month at the most. Then I might see to his trip across the Atlantic. He would return to you a much more valuable assistant this fall, let us say."

Nick Chance was holding his breath.

David sighed. "I had half promised Garnett that I would take my ladies to London for the Amesbury spring ball in April. Devilishly awkward."

"Not if I escort the ladies."

Alix joined Nick Chance in breathless suspense. David brightened.

"That would solve everything. What do you think, Nick? Say a three-month apprenticeship at the typing machines in New York."

Nick Chance could not have been more grateful. "And I could use my spare time to good advantage. The libraries in New York are said to be quite superior. I might return home — I mean to the village — with some interesting sidelights on your Aquae Sulis theme."

While Garnett, Phoebe and David were congratulating themselves, Alix grinned at her father but was caught by Nick Chance's fox-eyed stare. He knew that they were getting rid of him, but he was perfectly happy, for reasons of his own.

CHAPTER TWENTY-SIX

Alix's concern about one possible guest at the Amesbury ball was strictly private. Phoebe and Lady Amesbury, on the contrary, were beginning to worry about the only guest superior in station to the ruler of Lichtenbourg, who might not attend after giving Her Ladyship his word.

"My dear Phoebe," Lady Amesbury confided when visiting her friend's suite at the Savoy, "poor Bertie had a dreadful time of it in Paris. He attended the conference on Balkan problems, particularly that dreadful Black Hand Society in Serbia, and they say he has been simply racked by bronchial spasms."

"Frightful weather in Paris, I always thought," Phoebe reminded her. "Not nearly so invigorating as our London weather. I have always maintained that fog is excellent for the complexion."

"Too true, my dear. Too true. Did you know that when he returned from the continent Mrs Keppel was said to be nursing him? Luckily, poor Queen Alexandra is on a cruise somewhere."

Alix was sorry for Bertie who had been kind to her, but at this time she was more concerned over another member of the Balkan conference.

"Excuse me, but we read that the chairman of the Balkan conference was our cousin, Prince Kuragin. You are expecting his son tomorrow night at the ball, aren't you?"

"Quite true, and a charming young man he is. You will be proud of Max. Both your Kuragin cousins are so delightful. I believe I wrote to you that we were invited to stay in the old palace while visiting their quaint country."

"Yes. I do recall," Phoebe remarked edgily. "Somewhat similar to our own visit. For my cousin's coronation, you recall."

Max Kuragin himself arrived at that moment, enthusiastic, handsomer than ever, and anxious to kiss all his cousins. Since Lady Amesbury had not yet taken her departure, she received her share of the attention and was pleased to spread the story among her London friends, that the dear boy had laughingly kissed her as well.

Garnett was more reserved than she might have been at home. She wanted to show him how grown-up she was now.

"I'll be writing even more perfectly after my tutor goes to New York with Grandpa Tiger. He's going so he can become better and teach me to be perfect."

"He helps your father, too," Alix reminded her.

Max held up both hands in protest. "Please, Garnett, sweetheart, I don't want you to turn into a prodigy. You will be far more brilliant than your old Cousin Max."

Garnett looked at him, starry-eyed. "I could never do that."

Alix watched her with gentle amusement. How well Garnett understood her cavalier! Better than I did at her age, she thought.

When Tiger came in he wanted to know whether "your father will reach London for that fancy ball tomorrow night? Old Frank said he'd be here if he had to swim the Channel, but I doubt if it'll come to that."

Max had been admiring the length and smooth texture of Garnett's auburn hair. He looked up to assure them all, "He seems very determined." Then he added, on a less happy note, "By the way, he and the French premier were worried about King Edward."

Tiger nodded. "All this politics at home. Lloyd George making trouble, along with that rascally turncoat, Winston Churchill. Something about these British political parties. Like our Republicans and Democrats. We men ought to give the ladies the vote. Then the boys will behave."

"Heavens, what an unladylike idea!" Phoebe sniffed but was soon teased into a good humour by Tiger's unfailing efforts.

He bowed to her elaborately. "First dance is mine at the ball," he reminded her. She was particularly flattered to be the first spoken for. Nobody had yet spoken for Garnett or Alix.

Max remedied part of this omission by remarking to Garnett, "Luckily, you are tall enough to dance with now. Even when protocol demands it, I detest dancing with short girls."

Alix was in a reverie. Would Prince Kuragin reach London in time for the ball? She could only hope and, like Phoebe and Garnett, wear her most flattering new gown.

She felt extremely guilty when Max said, "A pity Cousin David couldn't attend the ball. Everyone will be there."

Alix was quick to build her husband's reputation. She felt he deserved it. "He is in the midst of his most important research. I shouldn't be surprised if it earns him honours of some kind."

Tiger surprised everyone by saying roughly, "He's a fool, that boy."

They all looked at him, open-mouthed.

He explained, "Only a fool would let a woman as beautiful as his wife go to a ball alone."

Phoebe felt that the Miravels had been insulted, but since she shared Tiger's opinion to an extent, she contradicted him as softly as possible.

"David was always more scholarly than social. I'm afraid his grandfather was that way. Indeed, it was fortunate Mama insisted on Miravel being presented to me. If not, there never would have been a Bayard. David, that is."

Alix resented the slip, but it was an old habit of Phoebe's and no one seemed able to break her of it.

Alix spent the next day between hope and a determined negative feeling. Prince Kuragin still loved her. Wasn't that why he had told Max he would swim the Channel to get to England? Or was she as important as another of his meetings with King Edward who was due at the ball?

Most of the day was confined to the elaborate grooming and clothing preparations for that night. Pyncheon managed both Phoebe and Garnett, at the latter's insistence. Alix would not dream of relying on anyone but Mattie Fogarty, who would have been cut to the quick at being left out.

Alix did not have the inate sense of style possessed by both Phoebe and Garnett, but she hoped she possessed one quality they lacked. Her appearance had pleased Prince Kuragin long ago, then during the yearly visits to Miravel, and at last, most especially, at the old palace in Lichtenbourg.

When Tiger and Max seated their ladies in Tiger's Great-Arrow car that evening even the elegant guests of the Savoy stared.

The group was worth staring at: Phoebe, swathed in ermine over ermine-trimmed lace, Garnett all in sparkling fairyland white, with Tiger's present, a flashing little tiara, and Alix in deep sea blue satin, with a matched evening coat, her hair piled high in the Grecian style, with pearl accessories.

For once, Tiger permitted a chauffeur to get behind the wheel of his car. As he boasted, he was going to arrive in style, beside "his ladies".

"And mine, sir," Max reminded him.

Upon hearing this Garnett sat up straighter, vowing to her companions, "We're going to remember tonight every day in our lives."

Please let it be so, Alix prayed.

If Alix hadn't been so nervous, and so doubtful that Prince Kuragin would appear, she might have enjoyed the stir made by their arrival at the Amesburys' London town-house on Grosvenor Square, an elaborate monument to the prosperity of the new aristocracy following the upheavals of the Industrial Revolution.

There was a heavy flight of steps to the entrance, followed by the delicate, twisting staircase leading up from the Regency reception hall to the dining-rooms and ballroom on the floor above. Here, just beyond the head of the stairs, Sir Humphrey and Lady Mellicent Amesbury received their guests.

Sir Humphrey's father had been a stout, good-natured brewer whose ancestors were sheep farmers. Sir Humphrey was as jolly as his father, his manner always suggesting that he had just imbibed a dram of his father's brew. This appearance, not always indicative of Sir Humphrey, was the bane of Lady Amesbury's life, she having been the great-granddaughter of a belted earl.

Nevertheless, Alix liked her. She was a very civil, ladylike woman who had accepted Alix without the overt prejudice of many others who still called her "the Yankee" after ten years.

The Miravel party, having been divested of coats and furs, proceeded up the stairs, hearing the Amesbury butler announce them in his stentorian voice. When Max bowed to the host and hostess, he asked the question Alix was dying to ask: "Have you heard from my father?"

Lady Amesbury sighed. "Not yet. But I don't give up hope."

Max, who escorted Garnett, called ahead to Tiger. "Looks as though Father will have to swim the Channel after all."

Tiger laughed. "He could always fly across, like that Frenchman, Blériot, last year."

Alix did not appreciate their humour, nor her father's comment to her immediately after.

"Smile, honey. Don't wear your heart on your sleeve."

The long dining-room opened into the ballroom. The two matching chambers each had three chandeliers that sent dazzling sparkles off the bejewelled women beneath them. The Amesburys were celebrated for their excellent banqueting staff and the dining-room buffets were so crowded, the babble of voices and clink of dishes so loud, a number of the guests had taken to the ballroom and were dancing as the small but adequate orchestra struck up.

"It's like a fairy tale. Like Cinderella," Garnett breathed as she watched the dancers. Max took her white-gloved hands in his.

"Now that you are growing up so fast,

have you stopped thinking of me as your prince?"

"Never. Sir Prince Charming. As long as I live."

"As long as we live. Never forget that. Fifty years from now let's come back to this room and dance again."

She wrinkled her nose. "I don't like to be old. I want always to be young. Even when I'm not."

"You will be, Princess Garnett," he promised.

Tiger brought Alix a plate of pâtés and a glass of champagne and Phoebe, with well-meant insincerity, asked her to join their little twosome, but Alix took pity on her and refused.

"I am waiting for a real, live general. He seems to have been waylaid at the punchbowl."

They left her and soon she saw them join a group of dancers in a lively schottische. Meanwhile, two gentlemen collided in front of Alix, both asking her for the dance. Although both men were at least Tiger's age, their friendly pursuit was flattering.

The men worked out their differences and one of them, she had no idea which, led her out to join the bouncing round dance. She was looking over her shoulder at the open double doors at that minute.

Prince Kuragin had come in quietly in plain, immaculate formal eveningwear.

Would he see her? Should she apologise to her partner and go to meet Franz? Better not.

Suddenly, a guest in a uniform encrusted with medals hailed him loudly. "Your Serene Highness. Over here. Orchestra! Give our friend a drumroll."

There was no drum but somewhere behind the violins there was a piano. The pianist struck up the first notes of the Lichtenbourg anthem. Prince Kuragin stopped, looking angry and ignoring the summons. His dark eyes flicked over the crowd, many of whom had begun to applaud.

Lady Amesbury came to him. Lucky woman, Alix thought. Her Ladyship curtsied to him and began to speak. He was polite, kissed her hand, or a little above it, but he was definitely looking around.

He saw Alix at last. There could be no mistake, she told herself, and tried to make an excuse to escape her partner.

"Forgive me. I must greet my cousin," she said finally, just as the prince reached her.

Prince Kuragin bowed to her partner. "Pardon. My cousin promised me this dance."

Her partner was not quite so ready to withdraw. "Sorry, Prince, but Lady Miravel promised it to me five minutes ago."

Prince Kuragin smiled with every evidence of good manners. "But my cousin promised this to me five years ago."

Obligingly, the orchestra began a Lehar waltz. The prince whirled her out on to the floor. The music muted their voices and only she heard him ask, "Are you more beautiful today than when I watched you leave me on that cattle car?"

She poured all her feelings into one assurance. "I don't think I could have lived another night without seeing you."

At first glance he looked a little older, his hair a trifle tipped with grey. He was much more stern and serious than the dashing young prince without a country whom she saw first in her father's house the night of her engagement. His scar was still noticeable. Perhaps that made him look older.

It didn't matter. With her body held close against his, and shaken by her love for him, she felt his own bodily pulse, his tension as well. His words hadn't been the easy protest one makes to an old love.

"Do you get my messages?" he wanted to know. "Do you understand them?"

"I sleep with them. Like a girl with her

first love." She added a further truth, "You *are* my first love. How funny! At my age."

"I wish I could kiss you. I suppose you would be hopelessly compromised." They swung around the end of the ballroom near the long windows and started back.

"You could. If they only had a balcony in here. How could they be so thoughtless?"

He laughed. She thought of many things when she stared at his lips.

He said, "When can I see you again?"

"The family certainly expects you at the Savoy."

"That isn't what I had in mind."

"I know."

She had never been as happy as she was at this second in time. She wondered if she would ever be so happy again.

He said, "Is it possible for you to meet me tomorrow somewhere?"

"No. But I will."

His arm around her waist crushed her flesh but she made no objection.

"I want to kiss you. Now, before all these idiotic witnesses. But I want more than that. I want you to be my wife." He hesitated, made another sweeping whirl, and began again, "I have been grooming Max to take over my duties when Middle Europe is quieter. I can act in some capacity to see that he doesn't go too far off the track. But I want you as my wife."

She thought of David and his desperate threats at Lichtenbourg. And there was Garnett, not nearly old enough to be left with a father who loved, but took less interest in her than in his precious "Minerva Head" in some place called Aquae Sulis.

"It is really Garnett, while she is still so young. You see that don't you, my love?"

This time his arm hurt her, but he released her to a more gentle hold after a minute or so.

"I see it, but I don't like it." Then he smiled. She had forgotten how heartwarming his smile could be. "I adore the way you say 'my love'."

"My love."

He was silent. She felt his mouth against her hair. She wondered if anyone saw.

"Well, what are we to do? I won't give you up. I never have."

She became aware of someone crossing the ballroom towards them. The music faded. People were stopping to watch this odd interruption.

Lady Amesbury was pale and seemed frightfully unnerved. "Your Highness, I've already asked the help of Lady Miravel's father. He knows His Majesty, though not

440

as well as you do. Can you please come with me, at once?"

Prince Kuragin asked no questions. He took Alix's hand and strode off after Lady Amesbury. Alix remembered suddenly that there had been talk of His Majesty's illness in Paris. A bronchial cold. She felt a chill of horror. Bertie was a good man. A kind man. He had done all that was humanly possible to keep the peace in Europe. Had he suddenly been taken ill while enjoying a pleasant social evening? None of the guests had even known he was here.

The king was leaning forward to keep his back from touching the chair behind him and producing another fit of coughing. He managed to give Prince Kuragin a weak smile when Franz and Alix arrived. He gave the others in the warm, fire-lit study a casual wave that dismissed them from consideration: a woman servant with a champagne glass full of water, Lord Amesbury wringing his fleshy hands, Lady Amesbury standing by, almost blue-white with terror, and in the background, beside the mantel, a middle-aged woman, a bit heavy, quietly dressed in a dark gown jet-trimmed.

Alix had seen her picture several times: Mrs Keppel, the king's mistress.

His Majesty didn't seem surprised to see

441

Alix. He looked from her to Prince Kuragin. He grinned and smoothed his beard.

"Franz, my boy, I have the better of you. I was the first to kiss this little lady on her wedding day."

"I know, sir. I was there."

"I saw her before that, too. One night in the gallery at Miravel. Or was it a charming vision? I thought she was a servant girl."

"I remember, sir," Franz said, without looking at Alix. It was the first time he had ever admitted having seen Alix wrapped in towels and little else, that night before her wedding.

"Yes. You were there. I remember."

Mrs Keppel did not intrude but she took a step towards His Majesty.

"Sir, it is better not to talk. It only makes you cough."

He made a quick, impatient gesture, indicating her.

"Must get things done properly. Franz, will you see that this lady is safely escorted home without being seen? I don't like my loyal friends to be the object of gossip and speculation just because I came to have a quiet evening with the cards, and my old friend Amesbury. Don't worry so, old fellow. I'll be right as a trivet in the morning. Kuragin, can I count upon you?"

"You may, sir."

Franz looked at Alix. She nodded, understanding. Neither of them knew when they would meet again. Tonight a calamity threatened His Majesty's family, the empire, and perhaps, in many ways, the world.

The exertion of the king's conversation had brought on another spasm of coughing. Mrs Keppel tucked her handkerchief into his hand. She spoke to Alix.

"Your father is bringing His Majesty's physician and all restoratives."

"Is there anything I may do?" Alix asked. In such times the question was a stupid one, but necessary.

The king recovered weakly. "Nothing. Thank you . . . You were very sweet that night."

She had a sudden terrible urge to cry, but managed to curtsy and move back, out of the way of the emergency efforts that would soon be made. She and Franz looked at each other. Then she gave His Majesty her assurance.

"Sir, I will say nothing."

"Thank you." Mrs Keppel spoke for him.

Alix left the study. She had no idea when she would see Franz again. Too much was happening in which he would be involved.

CHAPTER TWENTY-SEVEN

"Nothing will be the same with poor Bertie gone," Phoebe repeated for what was probably the fortieth time. "And all this dreadful black we must wear. I do hate it."

Alix shared her feelings in some ways, though the revulsion against a black wardrobe was not necessarily one of them. However, some of her other reasons were as selfish as Phoebe's.

During those first weeks, the lying in state at Westminster Hall and the great funeral procession occupied everyone's conversation, but the changes were soon evident. The interests of King Edward's son, King George the Fifth, and his redoubtable young wife, Queen Mary, were domestic. The good of their own country occupied them far more than the affairs of the European continent.

Admirable as this was, it had its effect on Europe itself. It became clearer after Their Majesties returned from the Great Durbar, a pledge of devotion given by the Indian subcontinent to the empire.

From this time on rulers like Prince Kuragin, who had based their efforts at peace on their personal relationships with King Edward, found it impossible to forge the same links with the new government.

David's work had, surprisingly, gone very well during Nick Chance's several prolonged absences, and he could afford to be generous about his Cousin Franz.

"I'm afraid this will mean the end of Lichtenbourg's independence, unless Russia steps in. The place is always an annoyance, even a threat, to the Austrians in particular."

When it came to political history Alix found David fairly astute. Still, she could not believe Franz would fail, after all his long efforts to forge treaties that would keep his country from being swallowed up by its neighbours.

"You mean there may be war? But no one wants a war."

David stopped working on the proofs of his new book on the perilous journey of the Ancient Greeks across what was now Persia. His theory was that the Greek historians had made a romantic drama out of ruthless history.

"Not war. No. They will use some excuse to gobble up Lichtenbourg. That little dot is an anachronism anyway. I hope old Franz doesn't lose French support. If he does, he's walking on a very high wire."

Alix sensed that from Franz's own notes and Max's activities in Paris where he was busy promoting his country's interests from the Lichtenbourg embassy. This position gave him entry to the French Foreign Office and, as a bonus, the Channel ferries to England.

Alix saw with affectionate amusement that month by month Garnett's photographs of Max were changed to more "immediate" ones.

Having gone so far as to give tacit approval of the warm relationship between Garnett and her third cousin, David became docile in connection with two visits by Alix and Phoebe to London alone, for "new wardrobes". He must have known from Phoebe's casual gossip that Cousin Franz was said to be in London also, but he ignored it.

During this time Alix and Franz met with every intention of doing no more than exchanging a few kisses and discussing a dubious future that seemed as far away as ever. There were two ecstatic hours with Franz while Phoebe was being fitted at her favourite dressmaker's. There was little time, and Franz was in England only for a long-overdue report to the Foreign Office, but Alix realised that nothing had changed for them in the two years since King Edward's death.

When she reached the hotel that unforgettable day and found she had still arrived ten minutes before Phoebe, she felt a deep twinge of regret that she and Franz had not spent the extra ten minutes in each other's arms.

Phoebe dwelled once more on her favourite theme: "London simply isn't the same without Bertie. They tell me Their Majesties are strictly bourgeois. No balls, no whist parties, no baccarat or roulette. Just boredom."

Remembering her hours with Franz, Alix knew Phoebe was wrong. Nothing had changed. She and Franz felt as secure as ever in each other's love. Once again, Franz had asked when they were to make these liaisons legitimate, but even that had not changed.

Nick Chance returned from his third "training summer" in New York to work with David on a new idea about the "lost Atlantis".

Alix still felt uncomfortable in his presence, wondering when he would produce some unpleasant surprise, but David and Garnett were happy to see him. Garnett couldn't wait to show him the little twist of gold that Max had put on her finger, calling it a "friendship" ring.

Nick smiled grimly.

"And soon we'll see little Kuragins running about here as Miravel heirs."

It was the first time he revealed in Alix's presence the real bitterness he felt about the Miravel estate. He caught himself at once and glanced at Alix who did not look up.

When he and David had finished an outline of David's new work he startled David by saying, "I'm told I have a talent for cryptography. Mr Royle says he can help me get a post. Of course, he wants it in New York, but I suggested London. In case of war sometime, you know."

David and Alix were both disappointed. Alix had hoped he would return to New York.

He must have guessed this. He went on casually, "I thought I'd take Mother up to London. They have a clinic there for her problem."

"Problem?" David asked.

Watching him, Alix was more than ever convinced that he had somehow erased from his mind any responsibility to Glynnis Chance. The woman had enough money. She was not in need, but if he wanted to be kind to his mother, David saw no objection.

Nick reminded Alix in the wistful manner she never trusted, "Of course, if I take my cryptography in New York I couldn't look out for Mother. It would be better in London."

David agreed. "Much better, my boy. By all means. And when I am well along in this new one, you might drop by and lend me that expert young brain of yours."

Alix had very little to say about it.

Nick Chance took his mother away, but Alix could not believe he was entirely gone from their lives.

Mrs Tether made the comment most of the village shared: "Good riddance there. I don't know why, but I never have trusted that boy. And heaven knows, his mother is no better than she should be."

There may have been method in her unsympathetic view. She had no more interference in Garnett's teaching and she was very fond of the girl. Her theory was that Garnett's future might require more "manners" than mathematics.

She may be right, Alix thought.

Early in 1914 Tiger Royle said, "Sorry to lose the boy. I've been told, roundabout and very hushed, that Chance is being useful in the decoding field in London. Seems to be something driving him. I sure hope it isn't the Miravel estate. If so, I'll have to get him shifted about, somehow. Get him off that track. Oddly enough, he seems to like me."

Alix wished they would all stop hinting

at war. Only David consoled her with the reasoning that most of Europe was like a child building blocks. He explained, "Germany with Austria-Hungary. Russia with France. Britain with Belgium, France and, by extension, Russia. And God knows who the Balkans are cementing blocks with."

One June day in that momentous year Mrs Tether came home from the village reporting that there was only one letter for the Miravels at the post office.

The day being warm and sunny, David had been out for a stroll while he considered what subject would be most likely to sell as a manuscript on its own. It would be a triumph if his next book did not have to be subsidised. Alix was in the herb garden cutting watercress for tea sandwiches.

"Only one letter, sir. And it's for you."

He took it, showing little interest. Alix went on cutting watercress. A sudden whoop of joy made Mrs Tether trip on the door sill and Alix dropped her shears. For a minute she thought David had lost his senses. She ran to him. He was waving the letter above his head.

"Honours. For me. A splendid Greek plaque for the body of my work. That's all of them, from my very first to my latest, which, luckily, was about Ancient Greeks."

"Wonderful! Who is it?" Alix hugged him, thrilled for his achievement. It was such a triumph for him, whatever it was, that made him look so happy. He had spent a lifetime in the shadow of other men. Even his Cousin Franz, whom Alix adored.

There had been some valuable assistance from Nick Chance, but there were books before Nick came into the picture, and much of the groundwork had been done by David without anyone else's help at all. It was truly David's triumph.

"Who are these people?"

David read it to her. "Very impressive. It's a genuine society. The Society of Athena. I tried to attend one of their meetings once, here in London, but I was denied. This comes from Athens, the home of all genius. All brilliance."

Mrs Tether shrugged, said, "Very nice, Your Lordship," and went inside, but Alix was delighted for him.

"When do you receive it? And where?"

"That's the best part. We go to Athens. The Athens of Pericles and Herodotus."

"It sounds thrilling."

"You and Garnett will actually see me receive the award. It is a plaque with chips and earth from the Acropolis itself all enclosed in glass."

She found herself with tears in her eyes. He was so terribly happy. "I just can't comprehend it. Such an honour, David. When does it take place?"

He looked back at the letter which he caressed with the palm of one hand. "July 25th. We'll take the Orient Express and change somewhere in Macedon or wherever it is. Then we can return the same way." He had a sudden idea. "How would you like to stop off in Lichtenbourg? I could show Franz the plaque. I'll wager that will impress him."

"It certainly should," she told him sincerely.

She knew Franz would be pleased for him. But to see Franz and not be permitted to love him, would be painful. She must take care to act with great restraint. There mustn't be another episode like David's attempted suicide. He had been too generous about including Lichtenbourg in this momentous event in his life.

David's emotional excitement spread throughout Miravel village which regarded his triumph as a part of its own heritage. He was one of their own, after all.

Phoebe thought the entire affair was rather too "intellectual" but she was the only one.

This beautiful climax to his life's work

(and at such an early age) lasted for ten days. What appeared to be the awakening came on the morning of 29 June when Alix herself saw that day's London papers, one of which lay on the housekeeper's desk at Elder Home.

Mrs Tether read over her shoulder. The article was on an inside page, but as startling as though it had been spelled out in capitals, as it would have been in New York or San Francisco.

"Somebody assassinated?" Mrs Tether asked. "Anybody we know?"

Depression gripped Alix. She sensed that this news was far more important than its position in the paper indicated.

"The Austrian Archduke, Franz Ferdinand. He's the heir to the Austro-Hungarian throne. I saw him and his wife at Franz's coronation. His wife was rather sweet in a quiet, motherly way. Good God! Both of them. Shot by anarchists, or one, anyway. Something called the Black Hand."

Mrs Tether grasped something even more important. "They weren't shot in Austria, either. Says the assassin was a Serbian terrorist. He killed them as they were driving through Bosnia. That's next door to Serbia, isn't it? Anyway, the Austrian government claims Serbia was behind it."

Alix's thoughts were more personal. "This will kill my poor husband. He never wanted anything in his life as much as to receive those honours from the Athenians."

"If it was me, I'd tell them to wrap the award up and send it."

Alix laughed, but explained, "Part of the glory for him is to receive these honours on the very soil of Ancient Greece. The train goes through most of those countries involved — Austria, Hungary, and the Balkans."

"Well," Mrs Tether added optimistically, "maybe they won't fight. Why should they? Those big countries haven't had a real war since Hector was a pup."

Alix was thinking of something else. Franz Kuragin's little country was almost in the middle of the area between Austria and Hungary. Many of his people were of Slavic blood, probably Serbs. His dead wife's aunt had been a Serbian queen. She had been the godmother of Max Kuragin.

She took a long breath. She had no heart for seeing the work of the Elder ladies today. She dreaded telling David, but the sooner she did so, the better.

Mrs Tether walked with her, remarking, "I swear, those Balkans like Serbia and the rest, can cause more trouble."

"Sometimes I think they all do."

Alix was too discouraged to discuss it.

They walked home in silence. Mrs Tether realised that nothing she could say would solve the problem, and Alix was trying to find a way to persuade David that receiving the award in London would be just as thrilling.

The one thing she didn't count upon was the fact that David might feel all was far from lost.

She went up to his study just as he was coming out to meet Alix and Phoebe for tea. He was still in that stage of euphoria which had pleased her so much. She said nothing but showed him the newspaper, folded to the story of the assassinations.

He read it in the upper floor hall by the light of the high chandelier above the double staircase. To her amazement, he handed it back to her with the comment, "Brutal as ever, these Central Europeans. I wonder what Franz thinks of it."

"But won't this bring war?"

David stared at her. "Why? This archduke isn't old Franz-Josef himself. There are always more archdukes where this one came from."

"But it's so horrible, and killing his wife, too. Not to mention the Black Hand connection."

Suddenly, he guessed what she meant. "You don't mean that a thing like this will ruin the Athena award."

She tried to be very gentle about this. She had only once known him to feel as strongly over something, and that had brought on a suicide attempt.

"I only thought London is so much bigger than Athens, and so — " She had almost said "so much more important." That would never do in this case.

"Nonsense. We are English citizens. It can have nothing to do with us."

"Then you think it is safe to take the train through all those countries on the verge of war?"

He started down the stairs with Alix trailing him, trying to reason with him.

"Of course it will be safe. I have the tickets. We have the reservations in Athens. If, by any ghastly chance, they start their damned war before we leave — and we still have an entire month in which they can start it — we won't go. But there are a great many 'ifs' in that. Besides, we will check with Franz and the Orient Express people just before we leave." He turned and took her hand. "There. Does that satisfy you, dear?"

It seemed to her, on consideration, that if no war had started, and they had plenty of time, as David said, then both Franz and the train people would have better information than her family in Miravel.

She was almost sorry she had let herself get so excited. But it was horrible, no matter how people dismissed it and she had no desire to travel through the very heart of this bloody dispute. Her next concern now was to persuade Franz that he would be safer out of that hotbed.

She had a feeling, though, that he was fully as stubborn as David.

CHAPTER TWENTY-EIGHT

"A pity the local train was late," Mr Minos apologised. "It is always late. Now, the day is too far gone for you to see the Parthenon. But tomorrow will be more appropriate, the day of your award and the society dinner."

Mr Minos, the presiding officer of the Athena Society, spoke excellent Greek, English and a smattering of twelve other languages. He had met the Miravels with his impressive touring car imported from the United States, and personally drove them through Athens to the hotel chosen for the guest of honour, the recipient of the prestigious Athena award. At the same time he explained carefully that the society was not a rich one, and the same could be said for the hotel. He added, "You are to be congratulated, Lord Miravel, on not letting the alarmists keep you from this great moment in all our lives."

David, sitting beside him, vowed, "Nothing could have kept me away, I promise you, and it was exceedingly important that my dear family see me receive this award. I might say, it is the climax of our lives."

"You saw no trouble on the journey across Europe?" his host asked casually. "It is regrettable that we do not have an express to Athens. Perhaps in the near future. You must have found local lines tedious in the extreme."

"And adventurous," Garnett put in, to which Alix agreed smilingly. It had not been comfortable and there were no sleepers, but she and Garnett made up their minds very early that this was to be David's great moment and nothing like complaints should ruin it for him. They would only be here a couple of days anyway, depending on conditions. David had agreed to that.

"Frankly," David admitted, "I've never heard such alarmists. Most of them civilians, without much information. The only man in authority, my cousin, the Prince Royal of Lichtenbourg, seems concerned, but I suppose that is to be expected."

Minos agreed. "A real hero to us, but in this case, over-anxious, perhaps. Not that I blame him. He has been in the arena of our struggles through this part of Europe. Now, just as we were settling down with our king, he was assassinated, very like that unfortunate Austrian archduke, and now we have King Constantine, a worthy young man who led

459

us against the Ottoman Turks recently. We fear nothing now, however."

His confidence was all very well but Alix reminded him nervously, "The Prince Royal has advisers in Vienna, very close to the imperial Government. They seemed determined, as they call it, 'to punish Serbia for its insolence', although the Serbians don't appear to have instigated the attack. Personally, I would think the assassination of the heir to the throne would be more than 'insolence'."

But nobody wanted to hear this kind of talk. Nor did they want to hear her own observations as they crossed Europe on the train.

While the sleek Orient Express made its circuit around Paris those in the train clearly heard the cries of *"Revanche!"*

Crossing Germany, they saw similar signs carried by gangs, mostly youths, and heard them yelling, *"Nach Paris!"*

Alix didn't like to quote Franz. She was always afraid her deep feelings for him would betray her, but the pleasant, confident Greek scholar was nothing if not reassuring, even about Franco-German feelings.

"One must remember, *madame,* that they are not actually involved in this dispute. It is really not their business. Why should they plunge into trouble? Or why should we, I thank the good God."

To Alix, probably the most important worry was the failure of Franz Kuragin to meet the Orient Express at Lichtenbourg City's station. His presence there had meant so much to her at the end of their coronation visit.

In the last month David had received several telegrams from Franz, warning the family not to cross the Channel, but when David persisted, along with thousands of other summer visitors, there had been the prince's last message, a promise to meet them during the train's brief stopover. Alix still thought his failure to meet and reassure them was a bad omen. Something of great importance must have kept him from the appointment.

Meanwhile, Garnett missed none of Athens's dry, austere beauty. She was looking too young and pretty to be found amid ruins, as Mr Minos said, a thought that made her laugh delightedly. She wore a saucy, tilted little feathered hat and a crisp tunic suit of lemon yellow that complimented her auburn hair and created a good deal of attention from the Athenians and a sprinkle of optimistic tourists.

Her father, forgetting his former boasts about the Pyramids, the Nile and the glory of the pharoahs, had switched his allegiance to the intellectual favourite, Athens. To the pleasure of Mr Minos he began to tell Garnett why the city was heroically shabby. It had so long been a battleground between the Ottoman empire and the European powers.

Garnett was not sure what he was talking about, but acted properly impressed and was even pleased about the "quaintness" of the hotel. To her mother, however, she remarked that it did remind her of the ancient back rooms for which the Old Tudor Inn over-charged its patrons.

Alix too was glad that they could bathe, in water brought up by the hardworking chambermaid, for all the world like her first night at Miravel. The next day they got an awe-inspiring view of the Acropolis with its magnificent crown, the Parthenon and the remnants of past splendour half destroyed in two thousand years of wars. At last, David was able to explain to Alix the difference between Doric, Ionian and Corinthian pillars which had so baffled her at their engagement party. The Acropolis was surprisingly crowded. War or no war, many people from many lands seemed to have risked everything to walk among the wonders of the ancient temple.

They were not to spend enough time there,

however. They had barely begun their circle of the priceless columns when Mr Minos came hurrying up to warn their guide that he had been advised to bring forward the ceremony. It would be this afternoon, before dusk.

David was shaken with excitement and started down the hill even before Garnett and Alix understood what was happening.

Mr Minos explained to Alix, "I do not like to disturb Lord Miravel's process of thought at this time but your informants seem to have been more correct than mine. His Serene Highness, Prince Kuragin, has tried to contact you through his embassies at Budapest, Bucharest, and finally here. He asks that you reach the express from Constantinople tomorrow. The company will not be responsible for the exactness of future schedules . . . I think, *madame,* that you know what that implies."

"Then there will be war."

He shrugged hopelessly. "You must leave tonight and tomorrow take the appalling local train in which you arrived. But it is imperative, I think, that you do arrive at Sofia in Bulgaria, and then at Bucharest before the Orient Express arrives late tomorrow night. I suggest we arrange a comfortable touring car for the first lap of your journey."

Garnett's eyes sparkled. "What a story this will be to tell them back at Miravel."

Mr Minos agreed with a sad smile. "They say the German kaiser has returned to Berlin from a yachting cruise. His Majesty the Tsar is in St Petersburg. The French premier. The British. Who knows?"

"Only the two quarrelling children," she said sharply. "The Austrians and the Serbs."

Alix and Garnett returned to the little hotel while David was rehearsing nervously in Mr Minos's company.

Garnett was amused that she wouldn't be able to try out once more the lumpy mattress of the brass bed she had shared last night with her mother. She was a good traveller, seldom complaining, and regarding everything as a new story she could recite to everyone she knew.

The amphitheatre in which the great event of David's life would take place was newly restored. With a true artist's feeling the Greek members of the Athena Society had decided that before homes, restaurants and places of work were repaired in the wake of their recent freedom from the Turks, their very own Athenian theatre for lectures and awards et cetera would be ready.

Part of the seating was unfinished and the eager members plus those invited guests took

464

seats on the ground with its rough, occasional tufts of grass. Garnett called it cheerfully, "one of the horrors of war".

David was introduced with a flourish, mostly in Greek, but with some remarks, certainly the most flattering, translated into English and French, for the sake of the guest members of the society. David looked more dignified and certainly more dominant than Alix had ever seen him. She was sure his mother would respect him a great deal more if she could have seen him.

A woman sitting just below Alix turned to remark, "How fortunate you are, *madame!* Such a great man to have brought back from the dead past all these moments and truths which have been denied to us for so long."

"He is one of our great scholars in England," Alix told her honestly. She had scarcely more knowledge on that subject than Garnett, but she respected his long years of slavery over the ancient world.

David was a little nervous, but once he began his story of the Greek escape across half of Asia, "correcting" the original historian, Herodotus, as politely as possible, he was fiery and held the audience's rapt attention. They did not always agree, and occasionally called out a contradiction, but he answered these with ease. He certainly knew his subject. Whether he was right or wrong in his conclusions, Alix had no idea.

In spite of her pride in his personal triumph, a part of her mind was working on the journey to come. She dreaded the possibilities. Since the Compagnie Internationale des Wagon-Lits could not guarantee the schedule of any trains beyond the one they would catch tomorrow night, Alix had even less confidence in all the people who informed her that the Compagnie was worrying needlessly.

They had scarcely finished applauding David and were standing around him, chiefly congratulating, but some arguing their own viewpoints, when Mr Minos, sweating a little, came to speak with Alix quietly.

"It is a bitter disappointment to us, Lady Miravel, to have you arrive and depart in two days, so to speak, but we have every confidence that this little affair will be over in six weeks. They usually are. At which time, you may count upon our invitation to be repeated to yourself, your lovely daughter and, of course, His Lordship. We have so many questions unanswered that we would like to put to him. Any number of our members seem to feel that they have been cheated of their chance to talk with this brilliant man."

Dear David. He had proven himself as good as Bayard at last.

Meanwhile, Franz would be near some time the following day after they left Bucharest. In spite of Franz's own danger, she felt safer, knowing he was no further than two days from them.

She said, "Thank you, sir. My husband will be profoundly grateful. Please tell him we leave within the next half hour. Is that satisfactory to your driver?"

In twenty-five minutes Mr Minos and a horde of David's admirers had got the family to the touring car which apparently was owned in common with the entire Athena Society.

The most important problem, thus far, in this entire trip, would be coming up. Could they possibly get to Bucharest in time to catch the speeding Orient Express from Constantinople? The Miravels might be reasonably well known in Britain, but they would mean less than nothing to the Orient Express which was apparently racing back to Paris to beat a war.

Once they were reasonably comfortable in the back seat of the car Alix tried to calm what she supposed would be David's nervous qualms. He had certainly been busy today.

"Let's just assume things will go well. You

did wonderfully today. We were so proud of you!"

He blushed at the compliment and then said an odd thing that made her feel deeply ashamed. "You really mean that, don't you, dear?"

"Of course, I do." She kissed his cheek, trying not to think of anything else that might give away to him her anxiety to see Franz, to know he was safe and still loved her.

Garnett, who had tied a length of ribbon around her flying hair and managed to get the front seat of the car, now laughed at her father.

"How can you be so silly, Papa? Mother would never lie to you. If she says she loves you, she loves you. Isn't that true, Mama?"

"Yes, dear. Now, can we get on to Bucharest, piece-meal, as it were?"

CHAPTER TWENTY-NINE

Young Stavros, Mr Minos's son, was a jolly young man whom even the bumps and rattles caused by the unpaved farm roads did not disturb. He was quite sure they would reach the local train in time. They missed it by more than an hour.

"And after that night, too," Garnett remarked. She was trying to pull herself together.

Stavros agreed proudly. "Wonderful to ride in one of these American cars. Like flying along."

He sounded so like Tiger Royle with his early cars that Alix found him endearing. If Tiger were only here now, she felt that he would get them out of their scrape. Now, Stavros was philosophical. He said, "It is a pity we missed the local, but that is life, as the philosopher says. Even an American could not do better. There must be some way to beat the express."

"There had better be," David muttered. "That was a ride!"

"Unforgettable."

"That's the word I was searching for."

Meanwhile, the solution seemed obvious to Alix. "If we could pay you what your time, and what the wear on the car is worth, perhaps you could drive us on to Bucharest."

Garnett groaned but seeing Stavros look doubtful, she became the charmer and told him that he was "really the only person with the talent to drive us there. I wouldn't trust myself to anyone else."

"Congratulations," Alix whispered as Stavros became more receptive.

"I see no reason why I could not, sir. *Madame*. As long as I do not return home with a car worn out and no money to show for the long time I have been away."

"Back into the seats of the mighty," David ordered everyone. "This time, I sit in front, in case our friend here becomes lost in this wilderness."

"Oh, Papa! You don't think you could lead us out," his daughter teased him, but any action was better than nothing so they all got back into the car, concealing their groans.

Stavros managed very well through much of the day, and eventually acquired their trust in spite of the Balkan roads. He managed to find strange peasant houses where food was obtainable, and though they couldn't identify much of it, there was certainly lamb here and there as well as Levantine types of rice and wheat.

None of the Miravels let himself, or herself, get downcast for the sake of the others. In some ways it was a curiously satisfying journey in which they actually felt like a family.

This had never quite happened to Alix since she discovered that their married lives were not what she had expected when she married him.

Long after dark in the evening, with a strange, firefly glow along the horizon, Stavros called out, the victor at last.

"Behold, *madame. Monsieur. Mademoiselle.* What you see is a city. And that city is Bucharest. It was in Turkish hands for centuries. There are buildings with onion domes. Very interesting. Not the great white lights of Paris, but well enough. I have been to Paris, you know."

"How nice!" Garnett told him, managing to smile her sweetest. "Can we possibly reach the railway station? Please?"

Alix's hands felt moist with perspiration. Now that they might actually be rescued, actually see Franz, she could scarcely believe it. It was too much to hope for. Of course, she had her aching body to remind her of the last twenty-four hours in which they had tried to reach this metropolis.

Stavros reached his apex when he found the railway station with little effort and was only yelled at once by a stout woman on the street. No one could make out much of the city, but at least the station looked natural.

They all got out and surrounded Stavros so that they could discover, as quickly as possible, the answer to the all-important question.

"Has the Orient Express come in from Constantinople yet?"

The first station attendant they met replied with a torrent of words in some incomprehensible language. Alix was not made any more confident when she saw the perplexity of their chauffeur-guide.

"What did he say?"

Stavros looked down like a naughty boy. "It is, I think, just lacking of an hour that you miss it."

"Oh, God!" Alix closed her eyes.

For the first time David was beginning to appreciate their real difficulty. Taking the lapel of Stavros's jacket, he demanded, "Now, we really must be on that train. It is the last scheduled train across Europe. Do you understand me?"

A well-dressed female standing nearby looked around and asked in English with a

French accent, "Why do you not take the Orient Express? The train you enquired about is most uncomfortable."

All the Miravels attacked her at once. "Is it true? We haven't missed it?"

"Certainly not, *madame*," the lady said, as though they had questioned her veracity. "I am to take the Express myself. I hope to be in Paris within two days. Safe from this middle European madness."

All Garnett could think of to say was, "Bless you, *madame*."

The woman eyed her suspiciously. "It was nothing, I assure you. In fact, I seem to hear that mournful whistle at the moment. Listen."

It was the Orient Express. A glorious sight, whistling and steaming its way along until it halted parallel to the frantic crowd. They all pushed forward dragging suitcases, baggage of every kind, and one pair of quacking ducks.

The unfortunate peasant pair with the ducks were left behind, but by elbowing their own way into the carriage their tickets called for, the Miravels fell on to their seats, breathless.

Garnett looked out. "Somebody just ran away with my vanity-case." She glanced over her shoulder at her mother and father who had risen at her cry. Then she shrugged. "Strictly speaking, we're lucky to get this far, baggage or no baggage."

Their heaviest suitcase had been left behind, but Stavros, waving to them frantically, promised by pantomime to send it along. Alix smiled. She had very little hope of ever seeing their things again. It really didn't matter any more.

"I agree, Garnett. We were lucky. Did you keep your plaque, dear?"

David was caressing the package. In spite of all they had gone through and were about to go through, Alix knew he had his magic amulet. She felt sad but tender about him.

As with most European trains the express moved rapidly and with almost total silence out of Bucharest and on to the tracks heading through Romania for Hungary, Lichtenbourg, Vienna, then across Germany towards France and safety.

Although Alix had never seen the train so crowded, the chatter in the corridors eventually stopped, and most of the passengers returned to their seats, profoundly shaken by the panic and what it implied.

They were too tired to eat that night and as soon as the wagon-lit attendant made up their beds they lay down, wondering if they could sleep. David, who would be sharing his compartment with an elderly German merchant, left his plaque in Alix's compartment although the merchant had no interest whatever in why this Englishman had been to Greece.

Alix was amused when Garnett, in the upper berth, awoke in the middle of the night and, seeing Alix looking out the window, whispered, "That's Dracula country out there. See any bats and weird people?"

Alix laughed. "It's too dark to tell. I haven't seen any castle or any lights at all for ages."

"Too bad. Better luck next time, Mama," and Garnett went back to sleep.

The attendant in his neat brown uniform stopped by after Alix and Garnett were awake and dressed in the morning.

"The dining car is crowded, as you may imagine, *mesdames*. And very shortly, the passengers will be ordered back to their compartments. I had better bring you something."

"Ordered back? Why?"

The attendant shrugged eloquently. "We are making a stop that is not on the schedule, to pick up the German ambassador to Austria-Hungary and a Hungarian general."

To Alix this sounded ominous. "Why? Has war been declared?"

"We are not informed, *madame*. I believe the German ambassador was inspecting

Hungarian troops and border defences. They are on manoeuvres on the Serbian border. There is a treaty between Germany and Austria, you know." He bowed. "I will bring rolls and *café au lait* to your family, Your Ladyship."

"Thank you."

David joined them for their typical European breakfast, remarking wryly, "I'd give a good deal if we were safe in London right now."

Garnett tried hard not to look worried. "Is it so dangerous here, Papa?"

"I've no idea, but of one thing we may be sure. The breakfasts would be better there."

They all laughed at that. It was a contagious sound, a relief that the other two could see the humorous side of it.

Since they had been crossing Hungary's rich plains for some time they were all wondering secretly why there had been no approach by the Hungarian border police, but no one liked to mention it. Each time the train came to a smooth halt the Miravels looked at each other, but it was not until the long stop in Budapest that Alix became aware of how close Franz Kuragin and Lichtenbourg must be.

David had looked out the window as the

train pulled into the great city on the Danube and was remarking, "I've never been in Budapest. I'd like to spend a few weeks here sometime. It has a very colourful history."

The two women looked out over his head, about to admire the city whose river divided it peacefully between Buda and Pest, when the attendant came in. He was in such a hurry he scarcely knocked.

"I regret I must close the blind. Please do not look from this carriage. It is forbidden to foreign travellers now."

Silently, they watched him lower the blind. When he left them he looked as uneasy as they felt.

Meanwhile, the noise outside the window was full of confused voices, shouts, and the train letting off steam.

"More passengers trying to get aboard," David surmised. "I'll make you a wager they are tourists like us."

The attendant returned in the afternoon, before they left Budapest, and set a tray down upon the shelf under the window.

Alix's throat was choked and she couldn't bring out her own question but she felt better when Garnett asked, "We will stop at Lichtenbourg, won't we?" To Alix she added, "I wish Max were here."

"If he were, he might be in danger too,"

David pointed out. "He's better off in Paris."

Alix said finally, "I only wish I knew where Pa is. He could knock a few heads together in no time."

They grinned at the picture in their minds but silently they agreed.

The long express finally got on its way but the compartment blinds remained down.

The next stop came suddenly, with an unaccustomed jolt. David looked out under the bottom of the blind.

"It's all fields but I think this is the Lichtenbourg border. There's a wagon road across the field and one of those black-striped bars just to the north-east."

"And signs of officers? Like Franz?"

He shook his head. "Several Hungarians. Mounted. Wearing uniforms and those odd baggy pants. They handle those horses superbly. Magyars, you know."

"Daddy," Garnett pleaded, "this isn't the time for history."

He reminded her huffily, "We are living in history, my dear."

The Miravels didn't have to look out to hear the heavy boots of the Hungarians as they climbed aboard the wagon-lit. Seconds later gloved fists pounded on doors along the corridor. The Miravel door was opened by the attendant. He was frightened but managed to keep his calm.

"Lord Miravel and his family," he told the young Hungarian officer in French.

"Anglais?"

David was surprisingly haughty. His very nationality had been challenged. "Certainly, I am English. What else should I be?"

"David," Alix murmured. "Be careful."

The Hungarian looked at her and smiled. He was considerably younger, but his eyes reminded her of Franz. He looked beyond her to Garnett and his smile broadened.

"So? I regret. Please to dismount."

The attendant began to panic. If any harm came to his British or French passengers he would be in great trouble with the Compagnie Internationale which had treaties with every country whose borders they crossed. "But they have done nothing. They are passengers through to Paris."

The Hungarian waved aside this technicality. In his fair English he said what they dreaded to hear. "As of today, the Austro-Hungarian empire is at war with the Kingdom of Serbia. We have treaties with our ally, the German empire. Serbia has treaties with the Russian empire. If the Russians go to war for Serbia, the French and the British will rapidly become our enemies as well, since France has a treaty with Russia and

Britain has a treaty with France. Do you understand this? It is most complex."

"But this has nothing to do with us. We are innocent bystanders."

"Innocent bystanders are not permitted in wars. As of the moment you will be interned with three others of your nationals — "

"What?" David demanded.

"Interned for the time until the disposition of your case is decided. In short, when your country goes to war with ours, or does not. Swords are already rattling, we are told, in Whitehall and the Quai D'Orsay. Come. I advise coats, *mesdames.*"

His dark young face broke into gentler lines. "It may all be over in hours, *mademoiselle.* Do not be concerned."

Even David realised there was no arguing with these galloping Magyars, but he was careful to put the light summer coats around the shoulders of his ladies and to take as much time as possible. Then he picked up his plaque.

When they were descending from the train which had seemed to be their salvation David gave back one last warning. "Wait until His Majesty hears of this outrage."

Garnett whispered, "My knees are shaky."

The Hungarian at once helped her down. When they stood between the rails of the opposite track Alix tried once more to reason with the Hungarian.

"We are closely related to the Prince Royal of Lichtenbourg. Are you going to make an enemy of him too?"

"Not so, *madame*. Lichtenbourg is an ally. What else? Austria is beyond. Our ally, the German empire beyond that. We all use these tracks you stand on. If he refuses to ally himself with us, we shall know how to protect ourselves in time of peril."

"Peril from little Serbia? And little Lichtenbourg? Really, sir."

The officer obviously wanted to make a good appearance before her pretty daughter. Alix could see that he was embarrassed. But he managed to reply stiffly, "The causes of war are not my business, *madame*. I follow orders. I obey. I regret. Come."

Beside the track they could see ahead of them a one-storey little wooden building that looked as if it might once have been a roadside tavern. Now, two guards stalked back and forth in front of it. The border crossing bar was only a few yards from them. About half a mile down the dirt road inside Lichtenbourg a troop of horsemen rode towards the border. Their uniforms did not appear to have the romantic flair of the Hungarians. As they advanced they looked much more modern and warlike in peaked caps, olive drab coats and what proved to be serviceable boots.

One of the Hungarians saluted. Alix clearly heard the word "Lichtenbourgers".

There must be a full company of them. It was true. Their uniforms were very like the one Franz had worn when he met the family at coronation time. She clutched David's arm.

"Look. In the lead."

He breathed a heavy sigh of relief. "Franz, of course." He added on a bitterly humorous note, "Ever the hero."

One of the border patrol ordered the bar raised but the company of soldiers pulled up at the bar and only Franz swung off his mount and came through, removing his gloves and slapping them against his thigh. He called out to the young Hungarian.

"Welcome to Lichtenbourg." He gestured towards the steaming train with its dozens of heads now watching from the windows. "Shouldn't they be on their way? They will be late to Vienna and I'm told you have important passengers aboard."

The Hungarian was confused but knew his job. "They may go with Your Highness's permission. We have only detained half a dozen possible enemy aliens. We have not yet received final word on their disposal.

Four British. Two French."

Franz was disgustingly casual. "Yes. I was notified. Three of them are related to me. You may release them."

The Hungarian looked around. Altogether, he had two border guards, a crossing guard and three more soldiers who had come aboard the train with him, removing three more of these "possible enemies". They were evidently waiting in the little frame guardhouse.

Against them were ranged a company of fully armed and determined-looking soldiers commanded by their country's leader. While the Hungarian debated, Prince Kuragin waved to the train's engineer.

"You may proceed into Lichtenbourg."

Alix could see the engineer's big, toothy grin as he saluted Franz and the train began to move.

"I must hold these aliens, sir," the Hungarian said again. "My orders, until we find out whether their countries are allies or otherwise."

"I understand. Call Budapest." He stared after the retreating train which had picked up speed and must be halfway to Lichtenbourg City by now. Then, still without looking at the Miravels, he repeated, "Call Budapest. In fifteen minutes. No sooner. No later. Meanwhile, suppose my family and I spend the next fifteen minutes resting in this little post house that you have set up against my ferocious country."

The Hungarian looked over at Garnett, gave a little shrug of defeat, and motioned them over to the guards' post.

When they were all inside Franz hugged each of them, then kissed first Garnett and last, Alix. David turned away as they kissed. He went over to the two stranded Frenchwomen and the Englishman from Derbyshire who vented his outrage in a chorus with David.

"My love," Franz whispered in Alix's ear. "Don't worry. It will go well for you." Aloud, he said to David, "Tiger is in Vienna now. When the express goes through Vienna he will be with you. At the French border you will be joined by Max and a French patrol."

"That is all very well, sir," the Derbyshire man snapped, "but why will they obey you? Those soldiers of yours out there?"

Franz laughed. "Because I am playing their game."

They had less than fifteen minutes to wait and so much to say. But David, with his plaque under his arm, watched his wife and Franz for a minute, then suggested to Garnett, "Come over and thank the French lady who told us we hadn't missed the express."

After a surprised minute she went.

All Alix could do was squeeze the prince's hand that held hers, and say while blinking back the tears, "I love you. There's so much to say, but I can't think of anything. Are you still engaged to that Princess Ilsa?"

"No, I promise you. I never was. Besides, I am too old for her."

"What?" He had never looked more magnificent to her.

"She now feels that Max is more suited to her."

"No." She began to laugh.

"She believes he needs maturity. That is Her Highness's word for it. Unfortunately, I suspect my son has other plans, when this idiotic war is over."

That terrified her. "You may be killed. Or imprisoned."

"My darling, I am a wily old campaigner. And very shortly now, I will prove it. But before that, I want you to know that I intend to finish grooming Max for my job. When that is completed, we will discuss our future, you and I. And no noble sacrifices on your part. I loved you before he ever did. And I will love you after."

The Hungarian had come from the telephone and saluted Franz. "Your Highness, I am told to remove our — er — guests

485

from detention and deliver them to the Orient Express which is being held for them in Lichtenbourg City."

Franz boasted to Alix, "What did I tell you? You hear? My cars have driven up. Well timed, I must say."

Everyone got up in a hurry and started for the door. The Hungarian, still puzzled, escorted them under the half-raised bar and on to Lichtenbourg soil.

There, surrounded by the prince's company of Lichtenbourg soldiers they crowded into two automobiles of a vintage similar to Tiger Royle's first auto-car.

It didn't matter. Alix loved them. She hugged to herself these few minutes with Franz.

It was not until they rode into Lichtenbourg City and were ushered back on board the waiting express, into their own wagon-lit, that David asked incredulously, "However did you do it?"

Franz kissed Garnett and clapped David on the back.

"For one thing, I have an engineer on your train in my pocket."

"You weren't here when we came through several days ago," Garnett reminded him. "We thought something awful had happened to you."

"Awful, indeed. I was in a strategy meeting with my staff. I rushed to the station but the infallible Orient Express had already pulled out and was across the border. I tried to telegraph at several of your stops but the lines were closed beyond Budapest. Eventually, my message reached you in Athens."

"And a good thing you did," David acknowledged. "How you got Tiger to Vienna so soon I can't imagine."

The prince dismissed this with a "business as usual" attitude. "After my last warning to you, I cabled Tiger in New York. He caught ship that afternoon. Arrived in Vienna at noon today. Being a non-belligerent, he can get you through Germany."

"But what threat could you have used to make the Hungarians release us?"

"Simple." Franz grinned. "My people had orders to take the German ambassador off this train as a Bolshevik spy."

"Good Lord! Isn't that dangerous?"

Franz denied this innocently. "Not at all. My police received a letter telling us that the German ambassador was a Bolshevik, masquerading as a nobleman. As for his valet, he was part of the Bolshevik scheme. That, at least, is to be our official view. Naturally, when the express reached Lichtenbourg City he was taken off. The two were taken off. My people here say they never heard such profanity. All in German. And the poor man will remain here until you are over the French border."

"And then?"

"We find the information was false, give him and his valet a sumptuous meal and send them on to Berlin full of good Lichtenbourg wine."

Alix knew there might be difficulties for him, but she also knew that there were men who must do the daring deeds of the world. Her father and Franz were two of them.

David turned away saying, "Kiss her goodbye, Cousin. You have earned it."

Alix walked out to the steps with Franz. They kissed. It was a long moment. She thought of the other moments with him. They would keep her warm in the time to come. Then Franz went lightly down the steps. On the bottom step he turned back to her. His eyes fixed on hers.

"My love, remember."

She nodded.

When the train started she got out her handkerchief and cleared her eyes before walking into the compartment.

David was saying to Garnett, "Wait until Tiger sees this." He held up the plaque. "If that doesn't impress him, I miss my guess."